BOURBON & LIES

THE BOURBON BOYS SERIES
BOOK ONE

VICTORIA WILDER

This is for the women who are brave enough to rescue themselves. It doesn't matter if it was from something life-altering or a small moment that felt big. You didn't need to wait for the cowboy to ride up and save you. You did that all on your own.

However, if you're still hoping for a sexy "cowboy" to reward you, then let Grant Foxx be your stand-in until one does...

A NOTE ABOUT BOURBON & LIES

While this story is a work of fiction, there are some heavy subject matters that you should be aware of before diving in.

First and foremost, a big part of this story centers around WITSEC or the Federal Witness Protection Program in the United States. This is purely an interpretation of this program. Neither I, nor anyone I know, have been a part of it, so when I list this story as fiction, I really mean it.

The following is a list of potential triggers that are not meant to be spoilers or tropes, but rather a warning in case you find certain aspects upsetting: Violence and death on page, descriptive gore, discussion of captivity, violence toward women, gun violence, violence against an animal, discussion of deceased parents and family, reference to sexual assault, discussion of cannibalism, discussion of homicide, main characters dealing with PTSD, vulgar language, and descriptive open-door sex scenes.

THE RULES OF BOURBON

Every bourbon is whiskey, but not every whiskey is bourbon. There are rules for bourbon to be called bourbon.

1. It must be made in the United States
2. The mash must be at least 51% corn
3. It must be aged for at least two years in a new, charred, oak barrel
4. The whiskey cannot enter the barrel higher than 125 proof
5. Nothing can be added but water and only to lessen the proof when necessary

In Fiasco, Kentucky there's one more rule that loosely relates to the bourbon that's made there: **Never fall for a Foxx brother.**

CHAPTER 1

GRANT

"Don't," I grit out through my teeth.

And for a moment, a short three count, I think she might listen to me. But I knew as soon as the call came in that she'd be the first on the scene. It didn't matter that she'd only been clocked in for less than an hour. I knew her better than anyone else here. She would be en route to the scene as soon as the location was out over dispatch. The intel lined up. It matched with the gathered evidence that shifted from a drug ring to the trafficking of human life. Women specifically.

A neighbor from two miles north of the old tobacco mill had called saying he didn't remember the property selling at auction, but there was activity there all weekend. Enough that his horses were spooked and stayed away from the pasture that had once been their favorite. The same pasture beside the tobacco farmland.

My walkie crackles as I stand, lingering at my desk and waiting to hear her response.

"I'm not asking, Foxx. I'm going in. There's movement, and I just heard a scream or pleading. It's probable cause."

"Goddamnit," I bark. "Fucking reckless." With a huff, I rush out of my office and into the pit toward the exit. "Del, you get your team at that farm right fucking now," I shout to my superior officer. "How are there no more patrols in the vicinity?" Everyone in the precinct is aware of this call. Fiasco is a small town considering its population, but there's a lot of land. Not too much happens around here that multiple cars would need to be on a scene immediately. But I don't think about what I'm saying. I'm reacting and trying to move. Fast. "Fiona and a fucking rookie are the only ones on scene right now."

Del's eyebrows hit his hairline. I messed up as soon as I said it. *Fiona.* It should have been Officer Delaney. *Not* Fiona. It didn't matter that I'd known her since we were in grade school together; more than half of these guys had been in school along with us. But I'll worry about that conversation later. It isn't the fact that I'm swearing at my lieutenant or pissed off that I wasn't called on the scene first. I run the K-9 unit. Any drug situation in town has Julep and me on the scene ahead of any patrol crew. But right now, they need backup. If this is gang related, they're walking into something they might not be able to control.

I curl my tongue and whistle out, rushing through the garage bay and toward my squad car. Julep is at my side in seconds, nails clacking on the concrete floor. "Time to work, Jules."

Once I open the passenger back door, she jumps into

her seat. I give her a quick pet along her dark brown head, hook her vest into the seatbelt harness, and I'm on my way. I'm a mile from the station when my radio channels start getting louder, the comms from other officers en route giving an update.

"Dispatch, we're eight minutes out."

It's too long. And I haven't heard a damn thing from Fiona. I look at the time on the dash. It's been four minutes since she last responded and nothing since. *Fuck.*

"Dispatch." Her voice sounds over comms and my grip on the steering wheel loosens. "The tobacco mill is as quiet as a mouse." But before I even exhale, I hear her voice back on the radio. It's a breathy whisper along with static that ratchets my nerves. "Dispatch—"

Julep lets out a short bark from the backseat.

"We're going to her, girl."

Julep had a good twenty minutes of belly rubs from Fiona this morning. It's been that way for the past six months. And before that, I had a feeling Fiona would still give her some extra pets before she snuck out every night.

I can see the tobacco farm in the distance. I flick off my sirens before I hit the main drag, but keep my lights on, especially now that it's dusk. I don't know what I'm coming into and the last thing I want is sirens to make this situation worse.

"Officer Delaney, do you copy," Dispatch responds again. "There are three units less than five minutes out. And the K-9 unit is less than two."

"Shots fired. Shots fired," comes over the next call, and I floor it as my heart races.

In the background, dispatch calls all available units to

the abandoned tobacco mill that I'm turning into. Cutting the engine, I'm out of my car seconds later. I choose to leave Julep in the back, since shots fired means K-9 stays put until there's an all-clear. She won't help in a shoot-out, but she's read my body language and heard Fiona's over the radio, so I leave her growling in the back seat as I quietly remove my gun and flashlight. When I move closer to the mill, the doors are wide open, and remnants of dried tobacco leaves still hang from rafters intermittently. There's forgotten machinery, old and rusted, sitting in the center of the space. Beyond that, it's empty.

Muffled shouts and two more gunshots ring out from an oversized shed at least a hundred feet away, along the edge of the farmland. I hear the sirens from the two squad cars coming down the same long drag. Screeching tires pull into the driveway, and seconds later, one squad car flies past me and directly toward the shed.

She's fine. "She gave her location" are the words I keep saying to myself as I sprint toward the officers entering the shed. I left my radio in the car so I can't be sure, but they have an exact location. *She's going to be okay. She's a trained, experienced officer.*

When I reach the shed door, gasping for breath with my flashlight raised and the gun cocked beneath, the situation in front of me is anything but controlled. "Jesus Christ," I mumble as I approach. Our newest rookie, Lee, is bleeding out on the floor in front of another officer, who's trying to make a tourniquet from his belt.

I don't stop to help.

Fiona.

"Mills, where's Delaney?" I ask, approaching the

double doors on the other side of the shed. A flashlight bobs in the distance as I spot small tracks of blood in front of me.

Mills shouts from behind me, "Del is following the tracks. Nobody else was in here when we pulled up."

And that's when I hear it on Mills's radio. Del radioing dispatch. "I have another officer down. I need paramedics. *Now.*"

I don't think. All my training—the caution that's necessary to override knee-jerk reactions and emotion-led actions —reduces to fragments in the wind. I run. I follow where the flashlight in the distance hasn't moved, rushing toward it at full speed. When I veer past a broken slotted fence, that's when I can make out the outline of them.

Del crouched over a still body in the grass. My eyes squint as my chest laces with pain. "No." I rush past Del and to his other side, and pull her away from him and into my arms. Tears that I don't remember falling wet my face as I shout at her unmoving body, "No, baby, what happened? Fuck. Fuck. No."

I don't care that I've just taken her out of her father's arms and into mine. I don't care that I've just shown all my cards that my relationship with Fiona Delaney had moved far beyond colleagues, friends, and even the ridiculous idea that it was only physical. I don't care that I keep repeating the same words over and over again. "I love you. You cannot die on me, do you hear me?"

I pull back to see where she's been injured, the small slit along her neck barely pulsing any longer as blood coats my arms and the ground below me. I push my palm against it to stop the bleeding. The shirt of her uniform is unbuttoned all the way down past her vest and a patch of wetness lines her side.

When I roll her toward me, Del's tear-streaked face squints in pain as he mutters out, "Jesus Christ, Fiona. My baby." We both look down at a piece of her skin that's shredded like she had gotten caught in a wired fence.

Her body grows heavier in my arms as I hold her tighter. "Just hold on, Fi. Just hold on."

I know she's not breathing, but I can't let go.

"She's gone, Grant."

5 YEARS LATER...

CHAPTER 2

LANEY

"You only lie when it's necessary."

I look down at my hands. Ballet slippers pepper my nails, colored with a pale pink nail polish I've grown to hate. My cuticles are a result of my nerves—freshly bitten and picked. I've been ignoring what was "right" for months.

"Might as well be a liar now," I mumble, shaking my head.

I'm frustrated, and that energy has my nerves graduating toward anger and sarcasm. A winning combination. I don't know where we're headed or for how long. The only certainty is the mess I'm leaving in my wake. I take a deep breath. *You can do hard things.*

The sound of the window cracking open drowns out the low bravado of Johnny Cash crooning away on the radio.

"He would be proud of you." The way she exhales while saying it makes it clear that encouraging or kind words are not something she typically offers. I would guess that needing to console an "asset" would be par for the course in her line of work. But maybe that's not her strong suit. When I study her from across the cab of the truck, it's too dark to tell if the way she grips the steering wheel tightly and scratches at the side of her face is her tell. If she's shoveling shit to keep me from spiraling, or if she's just not used to saying things like this to people like me. She may have known my father professionally, but she sure as hell didn't know him as a father.

My dad used to tell me regularly how proud he was—I don't need that reminder from her. Even when I was doing nothing other than giving him an ulcer. No matter how many jobs I cycled through, the end of one always came with a "you'll find what feels right, kiddo." Even when I'd come home crying and wouldn't tell him exactly why, he'd always say "that boy never deserved you." It didn't matter what it was, he always told me things would be okay. And that I'd figure it out. *You can do hard things, Laney. Never forget it. You're a Shaw.*

But right now, my dad would be disappointed. And he'd be angry. Pissed off that a monster crossed my path. The kind of monster that he spent his life trying to prevent from hurting anyone—and especially anyone he loved. He'd be disappointed at what I've become. I know I am. I blink back the tears blurring my vision.

"Agent–"

She cuts me off. "Just Bea. Get used to calling me Bea."

"Fine. Bea. I don't need you telling me what my father might have thought of this situation. That's not going to win me over. I'm on your side. I'm pissed at myself . . ." I grit out. "No, you know what? I'm pissed at a lot of things right now. Myself for—" I shake my head at the reason why I was even in that place for as long as I had been. "I'm pissed at that monster for existing, for hurting people and uprooting my life. But I know exactly how my father would be feeling if he were here."

She gives me a tight-lipped smile. "I know you didn't ask for any of this, and you had a life—"

I lean my head back against the headrest with a small laugh that stops her from finishing that sentence. My life was in the midst of the deepest nosedive. I had a life. One I was finally proud of building, and I tarnished it. I justified doing the wrong thing. Maybe that monster was my punishment. I cringe at the thought of the universe being so cruel. I made some bad decisions, but I didn't deserve this. His victim didn't deserve this. Squeezing my eyes closed, I pinch the bridge of my nose. The headache that's been dull and throbbing has moved to a more stabbing pain behind my right eye. *Great, a migraine to add to the fun.*

Being awake for more than twenty-four hours, I'm emotional and not thinking logically. The adrenaline that buzzed through my veins, pushing me through this nightmare, has worn off. I just need sleep.

"I have always listened to my gut, Laney. And it's telling me this relocation needs to stay quiet and away from any official channels."

My gaze flicks to her again. I should feel relieved to see a familiar face in all of this, but I don't. I wish it were my dad getting me out of this.

"The woman you saved that night will never forget what she went through. Remember that."

"I know." My skin breaks out in goosebumps when I think about the way that woman screamed and ran right at me, pleading for anything that resembled help. I should have never been there in the first place. I never wanted to be a hero. I wanted to feel close to my dad. I wanted to be picked.

But she's making me curious. "What's your gut saying that doesn't feel right?"

"That it's been more than seventy-two hours now and nothing has happened. Someone had brains enough to get the U.S. Marshall Service involved because something isn't right." When she glances at me, I'm studying her profile and trying to read between the lines of what she's not saying. She shakes her head, like she's shaking off what she really wants to tell me. "With the type of evidence they found, you and his victim shouldn't have to be relocated." She pauses for a moment, swallowing audibly. "They couldn't get him to give a name and they can't find him in the system."

The hairs on my neck stand at the thought of him. I can still feel the way my lungs burned from running with the weight of another person draped over me.

"No name. Only partial fingerprints that haven't connected him with anyone in any system. There's no credit history or money trail. No rap-sheet. But the consistency in his victims' wounds are—" She cuts herself off. "Until I know that your risk is limited, I'll make sure you're out of sight. I owe at least *that* to your father."

She lights her clove cigarette, and I pull out my bag of sour gummy bears.

I don't know the details of the relationship she had

with my dad, but he was a respected federal agent, and I have a feeling he left a lot of people owing him favors. That part, out of all of this, isn't what surprises me. It's the fact that she doesn't want a paper trail about where I'm going. Hell, I don't even know where we're headed.

Heaviness settles on my chest like I can't take a deep breath. I want to scream at her and tell her that all of this isn't okay. I feel like I'm being punished for doing the right thing, which isn't fair. And as much as I'm relieved to not be dealing with the mess I left, I don't want to disappear.

Memories would be harder to remember when I wasn't there to see the things that brought them back—blankets on the grass in Bryant Park, wandering around The High Line, eating our way through Chinatown. I didn't even get a chance to bring things with me.

"The color suits you," she says, knocking me from my thoughts.

Pulling the visor down, I pop the mirror open. I look... different. Still me, but older in a way. Less like a woman trying to look like other people, to fit into a mold or keep a man's attention. I look like someone who's confident in her own skin. *I like it*—my hair an orange-red tint instead of the platinum blonde I've maintained for most of my adulthood.

I'm someone new all over again and I don't recognize her yet. But I will. Eventually. If I'm being honest, I hadn't recognized the person I became. It's felt that way for a long time, maybe even before I lost my dad.

"You can keep your first name." She tucks her clove between her lips and leans over me, plucking a cloth zippered pouch from the glove compartment. "There's a new social, license, and passport..."

Thinking about my name, I tune out the rest. My dad called me Laney, but I hadn't gone by the nickname in years. There's only one person alive who knows me by that name, and I never want to see him again.

I close my eyes and try to breathe through the disgust I feel when I think about what I had been doing with Phillip. I spent so much time trying to smudge out Laney from Coney Island and fit in as Eleanor Shaw from Manhattan. I'm neither of those people anymore—Coney Island Laney nor Manhattan Eleanor. The high-profile events, society weddings, and the wealthy clientele I had catered to allowed me to build a lifestyle, but it didn't feel like a life. It felt like name-dropping whenever possible, materialistic, and after a while, it was easy to mistake hard work for happiness.

Feeling a sense of relief, I flip through the laminated pieces of paper. I still haven't processed everything, and that's going to hit me like a freight train when it all sinks in. I'm smart enough to know it's why my emotions are all over the place—lack of sleep and an intensely traumatic event will do that to a person. But as I watch the dark highway blur by, it's erasing my piss-poor decisions and priming me for what's coming. If Laney Young from Colorado had to be a lie, then I'd lean into it.

It took me until West Virginia to finally doze off. It feels like a span of only about five minutes between my eyes closing and the sound of arguing to nudge them open again. I rub away the blur from my eyes as I focus on the dashboard clock. Five minutes was more like six hours. The car is warm, borderline sticky, like the AC has been off for more than a little while. *Where's Agent Harper?*

Unbuckling my seatbelt, I look out my window at where we've parked. No mountains or oceans. From what I can tell, everything looks flat. I've only ever lived near water and in a city. But here, there's no cityscape nor tucked-away parks. No skyscrapers nor light pollution of any kind, only the massive farmhouse ahead of me.

When I open the truck door, the humidity hits my skin like I've just walked into a screen door. A layer of sweat is already forming under anything that's clothed, especially right under the band of my sports bra and along the back of my neck.

The East Coast can be brutal in August, but it's only the first week of June, and that twelve-hour drive felt like it fast-forwarded me right into the dead heat of summer.

I stretch my arms over my head, lifting my hair as I do to air out the trapped warmth. Inhaling deeply, I try to calm my anxious thoughts about where I am or how annoying it is being this hot in the middle of the night. And then it hits me: the smell. It's like a motionless breeze just kicked in as the scent from a bakery permeates the air. Like yeast from baking bread, it carries a hint of chocolate with a tangy sweetness. It's not the savoriness of salted air or the pungent odor of a low-tide marsh. It's far better. *Maybe I won't miss the ocean, after all.* This smelled delicious and inviting.

Anything that smelled this good now must be beautiful in the daytime. "Damn," I say to myself as I look at what stands before me. The opulence seems like something you'd see along the Gold Coast or the shores of East Hampton. The manicured lawn and landscape are uplit, as if each shrub and tree are meant to be honored and displayed. Black-framed windows contrast the white siding, and a black metal roof has that modern farmhouse style. It's the kind of house that touts simplicity, but I know how expensive "simple" can really be. Farmhouse, in this case, was a design choice and not a literal house on a farm. Without even meeting its owners, I know farmers aren't living here.

There's barely a chirp from crickets or a hum of the wind that would rustle the trees. It's quiet and calm. That late-night or early-morning peacefulness that can be easily mistaken for safety. Will I be safe here? There isn't a single streetlight or neighbor's porch lit. There's no dusky rose-colored hue along the horizon, polluting the edges of the landscape into the dark sky. Everything is black and speckled with stars of various sizes.

A man's deep voice raises and has my head whipping toward where it came. The tone of it has me moving around the parked truck. "Bea, you're only hearing what you want to hear. I said no. Why are you at my front door and not Grant's?"

It's not rocket science to know this argument is very likely about me. She said she was doing this her way, but I thought she would have phoned ahead to make sure wherever I was going, I'd be welcome.

"You know why. And Ace, I'm not asking here," Agent Harper's voice rasps.

At the foot of the stairs, I stop in my tracks. Who is he?

"So you're threatening me?" the man says, just as he notices me. He does a double take. His dark hair with streaks of silver is combed back and cut short. But it's not the matching scruff along his cheeks and chin or the way he holds himself that has my attention. It's the fact that it's the middle of the night, and he's wearing suit pants and a white collared shirt, sleeves rolled to his elbows. *Definitely not a farmer.* He rests his hands on his narrow hips, looks up at the ceiling on the porch, and puffs out his cheeks, blowing out a breath. When his head tilts back down, eyes shifting to mine, he says, "Jesus, Bea. She looks like a fucking kid."

Maybe to him. But I've seen plenty of life at twenty-nine.

Bea turns to me and pulls out her silver case of cloves with a smile. When she lights it and takes a drag, plumes of smoke trail from her mouth and behind her with the slow, warm breeze. "She stopped a monster a few nights ago, Ace. She's not a kid, I can promise you that."

It's the first time I feel good about what I've done. It's the first time in two days that I don't feel like I'm drowning in uncertainty.

His mouth tips up into a sympathetic smile that almost looks like an apology. It reminds me of how my dad would smile when he knew I was going to tell him some not-so-great news.

He side-eyes Agent Harper. "You need to quit that shit, Bea."

"Shut up, Ace," she barks back. "Are we good here?"

"Del know you're here?"

She gives him a quick tic of a "no."

Ace takes a deep breath and holds it. "How long?"

Harper walks down the steps. "That'll be up to her eventually. But for now, it's until I can guarantee she's out of harm's way."

Keeping his eyes trained on me, he asks, "We in any danger by having her here? You know we've had enough bad things happen to last a lifetime. And Lincoln's got kids—"

She cuts him off, "I need her to be somewhere I trust, and away from people I don't."

I don't miss the fact that she doesn't answer his question about being in danger.

He smirks at her. "So I fall into that category now? In that circle of trust?"

"It's really fucking small, Ace. You know that." With a begrudging tone, she says, "Plus, this means I'll owe you. You know how much I love that kind of currency."

"You really think Fiasco is a good idea to hide someone?"

"What fiasco?" I interrupt. She better not be dropping me into something worse than what I just came from, if that's even possible.

"It's not unheard of for a woman to be at your house late at night." She raises her brow, the insinuation lingering as she pats his arm. "Do what you can. I know how rumors work here, so keep her away from anything that looks like the truth."

"I assume I don't get to know what the truth is, then?"

Harper meets my eye. "It's whatever she tells you." She winks at me.

He looks me up and down like he's sizing up what to do with me. I shift my weight and square my shoulders, wordlessly telling him that I'm not intimidated. With another smirk, he shakes his head, extending his right hand. "Atticus Foxx. You can call me Ace."

It takes me a few seconds to remember the lie. "Laney. Young. Laney Young," I stammer out as I take his hand.

His eyebrow quirks at the delivery.

Yeah, I'll need to work on that. I need to get better at saying a name that's not quite mine. The problem is, I'm not a liar. Of all the things I've been—an opportunist, a hopeful romantic, a cheat—I've never been a liar. Until now.

"Alright then, Laney Young. Welcome to Fiasco, Kentucky."

CHAPTER 3

LANEY

"You're in good hands here, Laney," Harper interrupts.

I don't mean to snort a laugh, but I do. It's funny and nerve-racking to think I'm supposed to trust anyone now. I had done that—trusted someone, trusted my gut—and look where it landed me.

I shift my eyes to Ace, who tries covering a smile in response. At least he's not opening wide for this bullshit. He didn't plan on any of this either. He sure as hell hadn't planned on me showing up on his doorstep in the middle of the night.

This isn't a hideout. There is nothing discreet here. I don't come from money, but I know what expensive looks like. I've spent the last handful of years trying to fit in with some of the wealthiest families and inner circles in Manhattan. Modern, clutter-free, amplified by deep, masculine colors and complimenting details. From the brushed gold and matte black metal fixtures on the doors and lighting above, to the layout of the lightly stained wood that makes up the floors, the wide foyer and sprawling staircase. This place is not a government-funded halfway house or a community with a budget.

Agent Harper ignores my response as she types out a text on her phone, giving me a few seconds to really look around. The place shouldn't feel welcoming, but it does.

While the humid air outside wraps around my skin and smells of chocolate croissants, in here it's a few degrees colder than cool, and it carries the faintest smell of a man's cologne. Something earthy, woodsy, with a hint of tobacco from cigars instead of Harper's cloves. I like this better. I picture my apprehensive host with a cigar draped in his fingers while he sips on something strong and dark.

"Your burner," Harper says, pulling it from her pocket. "Stay off anything that looks like social media. Don't start posting videos about food or trending dance moves. If you feel anything that seems out of sorts, you text me. *Me* first, and then you don't hesitate. Find Ace. If there's a real urgency, dial 911."

As I stare down at the phone, I can feel her attention zeroed in on how I'm reacting. "What aren't you saying?"

"I have a very small circle of people I trust. Ace and his family are in that circle. And a select few in this town will ensure you remain safe here." She gives me a sad smile. "You'll get through this, Laney. And I will make sure you end up on the other side of it." When I glance at Ace again, his arms are crossed, just observing the exchange. I wonder what I look like from that perspective. It feels like a new beginning, but a tentative one.

She follows my line of sight. "She's smart and could add

some real value to your brand. Keep her tucked away, give her a job, and I'll do my best to keep her chaos out of here."

Ace clears his throat. "Any smell of something dangerous, she's gone, Bea. My family is here. My brothers. My nieces. And even my crotchety old grandfather."

"Fuck you, Atticus," a loud, deep voice with a slow, southern drawl comes from down the hall. It startles me. I hadn't expected anyone else to be here.

Ace mutters "fucking hell" under his breath before he speaks up louder. "Griz, this isn't the kind of conversation to be eavesdropping on."

The ominous, albeit hilarious voice responds, "Ya'll are the ones shoutin' like you're livin' alone. And you damn well know this is my house as much as it is yours." Around the corner from the long hallway, a man with white and silver-streaked hair stands against the archway. Tall and lean, with a thick, more-silver-than-white mustache hiding his lips. They resemble each other. Good looking in a way that makes you look twice. "When you put out your business like it's a breakfast buffet, I'm gonna help myself." The side of his mouth kicks up, his cheek moving so that the skin crinkles around his eyes. "Now"—he shifts his attention to me—"who's this lovely thing?"

Simultaneously, Atticus says, "Go back to bed, Griz," while Agent Harper huffs out, "Jesus."

But I ignore them and answer, "I'm not a thing. But thank you for calling me lovely."

His chin tips down as his eyes meet mine. "I didn't mean any disrespect by it, darlin'. I'll make sure not to make the mistake again." Griz walks toward us with two small crystal glasses, one in each hand, filled with just a sip of a deep caramel-colored liquor. He shifts his attention to Agent Harper. "I see you're thriving in what looks like trouble, as usual, Beatrice."

She smiles to herself. "You know it, Griz," she says on an exhale.

The anxiety of my arrival all falls away. The history between these three, that I'll probably never know the extent of, aside from igniting my curiosity, also calms my nerves.

Griz holds out a glass for me to take. "You're gonna have to forgive us for not welcoming you properly, darlin'." When I take it, he clinks his with mine, and sips.

The slight smell of burned oak hits my nose just as the bite hits my tongue. I knew I should have sipped it the moment it shot to the back of my throat. It takes my breath away and forces me to hack out a cough that feels like fire. My eyes water as I try to recover. It's a novice move for someone who spent most of her early twenties pouring alcohol.

"Let it coat your tongue this time before you swallow," Ace says. My cheeks warm at the direction, and I do as he says.

"Feel that warming in your chest?"

I nod yes. It's a better kind of warmth with this sip.

"We like to call that a Kentucky hug."

Griz pipes in, "And that, right there, is the one-hundred-year-old anniversary batch I tapped this morning. You're only the second person in that amount of time to try that barrel."

"Wow. Thank you." I wipe at the corner of my eye that watered from my very unlady-like coughing.

Griz looks at his grandson with disappointment. And then his eyes flash to Agent Harper on the other side of me. "She doesn't know who we are?"

Ace answers, "You say that like she's here on a tour or something. You realize this is a private matter, and again, in case you didn't have your hearing aids on, you're interrupting."

Glancing down at the floor, I look at the emblem there. *Well, I'll be damned.*

Griz bats at the air in front of him. "Shut it, Ace."

The way Ace huffs, it's hard to hold back my smile.

"Walk me out, Laney," Agent Harper interrupts.

"Pleasure as always, Beatrice," Griz calls out from behind us. She doesn't respond, but she gives Ace one final glance and a nod as she steps back out the way we came.

I walk her to the car in silence, then grab my things from the trunk. "They're good men. All of them," she says, starting the car and rolling down the window. She lights another clove, takes a pull, and on the exhale, she says, "You're safe, Laney." Looking around my face, she searches for something that says I believe her. "Try to live. Try to heal. And remember what I said . . ."

I nod. "Text. Find Ace. Call 911. Got it."

She smiles. "Glad you were listening. But I meant about your dad. He'd be very proud of you."

And I don't know if it's watching the dust kick up as the truck disappears down the long driveway or the fact that I know she's right, but my eyes water as I choke back a sob. It snuck up on me even with so many feelings whirling. *This is my new life.* I swallow the rest of the emotions that claw at my neck and threaten to spill over. *Not now.* I can fall apart later.

Standing there watching the taillights get smaller, the quiet plays tricks on my ears as the humidity in the air licks at my skin. I lift my hair and knot it high enough to keep it from sticking to my neck. *Now what?* My lower back is sore from sitting in a car for too many hours, and the fatigue hits me hard.

The shuffle of feet behind me alerts me enough to remember I can't sleep just yet. "We've got an empty cottage on the property that you can call yours while you're here." Ace's voice sounds from the front porch. "But it's after three in the morning, and I'll need to get it cleaned up for you first. I wasn't exactly expecting you."

"I could sleep just about anywhere right now," I joke.

He doesn't smile, just nods in response. "Need help with your things?"

I hold up the red bag covered in bullseyes. It's not even packed to the brim. But there's a week's worth of under-wear, deodorant, some black liquid eyeliner, mascara, and a bright red lip that looked like a good tone with my new hair color. I didn't second guess the color; I picked what I wanted. I also grabbed a bag of sour gummy bears, but I ate most of it already. A toothbrush and a curling iron. In a rush, apparently, these were my necessities. I'll figure out extra clothes eventually.

"That all?"

"I didn't get to pack before I left." Through the archway at the end of the hall is a kitchen on steroids, stacked with stainless-steel industrial appliances, all lowly lit by recessed lights peppered around the vaulted ceilings.

BOURBON & LIES 25

"Beautiful," I mumble. "How many people live here?"

He seems amused by my knee-jerk reaction to the impressive size and style of the room. Flicking on an electric tea kettle, he says, "It's just Griz and me in the main house." He pauses, mouth kicking up in the corner. "But my brothers aren't far from here. And they're here often. I host a lot of business things. Happy hours with my teams." He looks around. "The space was necessary."

Saddling up to the sprawling island counter, I choose the end seat from a row of eight. "It's big." I clear my throat and think about how the entire grounds, even in the dark, look like the perfect venue for a wedding. "Thank you for saying yes to me staying."

He pours the boiling water into two cups, with a tea bag in each. Giving me a tight-lipped smile, he says, "You overheard an argument that had less to do with you and more to do with Bea." His focus drifts to the steaming mug in front of him. "As long as you don't cause any problems, then you're welcome here, Laney. For as long as you need. As much as I don't love strangers on my property or in my business, I'll make an exception if it gains me a favor I can call in later."

The way he glances at the clock as he sips from his mug makes me do the same. And the fatigue, that bone-deep tired, crashes over me like I'm trying to stand up in the face of a tidal wave. I could sleep for days. My limbs are tired and sore, and my mind could use a break from hyper-fixating and overthinking. And that's when I suddenly feel nervous to sleep. To be somewhere new and all alone.

"I'll have a job waiting for you when you're ready. We work hard and it's busy, but this is a helluva place. Take a few days to get your bearings. It's not a big city, so it won't take you very long to get acclimated here."

He shifts his eyes to my neck as I nod at that suggestion.

I touch the small cuts that surfaced as she screamed and begged me to help her. Her nails grabbed onto whatever she could. It wasn't to hurt me. It was hysteria and panic. The only visible marks from a night I don't think I'll be able to scrub from my memory any time soon.

"I didn't mean to stare." He stands from leaning against the counter. "I don't know the details, but if I had to make bets, my money would be on you, Laney. You've got nothing but respect from me."

I look into the mug, and since I'm not much for a filter, especially right now, I ask, "Shouldn't respect be earned? Isn't that the saying?"

"No, not here. There are plenty of people I've lost respect for, but people don't have to earn it with me." The sincerity in his tone instantly has me never wanting to disappoint or lose it with him. Something tells me that having Atticus Foxx's respect might go a long way in Fiasco.

"I'm going to head to bed. There's a guest suite on this floor just on the other side of the butler's pantry. Down that hall. Help yourself to whatever you might need, and I'll make sure you get a full tour of the grounds tomorrow."

He walks past me with a nod goodnight.

"This is going to sound..." I shake my head and smile as I turn toward where he was headed. "When you say grounds...?"

He smiles and mutters, "Fucking Bea." Taking a deep inhale, with frustration on the exhale, he says, "That woman likes to leave nothing but questions in her wake.

You're at Foxx Bourbon. That includes the distillery, cooperage, and rackhouses, and all of it happens on this land. It also happens to be my home. And well"—he winks at me, lightening the mood—"looks like it's your home now, too."

If you're any kind of bartender in any large city where the patrons like to throw money around on expensive alcohol and not just happy-hour drafts, then you've poured Foxx Bourbon. I'm good at a few things and exceptional at a handful of others. Bartending fell into the exceptional category before I started planning events with limitless budgets. Foxx Bourbon isn't some up-and-coming brand or only popular in certain places. No, if you know the difference between scotch, whiskey, and bourbon, then you've heard the name Foxx.

I've ended up in the heart of Bourbon Country with a new name and a clean slate. And for some reason, when Ace calls this place my home too, my shoulders relax, the weight of what I'm hiding from easing up just enough that I feel lighter than I have in a long time.

Chapter 4

LANEY

MY BODY JERKS AWAKE, and despite the thick duvet and cool room, I can't get comfortable. Anxiety wakes me up every twenty minutes. My migraine has calmed, but the exhaustion doesn't keep me sleeping soundly. I keep seeing the same images over and over again from different angles: torn flesh and blood that wouldn't stop dripping. At the time, I hadn't known exactly what we were running from, but we had been leaving a trail. There wasn't enough time to stop it. The pace was on a constant loop every time I shut my eyes. I didn't want to fill the prescription meds that the government-issued therapist prescribed to me on our way out of town. Now I regret that decision.

I pull the throw blanket from the bottom of the bed and drape it over my shoulders, walking out the double doors to the patio. The transition from the cool hardwood to the blue slate is a welcome warmth under my bare feet. I tilt my head back, taking in a deep breath of that sugar-dusted smell. The sky's just starting to turn, with the faintest hues of peach and yellow painted along the dividing line that separated the earth from the sky.

Horse paddocks are to the left, far enough away that even if there were horses out this early, I wouldn't be able to see them as anything larger than a speck in the distance. The steps down to the grass are slick with the morning's dew, but I want to feel it between my toes. There are only a few times I can remember walking barefoot in the grass back at home; during concerts on the main lawn or lazy Sunday picnics in Central Park. Those were plans and a weekend destination. This is a stark contrast to all of it. A quiet change from the concrete, cabs, and smoking grates of a typical morning commute. This is steps from where I slept. It's Ace's overly exaggerated backyard.

A quick whistle, followed by "Whoa, girl," in a low, deep gravel has my head turning so fast it's entirely possible I'm going to have whiplash. Add it to the roster of things I'll need to work through. It seems far too early for someone to be riding up on horseback, but then again, I have no idea what people do in Fiasco, Kentucky. Maybe this is entirely normal.

After a short succession of whistles, a dog comes darting out of nowhere, running alongside the horseback rider. The pup's chocolate brown head is mismatched from the rest of its white-and-gray speckled body. It's keeping up with the speed of the horse and its rider, who is getting closer by the second as he crests the small knoll less than a football field away. With his body squared and headed right for me, he pulls the reins and instantly comes close to a stop. This isn't Griz or Ace. No, this man is bulkier, younger than them, but easily older than me. He looks pissed off, like I'm inconveniencing him for existing in his path. Even if I wanted to scurry inside, the way he keeps his focus on me, I have a feeling he's the kind of man who would follow. The kind who wouldn't ask, but demand answers to the question that's most likely: *who the hell are you?* And I'd have to lie because that's what I am now. A liar.

But I'm not going to run away. Even if I'm still trying to figure out exactly who this new version of Laney might be, I'm not going to let her be the kind of woman who runs away. So, I stand taller. I know what quiet judgment feels like as his eyes rove over me. Judge away. I'm doing the same.

There's a movie I saw as a teenager that I always watched whenever it was playing. The first time I saw it, I thought it was a western. It starts with a woman in a show-down with an outlaw named Rogan. The woman lets him believe he is going to get the peep show that he just demanded, but as she unties her skirt, she pulls out a dagger and throws it with perfect aim directly to his heart. She rescues herself. And as she limps out of her home, in the distance, she sees the love of her life on horseback. He waits for her to ride off into the sunset. He was there to be with her, but she didn't need him to rescue her. She did that just fine on her own. That has always stuck with me.

I always liked the idea of a man like that. A sexy femi-nist who doesn't need to boss a woman around or save the day in order to prove his masculinity. One who trusts and allows her to handle her shit, without having to rescue her, but is there when she needs him. I sure as hell haven't found any men like that.

The kicker in all of this is that the movie turned out not to be a western at all. It was an 80s rom-com about a recluse author who is forced on an adventure just like the storylines in her romance novels. She surprises herself by turning out to be a badass in the end. She rescues her sister, gets the guy, and becomes the hero of her own story. *I've always loved that movie.*

This isn't that movie. No matter how much I think this cowboy looks like a fantasy from far away, the closer he comes to me, the scowl on his face gets clearer. He's not happy. I'm not exactly sure who he might be, but if I had to guess, Ace hasn't given him the memo that I'm welcome. He slows his horse no more than fifty feet from where I'm sitting now, but his dog doesn't stop.

His eyes flick down, and I quickly remember that I'm wearing nothing more than an oversized t-shirt, my legs and feet bare. I ball up my fists, unsure what to do with my hands as he watches me. My cheeks flush as he commands his horse to step closer. I only realize I'm holding my breath when my lungs force out an exhale.

His dark hair peeks out from the edges of a worn royal-blue baseball hat. Broad shoulders and perfect posture make it look like he was born to ride a horse. The way he carries himself is confident and rugged. My eyes wander across his strong chest, up to his chiseled jaw that hides behind thick scruff. I do more than just glance down the length of his arms to his corded forearms and white knuckles gripping the reins. I'm staring. His grip seems as tense as my entire body feels. As his eyes roam from my face to my feet and back up again, the only sounds around us are the chirps of the waking birds and the wapping of the dog's tail in the air as its wet nose brushes a sniff along my leg.

"You lost?" are the first words the cowboy says to me. As intense as it is to have watched a man ride closer on horseback, I don't expect the biting tone of his question.

"At the moment, no."

His brow furrows into a deeper scowl. My bet is he's trying to figure out exactly who I might be. "Then what are you doing in your underwear on my property?"

His property?

I lift my chin, holding up my thumb to count off what I'm about to say with all the attitude that I can muster. "First, this is Griz's property," I add my pointer finger. "Second, I was enjoying the quiet morning." I drop the first two fingers and raise my middle finger all by itself. "And, third" —I pluck at the cotton hem with my other hand—"it's a t-shirt." I drop my voice lower, just north of a whisper when I add, "Not underwear. Not wearing those right now."

I don't miss his eyes flicking down to the hem of my shirt again. He grits his teeth hard enough so that his square jawline twitches, making it look even more severe against the shadow of scruff over his cheeks and chin. As he meets my stare, I can see how much that remark tipped him over the edge from annoyance to downright pissed.

I tuck my bottom lip into my teeth, trying not to smile. I am absolutely wearing underwear. And maybe I'm an idiot for saying I'm not to a stranger, but I'm running on little to no sleep. My lack of giving a shit has me feeling more than good. Why does it feel so good to just say what I want?

His dog nudges my leg again, knocking me out of the stare-down I've apparently entered. I let her smell the top of my hand first before I lean down to scratch behind the pup's floppy brown ears. "Hello there. You're awfully sweet, aren't you." Her muddy paws make a mess of my blanket, but I'm sure I can wash it. I whisper loud enough for him to hear, "Much friendlier than the cowboy staring at us right now, huh?"

Running my hands down to the scruff of her neck, I read the name, *Julep,* that's sewn on her harness. I smile and keep scratching as she leans into it. "Julep, is he still watching us?"

"I'm going to do you a favor and be honest with you."

I rub behind Julep's ears and flick my eyes up to him. "I'm guessing by your charming tone that this 'honest favor' won't be the kind that has me smiling or moaning afterwards?"

It takes all my energy not to slap my palm over my lips and apologize for just saying the first thing that popped into my mind. When I look up, I catch his gruff exterior crack for a moment as he clears his throat. The right side of his mouth kicks up just wide enough for the thicker patch of hair above his lip to move.

"Not interested."

I pucker out my bottom lip. "Is that your version of being honest?

He drags his gaze around my crouched body and lingers on my ass that's just barely covered by the way I'm perched in front of his dog. "I'm especially not interested in my brother's leftovers, honey."

What? Then it registers, that this is one of Ace's brothers.

"Not your honey, cowboy," I clap back as I stand back up.

This time, his chest moves and shoulders flex, amused at my response. "No cowboys around here. You've got horsemen and bourbon boys in Fiasco," he says with a little southern twang on the end. It's just enough bravado to remind me that I'm out here pantless and he's managed to switch on something within me that feels an awful lot like attraction. I really need to get some rest; I'm confusing insults for flirtation.

"Seems like you might have some assholes too."

I swear his lip tilts up a little more, almost rewarding me with a smile, but his phone alarm sounds from his back pocket, leaving his reaction and my question unanswered.

When he clicks it off, he spins his hat backward, giving me one more glance before he says, "Let's go, Julep." The baseball hat was cute. Flipped backward, it's hot. But if he were wearing a cowboy hat, I'd be squeezing my thighs together.

The dog barks, knocking me out of my wandering thoughts. She barks twice more at him, as if to say, "I'm coming."

Me too, girl. Me too.

He lifts his reins and lets out a short whistle, taking the horse from a dead stop to turning in a full circle. He moves past me with enough speed that my hair whips up with the wind and smacks me right across my face. I don't focus on the fact that I never got his name. Or the fact that I never told him mine. Instead, the only thing that has my attention is this zero-gravity sensation. A stomach swoop, cheeks burning, and the speechless state I rarely find myself in.

I let out a nervous laugh. "Who the hell was that?"

CHAPTER 5

GRANT

I WANTED THIS. I wanted this so fucking badly that my jaw hurt the second I tapped it. But the body wasn't right. It was close, but it wasn't ready. It wasn't the right time. I know bourbon better than I know myself sometimes. It's in my blood—the culture of it, the details and notes of what made a batch exceptional, defines our family. I never planned to make a living off it, but there's plenty that's happened in my life that I never planned for.

With bourbon, there are rules. And if those rules aren't followed, then it can't be considered bourbon. It's chemistry, oak, fire, and time. Chemistry is learned and manipulated. I know what it means to toast or char. And time is the only thing that feels too slow when you want to stop remembering, and too fast when you look back. Bourbon needs time, and no matter how fast or slow you want time to move, it doesn't make a difference. Bourbon has rules.

Rules keep our business moving. And rules keep people safe.

"You're up early," Griz says from the front porch.

I don't tell him that I've been up for hours. Went for a ride to check my bourbon, met one of Ace's women wandering where she didn't belong, and took a shower. A cold one at that. Hating myself the whole time, knowing I was hard thinking about that girl standing on my property in just a shirt and no underwear. A handful of rules right there I was breaking—hiding something from my family and looking at someone I had no business looking at in that way.

She looked too fucking young for him.

When I walk up closer, I see Griz leaning against the railing, barely sparing me another glance. "I should say the same about you. Or did you not go to bed yet?"

My grandfather's mustache is so thick that it barely moves when he speaks, but I don't need to see his mouth to know when he's laughing. His deep drawl turns from a low hum into a barked laugh. It's hard not to smile whenever I hear it.

He gives me a side-eye. "You know my bedtime is when the sun goes down."

That's a fucking lie. I came to grab a coffee before I headed into the distillery for the day, not to start word sparring with him, so I let it ride.

I grip his shoulder and squeeze. It's the typical Foxx form of a hello and goodbye. It's always been that way, even when we were kids. We were never overly affectionate with each other, but I always knew they had my back the way I had theirs.

He clears his throat before he says, "A bit of a heads up before you go in there."

I pause, eyebrow raised, already knowing what or who he's going to warn me about. "He has a guest."

My grandfather looks down at his cup of what I'm assuming is coffee, but with him, it's never a guarantee. "I don't know if I'd call her a guest, per se, but she might be the prettiest girl I've ever seen."

I hate myself for wanting to agree. I'm being an asshole for thinking it at all.

"That's a big statement, Griz," I say with a wry smile. "You've seen a lot of girls in your day."

Griswald Foxx is one of, if not the best, master distillers in Kentucky, but his second specialty is women. The man flirts with everyone, but it's women who love him. It doesn't hurt that he loves to gossip with them as much as he enjoys romancing them.

He doesn't meet my eyes. Instead, he just smiles into his cup like he's got an inside joke with whatever he's drinking.

When I lean back into the doorway, looking toward the kitchen, I see her again. Her long hair trails down to the center of her back. It's a warm copper with a few golden blonde strands that remind me of the color that makes metal bend. She looks to the side, studying something on the wall, as her bare legs swing back and forth on either side of the barstool she's sitting on. I wonder if she's able to hear us from all the way out here, or if she's in her own world right now. She looks innocent, but the way her mouth ran this morning, not holding back or mincing words, my guess is that she's the kind of innocent that gets you close and then eats men for breakfast. I couldn't stop looking at her as if I haven't seen a woman in years–in all honesty, maybe I haven't. I stopped looking a long time ago.

What is she still doing here?

I step back onto the porch, letting the screen door close softly, and ask, "Who is she?"

But instead of Griz answering, it's my brother's voice that comes from behind me as he climbs the porch steps. "A friend."

"That so?" I bite back my smile for the many ways the word "friend" can be used.

"Can you do me a favor and not ask any questions?" He rubs the back of his neck, his tell that he's uncomfortable. My brother doesn't do relationships. Never has for plenty of reasons, but one very distinct one. I've watched plenty of women be ushered out of here in the morning, but not a single one has ever stuck around. I should leave it. Stop myself before I ask more questions, and go jerk off again. But I pry anyway. "She's a little young, don't you think, Ace?"

Griz interrupts with another barking laugh.

I turn my head his way. "Why is that so funny?"

"You never ask about women. I haven't seen you even do a double take at one." He shakes his head, smiling, "Oh hell, this is going to be fun."

I point at Griz, eyes narrowed. "Don't start. I was only asking a question."

But Ace doesn't answer me, just changes the topic. "Where were you this morning? I had to open the studio house and Julep was the only one who answered when I knocked on your door. Then she ran off."

Shit. I need to start waking up earlier if I want to use

the horses and trek out to the falls. It's more peaceful than the ATVs. But I'm not ready for him to know what I'm doing out there. So I give him my usual lie. "Couldn't sleep. I figured I'd take Tawney for a ride. Clear my head a bit."

It's when he asks, "Nightmares starting back up again?" that my gut sinks. Worrying him that I'm falling back into a depression instantly makes me feel like a shithead. It's the last thing I want him to believe when he was the one who rolled up his sleeves to help pull me out of it. He was the one who forced me to talk to someone. Made me feel like taking meds for being depressed wasn't something to be ashamed of. Said trying something to make you feel better, a support tool to help you function, didn't look like defeat to him. It looked like a fight. And I was always a fighter. Not in the same ways as my brothers, but we all were.

I shake my head no. And it was true, no nightmares for a long time now. "Just a lot on my mind with the new guys starting this week." I rub at the sliver of oak that got embedded along my thumb this morning. "Plus, it'll be too hot to ride later." That part was true. The humidity was at an all-time high for this early in the summer. Tawney's a good horse, but all the horses that boarded here, regardless of their typical demeanor, are much happier in their shaded paddocks in the afternoons.

"Alright." He grips my shoulder and squeezes it once. "Lincoln and the girls are going to be here later for dinner, you coming?"

"It's Friday night. I'll be here."

"You want a coffee?" He points inside, and I give him another quick shake of my head. If he doesn't want me to ask questions, then it's best I avoid the entire situation. I'll never see her again anyway. That's Ace's pattern with the women he brings home—it isn't often, but they're never on repeat. For him, it keeps things light, and the ridiculous Foxx curse that Fiasco loves to gossip about at bay. We all believe in it. Each of us knows loss as our rite of passage. Every woman a Foxx man loved ended up dying. And for each of us, we learned our lesson once. That was enough. I don't think any of us want to try to survive another loss like the ones we've experienced.

I shift my eyes past Ace's shoulder and through the archway. I don't like that I look back, but I do it anyway. A wave of guilt runs through me for wanting to see her once more. I liked the way she talked to me—no trace of sympathy. Simply a stranger who had no problem clapping back.

I take a deep breath. This wasn't how I planned to start my day. Thinking about those pretty blue eyes and pouty lips.

I run my palms along the back pockets of my jeans. When I turn to leave, moving back toward the pathway that connects my house with the main, I catch Griz smiling at me.

Fucking shit-stirrer.

His eyes crinkle and his mustache widens.

Walking past, I point at him. "Don't."

"Didn't say anything." He holds up his hands. "But I told ya. Prettiest woman I've ever seen."

CHAPTER 6

LANEY

"THE STABLES ARE on the other side of the main house about a mile and a half down that way," Ace says as he points at a field of light green grass with a couple of trees every fifty or so feet from the next. The buzz of Cicadas always felt like the baseline of a summer's soundtrack, but the hum of them out here seems louder. They vibrate the grass, and it's an instant muscle relaxer. A nature-made white noise machine that calms my entire body. The two large oak trees on the far side of this plot of land would be the perfect place to hang a hammock. I close my eyes and let the sun warm my face for a moment. Even being so close to the horse stables, the only scent that permeates the air is that tangy, sugary smell.

It feels good to breathe, knowing you'll get something sweet as a reward. And despite the way this morning started, I feel good today. I don't have a job yet, or responsibilities. But Fiasco, Kentucky, might just be the life I never knew I wanted. I'm in the last year of my twenties and the idea of reading a book on a hammock connected to those two trees looks like my perfect end game.

"This is more than I was expecting," I tell him as I stare off at the way the landscape keeps going. And it's true, I had no expectations after WITSEC was mentioned. Witness protection seemed like overkill. They caught the bad guy, and the girl he held captive was safe. But the moment Agent Harper stepped into the picture, I knew it. I had only met her one other time before when she came to Coney Island for my high school graduation party. I remembered her because she was the reason my dad had to leave for work. The rest of my celebratory barbecue was with our neighbors. And Phillip.

"You should have plenty of privacy here. My brother is just across the way. He renovated this space. Added the Murphy bed, thought it would make the space feel larger if the bed could tuck away."

It may have been one big room, but it was well thought through, and the finishes make it posh and polished. Similar to the main house, the fixtures are modern and masculine. There's black metal hardware along drawers and pulls, and brushed gold lighting fixtures to accent the recessed lights on the vaulted ceiling. The height of it makes the one room feel like it's far larger than its modest 450 square feet measurement Ace had mentioned. A place like this where I was from was not cheap. If it had a doorman and a pool, it would have been considered luxury apartment living. "The rent—"

He shakes his head before I finish. "There are plenty of

things to do around here. We'll work it out." He flips the water on at the sink. "What did you do?"

The question has my nerves rising, but he must see it on my face, because he finishes his question. "For work, I mean, before you came here?"

It doesn't feel like I need to lie about this part. "Weddings, mostly." That piques his interest. "Large budget events, but mostly those were weddings. Occasionally, it was something . . ." How do I find the right phrase? I can't just come out and tell him that the agency I worked for ran the Metropolitan Museum's MET Gala or that we had been flown into D.C. for the second year in a row to plan and execute the White House Correspondents' Dinner. So I go with ". . . higher profile with a lot of very demanding guests."

"Did you enjoy it?"

In the almost eight years I had worked my way up from intern to running my own team, I don't know that I'd ever been asked that. It was a career, not just a job. And I was good at something for once. My dad wasn't around. I didn't have many people who cared more than to ask the somewhat rhetorical question of "how are you?"

I had set my sights on being successful at something and then just kept moving forward. "I liked the work, but the clients I had were . . ." I shake my head because I don't want him to think I'm not capable of dealing with all kinds of people. I am. I just lost myself along the way.

He gives me a nod that feels like he understands *complicated*. "People always have a way of fucking up good things."

My issue was that I blurred professional and personal

lines. Then decided to bathe in poor decisions and blurred moral lines while I was at it.

"You might have solved a little problem for me. When you feel settled, let's talk about what you could do for the Foxx brand." With his arms crossed over his chest, he looks lost in thought before the sound of a loud car engine revs up the private road and screeches to a stop out front. "It's like summoning Lucifer," he says under his breath. "That would be Hadley. She volunteered to pick up some things when I mentioned I had someone staying in the cottage." He glances around at the blank white walls and bare windows and then smiles at me. "We don't get many new faces that stick around longer than tourists. I think she's being more nosey than helpful."

Even with his reassuring laugh, my nerves kick in. "Does she know what I'm doing here?"

He looks at me curiously. "Laney, I don't really know the details about what brought you here other than an ornery U.S. Marshall. What I do know is that you need your past kept quiet, and I am more than equipped to keep secrets."

"Who does she think I am?"

The sound of a car door shutting has him moving toward the front of the cottage and out the front door. "A juicy story," Ace says as he steps up to a shiny, deep purple car that looks straight off the set of a *Fast and Furious* movie. "Hadley," he calls out.

"Present," a raspy voice sing-songs. "We doing roll call, Daddy?" A tall woman with dark hair piled high in a messy bun peeks out from behind the trunk.

"Quit it with that shit," Ace huffs with a roll of his eyes. "What's gotten into you lately?"

Sticking out her tongue, she laughs at him as she walks up the front porch steps, mumbling, "Nothing I want..."

She hoists an array of reusable bags along both arms. There's one slung on each shoulder, another hanging from each crook of her elbow, and then two in each hand. When she looks up, she smiles wide. "I am so damn happy you're here. This fucking town could use some new faces." Letting out an exaggerated exhale, she stops at the threshold. "Holy shit." She looks at me from head to toe, which would normally put me on the defense, but then she releases a small laugh. "You're gorgeous."

I'm taken aback at the compliment. "Thank you," I say with surprise in my tone. "I'm Laney."

"I already know." She leans close to me as she walks through the front door, tilting her head toward Ace trailing far enough behind not to hear. "But I'm wondering, Laney, are you a long-lost cousin, or are you sleeping with big, bad Atticus Foxx over there?" She keeps moving into the studio without giving me a chance to respond. But I have a feeling maybe she doesn't really want to know.

Yes, Ace is intensely handsome. I see the appeal; you'd have to be blind not to check him out. But he's not who caught my attention.

"Oh yeah, this place needs color." Barely taking a breath, she keeps talking. "I got some good coffee from Crescent de Lune in town, some loose-leaf tea. I didn't know what kind of caffeine you liked, so I also grabbed some energy drinks."

I smile at the thoughtfulness. "Coffee girl here."

"Me too. And then the rest here is mostly pantry fillers . . ." She goes off on a tangent, laughing, "Sounded like panty fillers." She wiggles her eyebrows. "Sounds more fun than canned goods, huh?"

What? I let out a clipped laugh, not expecting the quirkiness. It's refreshing. I was silently hoping for a package of red licorice—Red Vines or Twizzlers would have been good. But I am anxious, and candy is my vice.

"I thought you could probably use . . ." Dropping the bags, she starts digging through, holding up each item. "Last time I was in here, the place smelled stale. So, a candle." She opens the top and sniffs. "Yum." She passes me the candle and then pulls out a salt rock lamp. "These are so good for so many things. Felt kind of necessary." I couldn't think of anything a rock could do besides serve as a weapon. But she continues her show and tell, holding up everything from a box of tampons to dry shampoo. "I also grabbed my favorites. Don't worry, I have good taste. I've got condi-tioner, body wash, face wash, lotion, a good fluffy towel—" Then, she holds up a nail polish that I've never been happier to see. "Ruby slippers."

I smile. "I like it."

"It was that or pale pink." She sticks out her tongue, making a yuck face that has my smile widening into a knowing grin. There's nothing wrong with pale pink, but it's what I associated it with that has me revolting against it.

With a serious expression, like she's about to gift me a life-changing device, she holds up a black box shaped like a cube. "And a personal massager."

It's probably how I open my mouth and cough out a laugh that has her smiling back at me.

"I know, it's overstepping, but I went with my gut," she says. "Long-lost cousin."

"Hadley," Ace says under his breath from behind me.

She looks up and past my shoulder, winking at him. "Do personal massagers get your panties in a wad, big Foxx? They sure do special things to mine."

He shoves his hands in his pockets, and his buttoned-up demeanor shifts as he starts moving toward the front door. "You're in good hands, Laney. Find me when you're ready to talk about that job."

"Thanks again, Ace."

He gives me a curt nod, and then points to Hadley. "Please don't be a pain in the ass." I can read people fairly well and Ace Foxx is a confident man with what seemed like infinite patience—with the way both Bea and Griz managed to push him last night. But the woman in front of me, with her long legs and flirty words, set him off kilter.

"That's reserved only for you and your brothers." She salutes. And when he turns away, she flips him off.

I bite down on my lip to keep the smile from cracking. The entire interaction is hilarious, but I'm not about to pry.

Opening the small refrigerator, she says, "No need to worry. If you two are enjoying each other." She stops what she's doing for a second. "I've known Ace almost my whole life. His brother Lincoln is my best friend."

I ignore the remark about enjoying Ace and ask, "He's the oldest?"

"Yes. Then Lincoln. He has two little girls, Lark and Lily. And you already met Griz, I assume?"

I can't help but smile as I nod yes, thinking about the welcome drink he brought me in the middle of the night.

I notice how she doesn't mention a wife or mother of his daughters in that rundown. "Does Lincoln have a partner, or?"

"Widower," she says, her face turning sad. "It's been just him and the girls now for . . ." She pauses, grabbing a few more items from a grocery bag that looks like pears, strawberries, and some green lettuce. "Farmer's market from this morning." Holding out a small yellow berry for me to try, she pops one in her mouth. "Gooseberry. They're good." Chewing hers, she looks up. "Liv, or Olivia, Lincoln's wife, and the girls' mom, passed away about four years ago now." She looks up, as if trying to recall. "Yeah, that was a year after Fiona."

How am I supposed to keep track of all these people?

This isn't a borough or even a suburb. It's a small town. Small towns mean that everyone knows everyone's business to some degree. I can't understand why Agent Harper thought this was a good idea.

"And then there's Grant."

The cowboy. "Any chance he rides a horse?"

"Most people around here do. I have a thoroughbred boarding here, actually. Everyone knows someone in the horse business. Why?"

"I think I met him this morning." I gnaw at my bottom lip, thinking about the way he was kind of rude. And how he filled out that t-shirt he was wearing, and stared at my bare legs, trying to catch a glimpse of my ass when I asked him if his honest favor would have me smiling or moaning.

Why was it so much fun to say what I wanted and then see his reaction?

She looks past me and peers out the front double window. "He lives right down the hill from you. He's not the most social of this crew, so I doubt you'll see him all that much."

That's disappointing to hear. The last thing I should be thinking about is the way he rode in on a damn horse and was nothing short of arrogant, but I liked how it felt to dish it back.

"I can almost guarantee that you will see Julep on your front lawn from time to time. She loves to wander. But she's Grant's girl, so don't feel bad if she snubs you."

"Dog, right? Not daughter?"

She laughs. "Dog. No kids."

I like getting the rundown from her. She talks to me like we're already friends. And truthfully, a friendship sounds nice. Our conversation feels like playing catch-up from a place I haven't visited in a long while, not somewhere I had never been.

She asks, "What about you?"

I unzip a bag of sheets for the bed. "No dog. Always wanted one. No kids. The jury is still out if that's something I'd really want." The silky black satin is nicer than any sheets I've ever bought myself. "What do I owe you for this?"

She bats at the air in front of her. "A drink." And, before I can interject, she adds, "I can swing it." She points to her chest. "Rich girl."

I stare at her for a second, surprised by the honesty, and take in her appearance. It's not a typical response, especially from the stuffy rich people I was used to being around. She just said it; didn't flaunt it. And I respect that so much more. She doesn't scream stuffy or stuck-up. Her white Converse sneakers match her tucked-in tank. There are no designer labels, only a baseball jersey that hangs open like it was a short-sleeved jacket. Maybe it's a collector's item. Since I'm not a baseball fan, the last name Turner doesn't mean all that much to me.

She sees that I'm trying to figure her out, or at the very least figuring out how to respond. I'm being a judgmental twat, just like the people who used to do it to me wordlessly.

"I spend my money on things I like and not what people presume to be expensive and nice. I have a wardrobe to die for, with everything from Walmart and Duluth to Louboutins and Saint Laurent." She pulls at the front of the baseball jersey. "Signed. I went all the way to Maine for it. It means something to me." She clears her throat before I can ask any more. "My family does very well. I own my own business. So when I say that the best payment is good company, I really mean it."

The way that sounds so genuine makes me smile. "What kind of business?"

She hops up on the counter, and her long legs swing as she pops a grape in her mouth. "My family is in the business of horses. We raise, breed, and train thoroughbreds with a long history of producing Triple Crown winners. But my business is booze. I always thought I should have been born a Foxx for that reason," she says wistfully. "I own the best damn speakeasy in Kentucky." When she smiles this time, obvious pride beams from her face.

Owning something like that takes time, money, and real love. It's impressive. She's impressive, and I think I have a bit of a crush on her.

She pops another grape in her mouth. "Opened Midnight Proof a few years ago. I turned thirty and decided it was the one thing I kept saying I wanted to do." She shrugs. "So I did it. And my father was not the biggest fan, but I'm not the quiet little debutant everyone thinks I am. So I couldn't blame him for pushing back on the idea." Batting at the air in front of her, she says, "That's enough about me." Then she's pulling a bottle of Foxx Bourbon from her oversized purse like it's a completely acceptable thing to do. "You're living at the world's best bourbon distillery. You needed a bottle, so I snagged it from the main house. Ace said essentials. I consider it an essential."

Clapping her hands together, she jumps down. "Okay, I feel like I've barreled into your life without much permission." She smiles, reflecting the same one I've been sporting since she arrived. "So, I can get lost and come back another time. Let you get settled. Or you can escape with me briefly, and we can tour the distillery."

CHAPTER 7

GRANT

I'M IN A SHIT MOOD. That isn't new, but this particular sunny disposition I find myself in managed to seep in deep. It has my guys keeping a wider berth than usual.

A voice clears next to me. "Boss? I think there's something off with the machine. I've been trying to table the staves from this morning, and nothing's fittin' right."

I glance up at my new guy as he looks at me over his shoulder.

Sure enough, we have an audience. Jimmy must have picked the short straw to bring this to me.

As I stare at him, I try to get him to figure out on his own what he should be doing instead of me explaining. "You need me to do your job—?"

His neck ripples as he swallows.

"Jimmy," he stutters out. "It's Jimmy, sir."

I know his name is Jimmy. His dad, Jimmy Senior, runs Dugan's Hardware. He went to school with my parents, and as small towns go, he knows our story. But I'm not friends with people just because they know my last name or work for me. I'd been friends with almost everyone I worked with in the Fiasco PD. That ended up being a fucking joke. They just ended up giving me pitying looks and talking about me behind my back. I'm over that kind of "friendship." I have no interest in being friends with any of the men or women who work here now. I have my brothers. I have Griz and the guys from poker. Here, I'm their boss. That's enough.

He looks back at the crew as they all watch the exchange. "It felt wasteful to scrap all of it. I read the report that was posted about this season of white oak trees."

I move away from the hoop I was fitting and have a look. He's right, scrapping all that wood would have been a waste. There are shortages we need to be mindful of and making sure every stave has a purpose is one way to do that. Barrel making is like any job that requires manual labor. There's going to be hiccups. But these are the kinds of things I'm confident about fixing. Wood that doesn't sit right. A leaning barrel. Small adjustments that will have our output hitting the numbers we need for the day. I've always been good at solving problems, finishing puzzles, and finding answers. It's what made me a good cop–until it didn't.

When the lead cooper position opened, Ace wanted me to fill it. *"You're a Foxx. This is your family's company, Grant. And you're good at this."* I knew what he wanted, but I didn't have the energy to tell him I was nervous to have a team of people counting on me. I didn't want to fuck up that responsibility. I had done that already, and it cost a life. But *he didn't want to hear it anyway. "If you want to be here, then you're running it, not just treading water anymore."*

That was over a year ago now. I preferred just doing the job, but now I have people working for me. I assigned roles to each guy and trusted that they did what they were supposed to. I didn't hover. They're getting paid to do a job. It's that simple. If they don't do it, I fire them. Jimmy, apparently, didn't know that yet.

I nudge my chin toward the table. "Raise 'em."

Jimmy blinks at me.

"Stack them in the skirt." He looks barely old enough to drink what we make, but he jumps into action.

I never say much here, but it's more than that. Today, I'm distracted. The trip to the waterfalls didn't give me what I had expected, and then I ran into a fucking pin-up girl wandering around in a goddamn t-shirt. I tug off my work gloves and rub the back of my neck. Why the hell had my body woken up for her? I knew it wasn't going to be good the moment my cock twitched. I was hard the second my eyes hit the tops of her thighs.

"It's not always going to line up on the table. If you've got a few not cooperating, you can bang it out."

"Sir, it's the whole pallet that's not lining up," Jimmy says as he stacks.

I look over his shoulder, raising my eyebrow at the three who are watching Jimmy stack. "You sent the new kid to ask for help?"

I haven't given the new guys a full overview yet. I suppose now is as good a time as any. "Alright, listen up."

"That's definitely a tourist," one of the older guys, who's been here long before me, murmurs. I don't bother looking. Plenty of groups of women and men walk through, grabbing attention, but not much catches my eye. Frankly, I'm annoyed I don't have my crew's attention.

"If all of these aren't sitting right on the table, then you need to start stacking." I point at what I want. "You two, work those staves into the skirt. And then I want everyone adjusting their roles. We need them fired and steamed. Jimmy, you're taking lead on banging them to fit."

Around the space, I hear some of my guys adding to the chatter.

This is the only drawback of making barrels on site. Having a cooperage on the same premises as the distillery means plenty of onlookers from our distillery tours. While Foxx Bourbon sits on the farthest end of the bourbon trail, there are plenty of people just about any day of the week looking for a behind-the-scenes glimpse at the magic of this place. "There's a shortage, which means we need to make every stave count for us, even if that means we fit them this way from here on out." Not a single person answers, which has me looking up. Sure enough, the four guys huddled around me have their attention focused on something over my shoulder. Even Jimmy's wide-eyed, smiling like an idiot.

Another one of the guys firing up the barrels whistles. I already know I'm not going to like whatever it is. Maybe even a part of me knows what or whom I'll see.

As soon as I look up, it's like a punch in the gut. "Jesus Christ," I say under my breath.

She has on more clothes than this morning, but not enough to cover the shape and length of her legs or the way her tank top hugs her curves just right. That strawberry-colored hair that somehow looks like it has gold woven through it, flows wildly behind her. And her lips–I have to clear my throat and swallow because my mouth waters just seeing them tipped up and smiling at Hadley.

Ripping off my gloves, I grit my teeth. "Get back to work."

CHAPTER 8

LANEY

I WAS TOO interested in the Foxx Bourbon Distillery to hang back. Sleep would happen eventually. The universe somehow managed to drop me at the epicenter of one of the world's largest distributors and most respected bourbon brands. It isn't my first choice as a drink, but I've poured plenty of variations of whiskey in my lifetime. When someone asked for bourbon, if they knew a thing or two, they'd always request Foxx. Sometimes if they were cheap, they'd opt for another brand, but anyone who asked for rocks or neat always went with a Foxx label.

Instead of hopping into her muscle car, we walked along a stone walkway for about half a mile and ended up in front of the Foxx Bourbon Distillery. The entryway reminded me of the wineries in New York along the Finger Lakes. I did a wedding there last summer that was a "small elopement" ceremony of just under six-hundred close family and friends. That couple almost didn't make it when they argued for months about which vineyard would be the best for their vows. The West Coast was known for its vineyards and the way they were presented, but New Yorkers could only show off to as many people as possible if it was drivable. The Finger Lakes had won them over.

I feel warm here, beyond just the humidity. There's no pretension or sense of unwelcomed exclusivity. The beautifully curated landscaping ranged from perfectly rounded green shrubbery to wispy cherry blossom trees. Greenery with pops of color is what framed the massive oak double doors. It was quite simply...lovely.

At the top of the entryway was the Foxx Bourbon logo, the black metal bent and molded into the letter *F* with the profile of a fox head woven around it. It was grandiose and so different from the other side of the property, where the main house and cottage sat. This was for tourists.

The sound of cars driving over gravel and chatter from groups of people sitting along the patio along the perimeter greeted us. As soon as we walked closer, the air smelled sweeter and tangier.

"It smells so good here."

She closes her eyes and breathes in. "It's a combination of corn, malted barley, and rye that ferments when it's combined with yeast. Aside from making bourbon, it makes the air smell like you're being bathed in sugar." Holding out her tongue, she swipes at the air as her voice rasps, "Delish."

Just as she starts to say something more, a deep voice comes from behind us, startling me. I clutch my chest and close my eyes briefly. It's the first time a man's voice has made me feel jumpy. One of the consequences I hadn't realized I would need to deal with from coming face to face with a monster and living to remember it.

"The mash bill. It's always stronger the closer you get to the distillery."

He has a smile that pulls at shallow dimples and crinkles the corners of bright blue eyes. His brown hair is a little longer, and while he doesn't look like an exact replica, I know this has got to be the other Foxx brother. The same confidence and gait. All his features are distracting on their own, but add in the square jawline, and the Foxx men were all living up to their name.

"Laney, this is my bestest friend on the planet, Lincoln Foxx," Hadley says, smiling and wrapping her arm around him as she stands on her tiptoes.

Holding out his hand, he says, "My grandfather, Griz, told me all about the pretty new stranger staying in the studio. Thought that might be you."

Hadley opens her mouth wide. "Linc, are you flirting?" She points to me. "That was flirting, right?"

I can't help but smile and nod yes.

Lincoln drops the smile and gives her a sarcastic blank face when he tells her, "I hate you. And I'm welcoming your friend. Don't be a dick, Hadley Jean."

I shake his hand back, smiling at both of them. "It's nice to meet you. Your whole family has been really welcoming. Thank you."

They look at each other before Lincoln says, "Then you haven't met all of us yet."

The cowboy.

But before I can correct the assumption, Lincoln starts walking with us. "Can I tag onto your tour, Hads?"

Hadley gives him a knowing smile. And the way that his neck tints pink just above the neckline of his t-shirt, I think Lincoln isn't one to tag onto tours of his own distillery.

We follow him past the main entrance, where groups of people wait for their tours to start. "Laney, have you ever been to a distillery?"

Lincoln's face lights up as his smile lines crease and dimples tilt when I tell him, "This is my first. I've done a lot of vineyard tours and breweries, but never a distillery."

He claps his hands together and rubs his palms like he's about to unleash the ultimate entertainment. He's so much lighter than both of his brothers. "There's a helluva lot of fun in bourbon, but at the core of all of it is simple chemistry." He begins explaining the science behind it—where fermentation and ratios are what set bourbons apart at their core. He touts about the things that the Foxx brand does differently than all the rest. "Our ratio of corn to rye and barley is higher, which makes us sweeter. No matter what, in order to qualify as a true bourbon, one of the rules is that the mash bill needs to be 51% corn or higher."

He's charming. A natural presenter and captivating storyteller. There's no mistaking he loves what he does and is good at his job.

"So, Laney with no last name, how long are you planning to be in Fiasco?" he asks, just as we enter into a more industrial-looking space. "My brother was pretty vague, whether you were moving here or just visiting. Just that you'd be here for a while and to give you space until you started working."

"Nice job on that space, Linc," Hadley says, leaning into his side.

I knew the questions would come. I just wish I had thought through how I would answer. Without letting too much silence linger around the question, I settle on, "I'll be here for a while," shrugging. "I'm entering my 'don't over-think it' era," I add with a bright smile. "So we'll see."

Hadley chimes in, "I like that. I overthink everything. Usually, after I've already done it."

"So, ask-for-forgiveness kind of girl?"

Lincoln laughs and answers for her, "Rarely."

I slow down next to a massive silver tub. "Ace is doing a friend a favor by giving me a job and a place to stay for a while. I met him last night." Looking into the tub, I see it filled almost to the brim with a bubbling, thick yellow substance. When I hover my hand over the top, I can feel the heat radiating from it. "Getting involved with anyone is very low on my to-do list right now."

Hadley loops her arm with mine as we walk. "You, my friend, might want to consider a new to-do list. But fair warning, there's already gossip that Ace had a 'young thang' at his house this morning."

"News travels quickly here?" I had hoped this was more of a mind-your-own-business small town and not the stereotype in movies and books.

"Oh, Laney, it's the most fun part. I usually make up a couple of rumors about myself just to keep the old biddies out of my business." She winks at me as we leave the main building.

The clang of metal against concrete has me jumping. The echo grabbed most people's attention, but for me, it pushes my pulse rate into double-time.

"It's a bit louder in here. Between the wood that's

carved and slotted into staves and coming off the line to the barrels being toasted." Lincoln points around the massive workspace. Along the edges, several tour groups keep their attention on the center of the space as wooden barrels are being made in various stages of their process.

"This is one of the few distilleries that has an in-house cooperage. My grandfather decided it made more sense to do what we wanted instead of negotiating and paying for a product we couldn't control. It's one of our largest assets when it comes to making bourbon. The barrels are where everything changes. It gives us complete control on the level of char we have in our barrels and sets the plan for what we're making."

He talks as we walk, and I take in all the machinery and barrels that are rolled outside and off to wherever they're headed next. I'm fascinated by each piece of it. From the way he explains how the pieces of wood are held together by metal hoops and pressure, to the amount of time they're currently toasting their barrels for this batch. "Right there." He points to a conveyor belt that carries a newly constructed barrel. Someone pushes a button, and it immediately bathes the oak in a controlled fire. With a count-down clock on the wall of fifty seconds, the fire-roasted barrel is covered to tamp out the flames, and then when the cover is lifted, air ducts suck out the smoke as if it never happened.

But I miss what he says next, or whatever he wants me to see, because I'm watching as the cowboy, sans his blue baseball hat, yanks the barrel down and then rolls it from the conveyor belt, into the center of the room.

When he looks up, he pauses just long enough that our

eyes meet. Long seconds tick by before his gaze moves to Lincoln standing next to me, who I forgot was talking.

". . . that's the truth of it, Laney."

"I'm sorry, what did you say?"

He laughs, and then glances out to where I was focused. "Nothing. Come on, let's go tag a barrel." As we follow, he looks over his shoulder. "Perk of taking a tour with one of us."

Hadley leans into me as we walk behind Lincoln, adding, "That one, with the forearms and big shoulders, would be Grant Foxx." She must sense exactly what I'm feeling, because she sniffs a laugh. "Yeah, I know. All of them, right? It's ridiculous."

I widen my eyes, and whisper-shout back to her over the noise from the massive space. "All of them. What's in the water here?"

"Limestone," that voice from this morning answers. *How did he even hear that?* "These two are shit tour guides if they haven't already told you about the water here." His mouth ticks up to the right. "That's what you were asking —what's in the water here?"

Cocky bastard. He knows exactly why I asked that.

He looks down at my legs. "I see you found some pants."

He didn't.

Hadley and Lincoln look back and forth at us, clueless as to what he's talking about. "Linc, what am I witnessing here?"

"Honestly, I have no idea."

Hadley points between us. "So you've already met?" And since she is apparently someone who doesn't let people answer before she throws out more questions, she turns to me and says, "I thought you said you just came last night?"

And the minute she says it, that particular choice of words, I can tell exactly what Grant's thinking. His stoic expression cracks for just a moment as the tiniest smirk quirks the mustache that stands out thicker from the scruff along his beard. And I'm realizing really fucking quickly that Grant Fox is not just attractive. No, this guy is ruggedly handsome. Tall and built. Thick, dark brown hair long enough to thread through fingers and grip along the top. Hazel eyes shining with colors that make them pretty as they dance around my face. "That true, honey? Did you just *come* last night?"

"Sure did," I quip right back without missing a beat. "Not that it's any of your business."

"Honey? What did I miss?" Lincoln asks his brother.

The glare I'm trying to muster turns into a staring contest that, if I'm not careful, I might lose.

He keeps his eyes trained on me while he answers his brother. "She was wandering around the back of the main house in one of Ace's t-shirts. No pants. Thought she was still drunk or lost."

My hands ball up into fists and a full-body flash of heat flushes my face, staining my cheeks and up my neck too. "I was neither of those, fuck you very much."

He crosses his arms over his broad chest. "Didn't think I'd see you again. He usually doesn't like repeats."

Hadley barks out a laugh and slings her arm around my shoulders. "Well, it looks like you might be seeing even more of her since she just moved into the cottage across from your place."

The speed at which his eyebrows raise and lips part is priceless.

I smile with satisfaction.

Lincoln leans closer and quietly asks, "That true? You and Ace?"

There isn't anything discreet about him asking since Hadley and Grant are waiting on the answer and the fact that a few workers behind Grant have started paying attention to this exchange. Grant gives his brother a glare and Hadley can't seem to tame her smug smile.

This is going to be the beginning of my story in this town. The gossip will flow from this interaction alone, so I want to be crystal clear: what I'm doing here is none of their business.

"The last time I checked, Hadley," I say loudly while meeting Grant's eyes, "what a woman does with her body, whether it's with or without a partner, is nobody else's business but her own, right?"

"I knew I was going to love you," she laughs out. "And yeah, Laney. Sounds about right to me." She holds out her arm as a signal for me to loop mine in hers.

When we start to walk away, I pause and look at Grant from head to toe. I've been underestimated, overpromised, and left to pick up the pieces of a life that I don't recognize. He might be beautiful, but I'm not going to be intimidated. Been there, done that, wouldn't recommend. "Don't assume you know anything about me, *cowboy*. Because I'll tell you right now, you're going to end up being wrong."

"Not a cowboy, remember?" he shouts back at me, watching as I go.

"Might want to consider wearing a different shirt,

then." His chambray shirt looks damn good. Sleeves rolled to his elbows, faded and worn. As a man in Manhattan, he would have been chasing or starting a trend.

I shift my eyes to Hadley. "Want to do that tasting now?"

"Laney," Grant calls out.

When I turn back toward him, he looks like he's going to apologize, but instead, he stands there, the stoic look masking his handsome face, staying silent.

"My name sounds good coming out of your mouth like that."

I raise my eyebrows to challenge him to say something —go ahead, *try to have the last word, cowboy.* As I look over my shoulder at him one more time, I realize I've just figured out two very important things: I've definitely managed to piss off Grant Foxx just by existing in his small town. And I think I like it.

CHAPTER 9

GRANT

"YOU BELIEVE THAT NONSENSE?" Del asks, hunched over his slab of prime rib. Our dinners at Hooch's after his bowling league nights were a coincidence at first. A year had gone by after his daughter had been taken from us, and I still hadn't found the backbone to face him. I didn't get to her in time, and that wasn't something I wanted to forgive or gloss over. He was my friend, and I couldn't bring myself to talk about her and remember her. But Del couldn't stop talking about her. He wasn't ready to let people forget her.

Fiona's death was ruled a homicide by a meth-head junkie found about a mile from the old tobacco farm. An old farmhand who had worked there years prior was squatting and tweaked out when the cops arrived. It had nothing to do with human trafficking or a drug ring. Or so the story was spun. Apparently, the intel was bad, and it ended in unnecessary loss of life. The case was closed before the grass started growing on her grave. None of it sat right. I left the force a month later.

I look up at the flat screen behind the bar. "No, I missed it." But the truth is, I'm still thinking about the woman who crashed my day. *"My name sounds good coming out of your mouth like that."* I honestly still can't believe she said that.

But Del keeps talking, and eventually I stop thinking about those pretty lips and the way she stood in the middle of my workplace dishing attitude right back to me. "What they're not saying is that this guy is some kind of ghost. My buddy up in New York says that somehow his last vic gets out of the storage facility she was being held in and escapes. Fire department shows up on the scene first and holds the guy. NYPD arrests him, and based on all the evidence they found, they're looking to pin a half dozen missing persons on him. Not many vics because he savors them. You believe that fucked-up shit?"

"Jesus Christ," I huff out. "This is what you and your FBI buddies talk about?"

He takes a fry from my plate. "Yeah. And the shit season the Yanks are going to have." He cuts into his rare cut, and over a big bite, says, "That perp, though, there's no pattern. It's unclear if there are more locations—besides that one spot. It's a damn nightmare up there."

"Thought most of your guys would be retired?" I ask. Del knows everyone. It's in his nature to ask questions and be the friendly guy. He always told me the bad-cop schtick was bullshit. You always got better details with honey than spit. "Retired or dead, but what the hell else are we talkin' about besides cases and sports?"

"You boys need a refill?" Marla interrupts. She's already pouring the pitcher of Ale-8 into our mugs. It's one of four options at Hooch's: water, bourbon, coffee, or Ale-8.

Del smiles at her. "Thanks, Marla."

"You remember when Fi used to only let me put on football or Unsolved Mysteries," Marla reminisces.

My throat tightens hearing her name. Five years and it's still like a punch to the gut. The undercurrent of feeling like if I had only driven faster, gotten there sooner, she would have had backup. I tune out the rest of the conversation until Del nudges my arm.

"Anyway, the perp, from up north, the girl who survived, there were patches of her skin peeled off. The sick fuck wasn't just torturing and killing them. He was eating them. Found other skins that were brining. Like he was pickling them."

I drop my burger on my plate and give him my best *are you fucking serious?* look.

He barks a laugh. "You lose your edge, Foxx?"

"Just my appetite now," I tell him, wiping my hands on my wad of paper-thin napkins. I take a swig of my sweet soda. "And we didn't deal with that type of shit here."

He nods in agreement, looking down at his plate, and I want to pull back the words I just muttered. It didn't matter what we saw or arrested in Fiasco, no matter how mundane or fucked up a call might have been, none of them would compare to the one where his daughter was the victim. We may not have had cannibals or mass murderers, but plenty of bad things happen, even in our small town.

"Heard there's a new tenant living on the Foxx compound," he says, changing the subject.

I watch Marla dry the glasses that just came from the steaming washer beneath the counter. She's not fooling anyone, trying to listen to whatever gossip Del is pitching.

But before I can refute it, Wheeler Finch, Hadley's father, pipes in from behind us. "City girl. Heard she was keeping your brother company the past couple of nights too."

His laugh makes his stomach shake the table in front of him. I didn't realize he was here. Maybe I am losing my edge. I usually know exactly who and what's happening around me. And knowing when Wheeler and his business partner, Waz, were present should always be one of those times. I've never liked Hadley's family. Her father especially. He loves to throw money at anything that'll take it as long as it gets him what he wants. He owns most of the horse trainers working in Kentucky, which means he gets an inside ear on what thoroughbreds look like winners. He's built an empire, similar to what my brother has built, but they're nothing alike. Ace is respected. Wheeler is feared.

"Didn't realize you were taking over for the book club ladies and starting rumors around here, Wheeler." I hate that he's talking about her, never mind trying to fuel the fact that she spent the night with my brother. I hate even more that I can't stop thinking about her thick thighs and the way she had no problem trying to put me in my place.

"It's not gossip when I know it's a fact." *This fucking guy.*

Del moves his hand to my forearm, and then has a wordless exchange with Marla, who looks up from her phone and moves toward the tables. One more word. That's all I need and then I'll have no problem getting in

Wheeler Finch's face. It's clear as day that I need to hit my heavy bag.

Del leans closer. "Not worth it, Grant. I'm not going to be able to look past you decking that rich fuck in the face. You know he'll press charges. On top of that, you don't need to make that water between his family and yours any muddier."

To be clear, the only people I've ever punched are my brothers. When we were younger, it was over dumb shit. When Linc was nine and saw his first WWE wrestling match, he decided I was his ultimate opponent. It took a few years before I could really give him a run for his money. It was playful back then. As we got older, it was Ace who was the hothead. And Lincoln was always there for backup, regardless of consequences. They had gotten into their fair share of fights growing up, but none of them resulted in an arrest because of our last name. And into our twenties, I knew they skated over some legal lines, but they didn't involve me in that. I had always wanted to be a cop.

My brothers are the fighters, and they respect that I'm not. I wasn't getting into fights on their behalf, but they were there to either intercept or take over if someone said something out of line. That's the funny thing about Fiasco —there aren't many people backing down from a fight. Verbal or otherwise. When Fiona died, and then we lost Olivia right after, nothing made much sense to me. It was Ace who folded me back into the family business and then put up a heavy bag. He said, "Go to work, and then work it out. But don't get lost in the bottle or in bar fights." He was my big brother, and even though he was hurting too, he made sure we'd survive it.

The last name Foxx carried a lot of weight in this town. For most, it was who made the best bourbon in Kentucky. For a few who knew our history, we were the brothers who knew too much loss. But for those born and raised in Fiasco, it was the curse that we had been dealt. It was never discussed, at least in our presence, but Wheeler's lackey didn't get that memo. "She'll be gone soon enough. Everyone knows a Foxx can't keep a woman alive for very long anyway," he laughs out. Both men think they have the right to say that kind of shit and get away with it... Not today.

I'm moving for their table before I've even made up my mind to do it. At the exact same time, Lincoln walks through the front door, knocking Waz's shoulder, as he keeps the same fast pace moving toward me. His momentum with his hand on my chest pushes me back to the kitchen. "The fuck you come from, Linc?"

Wheeler laughs boisterously behind him and Waz has that smug look on his face, like this all is just a bit of dinner entertainment for them. If I didn't know any better, I would have thought it was perfect timing, but I did. I guarantee Marla texted Lincoln as soon as Wheeler opened his fat mouth. It would have been luck if he were on his way home from the distillery.

"Ease up," Lincoln grits out. My big brother isn't the bigger one anymore. He might have a couple of inches on me, but I had a good twenty pounds on him. When he shoves me out the door, I go back for him. He darts away, but he's not fast enough for the right jab that follows. It misses his nose, but nails him in the left eye.

"Fucking shit," he yells out and then crouches low.

I don't expect his shoulder to plow right into my gut. I hit the mud and gravel with a thud. It knocks the air out of me and embeds a good handful of rocks into my ass and back. I try to push him off me, but he gets in two punches to the kidney that'll likely have me hurting tomorrow.

"Fuck! Get off."

"You done?" he yells back, out of breath.

I sit up, resting my arms on my bent knees. "Yeah. I'm done."

"Weak jab," he says, spitting next to where he's kneeling.

"Fuck you," I laugh.

"You know I'm right." He stops smiling and asks, "What happened?"

I grab his outstretched hand to help me up. "That dipshit started running his mouth."

"Shit. Kinda wished you got a shot in before I got here, then," he laughs. "'Bout what?"

I shake my head.

"Anything to do with the new girl you're acting weird around?"

"Who? No," I answer him too fast.

"Just haven't seen you talk to a woman, never mind flirt with one, in a long time."

"I wasn't flirting with her—"

"Not how I saw it."

But before he can get another word in, Del comes out through the back door, sizing up what happened. "Marla threw in a slice of buttermilk pie with your leftovers."

I take it from him with a tight-lipped smile. "Thanks, Del."

Lincoln nods. "Del, good to see you."

"You too, Lincoln. I'll catch you later, Grant."

I give him a wave.

"You need a ride? I just gotta fill up, but I can drop you."

"Nah, I got my truck," I tell Lincoln as we head toward the front lot. "Who's with the girls?"

"Ace has them tonight," he says, but doesn't meet my eye.

"You want company?"

He smiles at me with a look that answers before he does. "I do, but you're not the kind I'm looking for, little brother."

"Fair enough. Be safe."

Twenty minutes later, I'm pulling up to my house. The only lights on are coming from the studio cottage that sits less than two hundred feet from my front door. Julep's head pops up from the cottage porch. *What is my dog doing up there?*

When I get out of my truck, Julep just watches me. I clap twice at her to come, but she ignores the command and puts her head back down. Giving a short whistle, I quietly shout, "Julep, get over here."

Instead of listening, she rests her head on her front outstretched paws. I scratch the back of my neck. It's not typical behavior for her. She always comes when I call. *Fine, stay there.* I'm still keyed up and could use another few rounds of hitting something. I have no business feeling this unhinged about Waz and Wheeler talking shit, especially when it comes to a woman who's little more than a stranger, but well, here we are. I need to work off some of this energy. Or anger. Whatever it is, it has me on edge. The only outlet I have, the only one that won't talk, cause more problems, or punch back, hangs in my workspace.

My fist slams into the black heavy bag hanging from the rafters in my workspace. I square off and rotate my hips, driving right hooks in rapid succession, running through a series of jabs, hooks, and uppercuts before one of my knuckles split. Fuck, I need to wrap my hands. My hair is damp from sweat. Taking off my shirt, I use it to wipe my face, and then press it against my bleeding knuckles. As I stalk back out to my truck, I'm somehow more pissed off than I was before I got home. I search my gym bag in the back, and no luck; which means my hand wraps are in the laundry. *Fuck it.* My knuckles are already ripped up a bit. I slam the truck door closed, and Julep lets out a bark, still sitting on Laney's porch.

When I walk over, her head pops up. "Jules, let's go."

But she's not interested in listening to me tonight, apparently. She puts her head back down and doesn't move.

"Is that how it's going to be?" I'm not in a good mood and I really just want my dog to follow me home. I nudge my head toward my house. "Let's go." But she's stubborn and just stares back at me. I grit my teeth. I can't believe I'm begging my dog to follow me. She always follows me. "I said, let's go, Julep." But instead of moving off the porch, she flops her body over, paws up, presenting me her belly. I drag my hands from the back of my neck forward. I'm already lingering here way too long. I don't want to see my new neighbor right now. But of course, when I look back up again, Laney's standing in the doorway, watching me lose my shit. She's in a tank top, with no fucking bra on and a pair of shorts so tight and form fitting it's more likely that they're underwear.

She smirks at me. "You lost?"

Funny.

I give her a sarcastic smirk right back. "Just here to collect my dog. You can go back to getting dressed." I drop my eyes to her bare legs and back up again. "Looks like I interrupted."

"You're on my porch—"

"Kind of isn't your porch." I tilt my head to the side.

"You woke me up." She shakes her finger up and down at me. "With no shirt on, by the way."

"It's hot out." I just continue to glare at her, not letting my gaze drift to those fucking thighs again or at the way her tits are awake, nipples hard, just begging to be sucked on.

"Clearly." Looking down, she does a double take.

"Let's go, Julep," I say again, trying to ignore the way just looking at her has my cock stirring.

"You're bleeding." She nods at my hands. I don't glance down at my numb hands. Instead, I just keep my eyes on her, trying to figure out why she would even care. What the hell is she really doing here? This isn't an Airbnb. Why the fuck would Ace move her in?

"Your right hand. Wait, I might have band-aids," she says as she moves back inside.

I turn and walk away. I don't need a damn band-aid. I can't do this. I'm going to end up trying to fuck her. "Julep," I shout out over my shoulder. "Let's go!"

I stalk back to my yard, around the back of the house, and through the screen door. Julep is nowhere in sight and still probably on that porch. Rifling around the kitchen, I look for a towel to wrap my hand. I throw on the faucet and watch the cold water turn from pink to clear. My hand starts to throb, but I'm so flustered that it barely registers.

"Shit." Leaning my hands on the counter in front of me, I hang my head. I need to calm the hell down. I try a deep inhale, holding for three, and a full exhale. But it doesn't do much. "Fuck my life, I want her."

The way her lips look puffy and pouty. Like she's not getting her way after just finishing sucking on a cherry popsicle. The way I want to see how she'd take me. If she whines or moans when she feels good. If she'll submit if I ask. The way it would feel to tuck my cock between her tits and then paint them when I'm ready. Make her lick me clean.

Fuck it. I can hate myself later.

I unbuckle my belt, flip open the button of my jeans, and let them drop. Once I kick off my boots, I step out of my pants. Then I'm spitting on my hand and gripping my cock. She's not dainty or fragile. I bet she'd grip me nice and tight. I can't hold back the groan, thinking about her on her knees in front of me, licking those lips and gagging on it as I hit the back of her throat. I close my eyes and imagine the way she'd look right up at me with those pretty eyes, her perfect goddamn tits out, and then how she'd slowly spread those legs for me.

"Fuck. That's it." My bare ass hits the counter, but I don't give a shit about where I am or that I'm not wearing a damn thing. I keep the pace slow and hard, the same way that I'd play with her. Rocking my fist back and forth, I edge myself, because I could have come on the third flick of my wrist. This is the second time that all I have had to do is exchange a few words with her and I'm hard. Ready to fantasize about how wet she'd be if I told her all the filthy things I could do to her.

Tightening my grip, I swipe my thumb along the tip and, shit, that feels good. This is what I get for being celibate for too fucking long.

I think about the way she'd smile when I'd tell her I wanted to bury myself in that delicious-looking cunt. *Fuck, I miss eating pussy.* I think about how she'd feel warm against my tongue and taste sweet like honey as I'd rub her arousal around my lips. How I'd sink inside of her and fuck her so deep that she'd lose her breath. I imagine the way a woman like her would feel if I came inside of her. If she'd milk me dry and then beg for it again.

I fuck myself faster. My body wound so tight that the tops of my legs feel numb, sweat slicks my body, and I'm ready to dive over and succumb to this. With my head tilted back and resting against the cabinet, I picture her looking at me like she'd never want anyone else. I

imagine her lying like an offering in the center of my bed as I watch my cum drip out of her and then how I'd push it back in with three fingers, just to see her come all over again.

"That's it, honey. Look at me."

Goosebumps run up my arms as scuffing sounds on the other side of the screen door, and at the idea of her seeing me like this, I come so fucking hard that my body shudders against the counter just as I splash my chest with my own cum. I gasp from holding my breath as I come down from the full-bodied orgasm that lingers, tingling across my limbs.

Holy shit.

It takes me a few minutes to realize I'm ass naked in my kitchen, before I wipe off my mess while moving toward the back door, checking for Julep. But instead of my pup resting on the stairs, there's a box of band-aids on the railing.

CHAPTER 10

LANEY

I LIE in bed and watch as the golden orange light starts on the left side of my room and bleeds up the wall as the minutes tick by. I haven't left my little house in days. Sleep had finally taken me. But every time I woke up, my mind reeled. Jumping from one intense thought to the next. The one I preferred was the one that came from my neighbor.

"That's it, honey. Look at me." I brought him band-aids, and just before I knocked on that screen door, my ears perked at his deep, guttural moan. I'm a stranger invading his life. And according to most, Grant Foxx is not going to be my friendly neighbor. But I knew he was getting off and the nickname he so casually assigned to me was what came barreling out. I slapped my hand over my mouth and stepped back down the stairs slowly. I wanted to be the kind of woman to walk in there and lick up the mess he made. But I'm not her. Not yet.

I peer my head up and over the fluffy pillows

surrounding me to look at the time. 10:47 a.m. A little more than five days since I've been in Fiasco. After my short stint as a Peeping Tom, I slept for a solid eighteen hours before I stepped outside again. I had a glass of water on the front steps of my porch and gave Julep about an hour's worth of belly rubs before I decided I wanted to go back to sleep. I earned a few lazy days, and sleep was what my body craved. Well, maybe not the only thing... *"That's it, honey."*

I'd do better with a routine, and time's the only currency I have a wealth of, so today I'll venture out and explore what Fiasco has to offer. Maybe find a grocery store so I can use the cute kitchenette in my new home and bake something. My eyes water when I think about the dinners I had as a kid. They were always simple and repetitive, but my dad had a sweet tooth and we got pretty darn great at baking.

I'll need to take Ace up on that job offer. The small amount of money I have from Bea won't last too long. I doubt Fiasco would be interested in bartering. *Barter.* Chills down my spine and make my stomach sour.

"You're taking something that's mine, pretty thief? You planning to barter?"

How could something as small as a single word drive me right back to the night that got me here? I want to erase it. What that monster said and the way he said it. How the calmness of his voice made my skin crawl even over the chaos. I hate that these thoughts and memories are sitting on the sidelines, waiting to remind me.

I just reacted. Swallowed the fear and moved as fast as I could. I squeeze my eyes closed, feeling disgusted by my choices. I keep thinking about the scream that came shortly after I yelled at Phillip to leave. A blood-curdling shriek that sounded as if someone was being tortured. And someone had been.

I don't know if I'll ever forget the way she collapsed into my arms and how I dragged her through the exit. The relief I felt as the firemen rushed toward us. The chills that worked their way around my body, burrowing deeper into my bones, the same ones I'm still experiencing. I'm banking on the idea that time will help erase some of it. Maybe not all of it, but enough that I'll stop jumping at loud noises and unexpected deep voices.

"Hello?!"

I sit up at the thumping knocks at my front door.

"Maybe she's not in there," a little voice says. Its tone instantly relaxes my shoulders and pulls a small smile from my lips.

"Maybe she ran away when she saw Uncle Grant so gross and sweaty," another little voice says, giggling. The idea has me shamefully trying to look out the window to catch a sweaty Grant Foxx.

"Lark, if we can balance on the railing, we might be able to see inside." I hear feet move around the small front porch.

My stomach rumbles as I drag my hands through my greasy hair. I could use a shower after spending so much time in bed.

"Miss, are you alive? Uncle Grant says he hasn't seen you all week and we've been waiting for you to come out."

The other voice chimes in, sounding defeated, "But you never come out."

I twist my hair into a bun as I open the front door, the

humid air slapping me. But I recover quickly as two smiling little blondes stare back at me. I can guess how crunchy I must look by now based on how quickly their smiles shift to a horrified surprise.

I pull my sweatshirt up over my mouth. "Hi."

"Hi," the shorter little blonde says. "I'm Lily."

"I was just getting up." I look back at the rumpled bed.

"It's closer to lunch than breakfast," the older one says. "Our grandpa says the only people who sleep until lunchtime are lazy or depressed."

I snort a laugh. "Who's your grandpa?"

They both rush past me and through my front door. I look outside and don't see any adults. "Grizwald Foxx," the older one says with her shoulders back and chin up.

"Sounds like something my dad would have said." I smile at them.

They've clearly moved on from that discussion as Lily says, "We're so bored. We came looking for Uncle Grant, but he wasn't home."

While I'm usually not the biggest fan of kids, I'm relieved to have some company.

"How about I meet you both outside when I'm done showering? I'd love to pick some of those flowers you have tucked in your pocket." I tilt my chin toward the front pocket of Lily's shirt. The wispy yellow and purple flowers look like they're barely holding on to their stems, but if they're bored, that's something I know how to do.

"How did you learn to make these look so pretty, Laney?" Lark asks as she wraps the stem of a purple aster around the wire hangers that were hanging empty in my closet.

Two hours after what felt like a life-changing shower, I've been talked into setting up a stand on the side of the road to sell flower crowns.

"I had a lot of jobs, but one of my favorites was working at a flower shop in high school. I mostly filled buckets and cleaned roses for the first few months, but after a while, I started paying attention to the way the designers would make bouquets." I pull a few stems of daisies and yellow aster together, balancing the colors on each side. "Anyway, it was a little shop, and I had a big, huge crush on one of the delivery drivers, so most of my attention went to him."

Lily laughs. "Gross."

But Lark just listens and watches as I pull the stems together to make a small, handheld bouquet. "What was his name?"

"Jonathan Gofronty." I smile, thinking about him. It feels like an entirely different life having that crush. "Anyway, I worked there until they fired me for spending most of my time flirting with him." I move around the flowers so the colors and sizes of the buds are balanced. "Well, flirting, and for telling customers to go to the bodega around the corner because it was cheaper."

"I don't even have a job yet and I would have told you that wasn't a good idea." Lark laughs. "Here, you need to reapply," she says, pulling the sunscreen stick from her backpack. It's not lost on me that I've been out here with these girls for a while now and not a single grown-up has come looking for them.

"Who is supposed to be watching you two today?" I ask her, but Lily interrupts before she can answer.

"Customer! Customer!" Lily shouts at us, waving at the car coming down the road. Her handwritten sign waves high above her head that reads: Flower Crowns $5. The black Ford F-150 slows down. Grant Foxx. I've learned a few things about the girl's Uncle Grant while we picked flowers behind his house today.

"Are you sure your uncle won't mind that we're picking all of these?"

Lily laughed like that's the funniest thing to say. "No! Uncle Grant lets us do whatever we want. And he'll be happy we picked these. He says," she lowered her voice, "Whatever makes my little flowers happy, makes me happy."

Little flowers. This man and his nicknames.

The truck comes to a rolling stop in front of our makeshift stand–two camping chairs they took from his back shed and a piece of plywood that balances on two upside-down sand pails. It's probably the most time I've ever spent doing anything with kids and it's the most fun I've had in a long time.

Julep barks from the front seat.

"Well...would you look at that? I've been looking for flower crowns," he says with a lightness to his tone. That damn baseball hat is back and all I can think as he comes around from the side of his truck is that a cowboy hat might look better. He lifts Lily in one arm and wraps his other along Lark's shoulders. "First week of summer break and you two are already trying to start a hustle?"

He spares me a glance as he smiles at the two girls. And my eyes jump to his forearms as they flex. I can't help but take him in. From his boots to the scruff along his jawline. It's shaved tighter than the last time I saw him. The thicker mustache is tamed back to the same length. "Haven't seen you in a while," he says without looking at me.

"Haven't heard you in a while either."

I watch as he swallows, his Adam's apple bobbing. He glances at me again as he hoists Lily up higher in his arms. That's when I notice the back of his neck is flushed red. And maybe I shouldn't push it. Maybe I should just let what I heard and the way this man clearly doesn't know what he thinks of me just fizzle out. But I'm feeling good, well rested, and a little more at ease today.

"How's your hand?" I ask, looking at his knuckles that were bloody. It takes all of my power to keep a straight face as I trail my eyes back to his.

His eyes flit to mine, tilting his head just a pinch to the side. "Got your band-aids, but I didn't need them. I took care of it on my own." And it's like I just got sucker punched, right in the gut with massive butterflies that swoop low and with so much force that they turn my cheeks hot.

As he starts asking the girls questions, his eyes stay trained on me. "Lark, your dad knows you're down here?"

Lily shifts her eyes to her older sister. And it's pretty clear by just one glance from one to the other that their dad has no idea where they might be. *Shit*.

"I should have asked them that sooner. I really hadn't thought about it until you were pulling up." I smile at Lark. "We got caught up having so much fun, time seemed to get away from us."

"I told him we were coming to your house." She holds

out her arms, getting defensive. "Which is where we started, but then you weren't home, and Laney said she wanted to pick flowers."

I raise my hand. "Guilty."

"Next time, if I'm not home, just check in with him, okay? And as much as I'm glad Laney was nice and hung out with you guys, she's new around here and might have had things to do."

"I wasn't busy. Thank you for the company, girls," I say as I stand from behind our little table shop.

Lily smiles at me, speaking up eagerly before I go. "Laney, do you want to come to Uncle Ace's breakfast barbecue tonight?" She looks at Grant. "She's new. Like you said. And we can get to know her better that way."

He smiles at his niece, and then tilts his head my way. "Miss Laney probably has plans."

Lark chimes in, "She doesn't."

"I don't," I say with a laugh. "And breakfast for dinner sounds amazing."

He clears his throat, and then walks away with the girls. Julep jumps up and starts barking after them.

"See you at dinner, Laney," Lily yells out, followed up by a giggle as he hoists her over his shoulder.

I can't stop looking at him as he jokes around and smiles with his nieces. It's almost as sexy as hearing those words again. *Almost*.

CHAPTER 11

GRANT

"It's going to be the biggest party this county has seen in a very long time," Lincoln says as I meet Griz's eyes, and he rolls them at me. Lincoln likes to showboat. He's like Griz in that way.

"You picked a good time to show up, Laney," Ace chimes in from the head of the table. "You'll get a taste of what a real Kentucky summer feels like, and then at the end of it, we celebrate." Then he fucking winks at her. And it pisses me off way more than it should.

"Isn't that what you're doing?" I chime in. "Asking one of your . . ." I pause. I know I'm being a dick right now. ". . . *friends* to stick around."

Ace's eyes move over to Laney's, and they exchange a look that says something's there. And that makes my stomach sink. My brothers have plenty they keep close to the vest. Ace keeps things about the business from me. He and Lincoln have plenty of dealings that I haven't been

privy to. At first, it was because I was the youngest, but
then it was because I was a cop. We agreed to keep me away
from anything that I wouldn't approve of or would have to
turn a blind eye to. They're good men, and I knew they
didn't want to put me in a position that would jeopardize
my moral compass. But right now, whatever exchange Ace
and Laney just had has my leg bouncing. I'm more annoyed
than I should be.

"Is there going to be a carnival too, Dad?" Lark asks
Lincoln, waiting for another pancake from the griddle.

"What about animals?"

Lincoln turns, wearing his 'Grill Daddy' apron. Ridiculous, but it was a Father's Day present from the girls a
couple of years ago and he won't grill without it. "No
animals, Lily. But there will be carnival rides during the day,
and then we'll have a movie projected on a big screen on the
great lawn of the distillery."

"Sounds like fun," Laney adds with a wistful smile. "I
used to watch movies in the park every summer. Wednesday
nights with a blanket and some wine. And there was always
the most delicious food. My favorite was when Taiyaki
would do a pop-up." She smiles at Lark and starts using her
hands to describe it. She's frustratingly captivating. "They
do soft serve ice cream, but in a fish-shaped, soft waffle
cone."

"Yum," Lark says back with her chin resting on her fist.

"So much yum."

"Dad, can we get Taiyaki to come here for our festival?"

Lincoln gets cut off by Griz when he says, "Lark, the
important piece is the anniversary batch we'll be releasing."
Griz sits back in his chair from the head of the table, oppo-

site Ace. "The whole point of it is to release some barrels that haven't been sampled since *my* grandpa started this place."

"Griz, of course, we know the most important part is the bourbon, but you do realize that if we don't make a big-ass deal, nobody else will. Also, Taiyaki sounds delicious, Laney." Now, he's winking at her.

Laney clears her throat, her eyes shifting to me briefly, as she plays with a braid underneath her hair that still has wildflowers woven into it. "What about fireworks?"

Her eyes meet mine again. *Yeah, there're fireworks.* I can't help but study the way she interacts with my family. She's fucking beautiful, but there's something not right here. I can feel it in my gut, and I refuse to ignore it. Maybe it's that she has no problem with eye contact. I don't intimidate her, which is new for me. Not many people have balls enough to keep looking or to follow it up with a smile. She just keeps looking. And dammit, I like that about her.

"The Fourth of July jamboree is coming up. There're fireworks then," Ace interrupts. "Laney, you'll have a chance to go to the largest fair in all of Kentucky's 120 counties. Craft tables as far as the eye can see. There's tractor pulls, fireworks, and—" He looks at Lincoln. "What bands are coming?"

Lincoln shrugs.

"Not sure who the bands are this year, but there'll be some dancing, too."

"Save me a dance, Laney?" Lincoln says from his seat.

A growl escapes my throat as I watch her smile at him with a nod. I wipe my mouth and throw my napkin on my plate to play off the noise.

Lincoln looks at me with his brow furrowed, like *what the fuck?*

I don't know what the hell is wrong with me.

"Me too, Dad?" Lily says.

"Always, Lily. You too, Lark? You'll save one for me too?"

With my eyes trained on my brother, I ask, "You still planning on being here by the 4th?" But the question is aimed at Laney. I turn my head, focusing on her, just realizing I've shifted my attention. "Or are you planning to be gone by then?"

She shifts another quick glance at Ace.

Everyone at the table halts their side conversations, rolling out a nice stretch of silence for her to answer. She looks immediately uncomfortable. I watch her rub the tips of her fingers on the arm of her wicker chair, funneling some of that nervous energy. She's working hard to keep her facial expressions neutral. But then she clears her throat. And I may have just discovered her tell. The nervous energy moves quickly, though, as she raises her chin and keeps her eyes on mine. "I'll be here for a while."

My mouth ticks up on the right side, challenging her to keep going. "You know, I never got your story, Laney."

With seven pairs of Foxx eyes on her, she stalls by taking a bite of my bacon.

Griz interrupts, "Laney, can you pass me that plate of biscuits in front of you?"

She passes the biscuits down, but I have another question. "Where was it you were living before here?"

"Colorado," she clips out, clearing her throat. Again.

I push for more. "Whereabouts? I've got a few friends who run a winter sports business out there."

"Laney, that bowl of sausage gravy too, if you wouldn't mind," Griz interrupts again. She gives him a tight-lipped smile, passing the bowl down. He's trying to keep this less awkward, but I thrive in these moments. Truths always trickle out one way or another when someone is on the spot.

I sit back, taking a sip from my cup as I wait for her to answer. She plays with that piece of braided hair and some of the small white flowers drop as she does. That's when she lets out a small yelp. Julep barks in response from her spot on the patio, just adding to the attention. Laney pulls her phone from her back pocket. Whoever it is, she's not happy about it, because while she may be able to school some of her features, the way she's staring at her phone makes it obvious that she wasn't expecting whatever is waiting for her on that screen.

"Laney?"

She looks up at me, confused and surprised. *Who the fuck is texting her?* It's one thing for me to push her, but I'm not a fan of someone else shaking her up. "I'm sorry, what did you ask?"

"How'd you make a living in Colorado?"

Lark chimes in, "She was a florist. That was her high school job."

Lily adds, "Plus, she was fired."

She sips her sweet tea and takes a quick, shallow breath, looking around the table, and then starts talking. "I don't have a job right now. I didn't think I'd be a career girl. I liked jobs that you could go to and leave. But then, after college, that was . . . not reliable. I was good at planning details for parties for our neighbors growing up. Like baby showers and retirement parties." Pausing, she waves at the air in front of her.

"Anyway, I liked planning events and found an internship with a prestigious company that did weddings and some larger-scale parties. But I've done lots of things. That was the last. The one I worked hardest for. And it made me the most money. But waiting tables and bartending were the main earners for a while before that. I was also a concierge at a hotel."

She looks down at the table and away from me, but then smiles at Lincoln and Ace. "That one was awful," she says more quietly. "There was the short stint as a hairdresser, but I was young and had a bad semester at school, so I thought I'd try a trade. I ended up washing a lot of people's hair. Botched a few bangs and almost threw up when I was giving someone a perm. I was good at hot shaves, though." She puts a strawberry in her mouth, and it bulges out her right cheek. She's rambling. If she didn't look so anxious, she'd be cute. I want to see her fumble over her words, but at the same time, I can't help but notice how enticing that mouth of hers looks filled with the juice from her strawberry threatening to escape.

I shift in my chair.

"The event planning was a lot of fun, but it took me a while to build up a reputation and client trust. Let's just say, I didn't have much mad money."

Lily pipes in, asking, "What's mad money?"

The fans are still oscillating above the long patio table, but Laney's sweating. And she keeps talking. "I thought I'd end up doing what my dad did, but that didn't pan out. I'm not always the best with patriarchal authority." Looking around the table of men, she snort-laughs. "Go figure." With a shrug, she tosses another too-big strawberry in her mouth and talks around it. "But I had a knack for people liking me."

I understood that. Felt it no matter how much I didn't want to.

"And I can pair things together well. Linens with signature cocktails. Colors that complimented moods or an aesthetic. That sort of thing. My boss liked that I was good at keeping brides entertained."

Under my breath, I can't help but mutter, "*This* is entertaining."

She squints a glare at me, and it's impossible to hide my smirk in response.

Then she continues talking with her hands, animated and keeping this conversation far from boring or forgettable. "I booked burlesque dancers for an event once and I really loved it. So I tried that for a while—I didn't sing or anything, but I loved dancing. I looked good doing it too. That was the job before I decided on weddings and events. When I started interning for the events company, I worked with a few headliners who had done private parties, but then one of the wedding clients thought they recognized me, and I had to make a decision."

At the thought of her dancing, or dancing for me, my dick slaps me like a distracted buddy, asking, *If I heard that!* Jesus, this is going the wrong way fast. I'm not supposed to be the one getting shaken up by my own question.

Lincoln's eyebrows are practically at his hairline. Next

to him, Hadley is smiling, borderline laughing. Laney must see it too, because she starts to backtrack. "Not like *those* kinds of private parties. It wasn't stripping. Those girls made good money in the city, but that was a different category of entertainment. My body is curvier, which is ideal for burlesque. Plus, I'm good at reading a crowd, and"—she slows her sentence, but instead of stopping, she decides to look right at me when she finishes—"I was a good tease."

I stare at her pretty lips still stained from her red lipstick that she wore over here, mixed with the juice from those fucking strawberries. My mind reels, thinking about her teasing someone else with that pretty mouth and her perfect tits. Fuck. This is a shit-show. I shift again, rubbing the back of my neck.

Glancing around the table, I'm met with a wide smile from Griz, as amused as can be. Ace rests his hand on his chin, probably trying to figure out what he's gotten himself into, or he's pissed I couldn't just keep the questions to myself. There's a dumbstruck look still plastered on Lincoln's face. Lily is drawing on her iPad, and Lark must have left the table.

"I've got some spots behind the tasting bar that I think would be a great place for you to learn a little more about our brand. My bartenders are troves of knowledge, not just about Foxx Bourbon, but just about every rule bourbon has and what we do to make sure we follow them."

I can see her smiling from my periphery. My focus, however, is on my brother and why he'd consider that resume ramble acceptable.

He shifts his attention to me, and then to Lincoln, before he adds, "I'd like you to help with our events as well.

We have a Women in Whiskey dinner at the distillery next week that needs some last-minute support if you're up for it."

The sound of her phone buzzing has her standing from the table. "Absolutely. I'd really love that." She glances down again at her phone before she says, "I'm sorry, my aunt just asked me to call her." The sound of the chair dragging disrupts everyone and has them looking. "Ace, would you mind if I just take this inside?"

He gives her a nod to go ahead.

"I'm here," she says as she closes the sliding door behind her.

"The fuck was all of that?" Lincoln asks, pulling my attention from Laney back to the table.

I sit up and take a bite of the piece of bacon left on my plate. "What was what?"

Griz barks out another laugh. "You just turned back into Officer Foxx, that's what."

I shrug. "You want to keep me out of the loop, that's fine. But then I'm going to get answers to things"—I look back at her pacing inside—"or from people who don't sit right with me."

I look down at the other end of the table to Ace. "You've got nothing to add?"

"I haven't seen you get worked up like this in a while."

I shove out of my seat and stand. "You enjoying the show?"

He smiles. *Dick.* But before I can say anything else, I catch a glimpse of how Laney stops her pacing and sits on the couch, like she's being served a heaping dose of shit news. I'm not going to overthink why that bothers me, but

I'm moving inside before it registers how much of a contradiction this is. Checking to see if she's okay, even though I just interrogated her over pancakes.

She's so wrapped up that she doesn't see me. It's why when I hold a rocks glass with two fingers of bourbon in front of her, she sucks in an audible breath.

As she takes the glass from my hands, my fingers brush hers, and I watch as she swallows down the emotions that her conversation was causing.

She mumbles, "I really loved that apartment." And then, clearing her throat, thinking of only one other thing, she adds, "The things from my storage unit. Are they…"

"Thanks again," she says in a lighter tone. "Appreciate the heads up."

Hanging up, she pushes the phone into her back pocket before taking another sip of the bourbon. I wait as her throat works it down until the glass is empty.

She holds up the glass. "Thanks for this."

I don't know what else to say to her, so I keep it simple with a nod and a tight-lipped smile. The annoyance from dinner is gone, but my curiosity is spiked as I hold contact with those blue eyes. Staring any more at her isn't going to do me any favors, so I push off the arm of the couch I was leaning on just as Hadley and Ace come inside.

"You trying to scare off my new friend, Grant?"

"A little quick to be adding someone to your friend list, Hads."

She stops next to me with a leveling glare, and I already know I'm going to hear it. "Just as fast as you've been to add her to your suspect list," she whispers.

I ignore her, but everytime I try to move back outside,

more of my family filters in. I keep my mouth shut as I hear Ace talking with her about what time she should get to the distillery on Sunday. I do my best to ignore the way my nieces vie for Laney's attention. When she finally says her thank yous and goodbyes, she turns to me and says, "Don't worry, Grant, I'll stay out of your way."

Don't. It was the first word that came to mind when she said it. But I kept that to myself.

Ace is staring at me when I finally look back from watching her leave. I clear my throat. "You planning on telling me why a girl, who is clearly hiding something, who you had a sleepover with last week, is just welcome now to Friday night dinner with us?" I don't let him answer just yet. "And is living in our guest house as *my* neighbor?"

My brother gives me a side-eye without a lick of amusement on his face. "Aren't you the one who invited her to dinner?"

"That was the girls." I rub the back of my neck.

"Grant, this isn't me trying to be rude, but it's really none of your business what she's doing here. We have an agreement, baby brother. I don't overshare. You don't ask too many questions. It's always worked." He's focused on his phone when he says, "She's here. Deal with it. You were a bit of an asshole to her at dinner, which was unnecessary."

I know when someone is lying. We're not Fiasco's welcoming committee. If Fiasco had one, at least. Most locals barely tolerate the tourists. Never mind unexpected freeloaders with a pretty face and a tight ass. She had every single tell there was with her vague answers followed up by nervous rambling. She cleared her throat more times than I could count. She was uncomfortable, and she's somehow folded herself into our lives without any questions. "Since when are you okay with having women you slept with stick around like this?"

I'm pissed. Ace knows it. I've always hated how he makes big decisions about all our lives.

He flicks his eyes up and gives me that fucking parent glare. The one he's always done when I'm being an asshole. For the record, he's always the asshole and there's nobody there to glare at him. Griz always seems to egg it on. "Like I said, not your business." He finally puts the damn phone down. "Why are you pushing? Linc is usually the one with too many questions."

He's right. This isn't me to be so interested in someone. I'm frustrated by my attraction to this woman.

"She's harmless."

We both know there is no such thing as a harmless woman. Not one who spoke the way she did, her Yankee accent evident. Or the way she's so effortlessly charming and how it made my family instantly like her. Harmless doesn't look like that. Harmless doesn't linger like this.

I pick up pieces of white and purple flowers that must have fallen from her hair and twirl them in my fingers. "You know she was making flower crowns with Lark and Lily today?"

He laughs. "That's...creative."

"Unsupervised."

He looks at me like what I'm saying is boring him. "If Lincoln didn't have a problem with it, then I'm not sure why you do."

"Ace. Come on. It's a weird fucking situation. Unless you were sneaking into her place without my knowledge, the girl didn't leave that one-room cottage all week long. And it doesn't look like you two are into each other." I rest one hand on my hip and drag the other across the scruff on my jaw. "Unless I'm losing my edge and totally misread—"

"You like her."

"I don't know her. And the whole point is, aside from fucking her, neither do you."

"So what?"

I give him a deadpan glare.

"I didn't, by the way." He clears his throat. "Nothing happened between us if that's what has you so pissed off." Then he gives me a knowing smile.

I exhale and try my best to school the relief I feel at hearing that. "Then why help her? Who is she?" My brother doesn't open his door to people. He isn't the nicest guy. He's good to his family. But other people? Not so much. We've had plenty of disagreements over the years about the lines he calls gray and the ones I referred to as the law.

I know when he shrugs one shoulder that it's all I'm going to get. And quite frankly, I don't want to unpack my feelings with him as my audience any longer.

I walk out the side door and down the pathway to my place. It only takes a few feet before I hear Julep shooting out the dog door behind me to catch up. I make up my mind before I even make it past the front porch that it doesn't matter if she was involved with my brother or not.

The only interest I have in Laney Young is keeping my distance.

CHAPTER 12

LANEY

"The tastings were out of order. We wanted to start with the 1936 blend and then work our way forward," the PR person from Women in Whiskey said as we finished cleaning up. I tried to keep my attention on her and Lincoln, but I couldn't help but glance at Grant. There was no way he could overhear this conversation from where he was walking with his team, but I felt embarrassed.

I realized I messed up the moment I heard the chairwoman describe the color. The bourbon being swirled wasn't an almond color like she described, but a deep caramel. Just like the one after that wasn't the "white dog" raw, unaged whiskey that went into the barrels. White dog probably should have been clear and not the darkest bourbon that was poured. It was a simple mistake for someone new, but to me, it felt like a failure. I had flawlessly handled everything for my events. The biggest requests executed perfectly, down to the tiniest details without a hiccup. Screwing up a luncheon for fifty respected women in the bourbon industry was a blow to my ego. But it stung more, knowing that Grant was aware of what was going on. He wasn't my boss—not directly, at least—but I still wanted to show him I was more than capable of doing this. It was the first time this week that he even looked at me. After dinner last week, he didn't care what I was doing here anymore. He ignored my presence. I also didn't want Ace hearing about this and think he'd made a massive mistake by offering me this job.

When the conversation wrapped, Lincoln grabbed a bottle and two glasses from behind the bar.

"Are you going to fire me?"

Lincoln smiled, calm as can be. "Not yet."

"You should have her pour some rounds with the tour guides at closing time each day." Griz winked at me from the end of the tasting bar. I hadn't even realized he was there.

Lincoln tilted his head, thinking through it. "I owe you a little more time to learn all of this. I shouldn't have just assumed you knew what they expected. There are some folks that come here and want to lazily enjoy some bourbon and our vibe. But there are plenty of others that take this very seriously. Those ladies are the serious bunch." He leaned in closer. "Truthfully, the head chairwoman is not my biggest fan. She wanted a second date a year ago, and I didn't. It was a whole thing." With a wince, he batted at the air in front of him.

That was enough to push me to know more. I wasn't someone who accepted mess-ups like that and shrugged it off. So, every evening since, right before the last tour of the day, I wrap up my emails and I tag along. I listen to the history of the brand. The nuances of choosing the right mash bill, why Foxx is different, and then I usually help with pours behind the bar. Sometimes, I'll make a Foxx old fashioned or two, but usually, it's a flight of their bourbon that ranges in a series of years they were made.

"Put it in storage," the tour manager yells out to the barback behind me. It shouldn't have pulled my attention, since I'm busy helping clean up. But it does, and I become fixated on the word *storage*.

That's all it takes to go barreling down the rabbit hole of a memory, leaving me crawling out the other side feeling anxious and unsettled. It instantly makes me think of the storage facility back in New York. I've realized that loud, unexpected sounds make me nervous and urge me to walk faster, maybe even to run. But a simple word, and I felt uneasy? Over and over again. I hated this.

How am I going to live in this bubble? Just when I start to forget about what happened, I'm sucked right back in. I start thinking about the what ifs. What if I hadn't pulled the fire alarm? What if I hadn't heard her scream?

I asked Bea, "Am I in any danger?" and she didn't give me a straight answer.

"This case isn't wrapped up. I'm telling you all of this because you're smart, Laney. Be selfish with who you allow to know the real you. The truth makes you vulnerable, and it's in your best interest to keep it to yourself. Lies will keep you safe."

Now that my day's over, I can't go back to my cottage and stew. I need to work out the nerves somehow, so I start walking. I used to walk everywhere. Streets and avenues.

City blocks that bled into new neighborhoods were nothing compared to traipsing through horse paddocks and the flat fields of Kentucky. But it worked just the same.

By the time I notice how far I've gone, I'm feeling better. I like it here. The way it feels to wander without a destination. To feel the stagnant humidity blanketing my skin, smell the sweet and tangy air when the wind remembers it has a purpose. It's all enough to be present and not pay attention to what's behind me.

It's also probably why I haven't noticed the dark sky looming overhead, or registered the low rumble in the distance that wasn't a loud muffler or big truck driving by. The whirl of a subway beneath rickety grates, blaring fire engines, and horns honking from impatient cab drivers, my ears had been trained to mute it all. Everything is so quiet here. Especially the way the atmosphere changes. It's instant. Suddenly, rain pelts down so fast it looks like it's rushing down sideways.

When I reach the stables, they're cool and dry. If they didn't smell like hay and echo with the sounds of their occupants, I'd think they were another vacant dwelling on the Foxx property.

The lights are on and every stall is occupied with horses, all curious about me as I make my way down the center. Hay spills into the main drag, and I find a large fridge next to a worn leather couch at the end. It's the only spot that depicts humans and not just horses who've spent time in this space. I pluck a handful of peppermint candies from the overflowing bowl perched on top. Mint isn't my top choice as far as candies go, but I take them anyway. With a sigh, I start walking slowly back down the center aisle and read the names of each horse above their doors.

A massive crack of lightning makes me jump, and a yelp escapes me as the thunder follows. It sounds more like a beast waking than the mingling of warm and cold air. I know logically, it's just a noise, but my heart beats wildly. I can't catch my breath, and I'm feeling lightheaded. *What the hell is wrong with me?* Squeezing my eyes shut, I try to take a deep breath, but it can't get past my throat. I brace my hands on my knees. I refuse to pass out. I've never felt panic before. I faced a monster who stared right back and didn't stumble. I wasn't going to let thunder and lightning knock me around.

"Close your mouth and breathe through your nose," a deep voice says softly to my right. *Grant.* I don't want to think about anyone seeing me like this, but I don't have much of a choice other than to listen to him. I give it a try, but the air still won't move past my throat. It has my eyes blurring with tears.

"I need you to relax, and then purse your lips like you're going to whistle, Laney. Breathe out." He smiles. "Tawney can smell those peppermints in your fist. So let's take a deep breath, and then you can be her favorite person today." Reaching out, he pushes a piece of hair back behind my ear. "Do it again, in through your nose. And out through your lips." His fingers trail down my hair to my shoulder and then farther down to my arm. It's a distraction that I don't think he intended, but in the wake of his fingertips, he leaves goosebumps. And I start to relax.

When a snort over my shoulder blows hair across my face, I laugh lightly. It eases my heart rate. The next breath pulls in deeper, and the next comes easier. My eyes clear. I watch Grant as he watches me, inches from each other. No judgment or scowl anywhere, just kindness. Maybe even a sense of familiarity, I'm not sure, but it makes me feel less alone than I have in a while. I don't know what to say. I don't understand this moment of peace between us, and I want it to stay this way.

My limbs are shaky, a sheen of sweat coating my skin, but the worst part is over with, I think. He's gotten me through it.

"It was early in the morning when I would struggle most. It had me stuck in my house, in my bed, for longer than I'd care to admit." He keeps talking and sharing as he gets up from being crouched in front of me to rub a hard-bristled brush along Tawney's body. I like hearing him talk to me like this, but I already miss the comfort of his touch. "She won't bite," he says with a smirk. "Just nibble, if you don't give her one of those." He tilts his chin toward my closed fist.

I open a red-and-white candy and hold it out to her. It disappears in seconds. I laugh when she snorts and nudges my hand for more. Instead, I glide my hand along her head. Her big black eyes look into mine, and it's like we exchange something. Another laugh escapes me, this one filled with hope. Like if I don't laugh, those tears from moments ago will fall. This entire situation has my emotions all over the place.

When I look away from the massive horse in front of me, Grant's hazel eyes study me, searching for a reason for my strange reaction. Maybe even why he shared any of himself with me. Maybe both. I know he wants to know more about me in return, but I heard Bea—*keep the truth close.* The silence lingering has me wondering if I'm not cooperating. He shared something with me, and I can't reciprocate.

His jaw tenses, and I can see the muscle tic. I can't tell what he's thinking or if he remembers he's been ignoring me this past week.

"She's impressive," I say, trying to lighten whatever just happened. But he doesn't let me escape that easily.

He searches my face, his eyes landing on my lips, before he says in a low gravel, "She is. Impressive. Strong. So fucking beautiful."

CHAPTER 13

LANEY

"THIS MANHATTAN IS the best I've ever had." I shed the black leather jacket I borrowed. Hadley demanded that I wear this very low-cut black dress, because "my tits will look impeccable in it." I couldn't say no after that and, really, they do. It's the best I've felt about myself in a while.

Grant looked at my lips and then I swear his voice dropped an octave when he said, *"So fucking beautiful."* I nearly passed out again. I would have let him kiss me. Truthfully, I would have let him do a treasure-trove of things to me after the way he talked to me in the stables and made sure I was okay. It only took his horse to kick her stall that had him snapping out of whatever trance he was under. He pulled back so fast, I'm not even sure he said goodbye. Maybe I had blacked out and dreamt the whole thing. If it hadn't been for Julep walking next to me on the way back to the cottage, I would have second guessed if it actually happened.

Hadley texted that she was kidnapping me tonight, and I let her. Getting away from the Foxx distillery and anyone with the last name Foxx for the night sounded like a great escape. I needed a breather from the heaviness of the day, that thunderstorm, and the stables.

As soon as we walked into the front of the small French bakery and toward the back hallway along the kitchen, I knew this place was going to be impressive. Most speakeasies are a throwback to the prohibition era, when alcohol was illegal and any establishment that wanted to serve it had to be hidden in plain sight. In Fiasco, Midnight Proof can be found down a flight of stairs in the back of Crescent de Lune.

The black-painted walls that greeted us as we were buzzed in set the mood for the kind of place this was going to be. I haven't seen anywhere as impressive as Midnight Proof, and I've been to plenty of places in New York City that held year-long waitlists. No, Midnight Proof is a clash of the late 1920s Gatsby-style with a ceiling that replicates the starry night sky and the live music of a three-piece jazz band as its soundtrack.

For the past couple of hours, the mix of tourists and locals has kept the room buzzing. Low conversations and laughter just a notch louder than the band. Hadley greeted everyone with either a beaming smile or a two-cheeked kiss. "It's a tie between the sour-cherry smash and this one for me. Here, give me one second." She walks to the far end behind the bar and shakes up a dirty martini for an older man who's been shamelessly checking her out since we arrived. He wasn't the only one. Hadley had fans—men and women who looked for excuses to get her attention. She was magnetic and her charm bled all over this place.

Whispering couples fill the intimate pink velvet booths peppered around the edges of the room. Toward the center are larger plush couches and low coffee tables between them for bigger groups. And around the sprawling bar, small couplings of friends gather out for the night or singles look to find a person to drink and flirt with. Between the crowd, the rich jewel tones, and the warm lighting, Midnight Proof makes you feel like you're the main character of a sexy evening you've randomly stumbled into.

"Looks like you have a fan," I say, smiling at my new friend. Her long black hair flows into pretty waves, offsetting her light blue eyes. Not a single person here would refute the simple fact that Hadley Finch is stunning.

She's easy to be around too. "I never take customers home, but that one is making it really hard to remember why."

"Does it have anything to do with one of those unnaturally attractive Foxx brothers?"

She smiles as she reaches below the bar in front of me, ignoring the comment. "Okay, this is my favorite new liqueur." Holding up a bottle, she starts pouring it into two shot glasses.

I hold up my hand. "I'm already tipsy. I can't."

"Sip on it, don't take it as a shot. It's a pistachio cream liqueur. If you sip it alongside an espresso martini, it's absolute heaven." With a tilt of her head, she smiles at me. "Next time for the espresso martini." She clinks her glass with mine and takes a small sip. "Can I say something if you promise not to take it the wrong way?"

My smile falters. Nothing good ever comes from a preamble like that. "That has to be the worst way to start a conversation, Hadley. And I'm almost drunk, so I can't be certain how well my filter is working." Although lately, I haven't been filtering much, with the exception of what brought me to Fiasco.

She nods and looks at me as if she's about to tell me something awful. Little does she know, awful things and I are well acquainted.

"They're my family," Hadley says, leaning on the bar. "I've been a part of the Foxx family since I refused to stop following Lincoln home as a middle schooler. They couldn't get rid of me if they tried. Luckily, they never did. Those men just folded me into their lives. I love them." She sips her light green liqueur, and I do the same, savoring the sweet, nutty flavor. "So if you're here to make any kind of trouble for them, then this is me kindly asking you not to."

I smirk, eyes narrowing on her playfully. "Asking?"

"Telling." She smiles right back at me. "I don't know your whole story, but if I had to guess, Ace is doing you a very big favor. So . . ." she pauses with a shrug, "don't fuck him over."

I didn't want to lie to her, so I told her a piece of the truth. "You're right, he's doing me a big favor, and I don't take that lightly. I wasn't planning on Fiasco, but, well, I'm here. Doing my best to live a quiet little life."

She watches me, looking for the lie in it. Then she shoots the rest of her drink and slaps the bar. "Good. Now let's talk about how you somehow managed to wrap four Foxx men around your finger in less than a few weeks."

I exaggeratedly scoff at that observation. "Hardly."

"Griz told me that you're the kind of stranger that small towns like ours can only hope to have crash into them."

That makes me smile. "I feel like Griz has some stories."

"Oh, he does. And that man loves to talk about them over some really old bourbon. That's pretty on par for him. But Ace"—she looks down at her nails—"he'd never move an overnight plaything into his guest house."

I raise my eyebrows at her. "I didn't sleep with him," I tell her with a coy smile. "He's all yours."

"No thanks," she says quickly. "Lincoln has a little crush on you, which is . . . shocking, really. He's become a bit of a slut. I'm not sure how I feel about it. He probably could use less of his dick and more therapy, but I've tried that conversation. It didn't go well."

I've never been close enough to someone like that. A person who would put things into perspective. Even if it was blatant honesty. Lincoln is good looking, sweet even. But I would guess she and I feel the same about him—a hot older brother who you can count on for a good time. Plus, he has the girls. I like them too much to muck anything up with their dad and hurt them in the process. It's the exact kind of complicated I can't do right now.

"And Grant, I'm sure he has women. I mean, look at him." My belly swoops with excitement at just hearing that man's name. Gah, it's a problem. "But he's not the guy to dance with girls at the bar and take them home. Let alone, word spar with one who shows up out of nowhere. The way he's been acting around you is . . ." She takes a sip of her water, eyebrow quirked. "It's just not like how he's been."

"Rude?"

She smiles, chuckling. "No. Just that he's been talking to you at all. He typically keeps to himself. A lot of grunts and annoyed looks are Grant's typical language."

I'm not sure why that makes me want to smile, but I bite my lips and hold it back.

Looking around the bar, she says, "They all believe it, too."

"Believe what, exactly?"

"I think it's bullshit, but every dumbass in this town has been force-fed the idea that the Foxx men are cursed."

I can't help the laugh that comes barreling out of me. "Seriously?"

"Griz lost his wife shortly after Ace was born. I actually don't remember how it happened." That admission has me feeling instantly awful for laughing. "Ace never married." She sighs. "And Linc . . ." Her eyes water as she tells me about his wife, Olivia. "She was everything good. I don't think she had a mean bone in her body. They loved each other since they were kids. The only reason I started following him home in middle school was because she begged me to come along." Tipping her chin down, she looks at the bar top. "God, I miss her every day."

"How did she . . .?" I ask quietly.

"Aneurysm. She wasn't even thirty yet, completely healthy. It was such an unexpected thing. And it happened just a year after—" But she's cut off when one of her servers interrupts an argument about a bill.

That kind of loss is one I haven't ever known. I missed my father, and while I still wanted him to be here with me, it wasn't the same kind of loss as a partner. But I understood what it feels like after someone you loved has passed.

To feel insignificant. To feel thankful for being here, but angry to be left behind. To want to grip onto something greater, something higher so that it didn't have to be a finite ending. All of it has me anxious to grasp how Grant factors into it. If he's been "cursed" in that same way. My chest tightens, but my buzz is stronger now. I just need some fresh air.

The air outside isn't cool, but it feels good to breathe in. The cocktails were delicious, but now I'm realizing that I haven't downloaded any rideshare apps on this phone, that would be a whole ordeal trying to figure out. Especially since I didn't have a credit or debit card to connect it to. *Shit.*

It only took us about ten minutes to get here from Hadley's place and the car ride from Ace's was less than five to there. Tipsy girl math brings that out to be about a half hour if I walk and don't get lost. There's only one main road in Fiasco, as far as I know, so it should be easy. I could start walking, and then pick up a cab if one comes along. On a Friday night, there have to be at least a few around.

"Hey there, girlie." Then the sound of someone's spit hitting the cement has me turning. "You new 'round here?" The slow drawl is much twangier than anyone else I've met in Fiasco. Either way, I know if I tried to ignore him, I'd quickly earn a follower. That was the absolute last thing I wanted.

So I flash a smile, put on my best I'm-not-as-tipsy-as-I-am face and pretend. I'm starting to get better at pretending, but I've always excelled at putting small men back into the Polly Pocket-sized egos they'd earned. "What gave it away?"

The twanger has a buddy, and the two of them look like the kind of trouble you never want to meet in the dark. It isn't tattoos or dark features–those were turn-ons. No, these guys look like bad taste just had a big payout. There might be a gold tooth, I can't be sure. I don't want judgmental glances to be misconstrued for interest on my end. I glance at the sign for the bakery, still lit, making the dark night around me feel less scary. But the reality is, nobody's around to step in and ask these guys to back off. When the one that spoke steps closer, I take in the dark slacks and black shirt. If it was on anyone else, it would be an attractive look, but he's the kind of guy that makes the back of my throat burn down to my belly.

"You're a pretty thing, aren't you?" His eyes drag around my body.

"I'm really not able to say the same about you." I smile. The sarcasm finally hits him as I flip him off.

"Now, now, new girl, I'm okay with taking Ace's seconds. Looking like that . . ." He licks his lower lip, and it sends a wave of nervous disgust through me.

If I didn't see the police cruiser parked down the block, I probably would have turned back inside, but I'm banking on the fact that there's an officer just a scream away.

So I don't hold back or cower. I lift my chin and square my shoulders. "Does this actually work for you? The sexual predator rapist vibe? Because I'm fascinated to hear about your success rate." I hold up a finger. "Forced customers don't count."

A bark of laughter sounds from behind me. "Waz, if it wasn't obvious by now, she's out of your league," Hadley says, grabbing my hand and pulling us toward her car just a few feet down from where we are.

His smile isn't one that greets an old friend, rather one laced with annoyance. "Hadley, you need a reminder that we used to play together?"

She mimics the sound of throwing up. "We never played, Waz. You tried to fuck me, and we both know how that ended." She tilts her head to the side. A nonverbal standoff that reads: *keep talking, fucker. Let's see who walks away with their ego intact.*

His mouth kicks up like he's got something funny to say, looking between the two of us. "You playing for the other team now?"

"Always been on the girls' team, Waz."

He ignores her. "Your daddy was looking for you today," he says while his friend just quietly stands next to him, observing all of it. I can't decide who is more of the stereotypical creep.

"Such a good guard dog. I'll be sure he knows you were looking out. And verbally assaulting women outside of my business." And with that, she slams the car door shut.

The engine roars to life, and she peels out of the parking lot. I'm not totally sure if it's to make a point or if that's just how she drives.

"While I love how you told him to fuck off, he's dangerous, Laney."

I rest my head back. "An ex?"

"He wishes." She rolls down the windows and the warm air whips, so she has to yell over the sound. "My dad's got a bunch of guys working for him. Waz handles a good portion of the business. He's a shit-stirrer. Plain and simple."

I pick at the cuticles of my nails, looking over at her driving like she doesn't believe in brakes. "Thanks for the rescue."

She smiles, flicking a glance at me from across the front seat. "Laney, you didn't need any rescuing. I wish I could have caught everything you said, because there is nothing more beautiful than watching a guy like that get verbally spanked."

It's another time in just a few days when I feel strong. Less like a people-pleaser or someone to fall in line and more like someone I could start respecting again.

CHAPTER 14

GRANT

MY LEG GETS WARMER, wetter. My hand holding her back is soaked in black. Blood gushes out so heavily that it doesn't have time to turn red. "No. No. No."

I jolt awake in my hammock. I must have dozed off just for a few minutes because the firepit still roars in front of me.

With a heavy breath, I drag my hands through my hair. I don't have many dreams anymore about that night. Rarely are they full-on recollections, but sometimes, like just now, I'll get a small reminder of what I lost. Fiona had bled out with an almost perfect incision that nicked her carotid artery. It seemed too clean for her killer, who was chock full of methamphetamines, to pull off. Between that and the torn-up skin along her side, it was meticulous.

When I look over, Julep is sprawled out on her patch of grass, belly up, tongue out. I let my attention linger on the guest cottage. The lights aren't on, but someone's living there now. Memories from that night pop up whenever I start to think about moving my life forward. Maybe it's my punishment for not being able to get to her in time. I had failed someone I loved; there was no do-over nor apology. I didn't get there, and I couldn't fix it. Early on, I needed therapy and to learn some coping tactics. Now, my therapy is my morning rides and making bourbon.

I didn't want to factor in anything else. Anyone else.

When I saw Laney last, I couldn't stay quiet in the stables any longer. I watched her explore the place soaking wet, her shirt molded to her skin. I was just fine minding my own business as she hummed down the main corridor. Until the crack of lightning. The way she screamed made the horses even more uneasy than the weather did.

And then I was beside her, my feet taking me there on their own, the urge to help her overwhelming. Being so close, sharing a vulnerable moment with her, I was seconds away from kissing her. She was having a panic attack one minute, and the next, I'm staring at her like a fucking creep.

The sound of Hadley's obnoxious Camaro roars up our otherwise private road. I still don't know how she has a license. She has one speed—too fast. From the back of my yard, I have an unwanted view of Laney shuffling out of her car and dancing up the front steps. I should go inside.

But I'm frozen in place. My new neighbor is impossible to ignore. Especially in a little black dress that might as well be categorized as body paint. I scrub my hand over my face. *What is it about her?* My dick is slapping me in the leg with the obvious answer.

After the stables, I felt too much. I talked myself down from plenty of panic attacks over the years. I didn't care what she was doing there, or who she was in that moment, I didn't want to see her scared or watch tears pool in those pretty eyes. I let her see me for a minute. Touched her skin and held her hand long enough to make sure she was okay. Then I said too much.

Laney waves at Hadley from the porch and then searches her bag for keys. She fumbles for a good few minutes before her head tilts back and she starts laughing. Throwing up her middle fingers high in the air, she says into the sky, "Fuck you, universe. Seriously. Fuck. You."

That has me smiling. "Lock yourself out?" I shout from my hammock.

"Holy fucking shit." She jumps, pressing her hand to her chest as she turns around. Now I feel like a dick for scaring her. She looks around and zeroes in on the firepit in my yard, and then finally sees me.

I hold up my beer as a toast hello. *Maybe I should have stayed quiet.*

She stares for a second, and then starts moving down her porch steps. "Any chance you can help me?" she shouts back.

Her long hair is wavy and a bit wild. She looks good even from this far away. My lack of response keeps her walking over. Her heels must be giving her a helluva time, getting stuck in the grass every few feet because halfway here she finally gives up, takes them off, and just leaves them there without bothering to pick them up.

I can hear her talking to herself as she gets closer. "Grown-ass woman can hold her own, but can't remember a key . . ."

She inhales like she's already annoyed and it has me

biting back a smile. Why do I find this amusing? "You seem a little angry over there."

"I'm thirsty. I want to get out of this suction cup of a dress. I could use something greasy in my life, but seeing as how I haven't gone grocery shopping, that's not happening." Looking down at her bare feet and then back up at me with the most defeated look on her face, she says, "And now my feet hurt."

Julep sits up and her butt and tail are moving so fast that she looks like she's going to take off if I give her the command that she can go.

"Hello, sweet girl," Laney says to her. She looks back at me. "Is it okay?"

I nod for her to go ahead. "Ease up, Julep."

She smiles up at me from a crouched position, giving my dog a full head rub, and I'll be honest, she could ask me for just about anything right now, and I'd get it for her. "I've got a spare key inside. Water?"

It takes just a minute to find it, but when I come back out, she's sprawled out on the hammock, swinging it slowly back and forth with one leg draped over the side. The entire scene has me stopping in my tracks because this woman is more than beautiful. And trying to look away is impossible.

Sitting up from the hammock, she takes the glass of water I brought and chugs it back. "I think I want a hammock. There's a spot over there." She points into the dark at what I'm assuming are the two big oak trees near the cottage. "This is the first time I've ever had the pleasure of being on one of these. I get it now," she says, resting her head back, brushing her foot a bit faster to pick up the motion.

"They don't have hammocks in Colorado?"

She tries to ignore me, but I'm really good at silence. It's a learned tactic, one that still works in my favor. Especially when she says, "I would think they do, but I've just never been on one. Just like I know there are nice guys in the world, but I've never been on one of those either." She slaps her hand over her mouth. "I said that out loud, didn't I?" *Certainly did. And now I am picturing myself as someone she'd want to be on.*

"How was Hadley's new summer drink menu?"

I laugh when she emphasizes, "Too good." Her hands explaining what she's most excited about. "There was a pistachio thing at the end that I could have kept sipping on if Hadley kept pouring."

Jesus Christ, I can't stop staring at her mouth.

"You keep looking at me like that, cowboy, and I'll get the wrong idea."

I swallow and already regret responding, "And what idea is that, honey?"

She lifts her head up and smiles. A wide and full grin that's laced with mischief. "Say that again."

It takes whatever is left of my reserve not to smirk at the way she flirts with me. But I stand there, not tipping my hand, and let her bring up what I know she overheard when she left me band-aids. "Say what again?"

The word comes out breathy. "Honey."

I remember exactly what I said, and I can't help repeating. I smile, dropping my tone lower when I say, "That's it." Her eyes widen as they meet mine, and I cross my arms. "Honey."

Her thighs squeeze together. Did that turn her on?

She clears her throat and then rests her head back against the hammock. "Midnight Proof is incredible," she says, pivoting the subject. "But then I wanted to leave. And then when I got outside, I realized I didn't have a credit card for a ride-share so I thought I would walk—"

"You thought you were going to walk here?"

She nods.

"Alone? From Midnight Proof?"

Absolutely not.

"Yes, but then there was a guy—"

"What guy?"

She squints her eyes at me. "What are you, a cop? Yes, a guy."

"I was," I snap back at her.

"You were what? A cop?"

I nod, sipping the ass of the beer I'd been drinking earlier. Tossing the empty bottle to the side, I cross my arms over my chest once more, watching her swing in *my* hammock.

"Hmm," she laughs. "I would have thought Bea would have told me that. My dad would have liked you."

I can only stare, because that was the most information I've gotten out of her. And if she's talking about the Bea I think she is, then this would explain a bit more about what the hell she's doing in my town. As I look her over, the firelight hits a small, jagged scar along her neck. One I hadn't noticed before now.

"Bea?"

"What?" Her eyes flick to mine. "Where?" She swats at the air.

"Bea Harper?"

"What?" Yawning dramatically, she tries to play off what I just caught.

"Are you talking about Bea Harper? The U.S. Marshall?"

She stretches her arms above her head and shuts her eyes, mumbling, "So tired," and then lies still. *She can't be serious?* What the fuck?

At least a minute ticks by. *Goddamnit.* "I know you're not sleeping." I shift my weight and stare down at her, taking in the way her hair falls through the roped holes of the hammock. Her legs cross at the ankles and her face is slack without a trace of tension. "Are you in trouble, Laney?"

I walk closer so I'm standing right over her. "This isn't going to work. I know you're awake. Just answer my question."

Another minute passes, and she's still just lying there like she's fallen asleep. Apparently, I'm not the only one good at the silence game. I make up my mind.

Fine.

I'll play.

Reaching down, I loop one arm under her knees and snake the other across the middle of her back as I scoop her up and into my arms. "I don't like being ignored, honey. And you and I both know you're not asleep." I stride around the side of the house. "This is your last chance, Laney."

With a sigh, she snuggles into my arms. I stop and hoist her higher, which prompts her to lift her arm from dangling at her side to rest it across my chest and neck. I'd be the liar if I said holding her like this didn't feel good.

There's something about picking up a woman that makes a man feel like a man. Tack that onto carrying her and then dropping her onto something soft, just to fuck her hard, it's a feeling I haven't had in a long time. But something soft isn't my destination. I lean forward so that my thighs brush against the metal. Holding her over the filled horse trough, I give her one last warning.

"Laney, you're going to get wet if you don't answer my question."

A smirk plays across her face before she whispers, "Don't threaten me with a good time, cowboy."

Jesus Christ. It has me rethinking what I'm about to pull for the briefest second. But not enough to stop it. The splash, followed by the immediate screech that comes pouring from her mouth seconds later when she's dropped ass-first into the cold water, almost makes me feel bad. *Almost.*

She raises her arms and slams them down like she's throwing a temper tantrum. "You dropped me in a tub of dirty water."

"I did." I try to stifle the smile teetering on the edge of my lips. I'm not as wet as she is, but the front of my shirt and jeans took on the wave of water from when she went in.

"Are you going to waterboard me now?" She splashes at me, and I lunge backward as much as I can, but she still manages to wallop me with a good soak. "Why aren't you a cop anymore? Let me guess. Cruel and unusual punishment?"

I grit my teeth and try not to laugh at how pissed off she is.

She stands, fuming as her soaked hair drips down her

body. As she moves to lift her leg over the side of the trough, I quickly grab her arm to help her balance the rest of the way out. Her skin is cool to the touch, but it's not enough to ignore the heat that's sparked between the two of us. Attraction, anger, and annoyance linger as thick as the humid air. It was an asshole move, I know that, but I don't regret it.

When she stands straight, both bare feet on the grass while rivulets of water run down her skin, I can't hide my smile in response to her threatening glare. Her tight black dress is plastered to her curves, almost the same way it did when it was dry. Only now, her nipples are hard and poking through. *I didn't think this through.*

"Be a gentleman and give me your shirt," she demands.

I laugh. "It's almost as wet as you are."

"Fine." She hooks her finger into the strap on her left shoulder and lowers it.

Fuck, did I want her to keep going.

"Alright. Alright." I grip the hem of my damp shirt, whipping it over my head and tossing it to her. She stares at my bare chest, and it fuels my self-esteem. Something I never typically struggle with, but damn, it's nice to see it up close and feel it. There was a time when the gym and working out was a part of my job, but the physical labor of the cooperage does plenty to keep me in shape. Snapping out of her perusal of my arms and chest, she balls up my shirt to wipe her face. Then she moves it down each arm and bends to wipe her legs.

Once she's done, she throws my balled-up shirt back at me and starts to walk away. "Haven't gotten that wet for a man in a long time. So, thanks!"

I look up at the pitch-black sky. What am I supposed to do with that?

"Laney," I call after her. When she turns, I toss the spare key for her place. "You know I'm not going to let it go, right?"

She catches it with a smirk. "Neither am I, cowboy."

I snort a small laugh to myself. That ridiculous nickname.

Turning around, she yells over her shoulder, "And I'd be very disappointed if you did."

CHAPTER 15

GRANT

I STOMP through the front door and find Griz on the couch, reading a floral-covered paperback with big, bold purple letters that reads: "Marriage Assault."

"Where's Ace?"

"Fuck if I know." He lowers the book just enough to give me an annoyed glare. "What's gotten your panties in a pucker?"

"You're in everyone's business." He has to know at least something about Laney that I don't. It's not in his nature to be out of the loop. I put my hands on my hips and square off with him. "Did Bea Harper happen to fly into town with our newest resident in tow?"

"That's a very specific question," he drawls out. "Sounds like you already have the answer. So what the hell are you really askin', Grant?"

Raising my hands, I rest them on top of my head like

I've just run miles and need my lungs to open up and make room for air. "The last time Bea fucking Harper decided to rustle shit up in this town, people ended up out of sorts and dead." As soon as I say it, I regret it. I stopped being angry at Fiona for going out on that call, but I'm not even close to forgetting.

"There are three girls who have gone missing in this county in the last six months and not a single person is asking the one question they should be," she said, biting on the end of her coffee stirrer.

"I'll bite," I teased with a smile, kicking my feet up on the desk. "What's the question?"

She gave me that signature 'don't be a prick' look. "Why here?" Standing up, she closed my door. "I've been looking into inconsistencies with property ownership in places that sit on city borders between Fiasco, Victory, and Montgomery. There are at least three of them that have sold in the past year."

"Fi, when do you have time to be looking into this? You're patrol, not detective." Not to mention, any time that she wasn't at work, she was either bowling with her old man or spending time with me. Not that anyone but me knew about the time we'd been spending together.

"I remember a long time ago, my mom talking about how they were always buying up properties in threes to utilize as relocation options. A single property purchase that wasn't used right away would normally look suspicious, so they bought in bulk. Like an investor might."

"So you think this relates . . . how? I'm not following."

"Grant, if we haven't found bodies, then they're still alive, being kept somewhere that nobody ever planned to look."

She looked at me with sheer excitement. The thrill of this line of work was always there for her. Before she ever considered the academy, she was hooked.

I was anxious about the idea. Without substantial evidence to even look in the direction she was suggesting . . . "It's a helluva reach, Fi."

"Yeah, but it's a starting point."

A starting point. I needed to know, *why here?* "I'm asking, what's Laney's story?"

"I think that story needs to come from her," Griz says.

Ace comes in from his office and looks between our grandfather and me. "What am I walking into right now?"

"I don't like being in the dark about this. What's going on with a woman being dropped on our front porch in the middle of the night by Bea fucking Harper?"

He ignores the tone in my voice as he walks toward the bar on the other side of the room, pulls out three glasses, and then chips out three rocks from the block of ice that's kept in the bar freezer. Each with a couple of fingers high, he gives one to Griz, and then to me. "You are left out of certain things because you like to play above the line, baby brother. Your moral compass doesn't have any fault points. You know that when you were PD, we didn't want to make any lines muddled."

"No shit, Ace. But I haven't been a cop in years." I take a swig of the bourbon and I can tell right away it's higher proof than the typical year he likes.

"You sure about that? You've been grilling Laney like you still are."

I hold up my glass to the light and then take a smell as I flip him off with my free hand.

With a laugh, he shakes his head. "I don't know all that much more than you. Laney isn't exactly an open book, despite the word vomit at dinner. But yeah, Bea Harper dropped her here in the middle of the night. You're right about that. Told her she could start fresh here, and now I have a favor to cash in whenever I might need it." With his hand slung in his pocket, my brother looks like a business-man. Buttoned up and always ready to negotiate.

"Why go to you and not me?"

He sips his bourbon. "You're really asking why someone would come to me and not the cop in the family? Wouldn't that be self-explanatory?"

"So she's off the books, then?"

The stoic expression that my brother has mastered gives away nothing. "I don't think she's here to cause any trou-ble." He looks over at Griz. They have a silent exchange that pisses me off, like they used to have when Lincoln and I were younger. "I know that you know what it feels like to want to start over. And to do it without having to answer a bunch of questions."

My gut sinks, and I immediately feel like he just put me in my place. My brother has a way of doing that. It's a talent. When an entire town wanted to be in my business, more than anything, I didn't want to have to explain why making barrels instead of being a cop anymore was the only thing that got me out of bed.

I finish the bourbon in my glass and walk it into the kitchen. I don't need to tell him he's right. "It's been a long time since I've seen this kind of life out of you, Grant," Griz says as he crosses the threshold.

"It hasn't been that long since you've seen me annoyed,

Griz. Happened last week when you decided to tell my guys to keep the barrels burning for longer than they should."

Swatting at the air in front of him, he pulls a bottle from one of the lower cabinets. "You want to play dumb? That's fine." He uncorks the unmarked bottle. "Maybe you don't see it because you're trying to fight it, but I can see when one of my boys sees something they want."

I'm not interested in Griz telling me all the ways he's reading a situation so I leave my glass on the counter, clap my hand on his shoulder, and lean in when I tell him, "Might want to switch to water, old man."

I'm halfway out the door when I hear him say, "Might want to stop being such a tight ass, Grant." Then he shouts after me, "Pretty things like that don't just show up and then stick around."

And all I can do is worry about what would happen if she does.

Julep's waiting for me on my front porch, and I bend over to scratch the top of her head. "You behave while I was gone?"

She gives me a little growl and leans into me. I could spend hours scratching the spot on the back of her neck where the chestnut brown meets the gray and white speckles of her neck, and it still wouldn't be enough. "What are you doing out here in the heat anyway?"

I look over my shoulder and see *her* singing to herself in the window, moving around the cottage like she's tidying up. There's a lightness to Laney in this moment, and I can't stop myself from studying the way she rolls her shoulders and stretches her neck while she pulls her long hair up into a messy bun.

"What's your story, Laney Young?" I say out loud, knowing full well she's not going to tell me. I shouldn't be so interested. I should chalk it all up to what it is: a new person in town. But she's got my attention. In too many ways that I'll never admit.

CHAPTER 16

LANEY

BOURBON WAS MORE than just a profession here, it was a lifestyle. Artwork and memorabilia that paid tribute to its evolution lined the hallways leading to every section inside Foxx distillery. From bourbon when it was sold in the prohibition era as medicine, to the way it was portrayed in movies and cultivated a subculture. It's inspiring to see it all laid out and honored. But I also know that if I don't watch how much of that "lifestyle" I consume, I'll end up screwing myself and confessing too many truths to Grant Foxx.

"Where you heading, Laney?" His ears must have been ringing. Hearing his voice behind me, that smooth, deep drawl that lingers when he's not busy trying to figure me out, makes my stomach flip.

"Exactly where everyone who works here should be heading."

He catches up in a couple of strides. "What are you eating?"

"The last of my sour gummy worms," I answer as I glance at his handsome profile. "Wait, are you actually coming? Hey!" I slap his hand away as he reaches into the bag. "Get your own."

He laughs and still manages to snag one, but he doesn't answer my question. Grant hasn't been to a single one of these sessions since I started. The already crowded space buzzes with chatter as I glance around and smile at a few of the tour guides I've become friendly with. And they all notice who's walking in with me, just about everyone is doing a double take as we get settled. Only, he doesn't acknowledge anyone. Proving just how much he likes to keep to himself.

"Most of what you're tasting in bourbon comes from the barrel aging process. I'll challenge anyone to tell me otherwise." Lincoln projects his voice as he looks around the massive room a few minutes into the meeting. I look around and almost everyone is fixated on what he says. These team meetings weren't in a boardroom nor needed someone to take minutes. This was how Foxx Bourbon made everyone feel like family—they simply talked. Lincoln and Ace made it a point to speak with every single person, from the tour guides and coopers, to the folks who worked the lines for bottling and labeling. I witnessed how they made their employees feel important. This was another way.

He's like some kind of homing beacon, because my eyes find Grant standing off to the side watching his brother. Casually leaning against a rack of wood staves, his arms cross over his chest. He looks like he'd rather be doing anything else than listening right now.

What's he doing here? He never joined these nor went back to the main house afterwards for happy hour. *"I'm not going to let this go."* I cringe, thinking about Bea's name slipping from my buzzed lips. I need to be smarter than that.

"We fire bend our barrels here," Lincoln explains.

One of the new social media managers asks, "It's not the metal hoops that bend them to their shape?"

But instead of Lincoln responding, Grant lets out a sound that grabs more than just my attention. He smirks while shifting his lean and crossing one leg over the other. "Grant, you want to take over here?"

He holds up his hand to his brother, gesturing no, but it's when his eyes meet mine again that I can't help but issue a non-verbal challenge with a raised eyebrow and lick of my lip. *Why are you letting Lincoln lead this? Isn't that a question for your expertise?* I rake my eyes down the front of him, all the way to his boots and back up again. For as much as I like that he isn't over the top like Lincoln, or needs to show people he was in charge like Ace, I hate that he wants to just fade into the background.

And that's when he does something unexpected. The quiet Foxx brother uncrosses his arms and says loudly, for the whole room to hear, "You're forgetting the most important part, brother." His deep voice is commanding and the cadence of it somehow has every part of me waiting on bated breath. "All of you know that in order for bourbon to be called bourbon, it needs to be aged in a brand-new, American white oak barrel. The second a drop of that white dog touches it, it's bourbon. It won't be good bourbon, but technically, it's bourbon." That garners a little laugh.

With his eyes still on me, he says, "We like fire around here." The statement runs up my arms and down my center, seemingly aimed right at me. I'm suddenly warm all over. My challenge just backfired because he's doing more than just talking. He's practically commanding me to listen. "Foxx barrels are fire bent, just like Lincoln said. We want them pliable. It's a tease for what's to come. Using heat to bend the wood exactly how we want starts queuing up those flavors early. We do that repeatedly. Fire them up. Get them nice and wet. It makes the wood relax. And then we fire them up again to get exactly the right shape."

I swallow, my throat dry as my pulse rate ticks higher.

Someone behind me shouts out, "Sounds like edging." That gets a round of laughs. And all the while, his eyes stay trained on me until he cracks a smile. And just like that, the spell, or whatever just had me tethered to his words, is broken.

"The caramelization begins then." He smiles again, and dammit, my panties are ruined. "We like to do this slowly. We don't rush the barrels. Just like we don't rush the bourbon."

He shifts his attention briefly toward Lincoln. "Your world, Grant, keep going."

Hell, it was his world alright. Almost an hour later, everyone was still talking about barrels. He didn't join everyone at the main house for burgers and beers afterwards, but he had everyone's attention. Mine included, long after I walked back to my cottage.

When I walk up my front porch, a shareable-sized bag

of sour gummy worms leans against my front door. *Nicely done, cowboy.* Julep's bark from his porch is her way of greeting me home. At least until my phone vibrates in my back pocket. Maybe she's his lookout.

UNKNOWN

Don't step on your present.

I can't keep from smiling. *Grant.*

LANEY

How did you get this number?

UNKNOWN

Used to be a cop, remember?

How could I forget?

UKNOWN

I also own the company you work for now. Plus, there's Hadley. Honestly, there are countless ways I could have gotten it.

I'm sure I look ridiculous, smiling at my phone like a fool, but I don't care. I like how it feels to be on the receiving end of sweet messages and gestures from Grant.

LANEY

Sounds a little desperate just to impress a girl.

UNKNOWN

Is that what I'm doing?

LANEY

I have no idea what you're doing, cowboy.

I decide to dish his words back.

LANEY

But I'm not going to let this go.

He doesn't respond. Candy shouldn't make me swoon, but here I am, hours later, lying in bed, swooning. I should have stopped thinking about Grant Foxx the moment I left the distillery, never mind ignore his text messages. And I definitely shouldn't touch myself with thoughts of his mouth on mine. Or imagine his hands playing with my body with his words from today on replay. But I ignore what's smart for tonight and enjoy Grant Foxx, even if it's just a fantasy.

CHAPTER 17

GRANT

"I'm all in."

Del doesn't budge. He stays steady with his cards fanned out in front of him, which means he's got a solid hand. For as long as we've been playing, Del never bluffs. He either plays a good hand or folds. He's always been straight-laced that way.

"Fold," Lloyd says, throwing his cards down.

The low chatter around the place is the soundtrack to our night. If I listen too closely, I'll hear some kind of blue-grass streaming on the transistor radio perched in the kitchen.

My buddy, Marcus, stares at me, trying to see if I'll give him anything. Right now, I've got a high two-pair of tens and queens. It's not enough to be going all in, but I like to play aggressively with these guys; otherwise, our poker games will go well past midnight. He gnaws on the tooth-pick left over from his turkey BLT, keeping his eyes on me, but I just stare back at him. I'm unbothered and ready to take his money tonight. I don't have any tells.

Lloyd lets out a low whistle as he looks over my head toward the front of Hooch's. "This ought to be good."

They all turn around to see who might have shown up. I'm hoping it's not Marla's ex. The last time that happened during our poker night, we spent most of it cleaning up shattered plates and glasses.

A familiar voice pulls my attention to the front dining counter. "What do you mean, I can't order?"

"Exactly what I said, big city. You're not a local, so you may not order here. This is a locals-only establishment," Marla says. She's nasty when she wants to be. Especially to out-of-towners. Standing there with one hand on her hip and a bored look on her face, Marla chews on her wad of sunflower seeds as Laney dishes a glare right back.

"There's no way that's legal," she snarks, dropping her arm full of shopping bags to the floor. "And what is considered local? I live here"—she twirls her finger in the air—"in Fiasco." She looks around the room but hasn't seen me yet. We're in the far back corner, the typical booth for poker nights. The way I can't keep my eyes off of her is a problem, but fuck it, I can't seem to curb the new habit.

Marla doesn't let up, and it pisses me off. "My money is on you passing through. Not staying put, which makes you a tourist. Part-timer at best. Not a local." She grabs a pitcher of water and a small plastic cup, fills it, and places it on the counter. "You can have water."

I've only been here a handful of times when Marla's shown people the exit. I never understood why she'd turn away money like that, but folks in Fiasco are territorial and, most of the time, kind of assholes. Most tourists have no interest in having food at a restaurant in the back of a gas station. Little do most of them know it's some of the best food in town, but that's beside the point. I never liked the idea of turning away people who didn't belong, but now I'm annoyed that Laney's on the other end of it.

"Isn't that girl the one you were complaining was your new neighbor?" Del asks.

I throw down my cards as I stand. "Two pair."

"Dammit, Foxx," I hear from behind me.

Laney catches my movements and looks relieved to see me. She lets out a sigh and says, "Grant, can you please tell this woman that I am not a tourist?"

I look down at the pile of bags, all from Loni's boutique and some from the soap store that connects to the flower shop. As I lean into her space, she takes a small step back, but I keep her from moving farther when I lightly press my hand along her lower back. She sucks in the tiniest breath as I say, "You're going to owe me."

Her eyes track from my arm that's wrapped behind her, then up to my eyes. She searches for what those words could mean. But then, she spins the tables on me with one small glance from my eyes down to my lips. That's all it takes to know that this woman has done something to me that not a single other person has—made me want them. Without confirmation, I turn back toward Marla, who first has a look of confusion that morphs into a *what the hell was that?* glare. And I bet that if I looked around the room, everyone would be paying attention to the way Grant Foxx just came to the rescue of the new girl in town.

"Marla, this is Laney Young. She's staying at our guest

house. For a while." I give her a look again. "Foxx property," I say with a smirk. She whips her head from Marla to me with that comment. "She's here for some food and a few hands of poker with the guys and me."

Marla stares at where my arm disappears behind Laney's back for a moment, but then that's all it takes for Marla to stand down. "You got it, Grant." This is going to queue up a phone tree of gossip by the end of the day, but I'll deal with that later. Marla looks at Laney as sweet as tea now. All that piss and vinegar in her attitude is long forgotten. "What'll you have?"

I answer for her because I'm having too much fun messing with her. "She'll have a hot brown and we'll take an extra mug when you come by with a fresh pitcher."

Picking up her bags from the floor, I start walking toward the booth.

"Let's go, Honey."

I hear her mumble behind me, "Not your honey, cowboy."

"Noted." I smirk back at her, clearing my throat as we reach our spot. "Gentleman, we have a fifth for tonight. This is the newest hire at Foxx Bourbon. Laney Young, meet the guys."

Lloyd snorts a laugh while Del covers his smirk with a cough. Marcus is the only one who stands, offering her a handshake and a place at the table. "Miss Laney, it's a pleasure. I'm Marcus. Any chance you good enough to beat our boy Grant at some poker?"

She smiles and scoots into the large horseshoe-shaped booth. "Maybe I'll have some new player luck on my side," she says while she shimmies into the center. The guys each introduce themselves, and I take the only seat rounding out our circle.

Del shuffles the deck and tells her, "It's a fifty-dollar buy-in, but if you'd like, you can sit out the first couple of hands if you need to see how the game works."

"That would be great. It's been a long time since I've played," she says as she rights herself in her seat. "Is this a regular thing, or is it a special night out?"

Lloyd chimes in, "We used to play down at the precinct on quiet nights."

"You boys are all police officers?"

"I was fire department," Marcus answers.

"All of us are retired now," Del says as he fingers through his hand.

I can feel her attention on me as we make our way around the dealt hand. She knows I was a cop, but I like that she doesn't know the whole story. Or how I took an early retirement because I couldn't do my job after everything that happened. It's nice that there's one person around here who doesn't instantly give a sympathetic smile or an assuming nod. A woman who doesn't see a man who couldn't keep someone he loved safe.

Two pitchers and a clean plate later, it's evident that Laney's new-to-poker status was a big fucking lie. She's already put Marcus and Del all-in after their second buy-in, and I'm down to just a few chips more than Lloyd.

"Raise," she says, splashing the pot with four more chips.

I look over at Lloyd, and I can tell by the way he's been twirling the corner of his mustache that he's bluffing. My guess is he's got a pair at best. She has a small tell; it's minor, but I've witnessed it enough times now that I knew she was bluffing. Both times she cleared her throat and touched her neck, she either folded or won the hand by everyone else folding. I watch her closely, trying hard not to stare too long at her dark lashes or the way her lips stay wet after she takes a sip.

"You going to call, cowboy, or is this too steep for you?"

Del sniffs out a laugh. "Cowboy?"

She rests her fist on her chin, staring at me when she says, "He's got the ornery, tough guy thing going for him. And the horse. Just needs the hat."

Marcus and Lloyd start laughing.

She can joke all she wants, but I'm waiting to see that tell again. I rest my hand on my chin, rubbing my thumb across my lip, mimicking her body language. I want to let a little bit of silence make her uncomfortable. Let's see if she'll give me something. And a moment later, she does. She glides the tips of her fingers along the side of her neck like she's feeling for something—her tell.

"I'm all in."

Marcus scoffs. "Fuck. Alright, let's get this over with. It's late."

She pushes all her chips in the center, with only a small stack left. "I think I may have just figured you out," she says to me. I drag my sweaty palm down my pant leg. Her tone is too confident to be holding a bad hand. And it's right then and there that I realize I've made a mistake. She was playing me.

I flip my flush.

She smiles. "Nicely done." But I know she's got me beat with that look on her face.

"Let's see it, honey."

She flips her cards. *Royal flush.*

Del and Lloyd hoot and laugh like me losing is the funniest thing they've seen in a long time. Marcus leans over and asks, loud enough for the whole table to hear, "We got played, didn't we?"

I keep my eyes locked on her as she starts stacking the chips. "We sure fucking did."

"Gentlemen, thank you for the game." She looks back at me, not breaking eye contact, and, *fuck*, do I feel it everywhere. Like a current that's just been flipped on, and it's rearing for more. "And your company. It means more to me than you know to have some fun for a little while." Del pays out her winnings as Marcus gathers the chips and organizes them back in his case. "Excuse me for a moment."

A few minutes later, Laney returns from the ladies' room. "Marla," Del calls out in the almost empty restaurant. "Can we settle up the bill?"

She shouts back, "All set. It's been covered."

We all zero in on Laney. None of us expected it. And in one small, selfless move, the little liar may have just made friends for life with these guys. Getting their asses handed to them by an unsuspecting woman *and* getting their dinner and drinks paid for, she's going to be all they talk about for weeks.

"Mind giving me a ride?"

"You walked?" It's at least a three-mile hike from our house to the center of town.

"I like walking. Helps clear my head and explore Fiasco at the same time." She moves to pick up her bag, but I beat her to it.

"Feels like you bought out the whole store." Dropping the bags in the bed of my truck, I move around to open her door.

"I got paid today." She smiles proudly. "Even before I took all your money." As she hops in the cab of the truck, my eyes follow her ass hitting the seat. I clear my throat and shut her door, telling myself to calm the fuck down.

The rest of the quick ride is silent. Between the flirting and unanswered questions, I'm all over the place with how I should be around her. It felt wrong to try to romance the truth out of her, but I want to know what the hell she's doing in Fiasco. "Stay right there for me," I say, hopping out of my side.

I open her door and she gives me a questioning look. "You wanted me to stay right there so you could open my door for me? That's a real thing?"

"Yeah, Laney, that's a real thing."

She slides down, and I take an immediate step back. If I stand too close, I'll do something stupid like close the distance and kiss that pretty fucking mouth of hers.

Looking up at me, those blue eyes meet mine, and I swear they sparkle. "Have a nightcap with me?"

I don't know why it catches me off guard. It's one thing to flirt and push, but to step up and take what I want . . . I don't know what the right call is here. I haven't been with anyone in this long for a reason. "I . . . um . . ." I stutter out as we grab her bags out of the truck.

"It's okay if you'd rather not. I won't hold it against you," she says playfully, with a smirk.

Fuck, what am I doing?

She's exactly the kind of woman I'd want if I thought

being in a relationship wouldn't end up in a flaming disaster. We would be fucking fire together; there's no doubt about that. The skin along her neck flutters with her rapid pulse. Her red lips slightly part and I think about all of the things I'd like to have glide along them. Yeah, she'd probably be the best I would ever have. But I wouldn't be satisfied with just fucking her. And that's the problem. I've been ignoring the way I can't stop myself from looking for her in the mornings, then at the distillery, and glancing to see if her light is off before I go to bed. I haven't been able to stop thinking about what brought her here. Or the way I'm going to be pissed off if she's not okay and in real trouble.

She looks down at her fidgeting fingers before she lifts her chin and steps a little closer. "I know a nightcap could mean a lot of things, so let me make it clear for you, Grant."

Shuffling closer, the dirt and gravel shifting under her feet makes the move sound as loud as it feels. "I'm starting to like you. But whenever I'm around you, I can't figure out if you're trying to catch me in a lie or eye-fucking me."

I bark out a laugh, squinting one eye. "If it's both?"

It's the truth. She pulls in a deep breath, her chest rising slowly. "Alright. I'd like to be friends, then." But it's the way she exhales and forces a smile that doesn't reach her eyes that has me hating the idea of *friends* even more. "What do you say?"

I shake my head no and grind down on my teeth. What I really want and the smart move here are wildly different things. "I don't need any more friends, Laney." Taking a small step back, I clear my throat. Keeping some distance is the right call. I need to pump the brakes. I rub at the back of my neck, and when I look back at her, she's biting her lip like she's stopping herself from laughing.

I tilt my head to the side. "That's amusing?"

"Do you know how I beat you at that poker game?" Her grin grows into a full-blown smile as she starts walking back toward her cottage.

I wait for her to say more, but she keeps stepping backwards, that smile never faltering. She's looking at me like she's got me all figured out.

"Are you going to tell me?" I shout, since she's almost to her front porch.

"I can tell when you're lying, Grant Foxx," she shouts back.

The distance between us is wider now, yet the pull between us feels like it's growing stronger.

A smirk tugs at my lips at the way she's so impressed with herself. "Is that right?"

She nods, head tilting with that bright smile.

I'm playing with fire here, but holy hell, is she fun to play with. "Laney, there's no way that being your friend would ever be enough for me."

Eyes widening, her mouth opens slightly.

It takes every ounce of my willpower to turn away from her. My body screams at me with every step that brings me closer to my front door. I don't look back over my shoulder or check to see if her lights are out before mine tonight; otherwise, I'll rush right back to her, slam my mouth to hers, and fuck the truth right out of both of us.

Chapter 18

LANEY

The oven timer has been buzzing for more than a minute when my shower turns from warm to freezing while I'm still rinsing the red-tinted conditioner out of my hair. Keeping the red, strawberry tint to my hair is more demanding than I expected, but I like it. It's worth the upkeep. In my rush to reach the timer, I forget to grab the fluffy pink towel hanging on the rack next to my closet.

Barking at my front door is the least of my problems, but it adds to the noise, which then adds to the anxiety to make all of it stop. I've felt so much better with how quiet things have been lately. I used to thrive on the buzz of the city, but now I crave the stillness of this Kentucky summer.

I glance at the clock right before I wrap my hair in my towel. It's only 6:22 a.m. I've had Etta James's Greatest Hits on repeat since I woke up to give me the attitude boost from the shitty night's sleep induced by massive amounts of overthinking.

A few days ago, I ventured to the Fiasco farmer's market and picked some of the prettiest looking basil and sweetest smelling peaches. Between the peaches and the loaf of sourdough from Crescent de Lune that I couldn't say no to earlier in the week, I had the perfect distraction when I rolled out of bed. It was easy to get lost for a little while doing it, and baking reminded me of my dad.

My skin is still damp, but I throw on a pair of cotton shorts and a tank top from my floor because, again, just that one damn towel. I flip off the timer, toss on oven mitts, and pull out the baked French toast. Julep sits at my front door, and her butt wiggling and tail wagging is a heck of a greeting. I extend the top of my hand, letting her smell me first. "Hey, pretty girl."

In front of her is an interesting-looking piece of gray cloth. "What is thi—Oh! Fucking gross," I hiss and shimmy back as I reach it to pick it up. It's not a cloth. "Did you bring me a present?" Yup, that's a shed snakeskin. *Awesome.* Now I can overthink about how there are snakes out here. I look at her big brown eyes, and she really is the sweetest dog I've ever met. "You thirsty, Julep?" She gives a little high-pitched whine and a bark, as if she can understand me. "C'mon." As I open the door wider, she follows me in. I fill up a bowl of water that she sniffs but doesn't drink and then makes herself at home smelling around the cottage.

"Where's your big, flirty daddy?" I ask in a playful voice, and then laugh as soon as I say it. Even losing sleep over it, I can't help smiling, thinking about the way he stood there, his hands in his back pockets, squared off and shouting back that friendship wouldn't be enough. He knew what I was asking when I offered a nightcap, but he didn't go for it.

Grant Foxx is nothing like the type of men I'm used to being around. One, in particular—more polished, seemingly sweet, and taken. Also, a liar. A cheater. I squeeze my eyes shut tight. Exactly like me now.

Whisking together a shot of bourbon with some powdered sugar and a dash of vanilla, I thin it out with some water, then drizzle it over the warm and gooey bread. *Damn, this is going to be good.* Julep sits on the floor next to me and whines. "I know, it smells yummy." Grabbing a leftover slice of peach, I give it to her. "I think this will earn me a favor and serve as a thank you, what do you think?"

She barks back.

"Exactly."

I slip on my flip-flops and make a smooching noise for her to follow me. The humid air feels almost as damp as the dew-slicked grass, as my feet get wet traipsing from my place to his. It's going to be hot today if it's already this warm. Maybe I shouldn't even bother with finishing out a shower; I'll be sweating and in need of another by the end of the day anyway.

What if I told him? All of it. The truth of what brought me here and everything leading up to it? I'd be trusting him to keep a secret. He'd have to lie on my behalf. He wouldn't like that. And then what if it all just ends up being a good time and nothing more? Then someone will know who I am. That's a gamble I'm not ready to take.

I make a fist and give his front door a good tap. *I wonder if he's even home right now.* On my second round of knocking, I hear movement behind the door, and Julep lets out a short bark. She stays next to me on the porch like this isn't her home, even though she has a doggie door she could have entered through.

"Jules, you're knocking now?" Grant says with a laugh, opening the door. His hair is wet and messy. But that's not what I'm focused on. It's the tattoos that spread from his biceps and up along each shoulder cap. Outlines and shading of shapes that if I could freeze time, I'd trace with my finger and try to find their meaning. This isn't good. I'm trying to swallow the lump in my throat. It doesn't help that he's also standing right in front of me, half leaning against the doorframe with nothing more than a navy-blue towel knotted along his hip.

He holds the door wider, the muscle in his sculpted arm jumps and draws my attention down to his broad chest. It's the dusting of dark hair along his chest that operates like a roadmap for his body, allowing me to confirm where it ends and his abs begin. He's so much bigger than I am. Taller. Broader. With a trim waist and a *very* well-kept physique, Grant Foxx is intimidating.

"You here for something, Laney?"

I give him a tight-lipped smile. What are words? What am I doing here right now?

"I made a bourbon peach-stuffed French toast." I tilt my head to the side. "For you. For stepping up at Hooch's last night. I appreciate you doing that for me." I hand him the warm pan, and the surprised look on his face is endearing. So I push my luck and hope for the best. "And my hot water turned off, so I need to use your shower and finish rinsing the conditioner out of my hair."

"That horse trough has fresh water from the morning," he says so quickly that I think he's being serious.

I give him a wink. "Maybe next time."

With a chuckle, opening the door wider, he gestures for me to come inside. "It's just a valve adjustment outside for the well. I'll do it for you once I'm dressed. But go ahead, you can use my shower for now."

It's brighter than I would have expected when I walk into his place. The brooding, quiet man has nice taste. Its ranch-style layout has everything on one sprawling level. Windows that face the east make up almost the entire wall of the large main room. It's the perfect view of the property at sunrise, with the sky tinted the prettiest hues as the sun finally crests above the horizon line, burning off the night and leaving a smokey haze in its wake.

"This is beautiful," I say as I look around the room. To my front is a fireplace. No television or entertainment system in sight, just a large leather couch and coffee table covered with papers and books. The leather recliner next to it has a thick blanket thrown half on the ground, like he had been relaxing there and then went to bed.

"I like it," he says in a rasped voice behind me. Like morning came too soon for him. "It was the original house on the property. Griz and my nana's house." Turning around, I watch as he pulls plates from open shelves.

Why was it cute to hear him say "my nana?"

"It looks much different now, but when Ace wanted to build his own spot, I asked Griz if he wouldn't mind selling it to me when he was ready. That was just over five years ago." He smiles. He's handsome when he smiles, that's for sure. "It's been an ongoing project, but it's kept me busy.

Built out the garage into a workspace. It was a massive amount of updating."

"You did all of this yourself?"

"Most of it. Had some help with the electrical and plumbing, but the rest was me."

It's not something I've thought of as a turn-on before, but that's attractive to me, someone who can fix up their own home.

As we both look at each other for a moment, I remember why I'm here. "Shower?"

"Just down there, the first door on the left is the guest bathroom. Towels are in the closet behind the door."

"I'll be fast. It's just a rinse."

His eyes pull up from my legs as he clears his throat. "Take your time."

The bathroom is just as well-curated as the rest of the house. Simple white walls and matte black fixtures. A clean white tile shower and a half-glass wall instead of a door. It's a no-frills space, but that feels very on-brand for him. Grant doesn't strike me as a guy who likes too much extra of anything. It only takes me a few minutes to rinse out my hair and towel dry off.

When I come out from the bathroom, Grant is sitting at his small kitchen counter on one of the two stools. He managed to throw on shorts that look like swim trunks and a t-shirt that reads *Fiasco PD* along the back.

"When did you retire from the police department?" I ask as Julep sees me and stands, trotting over to my side. I give her a scratch along the top of her head as I meet him at the counter. "We both retired around five years ago now."

I smile at that, and then look down at Julep's panting face. "You're such a smart girl, aren't you?"

He gets up, rounding the counter. "She likes you."

"The feeling is mutual. I always wanted to get a dog, but I didn't have the kind of lifestyle that allowed it. I didn't want them to just be alone all day or night while I worked."

I look at his empty coffee pot on the counter. "Any chance that thing works?"

"I'm sure it does, but I usually grab a cup at the main house. Gives me an excuse to see Griz for a few minutes in the morning before I head into the distillery."

"It's nice that you're so close with your family."

His eyes flick up to meet mine for a second, and then back down to cutting a piece of the baked French toast. There's already a decent-sized square missing. "What about you? You close with yours?"

I swallow and think about how to answer that. There's no lie needed here. "I don't really have one. My dad passed away right after I graduated. He hadn't kept a great relationship with his family, so it was always just the two of us."

"Must have been hard. I'm sorry to hear about your dad." Bringing both plates over, he reaches back to grab another fork for me.

I give him a small nod and a placated smile. I never knew how to respond when people said they were sorry about my dad. I didn't want to say it was okay, because really, there wasn't anything okay about someone dying. He wasn't sick and hadn't suffered. He was honored for the way he died, in the line of duty. A negotiation that had resulted in a stray bullet that hit him just above his bullet-proof vest. I could never tell anyone that it was okay that I had lost my only family. My favorite person in the world. So I just accepted their condolences and tried to remember that he died trying to save someone. If there was any way to go, that would have been his pick. And until recently, I never understood it.

I look up from my plate, trying not to get sucked into my memories. A magnet on the side of his refrigerator snags my attention—a Princess Crown Pez dispenser.

He follows my line of sight. "Lily had really bad nightmares right after her mom passed. Lincoln told her that Pez have superpowers. We kept them just about everywhere after that. She really believed it." His eyes meet mine. "We could all use some of that superpower sometimes. So that one is still where she left it. In case of emergencies."

How am I not supposed to melt after hearing that? "My dad took me to the Pez factory when I was a kid. I had thought it would be this massive place like Willy Wonka's chocolate factory, but it was more museum-like than a candy factory. Bit of a letdown, now that I think about it. It was a good day, though, and I got a Star Wars dispenser. Saved it in our memory box."

"You should show it to Lily. Maybe she'll believe me now that they don't just automatically refill themselves."

I clear my throat, my chest tightening. "Don't have it anymore." I hate that I had to leave it behind, along with other items that helped me remember my dad when I touched them. Releasing a breath, I take a bite of the bourbon-soaked peach, coated in a cinnamon sugar syrup, and hum at the flavors. "This came out better than I thought it would."

Turning to Grant, I find him staring back at me. I've never been brave about eye contact. Except when it comes to him. A simple studying of the shade of hazel green his eyes are. The way the thicker scruff around his mouth leaves enough of an outline around his lips that has me wondering if I'd feel the bristle of it if I kissed them. Maybe it's the proximity of where he's sitting and staring back, or the fact that I haven't felt confident enough around anyone before him to keep from looking away.

He swallows, and I follow the movement of his Adam's apple. When I look back up again, he's staring at his forkful of drippy bread and peach just before he shovels it into his mouth. I try to ignore the bourbon glaze that's dripped onto his lower lip or the way his tongue peeks out to snag it. "So you don't have any family, but how about friends?"

Friends. Actual friends without gray lines that will inevitably get me in trouble, or worse, confuse me all over again.

I clear my throat, and his eyes rove down toward my mouth. "The people I thought were my friends, were acquaintances at best."

"Colorado doesn't sound much like home, then. No family or friends."

"No, it doesn't." Fiasco is already more like home if friends are a way to gauge what a home should feel like. I may work with Ace and Lincoln, but Hadley is becoming a fast friend. And despite what he said last night, Grant might not want to be friends, but we are . . . something.

He turns his attention back to his plate and takes another forkful. With a mouthful, he says, "This is damn good, Laney."

The compliment makes me sit taller. Baking felt good. Sharing it is even better.

"That's the beauty of something new. You get to start fresh. Make new friends," he says with a wink.

"Speaking from experience or a Snapple cap?

He laughs at that. "I did always have a thing for that peach iced tea."

But that's all he gives me. I know there's more to it. He's a thirty-something retired police officer who has an entirely different career now. He started over.

The next few minutes we sit there polishing our plates clean, not acknowledging the buzz that exists between us just under the surface.

"I fixed up the valve for the hot water. Just text me in case it happens again." He shifts toward me. "I'll never say no to you making me breakfast." He smirks. "But it's not necessary."

"You should be learning by now that I do what I want." I nod toward his empty plate that he walks around to the sink, and shrug. "Plus, I've started baking again." As soon as I say it, I wish I hadn't. My thoughts go back to the last thing I baked with my dad, right before I lost him. He always loved breakfast foods. Damn, I miss him. I'm not sure if it's my tone or the look on my face, but now Grant's eyeing me curiously.

Julep's tags jingle, saving me from having to elaborate. She lifts her head, looking at the front door, listening for something.

"Thank you for the shower. And fixing the water for me," I say. But before I can stand to leave, the front door bursts open with a flurry of laughs and arguing.

"I want to knock on her door!" Lark screeches in Lily's face.

Lily hip-checks her into the front table.

Lincoln's right behind them with his arms full of bags and towels. His Ray-Bans push his dark hair out of his face, and the turquoise swim trunks complement his summer tan. Those aren't the only details that hint at them all planning on a trip to the water. The goggles dangling around Lily's neck and the towel draped over Lark's shoulders have me missing the ocean. And since we're landlocked here, I lean closer to Grant. "Is there a pool here that no one told me about?"

But he doesn't hear me with Julep still barking and the girls bickering. It's gotten so loud in here that Grant touches my fingers where I haven't realized I have a death-grip on my fork. When I loosen them, he takes it out of my hand for me. Our quiet exchange reminds me of how he was with me in the stables. *You're okay. Just breathe.*

"Jules, that's enough," Grant says. Followed by, "Halt."

"Girls, you don't need to fight about it. Laney is obviously already here," he says with a smirk and a glance at his brother, who's crossed his arms and is glaring back.

"Laney—" Lark starts.

"I want to ask her," Lily cuts off. "Will you come on a scavenger hunt with us?"

Lark finishes, "And swimming."

I give a quick glance at both Lincoln and Grant before I say anything else, but they're just waiting for my answer.

"There's a tire swing. And Uncle Grant and Dad are the motors for our bumper boats," Lily rattles off at lightning speed. "And we do a scavenger hunt. Uncle Grant, you have the cards ready?"

"All set, Lil."

Lincoln pipes in, "So whaddya say, Laney? Want to spend the day with your fan club?"

"Laney, can we make flower crowns again? There are soooo many flowers we can pick on the way. And we brought extra towels and snacks."

"C'mon, Laney. It's the weekend," Lincoln encourages with a smile.

I glance at Grant, trying to gauge if this is a good idea, but as I do, my eyes get caught up on his lips again. They shouldn't be pretty. Lips on a man aren't pretty, right?

"Come," he says. The tone of his voice practically commands me to do exactly that.

My eyes flick back to his at that simple word. He knows exactly what he's doing to me. "I'd love to."

CHAPTER 19

GRANT

"Not sure I've ever enjoyed watching that tire swing more than I have today," Lincoln sighs out like a lovesick teenager. I know for a fact that he's not pining away or holding out. My brother has plenty of fun, with plenty of women.

I look down at his wedding band still on his ring finger. The one he says he wears to make the girls feel better, but I know my brother. He keeps it on when he's the Lincoln I know. And not "the show." When he's being a dad. Nerding out as a master distiller. He takes it off when he's out fucking his way through whatever city he won't be recognized in, trying to forget about how much he misses his wife. I've gone in the other direction, so really, I have no business judging.

"You're not seriously considering messing around with her, are you?"

He sits up taller, now blocking the sun that was helping me dry me off. "What if I was? Why would you care?"

"Well, for one. Lily and Lark think she's their new best friend." I raise up on my elbows to look at who he's so intently studying. I swallow as my mouth waters, watching her too. Laney swings back and forth like a pendulum, hovering over the quiet river. Her fingers skim the surface as she leans back, smiling wide. Jesus, this woman is the worst kind of eye candy. The kind you don't want to just look at. The kind that I'm betting I'll want for longer than just a taste. *Dammit.*

"Exactly. The girls already like her," he says with a shrug. "Seems like a good choice."

"No."

He barks out a laugh. "What do you mean, no?"

I begrudgingly tear my eyes away from her. Away from her tank top suctioned to her like a second skin. Away from the way she's perched inside the hole of that tire, making her pink shorts ride nice and high on those thighs.

Pushing the sweat from my forehead into my already damp hair, I glare at my brother. "I mean no. You've got enough shit to work out on your own without involving a girl who clearly has plenty of her own baggage."

"Everyone who's a fucking adult has some kind of baggage, baby brother," he claps back. "Hello? Ace, you, and me are like those luggage handlers at the airport, for fuck's sake."

I know that's true. "There's something off. Ace knows more, but it's still not the whole story, I bet."

"You sure you're not trying to call dibs without actually calling dibs?"

Lark cannonballs right at Lily, leaving her job as a pusher of the tire swing. Laney's swing slows. "For your daughters' sakes, I hope you don't think calling dibs on a woman is in any way respectful. Not to mention, it makes you sound like a complete douche."

"Shut the fuck up, Grant," he laughs.

When I look back, Laney's swinging has stopped now, and she hangs there, suspended above the water, looking right where we're sitting. She's far enough away that it's possible she's just gazing in our direction, taking in the beauty of this spot, or staring off like I've caught her doing a few times. But there's a part of me that knows her eyes are on me. I can feel it, like a zip around my skin from every part that's exposed and beyond to the parts of me that are not.

"You're sounding like Officer Foxx again, by the way." He tosses a frozen grape into his mouth.

"What was so bad about that guy?"

"Nothing, just that you haven't been that guy in a long time."

I close my eyes and tilt my head up at the sun. "I don't like liars, Linc. She's lying about what she's doing here."

"That pisses you off?"

"That and the fact that she's everywhere." I think about her in my kitchen, using my shower, lying in my hammock. Laney's been in my head since she showed up, and I'm drowning in the idea of her doing more than just smiling at me. It's her body wrapped around mine. It's wanting to hear her story. It's the way I want her to see *me*.

"You sure you're not pissed off because she's the first woman in years you've paid any attention to?"

"That's part of it." I exhale heavily, frustrated that he can so easily read me.

He smiles, his eyes still trained on that fucking tire swing. "Everybody lies, Grant. Most often to themselves." Leave it to my brother to call me out and put me in my place with just a few words.

Getting up, he walks out toward the riverbank, right to where Laney is dangling.

The water is waist level here, but the current is so light, the surface looks like it's barely moving. With her head tilted back enough that the ends of her strawberry blonde hair dip into the water, the sun shines down on her face, making her glow. I love my brother, but I loathe every step he takes that gets him closer to her.

"Uncle Grant, can we please, please start the scavenger hunt now?" Lily says as she plops onto the towels we've laid out.

"Sure, my little flower," I say, watching as Lincoln says something apparently really funny to Laney. I bite down on my molars, trying to focus on something other than the way she's looking at him. "Why don't you go tell your sister we're going to start, and the winner gets to drive Griz's golf cart."

"Oh my gosh," she rushes out. At the top of her lungs, she yells, "LARK! Lark! Winner gets to drive the golf cart!

Lark comes running to where we're sitting and says, out of breath, "I'm so ready, Uncle Grant. Let's have it."

I glance beyond them, back toward the quiet river hosting the loudest distraction that's come to Fiasco. She glides through the air again on the tire swing as Lincoln pushes her, both of them laughing, and I wish it was me.

I've never been jealous of my brothers. We have our own lives, and different outlooks on what's important, but we always put each other first. No matter what. And in this moment, I want nothing more than to shove my brother aside and be closer to that beautiful liar.

CHAPTER 20

GRANT

"I FOUND THE SPIDER. That should make me the winner," Lark says as she shoves another spoonful of her mint chip ice cream in her mouth.

"Yeah, but I'm the one who got him to go on the stick and brought it back to my pile. So that makes me the winner," Lily argues as she licks around the cone, gathering up every last rainbow sprinkle.

"Alright, girls," Lincoln chimes in as he tosses his empty cup into the trash behind them. "It's late, and I can tell we're about ten minutes away from a fight that I don't have the energy to break up. So"—he claps his hands—"let's thank Laney for the company. And Uncle Grant for the ice cream dinner."

I get a squeeze from both of them just before they start bickering about who gets to pick their "before-bed show" on Netflix.

Linc gives me an exasperated look that makes me

chuckle. "I was off by a few minutes, I guess." After we hiked our way from my house to the river, we circled back and hopped in his Jeep for ice cream at The Fiasco Creamery.

Lincoln's attention goes to Laney on my right, giving her one of his charming smiles. "Laney, thanks for hanging out with us today. The girls think you're way cooler than the rest of the adults they know."

"They're probably right," she jokes back. She glances at me, and with a nod in my direction, adds, "Although, their Uncle Grant might have me beat."

"You sure you're good to walk? I can drop you guys back."

Before she can answer, I jump in. "You're in the other direction. We're good."

The look in Lincoln's eyes tells me he knows I just want to be alone with her.

We stand just a few feet apart from each other, watching as they leave, the girls waving until they're buckled in. "I can't remember the last time I just went with the flow and had so much fun doing it." Turning to me, she smiles softly. "Thanks for letting me tag along with your family time. It felt . . ." She takes a big inhale, and on the exhale, says, "Good."

I spent most of the day trying to steal glances of my new neighbor without obviously glaring at the way my brother talked and flirted with her. He was always good at that. Making people feel like they belonged. Feel wanted. That's never been me.

I rub the back of my neck because the two of us just standing here with the fireflies blinking at us in the distance makes me want to stand closer. Or hold her hand as we start walking.

Dark roads take on a whole new meaning here. There's not a single star out on a clear night like tonight that you can't see. "There's no light pollution out here. It's so dark," she says as her arm brushes against mine.

I pull out my phone to turn on the flashlight.

She laughs, then sighs. "Good idea. I don't think I've ever walked along a dirt road at night before. And I'll be honest, it was never on a bucket list. But now that I've done it. This might be one of my favorite walks."

"It's probably the company."

She barks out another laugh. A few seconds tick by before she says, "That's part of it."

I don't say anything in response because I meant what I said last night. Friendship would never be enough, and I'm riding a fine line between walking away or just saying fuck it. But I'm knocked out of my thoughts by the quick shuffling of dirt on asphalt, followed by a roster of swear words that come pouring from her mouth. "Goddamnit, motherfucking fucker..."

Shining the light on her scuffle, she reaches for her foot. I can't see her clearly, but it's hard not to start laughing. "Are you okay?" I ask with a smile.

"My cheap-ass flip-flop broke." With a small laugh, she holds on to my forearm and lifts her foot. They're dirty, but there's also a small slice along her big toe down to the ball of her foot that's bleeding.

"Alright, here," I say, handing her my phone with the flashlight still lit. "You be my light." I crouch down in front of her. "I'll be your ride."

She takes my phone and laughs. "You want me to get on your back?"

"You can't walk the rest of the way with one shoe and a sliced foot. So yeah, hop on."

She just stands there.

So I turn, still crouched on the ground. "Let's go, honey. My knees are getting pissed that I've been down here this long."

"Grant, I'm not dainty. I'm heavy. You're not going to carry me back." She starts moving forward with a hobbled step.

I grab her hand as it swings past me. "Laney," I growl out.

The tone of my voice has her stopping and turning immediately.

"There is nothing about you that I can't handle. You remember how I tossed you into my horse trough, right?" I don't let her answer that. "Now get your fine ass over here and hop on."

With eyes searching mine, she steps behind me. Her hands draw up and over the back of my shoulders and drape around my neck. Reaching behind me, I splay my hands along her hips and then move to stand. I drag my hands down along the outer side of each thigh, her bare skin warmer than my touch, as she gives a little jump to hoist herself onto my back. Before I start walking, I grab her tighter underneath each thigh and lift her with a bounce so she's wrapped higher, making her yelp.

"Alright, don't choke me out and point the flashlight ahead so we both don't go down this time."

She nods, and I'm painfully aware of how close her face

is to mine. I can hear her breathing almost as heavily as I am, even though she's the one being carried. She smells like the wildflowers that she and the girls were weaving through their hair, mixed with the vanilla from the ice cream cone she licked so damn well, it gave me a fucking hard-on.

"Am I hurting you?" she asks quietly next to my ear.

"You couldn't hurt me even if you tried, honey." I wince a little at the lie.

In a mocking low tone, she says, "Okay, tough guy." Keeping the phone light as steady as she can, she points to the uneven gravel of the long road to the distillery. "It's not a crazy question. I'm a grown-ass woman, and I'm thinking you don't give many of us piggyback rides." She laughs, then adds, "Unless I had you pegged all wrong, cowboy. You give lots of girls rides?"

"Do you always say whatever is on your mind, or am I just special?"

A hum sounds from her chest. "Lately, I say whatever is on my mind. No filter." Then, like she's so innocent, she says, "It was just a little question."

"Bullshit. And you know it."

She rests her chin on my shoulder. "Hmm, maybe not." With her arms holding me tight, I don't miss the way her mouth has inched closer to me. But it's her next few words that almost have me losing my footing. "Maybe you are just special."

Her arms squeeze me a little tighter. I relish the way her legs wrap around me. How her chest rubs against my back, and her palm and fingers grip onto my shirt just below my neck. An arm's length would be smarter. Less complicated. I don't want to be friends, and something more would be reckless. I made a decision a long time ago to close that part of my life off, but right now, it feels really fucking good to touch her.

My hands grip a little tighter on the backs of her thighs. She squeezes them around my sides in response.

"Who's watching Julep today? I'm surprised she didn't come with us," she asks, breaking the thoughts.

I give her a boost for a better grip as I keep pace toward the distillery. "Griz will stop in and see her a few times throughout the day if I'm at work or busy. She ends up going to him rather than the other way around, more often than not."

"So she keeps an eye on him, then?"

I smile at that, because that's exactly what she does. "She's smart and keeps tabs on her people."

"She's been keeping me company too. Do all K9 units retire together?"

"Usually, that's the case. If a dog has gone through training with their handler, living with them, it's hard to reassign them. She's stubborn and doesn't warm up to people she doesn't know." I turn my head slightly to glance back at her. "Except you, apparently."

We approach the rickhouse, our oldest building with some of our most aged batches resting, and the lights are on. Considering it's well past tour time, I doubt anyone is tapping any barrels this late. "You mind a small detour?" She looks up at where I'm focused. "One of the rick riders left the lights on the north end of the rickhouse."

"Rick rider?"

"I doubt they call themselves that, but yeah, rick rider. We have a crew that clocks the barrels. They move barrels around, rotate them in and out of our houses." When I walk up the ramp and through the double doors, the air is more stagnant and humid.

"Are all the rickhouses on this property?" While it's weathered and worn, she sees it for exactly what it is. "It's incredible. There's so much I had no idea about."

"We make a lot of bourbon. So there's another few dozen in the next county that house barrels that we're only aging four to five years." I look around the weathered space. "This might seem like the most boring part of the process, but it's where the most action happens."

She laughs. "You're almost too easy, Grant. How am I not supposed to make a comment after that? *Where the most action happens...*"

I can't help but smile. Hell, I've done a lot of that with her. I know there's more to her, somewhere underneath the part she's trying to keep to herself, but this is the light and playful version. I'm just as drawn to it.

I holler, "Anyone still working? Dave?" Pausing, I wait for a mumbled response. "Tim? Carter? You guys still here?"

I let Laney slide down my back, her feet hitting the cement floor.

She lifts her shoeless foot and looks at the slice that's bleeding a bit more than I originally thought. "Any chance you have band-aids in here?"

"Left them at home." Chuckling, I grab her around the waist and hoist her onto a bourbon barrel.

"That right there," she says, nodding to my chest. "You just walked at least a mile or two with me koala'ed on your back, and then picked me up like it was no big deal."

I smirk. She's giving me far too much appreciation for manhandling her. But I'll take it. "Wasn't a big deal, honey."

Her eyes track down the front of my chest and back up at a pace that feels really fucking good. She zeroes in on my lips as she says, "It was a sexy flex, Grant." That comment knocks me right in the gut and swoops around my body, landing right in my dick. "I can't figure out if this is just how you are or if you're showing off for me."

Jesus Christ, I want this woman. I grab the collar of my t-shirt from behind my neck and take it off, ripping one of the short sleeves.

She barks out a laugh. "Yeah. Okay, show-off."

I can't fight back the grin that pulls from me as I lift her ankle. "Here, let me see."

She sits there with a coy smile on her face, biting at her thumbnail as she leans forward.

With her foot perched on my thigh, I tie the torn strip of navy-blue cotton around the ball of her foot, bandaging up the cut and her toes.

"You didn't tell me why."

"Why what?" I ask as I focus on knotting the material around her foot once more to make sure it's tight.

She hesitates for a second. "Why 'friends' wouldn't be enough for you."

I keep my gaze on the tops of her thighs and think about every single reason as my hands move up her smooth skin and around her ankle. It feels like touching her right now isn't a decision I've made or a thoughtless choice, but a necessity. I stare at the way her skin feels under the pads of my fingers as they brush up the side of her leg.

"I don't think it would be enough for me either," she admits breathily. Without conviction. In fact, the way she says it seems like it's more for herself to hear than for me.

My fingers keep traveling up the side of her leg as I stand. The proximity reminds me of the kind of man I used to be—one who took chances, flirted with who I wanted, and then acted on it.

"This *isn't* how friends feel," she says. Her eyes watch my hands move as I watch her lips.

"Isn't that what you said you wanted?"

Her fingers brush over my hands, following the movement as they inch higher.

"Yes . . . I've said a lot of things since I've been here."

I'm so close to her that I can study the details of her lips, where the bow dips and how they're slicked pink and ready. All she would need to do is widen the space between her knees so I could slide closer. Press my lips against hers and taste what I've been wanting all day.

"I don't want complicated. I don't chase women. I don't like people who show up and crash into my life. I don't fall for strangers that are a pain in my ass."

As my hands continue up to her waist, my fingers pulse as I grip onto her. Slipping under the hem of her shirt, I feel the warmth of her skin again.

"Sounds like you might have a problem then, cowboy."

"Yeah, honey." I smirk. "Want to make a liar out of me?"

And that's what she does as her thighs shift just enough for me to get closer. A small invitation to take what I want. Her tongue runs along her bottom lip as she curls it into her mouth, dragging her teeth along it once it's wet.

There's still an irrational part of me that believes in this fucking curse that follows my family. That I couldn't survive it again if it were true. That if I let myself get lost in her, even just for a little while, I won't be the same.

But I'm bored of being cautious, tired of it. And, dammit, do I want to kiss the woman I can't seem to stop thinking about.

It's like being released from the gates. A shotgun call the second I decide I want nothing but this moment with her, and everything happens at once. My hand flies from her waist and my fingers clasp around the side of her neck as my thumb settles right where her pulse jumps. She reaches the nape of my neck at the same time and her fingers weave into my hair just as our lips meet in a kiss that has me hungry.

It feels like a reward.

The small noise that comes from the back of her throat as my lips rove over her mouth is what causes the last bit of my reserves to crumble. I brush my tongue along hers and it's like we've done this a million times before. *Perfection.* She tilts her head just enough that our lips can play deeper, and I pull back just enough to make sure she's feeling the same. That there is nothing else in this world but the two of us lost in a kiss that feels like a fresh start and an endgame all at once. When her eyes meet mine, she smiles, and I can't help but smile back and dip for another.

Shuffling of the dirt along the cement floor steals my attention instantly. Like cold water dousing us both. As soon as I turn, I see Griz waltz up the main aisle with a burlap sack in one hand and a copper whiskey thief in the other. "Well, well, well. Looks like you two are awful cozy." Leave it up to my grandfather to call it like it is.

Laney doesn't miss a beat as I back away. "Your grandson was just demonstrating something I've been thinking about since I showed up here." She gives me a wink, lightening the mood instantly. Wiping her mouth with her thumb as I regrettably put more distance between us, she asks him, "What are you holding?"

Griz walks closer as I cross my arms over my bare chest, now completely out of her atmosphere and hating it. I toss on my ripped shirt as he holds up the copper pipe with the pointed end.

"They call this a whiskey thief. We use it when we want to taste test what's in the barrels."

She smiles, moving her hands under her thighs as she sits perched on the bourbon barrel. "Taste anything good?" Her eyes dart to mine for a beat. *Yeah, honey, you taste more than good.*

"Darlin', there's always good bourbon in these barrels, even when it's early. But no, I wasn't tasting. Didn't get that far."

The tightened-up burlap sack in his other hand moves.

"Griz, you catch something?"

He brushes it off, walking past us. "Western cottonmouth is my best guess since I didn't hear the rattler, but you never know. Could be a young one. I didn't want to waste time and find out."

Laney looks to me with a cute furrow to her brow. "Rattler?"

With a nod, I tell her, "Snake."

"Real nasty one too," Griz says, moving toward the far aisle of the rickhouse. "She was pissed. It's the second one I pulled out of here this season so far. Usually, it's not until it gets cooler, but these damp, dark spots just call to all sorts of critters."

He holds the bag like it's filled with groceries and not a snake. "What are you going to do with it?"

Griz smiles at me, and then with a smirk, says to her, "They're mighty tasty."

"You're not serious?"

I can't keep the smile from cracking on my face. "He's probably going to let it go somewhere far from here. Don't worry."

Griz looks down at her foot. "What'd you get yourself into?"

"Small cut from walking back."

His gaze whips to me. "You let a lady walk with an injury. I didn't teach you better than that?"

She giggles at his tone. "He actually gave me a piggy-back ride all the way here."

With a nod, he turns back to Laney. "I've got the golf cart. C'mon, I'll give you a ride back to your place."

I help her down from the barrel.

"My back is shit now, so loop that arm around me. It's only out the side door."

Griz hands me the burlap bag. "What am I supposed to do with this?"

With her arm looped around Griz and a big smile on his face about something she said quietly to him, he says, "I'm sure you'll figure it out. Don't forget to shut the lights before you lock up."

I watch as he walks down the small path to his golf cart, helping her inside, just as the burlap sack hisses. She doesn't look back, already laughing at something he's telling her.

It's the second time today I'm jealous of another man taking her attention away. Only this time, my lips are still buzzing from hers.

It's the most reckless I've been in a long time, which isn't good for anyone. Mostly, me.

CHAPTER 21

LANEY

I LOOK FORWARD TO CAFFEINE, bright and early. And, if I want a good flat white, then I walk a few miles to the bakery. It's been one of my favorite things to do. A simple way to get me out and about, opening myself up to exploring my new home with a coffee in hand.

As I stop to look around my new town, it feels like a movie. A big-city girl plopped into a small town, trying to find her footing. I walked thousands of miles in New York. There was plenty to see. New restaurants, massive bill-boards, and hustling crowds, but there were also quiet parts. Never as quiet as the field outside of my new little cottage here in Fiasco, but there were parts of New York I loved stumbling across. There's less here. More space and far less to discover, but it's my way of finding something familiar in a brand-new place.

The mint green awning overhanging the little pink building smack dab in the middle of Fiasco's downtown should have been gaudy. With a neon yellow open sign and the shop's name painted in black block letters across the front, Loni's was charming from the second I opened the front door during my first shopping trip. The front table displays have clothing arranged by color, from red tops to pink shorts that lead to racks of dresses that aren't the conservative styles I had expected of a small southern town. They're trendy, even a bit edgy. I recognized some designer labels from storefronts in SoHo and other nameless styles that I wouldn't mind adding to my currently limited wardrobe.

As I walk past, the same black dress that I had borrowed from Hadley hangs on a headless mannequin. And then next to it is the prettiest floral dress that I had to find a reason to wear and come back for.

"You're the girl everyone in town can't seem to stop talking about," the woman behind the counter said as I tried to find my size in the bathing suit bottoms. I smiled at her, internally groaning at the idea of people talking about me. "Might as well lean into the rumors." She stepped over to help me. "Most gossip around here is based on a form of the truth and embellished because of boredom." I'm sure I looked uneasy at that, but she gave me a comforting smile. "We like our bourbon. We don't spill tea in Fiasco, we pour three fingers with intention."

It was just the right reminder as I cross the street and step into Griz's book club on Sunday morning.

I thought it was a pity invite for awkwardly inter-rupting the kiss between Grant and me. I can still feel the way his hand tilted my neck and how his thumb brushed so sweetly along my skin as his mouth devoured me wholly. I felt that kiss along every inch of my body. So when I was rambling and asking about Griz's weekend plans as he drove me back from the rickhouse, he told me all about his girls and his book club.

"You must be Laney. I'm Prue. Welcome to our book club!" The unexpected excitement in her voice has a smile curling my lips. "The only thing Griz keeps talking about is how the prettiest girl landed in our small town at his distillery." She taps my hand. "And that she was going to be the one to break the curse."

I know what she's referring to, but I didn't think much of it or that I'd in any way factor into it. "The curse?"

She opens the door wider, taking the baked goods from my hands and smelling it. "Oh yes. There's so much to talk about. Is this a buckle? You baked a buckle?"

I'm not sure if this is a good thing or not, but I'll keep smiling anyway. "Peach. I hope that's okay."

The large and bright sitting room is packed as I walk inside. If it wasn't for the number of women that sat and mingled, I would have taken in more of the details. I only catch a glimpse of the pink paisley wallpaper and bookshelves overflowing with paperbacks.

"Laney is here," she sing-songs. "And she baked a peach buckle. Romey, come take this, and I'll grab a knife to cut it."

I slow my pace, smiling at the room, where their full attention is now on me. As quietly as possible, I say to Griz, who stands and greets me with a big bear hug, "You said book club. I thought you meant, like, five people."

His thick mustache tips up in the right corner, amusement dancing around his face. "Looks like everyone wanted to talk about this week's book."

"Or the new girl."

He laughs, lips pursing. "Yeah, probably the new girl. Don't worry, I'm right here."

Every single person is a woman other than Griz and ranges in age from early twenties to somewhere near Griz's age. "I'm sorry if I didn't read the book, but I would love to be a part of the next one, whichever you choose."

A woman close to my age, flanked by two Golden Girls, waves and smiles. "This was just a short romance novella. It was quick and dirty—"

"Just how I like it," another woman, crouched around a drink table on the far side of the room, chimes in. It makes everyone laugh and agree. I don't interject, but if I were more comfortable with this group, I would have joked right alongside them. *Maybe someday.*

"There's a brunch buffet back here," Prue says as she grabs my hand and loops it around her arm. "Darla brought her fabulous huevos rancheros, Tonya's deviled eggs, there's a French toast thing." She leans in and whispers, "That was Mary's, and it's always a toss-up whether she'll bring something edible." Then she mouths out, "Skip it." Leaning back, she speaks up louder with a playful smirk. "Griz, I see you weaseled your way out of bringing a treat this week."

"Brought myself and a new attendee." He winks. In his low voice, he flirts with her, "That'll have to be sweet enough this time, Prudence."

I don't miss the way she smiles back at him. Making assumptions, Prue is younger than Griz by at least ten years, putting her somewhere in her seventies. Silver strands streak her light brown hair reaching just to her shoulders. There's something warm about her that I can't put my finger on. Maybe it's the flowy green pants and floral pink blouse with a cream-colored cardigan pinned just at the top, but she looks and feels like a kind librarian.

"And Marla is behind the mimosa and Bloody Mary bar."

"Laney." Marla nods. It's pretty clear that Marla isn't my biggest fan, but it's a step in the right direction since she didn't tell me I couldn't have a drink or that I had to leave.

I load up a small plate and find a seat in between two women, who smile as I approach, and ask if I can squeeze in. As soon as I sit, of course, my phone buzzes in my bag. I try to ignore it, but then start to worry if it's something important. Not many people have this number—Hadley, Ace, and Agent Harper. Oh, and now Grant.

"Welcome everybody. I'm so excited everyone wanted to read this week's novella. I really enjoyed it, but the writing felt rushed . . ." Prue starts, but I quickly tune it out, over-thinking if I should check my phone when it buzzes again.

The brunette with the long curly hair to my right looks at me when it buzzes for the fourth time. "Are you going to get that? It's kind of distracting," she whispers. *Is it really that distracting?*

I can't help but smile when I see who it's from.

COWBOY

How's your foot?

LANEY

My foot is fine, but I'm in the middle of book club getting the stink eye from a leggy brunette for not paying attention.

COWBOY

Curly hair?

LANEY

Yes.

COWBOY

Nose ring?

LANEY

Yes. One of your exes?

COWBOY

She's tried.

LANEY

Not your type?

COWBOY

Depends. Jealous?

LANEY

Are you flirting with me, cowboy?

COWBOY

Depends.

LANEY

On?

COWBOY

You.

"What about you, Laney?" interrupts the text conversation with Grant.

"I'm so sorry, what was the question?" I look around the room and pocket my phone. Whatever that just was is something I can dissect later, but right now, all eyes are on me. I just went from a sense of ease to a nervous buzz starting to make its way around my body.

Griz interjects from his chair, "You know she didn't read it, Prue." The way he says it feels protective.

"I was just trying to include her. You don't have to have read it to have an opinion about a book that has a morally gray female main character. But it's fine." She waves at the air in front of her.

The brunette to my right chimes in to respond, "I personally think it makes her a weak character. When we've read morally gray men, they're usually strong mafia men or billionaires. She's none of those things."

Before I even realize I'm responding, the words are already out of my mouth. "That seems awfully patriarchal, doesn't it?" I glance around the room quickly to see if I'm going to die on this mountain alone. I see a few smiling faces, so maybe not. "We're okay with men who have questionable morals if they're rich and powerful, but we're not okay if those same types of morals are from a woman who isn't well off?"

"I'm not saying I'm okay with it. I'm saying I find it more attractive in a man. And that makes me want to read it."

I nod, but I can't just let it ride. "Okay, I understand that. Is it that you like the fact that most morally gray men have an innocent female counterpart in these dynamics?

Maybe you like the way they balance. But how do you feel about a morally gray female lead, whose male counterpart in a story has a perfect moral compass?"

She tilts her head to the side, her mouth pursed enough that it looks like she's thinking about it. But instead, she shakes her head no. "Nope, still not doing it for me." And all I can think to myself is that I've just described Grant Foxx and myself, or at least what I know about him and his reputation in this town.

Marla pipes in with a mouth filled with lemon poppy-seed muffin. "I'd read that story one-handed, Laney."

Enough laughs fill the room, allowing for that topic to die down, and thank goodness for it. I hadn't planned to go head-to-head with anyone about the moral compasses of fictional characters. When my phone buzzes again, I decide to excuse myself from the chitchat. I smile as I close the bathroom door behind me and pull out my phone, expecting it to be Grant. But it's not.

> BEA
>
> Has anyone from the U.S. Marshall's office approached you?

> LANEY
>
> I've only dealt with you, Bea. No one else.

Less than thirty seconds later, she calls me.

"Hello?" I say quietly. I can hear a few people outside the bathroom door talking now, and I don't want anyone to overhear this.

Bea's raspy voice cuts right to the chase. "You need to keep it that way."

My senses kick in, and I can tell by her tone and that simple sentence that something's happened, and it's not something good. "What's going on, Bea?" She starts to answer, but I cut her off, "Don't call me and say that shit to me just to keep me in the dark."

She lets out a huff. "I knew I was right to keep this out of the proper channels. *He* used to be in witness protection."

I lean my back against the door, trying to work out who. "The person who tried to murder that woman? The monster I rescued her from was being protected by the U.S. government? Are you fucking joking?" It almost sounds too ridiculous to consider.

"He did a lot more than *try* to murder someone, Laney. There are a number of missing persons that have been tied to him according to my contacts, after all of that evidence in the storage unit. But yes, he was WITSEC. Most of the people we relocate in the program have a criminal record. Usually, it's misdemeanors, rarely anything violent. This isn't something I've had happen before. Especially not at this scale."

My heart beats so fast, I can feel my pulse moving along my neck, hear it in my ears, and I've picked away at the cuticle on my thumb so viciously that it's starting to bleed. "Every time I think I can breathe and settle into this new life, I get a call from you." I lick at the wound I just created. "Am I safe here?"

"You're in the smartest situation I could hope for," she says without it sounding like she's done. "I'm not saying anything is going to happen here, but if there are any U.S.

Marshalls, FBI, authorities of any kind sniffing around down there, you call me."

"Dammit," I breathe out. *I wish my dad was here.*

"Somebody messed up and I don't know what it means in the long run. Everyone is keeping a tight lip on the whole thing, which makes my ass twitch. Hence, this call." I hear her light one of her cloves, and then seconds later, push out a breath. "I'm telling you all of this because you're not some victim, Laney. You stopped a murderer and saved someone who needed saving, and it earned you a life you never asked for. So I'm making it my business to be sure you're safe. And the best way I can do that is to keep you aware of the situation. Now tell me you can handle it."

She sounds like my dad. "I can handle it." My eyes water, knowing my dad would be proud of this. Not everything I've done, but being brave would make him proud.

"Good." Another puff. "If anything feels off, you find Grant or Ace and call me."

"Grant knows?" I rush out. "He knows about what I'm doing here?"

She lets out a laugh. "I knew one of them would sink their teeth into you."

"That's not—"

"Laney, I couldn't give a rat's ass what you do with the Foxx boys. They're good men. They only know whatever you told them. So unless I need to come into town because of trouble, it'll stay that way. Like I said, the less people who know the truth, the better. Safer that way. For everyone. Especially now."

Closing my eyes, I focus on the way I'm almost out of

breath. My adrenaline pumps in a chaotic rhythm. I exhale shakily as she says her clipped goodbye.

It takes me a second to remember where I am. In a bathroom, in the middle of a book club. I need to pull it together and slow my breathing down before I leave this room. There's so much pink as I look around Prue's gaudy bathroom. The soft pink tiled walls to the deeper mauve pink toilet and tub basin. Even the tissue box has a bubblegum pink knitted cover with white lace trim, and the hand towels match. There's a vase of baby's breath on the shelf above the toilet with a pink antique perfume bottle. I don't realize I'm smiling until I look up at myself in the mirror. Finally calmer than just a moment ago, I run the cold water and dip my wrists. I'm drying my hands when I hear my name outside the bathroom.

I stop moving and lean slightly closer to the door.

"I don't know. She must have left. I'm just going to say it. She's not some sweetheart she's pretending to be. Like, what was that patriarchal crap?"

Another voice says, "Do you think it's true? About her and Ace?"

The first voice says, "Definitely. He likes to slum it all the time. She's kind of fat too, right? I mean, she's not the usual for him."

My stomach lurches at being talked about and judged. I didn't do a damn thing to these women. I remember again why I painted my nails the pale shade of pink that I didn't particularly like and wore brands that were too expensive for my wallet. Why I worked too much, even though it didn't make me happy. I thought feeling seen meant I needed attention from people who signed my checks and rewarded me with more responsibility. It was why I couldn't recognize the things I wanted or truly liked. I didn't allow myself the space to figure it out. I had felt like an outsider, unwelcomed. And I let myself believe it. Maybe if I had family or a close friend, I wouldn't have given a shit. But I did. At least back then.

But then I hear them mention Grant's name, and I know I'm not going to be able to just stay here and listen. "I heard she was with Grant too."

Another person says, "No way. I would have believed it with Ace, but Grant?"

The first voice, who I'm guessing is my curly-haired brunette friend, says, "There's no way they would keep around someone like that. Grant has barely looked at anyone since Fiona. He was such a hot mess for a while, but he's looking good again. I did catch him smiling at me last week."

Doubtful.

"I'm not about to ask for forever from a Foxx, obviously, but I wouldn't mind a ride."

That's enough. I allowed these feelings time and time again in my old life. The bride who didn't think I was qualified to help her with her seating charts or the Maid of Honor who wanted to remind me that I was only the hired help. Even the groom who thought it was okay to treat me like I was nothing more than an expendable distraction. Racking up the negatives and unworthy feelings isn't something I have any interest in collecting anymore.

When I open the door, all three women stop with their drinks mid-sip and eyes wide. "Are you girls talking about me?" I don't have a plan here, but now that I'm looking at them, I wonder how uncomfortable I can make this. So, I smile. "You didn't have to be these women. The cliché villains. Women who feel the need to badmouth someone they don't know in order to make sense of their boring and basic lives." I look down the hallway, and I can see a few people eavesdropping in on this, but I keep going. "I would have liked some new friends here, but thank you for allowing me to bypass the wrong ones."

As I look at each of the three women, not a single one seems willing to respond with an apology. Might as well make this memorable.

"Fiasco is my home now too. And if you want to spread rumors about me, then let me make sure you've got them right. My name is Laney Young, and I'm from Colorado. The Foxx family are my friends. Except for Grant—you were right about that. He's . . ." I sigh because, really, he's sigh worthy. "Let's just say, the mouth on that man is quite delicious."

The three jaws dropping just enough let me know I've made an impression.

I turn on my heel, trying my hardest to keep my emotions in check. I can let my eyes water when I'm out the door.

I hear one of them whisper, "Did that just happen?"

"Oh! I forgot." I turn back around. "You can go ahead and fuck off for that fat comment." Tilting my head to the side, I point at her when I say, "Do better."

I swallow down the way I'd like to fall apart, and instead, I thank Prue for the hospitality and wave at Griz with a big, fake smile as I rush out the door. I'll wait until

I'm back in my cottage before I overthink the news from Bea and rehash the day's shitstorm.

I had never been invited to a book club before today, and as much as I would have liked to fit in, I like it better that I don't.

CHAPTER 22

GRANT

"I THINK WE DO A TASTING, and then we bottle everything on site, right there, as people are touring," Lincoln says. He wants to make the 100-year anniversary party as memorable as possible.

So, I back him up. "I'd remember that."

"Not if you've been drinking and celebrating all day. It's going to be time-consuming and take up way too much manpower to make happen. And for what? Some social media shit we can do ourselves?" Ace says with his feet kicked up on his desk.

"Laney said it would be a great way to involve people in the process. The exclusivity of that makes them feel like they're a part of this," Lincoln claps back.

The mention of her name has me thinking about those pretty lips and how much I royally fucked myself by kissing her. It won't be enough.

"Are you that hard up already?" Ace says to Lincoln. He

shifts his eyes to me, maybe thinking I'd find that amusing, but he's only met with a glare. The wordless exchange is all my big brother needs to know that he just started splashing in dangerous territory.

"Remember that time you said, when you start sounding more like a businessman and less like a bourbon boy to tell you?" Lincoln asks with his chin resting on his fist.

Ace leans back farther in his chair and raises his hands behind his head. "Yeah, is this where you're telling me that's happening now?"

It's my turn to chime in. "No, you've been more business than bourbon for a long time now. Almost as long as I've been on the team."

Ace narrows his eyes at me, and that's when I know it's coming. He's pissed at that remark. I always know when I've struck a chord with him. He's going to get nasty. "Is that what you're calling it now, Grant? A team? Because from where I sit, you clock in, do your shit, and then clock out. You haven't been in a board meeting, distribution meeting . . . Hell, I don't even think you've tapped a barrel in damn near a decade."

Not any of your barrels. But he doesn't know that. And neither does Linc.

"The fact that those are the things you think I need to do in order to be considered a part of the team is the fucking case in point, big brother."

Lincoln, the ever peacekeeper, stands a second after I do. Ace just smirks at me like an asshole, so I aim low. "No suit today?"

"Fuck off, Grant."

"Happily," I say as I move out of the office and into the main hall.

I hear Lincoln ask, "Was that really necessary?"

But it's Ace's response that has me turning on my heel and charging back into the room. "Those rumors are what's pissing him off. He thinks I slept with his new little friend." He watches me stalk toward him. "Go ahead, what are you going to say now that I know I've struck a nerve? Stings, doesn't it?"

That's what has me stopping from clocking him in his face. My big brother is only saying it because he didn't like that I was honest. He's baiting me. I can always tell because, while Ace can be a real motherfucker to other people, he's never said shit that's crossed a line. And right now, he's damn close.

Nostrils flaring, I point my finger at him. "You're not thinking like someone who loves this anymore. You're thinking like someone who wants a higher profit and a better bottom line."

"So what? This is a business." He raises his arms. "Look around, you asshats. How do you think we're able to live? How do you think the taxes for land get paid or that neither of you have to worry about budgeting? You're overpaid. You know that, right?" He drags his fingers in his hair. "Linc at least went to school and has his masters. If he went to another distillery, he could pull in something close to what he's making now. But you"—he points at me—"your salary is severely inflated, Grant."

I flip him off. "Should have done a better job negotiating, shithead."

He cracks a smile and looks down. *Got him.*

I look over at Linc, who's also smiling now. "He has a point."

"Fine. Then help me make this big ass 100-year celebration as big of a deal as I've been planning, and I'll ease up on the business side of things. It's going to boost us this year, and if we can keep the hype up, we may be able to utilize some bottles as barter for partnerships with other brands."

I send a look to Lincoln, eyebrow quirked. "You understood that? I'm just a retired cop who makes oak barrels in my spare time."

"Okay, fucker. I'm sorry. I know you're working your ass off."

Maybe now's a good time to tell them. But just as I open my mouth to share what I've been doing and where I've been aging those barrels, Julep comes charging in. Barking and nudging my leg.

"Hey, Jules, what's going on?" I ask, like she's going to articulate exactly what's up. I know my girl, though. Something has her riled up enough to come find me. She barks again and moves back out the door, waiting for me to follow her.

I look up at my brothers, waving as I'm already almost out the door. "Let me see what's going on."

Lincoln shouts, "Go. I gotta go get the girls anyway."

I pick up the pace, walking after Julep. She was back at the house after I finished up at the distillery today, but she has dog door access to our house and Ace's place. It's nearly eight at night, but it looks more like golden hour with the sun moving down to the horizon line.

Julep stops to wait for me, barking again. She's a smart dog. Even beyond her K9 training for the department, she has a way of reading people that I always felt gave me a leg up when she was around. It's more than just being hungry or wanting an extra greenie before bed tonight. Something's up. I jog to catch up to her and move down the paved pathway that connects the main house with mine. And the cottage. I don't see any doors or windows open at Laney's place, but I stop there first.

As soon as my foot hits the front porch stairs, Julep starts barking behind me, and I hear the music. Fleetwood Mac playing low and Laney singing loudly about someone going their own way. It's impossible not to smile at her when I turn. But it's when I see her that the smile falls away. I take in the full scene as Julep now lies next to the horse trough, where Laney sits in the water-filled galvanized tub, her strawberry blonde hair piled on top of her head in a messy knot, and her arms draped over either side. One hand holds a long rope of red licorice and the other a slice of pizza, her head tilted up as she pulverizes the actual words to the song. But that's not even the most distracting part. No, that would be her bare shoulders and back that sit tall and lean against the back of the tub. Is she drunk? She's skinny dipping in my backyard.

I step closer and she must hear me coming because her head turns to the side. A smirk lifts her profile. "Care to join me, cowboy?"

I can't hide the smile this sight is pulling from me, as I tick down the volume on her portable speaker.

"Looks a little cramped in there, honey."

Her head turns slightly more, a smile painted on those pretty lips of hers. The curve of her breast peeks out under her arm as she moves. "Not your honey, remember?"

I don't want to remember anything. I like the way she reacts when I call her that. I stop my steps because as much as I'd love to, I don't want to take advantage of this situation and see something I know I shouldn't. *Fuck, do I want to, though.*

"Fleetwood Mac fan?"

I can see the way her mouth ticks up from the side. "Everyone is a Fleetwood Mac fan." She takes a bite of her pizza slice. "My dad loved them too. And The Doobie Brothers. He used to get so worked up about them breaking up—it was long before I was around. But he said it was the saddest issue of Rolling Stone he'd ever read."

What is it about the little details she shares that have me so eager to know more? *That* shouldn't be so captivating. But the naked, tone-deaf woman sitting in a too-tiny tub and shouting lyrics like she's Stevie Nicks's backup singer steals way more of my attention than I've been letting on.

"Grant, come and have some snacks with me."

Shaking my head, I smile to myself. "I'm trying to be a gentleman here, Laney. I think if I come any closer, I'm going to see a whole lot more of you than I should."

She laughs and makes a mocking shocked noise. "Grant, are you a prude?" She takes a bite of her red licorice. "I'll be honest, I'm very comfortable being this woman."

I smile at the admission and a laugh slips out. "And what kind of woman is that?"

The hum she makes sounds wistful. "The kind that doesn't feel bad about her body. The kind that feels confident in her own skin. The kind that stands up for herself even if she cries about it later." She tilts her head back, and her eyes find me. "And definitely the kind of woman who doesn't care what other people think of her anymore."

I cross my arms over my chest. I'm just slightly behind her and to the left, enough that I can't see anything but the back of her and the side of her face when she turns her head to see me. "So how'd a woman like that end up topless and in the horse trough?"

She releases a long, exaggerated sigh. "I wanted to take a bath and have a drink. But I opted for what was accessible." Looking down, she waves around the licorice. Plus, the cottage doesn't have a bath. You weren't home. And I didn't think Julep was going to tell on me." She points at the dog sitting next to her. "Tattletale."

Julep lets out a bark, and then puts both her front paws on the tub, leaning in to lick Laney's face.

Laney squeals and laughs in response.

Seeing that makes me feel . . . something. Something deeper than attraction. Maybe it was appreciation. Witnessing my dog genuinely respond to another person like that. "I'm going to get you a towel. And then you can tell me what happened. How's that?"

Her smile this time is softer than the flirtatious grin from a few minutes ago. I rush inside, grab a towel, and I'm back out walking toward her. I'd be lying if I said I didn't see anything. The tops of her tits lift just above the water, but I don't dare allow myself to look for much longer. I wouldn't be able to stop. I know my limits, and I'm awfully close to them. Holding the towel up in front of the tub, I wait for her to get out. She manages to find her footing and steps into me with her arms raised above her head, bag of candy in one hand and the crust from her pizza slice in the other.

I don't care that she drips water all over my boots or the fact that I have to lean into her as I wrap the towel behind her body and tuck it in, holding it in place. She looks up at me with wet lashes that make me notice the little flecks of brown near the irises of her bright blue eyes. *Beautiful.*

"How chivalrous were you just now, cowboy?"

"You've been calling me a cowboy, not a knight." I wink at her. "Quick peek." My voice dips lower, quieter, "Was impossible not to."

"Should we pick up where we left off last night?"

I almost grunt with the way those words hit me right in the dick. And then her blue eyes gaze into mine as she licks at her bottom lip . . . Fuck, do I want to. But I need more from her. I hate knowing something's off—and not just whatever happened today, but what had her showing up with a U.S. Marshall in the middle of the night. Until I know more, I can't have a repeat of last night.

I rub my hand along the seam of my jeans because if I don't touch something, I'll take that towel right back and get my fill of her.

She bites at her thumbnail, trying to hold in a smile, then moves toward the chairs around the fire pit. "Am I making something hard?"

Jesus Christ, if she had any idea. I drag my hand along the back of my neck and take a few steps away from where she's sitting now. Grabbing two pieces of firewood, I toss them into the fire pit, then crouch to fill the space underneath with the kindling starters. I look up at her and the bottle she plucks from her bag. "Mind sharing some of that?"

She holds out the bottle of Foxx 1945.

"This one is Griz's year." My fingers drag across hers too slowly for both of us to ignore. I think about looping my hands with hers, propping her on my lap, and licking up the taste of this bourbon from her lips. But I resist, just barely.

"What does that mean, that it's his year?"

"We bottle up the oldest barrel that's been resting. A small run of only about a hundred or so the year that something important happens. Coming into the world is one of those important things, and Griz's year is 1945."

Her eyes go wide, sparkling with interest. Soaking wet, this woman is so fucking tempting. *Space*. A little bit of space from this moment would be good. "Let me grab glasses and a lighter." I walk backward toward my door, still watching her, remembering where she was going today. Maybe that has something to do with her being out here. "Griz said you went to book club with him?"

Her posture changes, and she looks up at the sky quickly, her eyes watery. I've never wanted to yell at Griz the way I want to right now for throwing her to the wolves. Because I can guarantee that's what it felt like when I heard about just a few of the women who were there.

I abandon the idea of getting matches and glasses. Instead, I'm in front of her chair in just a few strides, kneeling so she can see me when I say, "Whatever or whoever made you upset, I'm going to put money on the fact that they're not worth the tears."

Two tears fall from each eye as she looks down. There's

no part of me that thinks about what I'm doing or why I feel the need to do it, but I rub each of them away with the pads of my thumbs. "Or was the book just trash?" I ask jokingly.

She barks out a small laugh. "I shouldn't be crying about this."

I wipe a few more that track down the non-crier's face. "Just some leaking emotions. Happens to the best of us."

She laughs again, and those big glassy eyes find mine.

"Why are you crying, honey?"

I take the bottle from her hand and down a quick swig. Honestly, I need a second. There's something I'll always love about the way that first sip of bourbon hits your tongue and throat. But I just need it to help remind me that this isn't smart, getting so close to here, comforting her. "You upset I crashed your topless horse trough party?"

She barks out a laugh. "Naked. Not just topless."

I scrub my hand over my face and whisper out, "Fuck."

When I look back up, her eyes fall to my mouth before trailing back up to mine. Yeah, I could get in lost in this woman. The kind of lost that I won't find my way back from. That kiss was so damn good, but I could leave it there. I could ease back and try damn hard not to want more.

Changing the subject would be good. "Where else besides The Pez Factory?"

She smiles at me and leans back, a questioning look on her face.

"Thinking about my favorite things always makes me feel better."

Wrapping the towel around her shoulders tighter, she tilts her chin up to the sky. "Zoltar."

"The fortune teller machine?"

She points at me with a correction. "Not fortunes. Futures. Like when Tom Hanks wished to be big and he turned into a thirty-something the next day."

Well, now I'm curious. "What did your future say?"

She stares at my mouth again like she's zoned in on either making me wildly uncomfortable or imagining what I can't seem to forget. "Doesn't matter. I don't have it anymore." Her smile laces with sadness. "And it doesn't happen if you don't have the card anymore either."

I shrug. "Still curious."

"Can I ask you something?" she whispers.

I nod and take another drink before I look back at her.

"Do you think doing a good thing can erase when you've done a bad thing?"

My knees scream to get out of this crouched position, but I can't. Not when she's asking me things like this. I give her a tight-lipped smile and then sit back on the ground in front of her.

She holds out a piece of the red licorice in front of my mouth. I open for her, biting down on the chewy cherry rope.

"I think the world doesn't really work like that. Some things are black and white. If something is right or wrong. But reasons for doing them—the why—is what can be gray." I lean my forearms on my bent knees and watch as she nods at what I'm saying. "What kind of bad thing could you have possibly done?" For some reason, a few weeks ago, I could have imagined just about anything, but a little bit of time with her has me feeling like I want to do bad things to anyone who may have hurt her.

"The kind of thing that people tend to hate." She holds out her hand for the bottle. I pass it back to her, very aware of the way her fingers brush mine again in the process. Her tongue peeks out, brushing the rim just as she tips it back.

I can't help but swallow in response. That small movement alone hits me right in the gut and then travels down to my groin. Instead of filling the silence, I let her get comfortable with it and give her the space to tell me whatever she needs in order to feel better. I'm starved to hear anything that sounds like a truth from her.

"I was in love with Phillip when I was sixteen. He was my first . . . everything. I was blissfully naive to think I'd just end up with him. Even when his family moved away, I still wrote to him. It's what kept me single in college, and then I lost my dad." She looks up again, her eyes watering. She bats away a tear and glances down at her hand, the one I've just covered with mine.

"Go ahead, I'm listening."

Her brow furrows like she's remembering in real time, just playing it back for me. "We lost touch. I moved on with my life. Mostly. I moved into the city and started working for an event company that had clients who were very different from the kind of people I grew up around. I ended up being really great at it. People wanted me to plan their events and weddings. I was making a name for myself." She clears her throat. "In Colorado."

Liar. She was never in Colorado. But the rest of what she's saying feels too raw to *not* be true.

"I was given the lead on a wedding for a high-society

client. The bride's mother hired me, which was pretty common. But when I met with the couple getting married, it was Phillip. And his new fiancée. And in hindsight, I should have bowed out right then. I knew nothing good was going to come out of me planning that wedding."

"But you didn't?"

She takes another swig. "No, I didn't." With a sigh, she continues, looking at me warily. "You might go back to not liking me very much after you hear this."

I tilt my head. "I never didn't like you."

When her eyebrows raise, I explain myself.

"I don't trust many people. Least of all people who are hiding something."

She looks up from where my finger is running across her knuckles. The way this woman wears vulnerability is like a fucking drug. I want to experience it, consume it, and tell her anything she needs to hear to keep herself open like this.

"It started as text messages about the wedding. And then small inside jokes that turned into flirting. I didn't even realize that months had gone by, and I wasn't really dating anyone or even seeking out going on dates because I had started falling for him again." Pausing, she swallows roughly. "I looked forward to his texts. And yet I was still planning his wedding to someone else. The only time I was alone with him was the night that I told him I never wanted to see him again."

It's clear she's ashamed of whatever happened that night, because she pulls her hand away from mine, maybe needing the space. "He called, telling me his fiancée didn't understand him the way that I did, and that he should be marrying me and not her. That he needed to see me and talk through his feelings."

I really fucking hate this guy.

"He said wherever I was, he'd meet me. He just needed to talk to me. And I stupidly said yes." Wiping away another tear, she lets out a clipped, fake laugh. "I had hoped it was what I was waiting to hear. That he broke it off. That it was me he wanted." She looks down, picking at her thumb. "I was at a storage facility looking through some of the old things I had kept of my dad's." Her voice gets softer. "I hate that I was *there,* of all places."

If this guy put his hands on her unwantedly . . .

"He kissed me. And I wanted him to. It was the only time we had been physical. Everything leading up to that was conversations and texts." Her eyes meet mine, shaking her head in disbelief. "Maybe that's worse. I assumed if he needed to see me that urgently that he had ended things because the Philip I knew was a good guy. The one I had known as a teenager was." She stops there and waits a moment, and I hold myself back from holding her hand again. "Things got heated, and he said he needed this with me. Just this once . . . to get me out of his system."

The anger I felt when she started telling me about wanting this man is nothing even remotely close to how pissed off I am at hearing that someone could fucking say this to her. Someone who was already planning a life with another woman.

"I've never felt more ashamed of myself." Another tear drops from her cheek. "It didn't even register what he had said until his hand was down my pants, and he was . . . I didn't even have a chance to register what was happening, much less enjoy it. And he was already done." She tries to laugh, but it's more like a wince. "He jerked himself off with two pumps and came on my leg. I'd never been more disgusted than I was in that moment. I told him that I thought he cared about me, but when he looked at me with sympathy, like he felt sorry for me for misunderstanding what this was, I snapped. I yelled at him to leave and that I never wanted to see him again. And he told me that he would always care about me, but he had to take the opportunity he was given."

"What the fuck does that mean?" I stand up, swatting at the mosquitos getting on my nerves, and remember I had left a lighter in the tackle box next to the stack of kindling.

She smiles at me when I look up from starting the fire. "We were from a different class of people than the clients I was working for. His fiancée is the daughter of a pretty big name who runs a huge financial institution. What comes of his career and the lifestyle he wants was solely based on him marrying her. I was a coincidence or an inconvenience." She rubs her hands along the tops of her thighs, working out what else she might want to share. "I thought he cared about me, and I've never felt so stupid in my entire life for getting that wrong."

My head hurts from gritting my teeth so fucking hard. My fists have balled up at my sides, eager to punch the next Phillip I meet right in the fucking ear. I swallow it all down, though, because she's telling me something true, and it might be part of something I've been itching to understand. "How does that bring you here?"

She clears her throat and waits a few seconds before responding, "I needed to leave."

I can't tell if she's lying by omission or if the bourbon she's been sipping on is what's making her flushed.

The sun is barely left peeking as the sky above us deepens to a darker shade of blue, shades of pink from the sunset disappearing. And I can't for the life of me remember why I've been so hell-bent on figuring out what she's been hiding. That I assumed it was something dangerous and not a woman just looking to start over and forget some shitty choices.

"He never planned to leave her. I don't know if I ever really thought he would either. And I let it all happen anyway. And that's the part of it that—" She inhales a deep breath, and on the exhale, she says, "I knew better. I'm better than that. So today, at the book club, I overheard a few women talking about me, and it felt like . . ." I watch her shake her head, trying to get through what's triggered all of this. "It felt like I was that person again. The one who didn't fit in but tried too fucking hard, and the person who chose to carry on something with a man I knew was wrong."

Nervously picking away at the skin on her thumb, she blows out another breath, almost relieved to have said it out loud. I know what that feels like, having to hold something in because there's nowhere else for it to go. When the right person hasn't shown up to hear it yet. It feels good to be that for her. And what she doesn't realize is that a truly bad person wouldn't feel the way she does about her actions.

She stares at my chest, suddenly not wanting to look into my eyes, which is *not* okay with me.

"That's your bad thing?"

It takes a moment, but she nods, lifting her chin a bit.

"In the grand scheme of bad things I've witnessed, that one doesn't seem all that bad, Laney."

The flames from the fire behind me dance in the reflection of her gaze as it finally meets mine. "Cheating with someone is pretty bad, Grant."

"It is. But I don't think that was your intention. You were still in love with him. You wanted him to pick you. And he wanted to cheat."

She moves to take another sip of the bourbon, but pauses before it reaches her lips. "I haven't told anybody this."

I like that she wanted to tell me. "I'm good with secrets."

She stares at me like she wants to say more. I can feel that energy from her, almost pulsing between us.

"Is there more?"

With the way her eyes look between mine and the change in her body language from relaxed shoulders to a tensed hunch, I regret asking. The truth is, I care about her. So much so, I don't need to push. When she's ready, I hope she'll tell me. I'll be here to listen.

"Licorice. Is there more?" I back-pedal and look in the bag stuffed with candy, and a lightened smile pulls at her lips.

"There's more."

CHAPTER 23

LANEY

IT FEELS warm on my hands. Trying to hold her up and move with all this extra weight. I didn't expect the shreds of cloth and skin to feel so warm. I don't know where to hold her that won't hurt. But it doesn't matter. I only have one thought. Get out. Get out. Get out. My hand is so wet. And the whining. It won't stop.

I blink my eyes open when Julep licks at the palm of my open hand, putting me at ease. Her body sprawls across the mattress, leaving me limited covers and space. "Hey, sweet girl. Did you sleep in here?"

I move too fast, sitting up and instantly regretting it. My head throbs, my left eye twitches creepily, and my throat is dry and tastes disgusting. I look down and a navy-blue towel is loosely tucked around my body under the fluffy duvet. I don't remember how I got in here. And the idea of that makes me smile. I think I fell asleep outside.

When I eye my furry friend, who hasn't moved at all,

her light eyes just look back at me as I pet along the top of her head.

"Where's your handsome daddy?" I smile at the little twinge of nerves still lingering around everything that happened last night. Skinny dipping in his backyard, telling him all about Phillip. And choosing to leave out the rest. He knows there's more. I practically said as much, but he didn't push. Grant was the cop who made me nervous. The Foxx brother who didn't trust me. But last night, he was my bartender. My therapist. My...friend.

A succession of beeps from the kitchenette starts going off. And as soon as they stop, I hear water trickling. I sit up and look over, since it's not that far from my bed, smiling when I see it. A coffee pot. His coffee pot. The one from his counter that plugs in and looked like it had never been used. The time reads 7:10 a.m., which is still plenty of time for a shower before I have to meet Lincoln at the distillery for a touch-base meeting.

The smell of coffee permeates the room a few minutes later. Between the thoughtful coffee and that buttered croissant scent of the air outside my new home, I pause, recognizing how happy I feel.

I remember everything Grant said to me last night. Small things that I didn't realize I needed to hear. Big things I needed to say out loud, to anyone who would listen. And he listened. He listened and I felt lighter. We started talking about music, our favorite movies, and his family business. And now, the remnants of what triggered my pizza and candy binge aren't anywhere in sight.

"Do you like working here, or are you thinking you might want to do something else?"

I told him how much I really enjoyed learning about bourbon. That when I wasn't planning the 100th anniversary event, how I would pick up a shift from the tasting bar or help one of the new hires on a tour if they asked. *"It's exactly what I want to be doing. What about you? Do you like what you're doing?"*

When he answered, he stared at the fire pit, really thinking through his words. *"I thought for a long time that I was meant to be doing something else. But this healed me in a lot of ways. Helped me find a new version of who I was."*

Julep still hasn't budged as I get up to use the bathroom. When I shuffle my way into my small kitchen, there's a mug next to the coffee pot with a note tucked under it.

I never make good coffee so it's going to be gross, but the coffee pot is yours if you want it. Julep wouldn't leave after I carried you over. Hope you don't mind her making herself at home. Come find me when you're done with work today. - Grant

I read the note at least three more times, before a loud whistle has me turning and looking out the window.

The sheer white curtains don't give way to much visibility, but I'm guessing it's Grant by the sound of his truck. Julep heard it too—the truck starting, the whistle, and then the lazy morning lounger is long gone and at the door in seconds. Her front paws hit the center of the door and then at the knob, eager to get out there. When I open it, I'm greeted by the bright sun and the blanket of humidity, ready to assault anyone who dares to step out into it. Across the front grass, still peppered with wildflowers, is Grant standing next to his idling truck with the door open. Julep darts straight for it. She hops right into the cab, across the front seat, and into the back, where I'm guessing she has a strap waiting for her to be buckled into.

I cross my arms over my chest and lean against the door frame.

"Mornin'," he calls out to me.

"Morning, cowboy," I smile and lift my hand slightly to wave.

He's wearing his typical work attire. A pair of worn jeans and work boots, some variation of a blue t-shirt that fits just tight enough around his arms to let the rest of the world know that this man can lift plenty of heavy things. Today there's not a hat, but his dark hair is still damp at the ends, giving the illusion that if it were long enough, it'd be wavy. The scruff on his face is trimmed the same length—that mustache that looked thicker when I first met him is fully blended in now. It tickled my lips at first, but the scratch of it felt good when he kissed me. My cheeks heat just thinking about it again. And then I wonder if it would tickle or scratch between my legs. The way his tongue moved with mine and the mix of his beard and mustache. Was it horrible of me to want to see beard burn around my thighs? Maybe.

He smiles back at me, almost like he knows what I'm thinking. *Maybe not.*

"Thanks for the coffee pot."

"It'll save you a trip into town every morning." He's been paying attention. And I don't mind knowing that one little bit.

The big, fat crush I have on Grant Foxx is probably written all over my face as I watch him pull out of his driveway and turn down the road to the distillery. My smile stays in place until I take a sip of my coffee and cough at the bitterness. But then I laugh. *What the hell did he put in this?*

I promptly pour the rest of my mug and the pot down the drain and think about the way he waited for me to say more last night. I brace my hands on the counter and hang my head. He has to know at least what Ace and Griz do. How I got here and exactly who brought me. I basically told him as much when I was drunk and running my mouth.

It's just a matter of when, not if, I tell him the rest of my story. And the part where there's still something unsettled about what's happening back in New York that has my WITSEC handler on edge. Ace won't want me here if there's any hint of trouble. Hell, I wouldn't want me here if that meant any one of them could be in danger from it. I suck in a deep breath and count to three, because getting worked up over the unknown isn't going to make this truth any easier to share.

Especially when there's a chance it could risk my newfound happiness.

"I KISSED HIM," I mumble, looking through the binoculars.

"You're going to need to be specific with me, because there are a few Foxxes you could be referring to," Hadley says over a mouthful of popcorn.

I lean back and watch her shovel another handful into her mouth before she's even finishes chewing. "There is no way that Mr. Tall, Dark, and Flirty isn't in a throuple." She looks through the viewfinder of her telescope and points. "I just need to know. I'm going to be so jealous if the florist, who was actually really quite lovely in high school, is getting Eiffel towered tonight."

I bark out a laugh. "How do you know it's a Foxx?"

With her focus still on the people we're watching, she says, "Oh, the third-party is not a Foxx. It's got to be one of the firemen who just started. There were, like, three new ones who were just assigned to the Fiasco Fire Department."

"No, who I kissed. Why did you just assume it was one of them?"

She gives me a leveling glare. "They all look at you like you've brought some kind of magic to our small town. They're the most likely. If I had to guess, though, it's either Ace or Grant." She squints her eyes at me. "If it was Linc, I would have already heard about it. He's total shit with secrets."

I look back into the binoculars. "It was Grant."

"And?"

I inhale, and the sighing exhale is all I need to offer.

"That good?"

I smile, remembering the way he touched me, how our lips just went for it, the way his tongue made every inch of my body feel like putty while simply brushing mine. How not kissing him again last night was border-line torturous when I know how perfect it felt. "Yeah, that good." I clear my throat as I watch the tall, dark fireman come out of the florist. "Jackpot. It's the fireman."

"Oooh, which one?" She raises the looking glass to her

eye. "Nice. The dark-haired one. Tattoos. She's officially living her best life."

My phone buzzes.

COWBOY

I found a sour gummy worm in my boot this morning.

LANEY

Jackpot! Did you eat it?

I can almost picture his face when he reads that. His mustache lifting at the corners as his lips quirk.

COWBOY

There were also red licorice bits and smeared chocolate in the ropes of my hammock.

LANEY

Awesome. I'll come by and lick it up later.

Hadley interrupts, "Who has you smiling like that?"

COWBOY

I've already taken care of it.

LANEY

That's a shame. Cleaning up is sometimes the best part.

We've been on Hadley's roof deck for a couple of hours, sitting on pale pink lounge chairs decorated with plush pillows shaped like disco balls. There's a blow-up kiddie pool in the far corner with two swan floaties moving with the little breeze that's working through downtown Fiasco today. I knew some time with her would help to distract me, and it's been working like a charm. Grant was tied up with his brothers after work so I texted Hadley. She said she had worked super late, but if I wanted to come over and lounge with her, she was in "spy-mode." I didn't know what that meant, but I wanted to get to know her more. She's easy to be around. She wants to relax in the sun on her over-the-top roof deck on a hot summer's day in a bathing suit. And spy on her neighbors. I like that she's a bit of a troublemaker and caretaker rolled into a really fun package, who knows what it means to be curious and still kind. All of it equals me wanting to be around her. And it seems like the feeling is mutual.

"What about you?"

She kicks her feet up and tilts her head to the sun. "What about me?"

"Are you seeing anyone? You hadn't mentioned anyone, but—"

"Between us, I'm so single it's become my identity." She takes a sip of her Aperol spritz. "But if anyone asks, I enjoy plenty of company."

"Is that for your benefit, or . . ."

She exhales, long and loud. "You already know this, but everyone knows everyone's business here. It would make my father intensely happy to hear I'm looking to settle down. He's got plenty of douche-canoes lined up to marry me." She lowers her sunglasses to look at me. "And it's not because he wants to see his little girl happy. He wants me to marry into a family that'll benefit him or his business."

"That feels really archaic, Hadley."

I instantly feel shitty for being judgmental as she gives me a tight-lipped smile. She clearly already knows how it sounds.

"My father doesn't always play above the line when it comes to business. He has fairly misogynistic ideas about women. So my work-around is being the kind of woman none of his 'associates' would want to keep. Honestly, his generation says 'slut' with a negative connotation. Our generation says it and I'm ready to respect the shit out of whomever waves that flag."

I can't help but smile. There's not a category for her, and maybe that's why I like her so much. She has tiny tattoos peppered along her forearms, big, wild, curly hair, and this badass vibe that seems impenetrable.

She texts away on her phone. "Do you need a refill?"

"Sure, why not?"

"Press that button." She points to a framed black button. Across the top of it reads: *Cabana Boy.*

"So between us, I'm underwhelmed in the partner department. And I'm okay with that. At least for now, maybe I'll just live vicariously through you."

The door to her roof deck opens and through it comes a tall man with dark blonde hair wearing a Fiasco FD t-shirt. "Did I just beckon someone to bring us drinks?"

Her smile is mischievous. "You did."

"Ms. Wheeler, the lieutenant said I was supposed to come over here and help you with something?"

She turns to me with a smirk. "I may not approve of how my dad does business, but it has its benefits."

Looking back at him, she says, "Can you be a sweetheart and make us two Aperol spritzes?"

He smirks. "Ma'am, I'm on duty."

She sits up in her triangle bikini top, which he notices right away as his eyes drop lower and then flick back up. "Thank you for your service, then." She points to the bar cart in the south corner of the roof deck, sitting underneath a white sun umbrella. "Drink directions are right next to the glasses."

Kicking her feet back up on the lounger, she gestures for me to continue. "Now, did Grant kiss you, or did you kiss him?"

I bark out a laugh. "I think I love you."

She holds out her hand and wraps it around my forearm. "I think I love you too, babes. Oh"—she throws her arms up—"that reminds me. How would you feel about helping me out at Midnight Proof?"

CHAPTER 24

LANEY

I'M A DECENT BARTENDER, but it's been a while since I worked in a busy bar. The end of tour tastings at the distillery sometimes get rowdy, but it isn't anything like tonight. Midnight Proof is as packed as a new club's opening night in New York City. They're at capacity, between the private event happening on the second level, which took the attention of two out of the four cocktail waitresses. And the main level, which has every seat filled. Not to mention, the standing-room-only bar. It's chaos.

Hadley floats between helping me behind the bar and her waitresses on the main level. The outfit she plucked for me was mild in comparison to some of what the other wait-staff wore. Bustiers and fishnets, satin scoop-neck tanks that needed tape to stay in place, and skirts pinned high and fitted tight.

I didn't have a chance to look at the time, let alone at the people who came to sit at the bar. There have been plenty of open tabs and cocktail orders to fill for me to pay attention to who had tables on the main floor.

"Hey," a voice says a bit louder from the other end of the bar.

I glance over to make sure it isn't something serious. I had dealt with plenty of impatient people before. Usually, a smile and the fact that I was helping someone else would tone them down long enough until it was their turn.

"I said, hey!"

I finish straining the strawberry basil gin blossom I was making and slide it across the bar, grabbing their card. "Do you want me to keep it open or close it?"

The woman waves me off and tells me to keep it open. I look down at the bar and just about everyone is drinking something. I don't think there's anyone waiting now except Mr. Impatient.

"I know you heard me, girlie," he says as I walk closer, recognizing that I've met him before. Outside that night with Hadley.

"Waz, right?" I smile, trying to ignore the way I'd rather tell him to go away. "What can I get for you?"

"You already made me a drink, but I asked for a Manhattan, and you made me an old fashioned." He tsks. "I'd like what I asked for, Laney from Colorado." It's not a secret and people more than talked in Fiasco, but I don't like him in particular knowing any details about me. He has the ick-factor. "I didn't realize Hadley was hiring just *anybody* to work here now. Thought you'd need to have some experience bartending to pour twenty-dollar cocktails."

With a smile, I look down at the glass. It's in a coupe

glass with the pierced brandied cherry. I wouldn't have strained an old fashioned or put it in that glass, but I have a feeling he couldn't tell me the difference between the two drinks if I had the ingredients separated and laying in front of him.

"I'm so sorry about that. Let me make you what you asked for." I notice a few couples watching the exchange and another few people as I turn around, taking a peek at what is going on.

The jazz band starts a new set on the main floor with a heavy beat of percussion. It's loud enough that the chatter around the room dies off and pays attention to the new set.

The asshole takes a big sip of his "wrong drink" and pushes it across the bar right in front of where I set up the mixing glass with ice. He crooks his finger at me, motioning me to lean closer.

Jesus, I really don't like this guy.

"Want to play later, girlie?"

I can't even keep it together to quip back. I laugh at the question. *Girlie?* He can't be serious. I try to keep my decline as high-level as possible. "I think I'm good. You have a tab open, Waz?"

I reach for both the sweet and dry bottles of vermouth and a bottle of rye bourbon. When I move back to make the drink, a movement to my left catches my eye. The large frame in a black t-shirt could be anyone, but it's become a habit of mine to look for the way Grant stands so confidently. If I had looked long enough, my guess is that his hands are slung into the pockets of his jeans as his eyes lock on me, watching what I'm doing and who I'm talking to. I feel his attention on me, and with it, I feel bold.

So when Waz leans over the bar just slightly and starts talking, it's a foregone conclusion that I'm done being polite.

With eyes from the few patrons around who heard the initial exchange watching, I decide I might as well show off a bit. I slip the cap off the new bottle of bourbon and pop in a new pourer. Giving it a turn at its neck, I flip it over the mixing glass for an exact pour of two parts. That gains me a few more eyes from the folks sitting around the bartop closest to me. One would think that would have this asshole ease up a bit, but instead, he doubles down.

"Does it make your panties wet, honey, to show off that like that?" He drags his tongue along his teeth, and then says, "I hear you're sliding that sweet ass around to anyone who'll pay you attention."

Alright, let's play, you sleazeball.

I take a quick glance to see if I'm the only one who heard that. A few people have stopped their conversations, watching this little show, and I can spot a certain Foxx getting a bit closer out of the corner of my eye. That confirms it was heard.

Putting the bourbon down, I grab the sweet vermouth in one hand, giving it a nice flip for a splash. With my other hand, I select a highball and fill it with some ice. I had a fairly unhealthy obsession with watching the movie *Cocktail* with Tom Cruise when I was in college. As much as I swooned over the love story, I was just as intrigued with earning great money at bartending. It was easy to mimic, the flare of tossing bottles, but it took a bit longer to figure out how to make a great drink.

I toss the dry vermouth up higher with enough space

for a two-turn flip and a single shake. The soda water gun fills the water highball as I take the stirring spoon to mix the Manhattan properly.

I pause before I pour the Manhattan in the coupe glass. "Nothing sweet about me, Waz, so don't fucking call me 'honey.'" *That's reserved for someone else.* I hold the strainer and my arm up to pour high into the glass. He's stopped paying attention to my other hand. Bad call. A stream of soda water spouts out and soaks the front of his dress pants. Bullseye. Before he even reacts, I smile big and wide. "How do you feel about *me* making *your* panties wet?"

A barrage of swears pour out of his mouth as I grab a small metal pick and stab the brandy-soaked cherry to rest it across the top of the glass. One of the bouncers, whose eye I caught when this all started, along with Grant and Lincoln, drag the asshole out of the bar.

Damn, that felt good. A few laughs and hoots follow as the commotion moves away from the bar, and a round of applause rings out from the close spectators who got the full show.

Hadley is behind the bar just a few minutes later, looking like she just stepped out of a pin-up girl calendar. Her dark hair is pinned and curled, bright red lips matching mine with an exaggerated cat-eye. The corseted black one-piece is no more revealing than a one-piece bathing suit, but somehow, with the garter belt and thigh-high nylons, it makes every single person stare as she walks by. "You okay?"

"I'm good now. I hope I didn't just make a bad situation worse, but he was out of line."

"It looked like it was being handled. Lincoln and Grant

were ready to work out some bottled-up energy with Waz as tribute."

Shit.

"There's plenty of bad blood there. You didn't start anything." She smiles at me and lifts her shoulder. "Maybe just added a little fuel, that's all."

"You good, Laney?" Ace asks as he comes up to the bar.

I give him a nod. "Thank you."

He looks back at the door, where his brothers just left. "That was all them. I'm going to make sure they don't end up getting arrested."

"She's good," Hadley says, coming back to the bar from the kitchen.

"The fuck is that?" he barks at her.

"The fuck is what?"

When he looks down at her body, I can't hide my smirk.

She follows his line of sight and looks down at herself. With her hands on her hips, she pouts as she says, "Awe, what's wrong, Daddy? Don't like my outfit?"

He drags his hand through his hair, mumbling something that sounds like: "Fucking nightmare," as he walks away from the bar and up the stairs to the front door.

When I see her smiling, I ask, "What the hell is that about?"

"Just Ace being a tight-ass. And it's part of my molecular design to piss him off every chance I get. It's like a hobby."

I snort a laugh. "You're a troublemaker."

She winks as she grabs a bottle of tequila from in front of me. "From what I saw tonight, looks like we both are."

CHAPTER 25

GRANT

MIDNIGHT PROOF IS CROWDED TONIGHT. I should have known since it's July 4th week and the tourists are here for Fiasco's massive weekend celebration. I'm only here because I knew Laney would be behind the bar pouring drinks and dishing out that smile of hers. And honestly, I wanted one.

"I like her," Lincoln says as we both watch her move behind the bar.

Laney looks like she's been back there for years. Her bartending experience definitely wasn't a lie. Just like I wouldn't be lying if I said seeing her like this, with her hair swept behind her shoulders and that tight black tank top cut low enough to tease her full chest, is doing all sorts of things to me. She bites at her lower lip and fills up the cocktail shaker with vodka and olive juice, shaking it vigorously, up high enough that she has to put her whole body into it. I want to drag my hands up those hips again and capture her lips between my own teeth. Get lost for a while in the way she tastes and smells. I'm practically feral for her. Even more so now, after she opened up to me. Fuck, I want to do anything to make her feel safe, never mind wanted.

I want to understand how he means that. My brother is a flirt with everyone, but since the day at the river, I haven't seen him do too much of it with Laney. If he told me he wanted to pursue her, I don't know that I'd back off now. I've kissed her—that was better than dibs.

"Me too," I tell him as I watch Waz, that fucker, lean over the bar and say something to her.

"Thought so," he says. "You don't have to play it off like you're not obsessed with her."

"Obsessed is a little strong, don't you think?"

But I don't hear what else he says, because I'm observing the way her body language changes with whatever Waz just said.

I take a step forward, but Lincoln armbars me. "Don't start something in here, Grant."

I look toward the hostess station and catch the head bouncer's eye. *I'll start something outside, then.* With a tilt of my head, he looks over at the bar, and he knows exactly what I'm calling his attention to. Waz is a scumbag who likes to stir up trouble, especially for Hadley. I'm almost positive he's not even supposed to be here.

When I get closer, though, it's not the woman who confided in me with tears in her eyes. No, right now, Laney is in control of the situation. She smirks at Waz as she spins a few bottles in the air. I watch as she holds his attention and the rest of the bar within earshot. But it's her right hand that takes aim, and seconds later, she's spraying the front of his pants.

"Looks like she's doing just fine on her own."

Seeing Laney handle herself is such a fucking turn-on. But it doesn't negate the fact that this is the second time now that I've wanted to deck Waz just for him saying Laney's name.

"Guys, I got this," the bouncer says as he drags him up the stairs.

"Just making sure you're good, man," Lincoln says as he helps guide this asshat outside.

"Officer Foxx, so nice to see you again. Been cowering behind your brothers for long enough. You should know Mr. Finch isn't going to like hearing how handsy you boys are being right now."

I shove him away from my face and point at him. "Don't push it, Waz."

"Or what? We both know you're not doing anything. You too, Linc." He looks my brother up and down. "Still haven't thrown it in Hadley yet, have you?"

That's enough to get Lincoln fired up, so I hold him off. "Don't."

"Wheeler know how you talk about his daughter, you piece of shit?"

Waz spits at the ground in front of us and rights the collar of his shirt. "Mr. Finch considers Hadley a commodity. One that he'll be able to use when the time is right. He couldn't give a rat's ass what I say about her."

"Why are you even here? Hadley has made it clear

you're not welcome," Lincoln growls. "You think she's not calling her father about this?"

"I wasn't here for her." He smirks at me. "Nah, I was here for that sweet piece of ass. Little New York City girl."

What the fuck is he talking about?

Lincoln asks, "You want me to play interference?"

He shakes his head with a tsk. "It's a shame, really. Thought I'd try to take her for a nice ride before she gets what's coming for her."

Ace comes up beside me. "If you're not going to, I'll take this one."

I toss my phone to the bouncer. "Brady, if he's not out in two, call the department and get them to come down here."

I step forward without giving Waz a chance to register what's coming. I pop him right in the nose, and the crunch sound that it makes, followed by the spurt of blood that rushes down the front of him, lets me know I hit exactly where I thought. "That's one."

"You fucking broke my nose," he shouts, covering his face and pulling his hands to see the gushing damage.

"Now I'm going to make you piss blood for a month." I crook my finger at him in a come-here motion. The dumbass is pissed off enough to think he'll get a swing in, and he tries, but I move too fast for him, and as he overextends, I land a punch right in his side. He's on the ground, just as a black-and-white pulls up with the lights on but no siren. It wasn't going to take long. I knew there was a patrol car waiting a few blocks down for any drunks looking to start fights or drink and drive when Midnight Proof hollers last call.

The rookie cop drags Waz off and puts him in the back of the car. The other cop is a friend, a buddy from the academy, and he gives me a nod. "I'm guessing you didn't see what happened here, Foxx?"

I stuff my bloody knuckles in my front pockets. "He was inappropriate in the bar and caught a shower to the lap for it. Must have pissed off someone out here too."

"One of the negatives of the job"—the cop looks over my shoulder toward Lincoln, and then back to me— "can't punch a guy who really is asking for it." He gives me a tight-lipped smile and nods. "Have a good night, sir."

"You too, Cortez." As they drive off, my thoughts spiral about what he said—New York City. The last thing I should be doing is listening to anything Waz has to say, but it's too specific. Yelling a detail like that had nothing to do with his point. If there's substance behind it, then Laney's WITSEC cover isn't as solid as it should be.

"You coming back in?" Lincoln asks from behind me.

I look down at my hand. "Nah, I'm going to walk a bit. Get some air." I needed to clear my head. Laney handled herself in there just fine. That woman doesn't need anyone to swoop in and protect her, but damn, it felt good to play clean-up. The second I watched Waz move closer to her, I saw fucking red.

The way I feel about her isn't something I planned on happening, but here I am. Bloody knuckles, teetering on the edge of worried about what she's hiding from, and realizing that I can't go back. I don't want to. Lincoln's right, only obsessed isn't the right word. Falling for her is all-consuming.

He yells over his shoulder, "Text me if you want a ride home. I'm going to see if Ace is ready to go."

I don't know how my brothers would react if they caught wind of what was going on with Laney Young and me. I confided in them with just about everything, from the first time I kissed a girl to the moment I decided I wanted to ditch the family business and head to the police academy. They've always been the most important people in my life. But it's been years since I shared any of that with them. They didn't even know about Fiona until she was gone. Ace might have figured it out, but he never said anything. I'm afraid that if I put it into words, what I feel for Laney could easily blow up right in my face.

It's less about them knowing and more about that dumb fucking curse that always lingers in the back of my mind. Add that to the idea that Laney could be in real danger. And if that danger came too close, I'd have to say goodbye to her. Ace might have welcomed her here, but I know my big brother; he would have warned Bea that if trouble got too close, she would need to leave. Whether WITSEC approved it or not.

I'm so lost in thought and not paying attention to where I'm walking, that when I make it up to Hooch's, I do a double take. I see Del sitting at the counter. It isn't prime rib night or poker, but he doesn't do much of his own cooking. Since he's here anyway, I could use his thoughts on this. It always helps to work things out with him when I have ideas or hunches. He'll be able to help me. I trust him.

The bell on the front door chimes as I walk in, and the only people here aside from Marla and Del, are a group of kids home from college in the far back booth.

I clap him on the back, surprising him, and then I quickly realize what I just stumbled into. What I was missing. *Fuck, how did I forget?* I look at the specials board where Marla usually writes the date and, sure enough, it's July 2nd. *Fiona's birthday.*

"She would have been thirty-four today," he says, with a big piece of cheesecake sliced in front of him. How did I forget? I *never* forget. "Thought you might have forgotten," he says, his voice going softer at the end as he wipes at his cheek. It was too quick to see a tear, but I know it was there. My stomach sinks, thinking that seeing me just made him look relieved. And when I saw him, I felt guilty.

I clear my throat and sit down next to him with a squeeze to his shoulder. *I'm sorry.*

We never talked about what was going on between Fiona and me. It never felt right that I went ahead and fell in love with his daughter after months of sleeping with her and never took her out on a date in public because we were trying to keep it under wraps. But he knew. I didn't have to tell him I loved her. It was clear as day to everyone in town that I broke the day she died, and I had been continuously unraveling over the past five years.

Marla peeks her head from the kitchen. "Grant, there you are," she says to me. "I thought you forgot. I'll grab your piece now."

"You punch a lawn mower or somethin'," Del says, looking down at my ripped-up knuckles.

"Something like that," I breathe out. The questions that I had swirling about Laney are long gone and in their place are a ticker tape of feelings about today. The way I forgot about Fiona until right now, and if I hadn't walked here, I would have missed it completely. When I apologized for not telling him what was going on between us, I promised that I'd never forget what she meant to me. I feel like a liar.

"Here, honey," Marla says, pushing my cheesecake slice in front of me.

"Thanks, Marla."

She plops a bag of ice on the other side of me. "Heard there was a bit of a scuffle down near Midnight Proof."

I bark out a laugh. "How did you hear that so fast?"

"Police scanner."

Del laughs to himself.

"Did I ever tell you about the call where she couldn't get Loni's cat out of her Christmas tree?"

Del's already laughing before I even tell him the best part, but that's what we did. On her birthday, or her remembrance day, we always had a piece of cheesecake at Marla's since it was Fi's favorite, and told stories to remember her by. It was the only time I allowed myself to get lost in thoughts about her because, no matter what, the guilt I carried came in spades the next day.

An hour later and our faces numb from laughing as Marla pours what's left of the coffee and cashes out the college kids. Del looks at me, still smiling, and says, "You know, if you had other things going on tonight, I would've understood."

"Stop." I pat his arm. "I'm where I need to be." Del is one of my best friends. Even if there hadn't been something between Fiona and me, I'd still make sure I was here for him. I owe at least that much to him. I didn't protect his girl. That's never going to be okay with me. It's why I need to make sure that whatever put Laney in WITSEC, wouldn't find her.

"You still have a few favors up north that you might be able to call in?"

He barely lets me ask before he's saying, "Of course. What do you need?"

CHAPTER 26

LANEY

"HOW HAVE YOU NEVER TRIED A MODJESKA?" Romey asks from behind her table that's displayed with caramels and chocolates. And before I can even answer what was apparently a rhetorical question, she says, "They're divine. How long have you been in Fiasco now?"

"About a month now." I smile.

"Okay," she says, her hands fanned out in front of her. "Modjeskas are Kentucky's signature candy. Louisville, specifically, but in my opinion, these are even better than the originals. These have rules, just like bourbon. The basics have to be the same—marshmallow dipped in a soft, buttery caramel.

She points down at the far end of the table. "This one right here is a bourbon-infused dark chocolate." Covering part of her mouth, she leans in, whispering, "It's not Foxx bourbon, couldn't swing that, but it's still damn good."

My mouth waters as I take a taste of the sample she

sliced for me. There's no way I'm leaving here without being completely and utterly stuffed. I've already polished off a cheddar and jalapeno waffle on a stick, some thyme and local honey-infused kettle corn, and I'm managing to keep the sweat at bay with my quickly melting mint julep slushie.

"Romey, this is actual heaven."

She smiles big and wide as she moves to bag up a dozen or so for another few people who have huddled around her table. There are easily a hundred tables set up throughout Fiasco's downtown green, and I've only managed to hit a handful so far.

"It was nice to have a new face at book club," she says while tying a ribbon.

"I'll take a box of these and another one of these pista-chio-coated ones too." I smile at the two women who are sipping on their own slushies, looking out across the table of treats.

"Do you think you'll come to the next one?"

I answer her truthfully, "I don't know. I had some choice words with a couple of the girls who said some shitty things about me when they thought I wasn't listening, and I'm not interested in spending energy on things or people that don't make me happy. Not anymore."

"I can guess who that might have been." She gives me my bag as I hand her the cash for my chocolates. "I wouldn't worry about them coming to the next one. I think Griz may have overheard what happened. He was very clear about who is and who isn't coming to the next book club." She winks.

I raise my eyebrows. I wasn't expecting that.

"Plus, I don't think Grant Foxx goes around throwing punches, but he knocked some sense into that man, Waz, outside of Midnight Proof. I heard you were the reason why."

That's why he didn't come back inside? I knew he went out there, pissed off, but I've been racking my mind about why he didn't come back. I haven't heard from Grant or seen much of him over the last day or so.

And while I've been busy with a few last-minute items that Lincoln needed done for an upcoming event at the distillery, I'd expected to at least see him at some point. I look down at my phone and the unanswered texts.

LANEY

You disappeared on me. Thought you might be up for a nightcap?

LANEY

Julep left me another "present" this morning. How much skin can a snake really shed? It's borderline ridiculous.

LANEY

Do I need to send nudes for you to respond?

Now my text messages seem less amusing and more desperate without a response from him peppered in there. I told him a lot over bourbon and candy—more than I had planned to share. My stomach drops. Oh god—while I was naked in his horse trough. What was I thinking? How can I unsend that last message? Maybe I can pretend it was a drunk text. Those don't count.

But Romey smiles at me, and then nods over my shoulder, and I can guess who might be there if I look. "Let those women swallow that gossip. It'll sting going down knowing that they don't have any Foxx boys fighting over them."

My face must be showing exactly how I'm feeling, because Romey pats my hand when she says, "Laney, it wouldn't matter at this point if you didn't even know the man, when the gossip starts in this town, it's treated like local news. And *that* particular Foxx is not like his brothers. Grant ignores most people, never mind starting and ending fights over someone. I don't think he's so much as looked at a woman, much less dated one, since Fiona."

Fiona. Hadley had mentioned it when she told me about the losses connected to the Foxx brothers. "I wish he hadn't closed himself down the way he did. He's a good man. Quite the sight, too!"

That has me turning around. And she's right—a helluva of sight. Especially walking toward me. Lark is hoisted on Grant's back, while Lily is on Lincoln's shoulders. The way they love those girls is swoony, but even more so is how much everyone in that family cares for each other. It feels good to be in their orbit. To absorb some of that affection, even if it is fleeting.

When Lily spots me, she tries waving her hands, one filled with a stick of cotton candy and the other a stuffed giraffe. Lincoln looks over and sees that it's me who has her attention, smiling and waving. But it's Grant who stands just slightly behind him whom I can't seem to look away from. Grant lets Lark down from his back and suddenly I wish it were me still hoisted there. He held on to me so effortlessly; it was the most intimate I've been touched by someone without it being sexual. It felt good to be held.

"Laney!" Lily says, out of breath and giggling as she comes up to me.

"Hi, girls." I can't help but mimic their excitement. Glancing behind them, both brothers walking up in jeans like the material was specifically made for them. Lincoln, sporting a Foxx Bourbon t-shirt with the logo displayed prominently across the front, while Grant wears one more faded with the sleeves cut off. His thick, strong arms, that feel more than good wrapped around me, are a product of hard labor, and golden from the summer sun. It's entirely possible that I'm drooling. I've never wanted to lick a bicep and smell someone's skin the way I have the urge to right now. Jesus, I'm pathetic. Pair all of that with his blue baseball hat and he's easily the most handsome man I have ever seen. The brim is low enough that it casts a shadow over his face, but it doesn't hide the fact that he won't look at me for longer than a passing second. It feels like a gut punch.

"Hey, cowboy."

When his eyes meet mine, it's not the interest or fire that's usually looking back at me. This is different. This looks more like guilt, maybe even regret. I recognize it, as I've experienced plenty of both.

"Uncle Grant isn't a cowboy," Lily laughs out.

"No, flower, I'm not."

Ouch. That didn't feel playful.

I clear my throat. "I guess today he's not."

Maybe all that truth finally sunk in about what I had done—cheated with an engaged man. He didn't know about the brave thing that brought me here. The ugly thing was enough to push him away.

I'm not going to trash myself about this. If he's the one

having a come-to-Jesus moment about me, then I should be relieved that I didn't share more. I'll get over the kiss and the kindness. The sweet gestures and private moments. Eventually. But if there had been more than that? If I woke up next to him. If I had let him romance me right into bed, maybe not. Maybe he's saving me the heartache in the long run. So, I push my shoulders back, tits out, and shift my attention.

"Is that henna?"

Lark turns her hands over and shows me the prettiest designs that wrap from her fingertips all the way up to her wrists. "Isn't it so cool? And it'll last when it peels away too."

"Do you like my butterfly paint?" Lily asks with a mouthful of cotton candy.

"I do. I almost didn't recognize you."

Lincoln shoves his hands into his pockets. It's obvious that he can read the tension. "We were just going to head down to pet some animals. Apparently, they're also doing pet adoption today."

Even though it's Lincoln who asked, my eyes stay trained on Grant. I glance down at his knuckles, remembering what Romey told me just a few minutes ago. "What happened to your hand?"

He clears his throat before he says, "Someone crossed a line."

My cheeks feel warm as I try my hardest to bite back a smile. I liked that the quiet ex-cop went ahead and decked the slimeball that was coming on to me.

Lincoln interrupts, "Laney, want to join us?"

"I think I'm going to walk around here a bit more. I've

never been to a fair this big." I look around at the tables down this section and I feel like aside from spending some money, maybe it's a good time to talk. I can't figure out what's going on and I'd rather just get it out there. Rip off the band-aid. "Do you want—"

But Grant interrupts as he starts walking away. "Girls, c'mon!" His nieces use that as their cue to take off running ahead of him.

Lincoln lingers behind. "They're going to eat their way through the day."

I hold up my drink and bag of popcorn. "Same."

"You going to be here later for the band?"

"Maybe."

"Good." He smiles. "I know there's something going on between you and Grant. You'd have to be blind not to have seen it." Shaking his head, he sighs. "He likes you, Laney."

"He sure does know how to confuse a girl," I say with a side-eye. Lincoln's tight-lipped smile tells me he knows. I let out a breath and admit, "But I like him too."

"Something is eating away at him. When he backs off and gets quiet, he's working through something. It might feel like it's something about you, but I'd bet all my money that it's got more to do with him."

I nod because, really, what am I supposed to say to that? I couldn't begin to guess. I don't know enough. Most of what I've learned about Grant has been through others.

My phone buzzes in my bag. *Hadley*.

"I'm going to catch up with them." Lincoln points at me as he walks away. "See you on that dance floor later, Laney."

HADLEY

Okay, where are you? I'm almost done with my mint julep slushie.

LANEY

Craft tables.

HADLEY

Meet me at the slushie stand. And then we can hit Loni's tent. I'm hoping she brought some of her new stuff. I could use something cute for tonight.

LANEY

Meet you there.

THERE WAS ALWAYS SOMEWHERE to go in New York City. Somewhere familiar or somewhere new. There were after hours and there were early risers. I took for granted the constant state of motion the city was always in. It had been as natural as breathing to see something always happening —fairs, pop-ups, new restaurants, movie or television shows being set and filmed. But in Fiasco, life isn't like that. Except for this weekend. This weekend, my new small town is in a constant state of motion. And it made me savor the crowds and the way everyone was busy or curious. The craft fair turned into tournaments—from corn hole and horse-shoes, to an auction where bids went toward farming equipment and bottles of bourbon.

Hadley and I spent far too long in the tent for Loni's

Boutique. And then took a much-needed break to cool off in the AC and change into something that felt more like a night out and not a melted mess after too many hours at the fair.

There's still another entire day of this 4th of July weekend, but tonight seems like its party. There are only a few small kids left, all of them falling asleep on their parents' laps as they finish their late dinners. The air has the smell of burning wood from whatever the food tents still serve, and a twinge of spilled beer mixes with the ever-present sweetness that always lingers.

Lights are strung up high from one oak tree to the next. They hang across a makeshift dance floor in front of a stage, where a variety of bands play set lists ranging from cover songs to bluegrass. It's still warm, but with the sun already set, it only feels humid now. Everyone who spent time at the fair today has sunburns to show for it.

"Please tell me these cowboy boots aren't too over the top?"

Hadley looks down at my new black boots and drags her eyes up to the short little A-line floral dress I had my eye on from Loni's. "I think you look like some kind of southern goddess. I knew that dress would be fucking fire on you. Now we just need to find you a handsome cowboy."

I can't keep in the snort I let out because of her choice of words. Lost him before I even had him. And despite the ticker tape of emotions I have about what the heck he's thinking, I still want to see him. I scan the big open space sprinkled with groups of people. Mostly new faces and only a few I recognize—Prue is sitting with

Romey and a few other book club women, drinking at the picnic tables in the back. Del and Marcus are drinking beers and watching the dance floor. When they catch my eye, they both hold up their drinks in a hello. Ace stands at the high-top tables, along with a few colleagues from the distillery and a woman I don't recognize. But no Grant.

"Looks like a new one for his rotation," Hadley huffs.

"Admit that you like him."

"No." Instead of elaborating or letting me say anything more about it, she claps her hands. "I feel like dancing my face off. Should we do a shot and then hit the dance floor."

She pulls out a flask from under her skirt.

"You had a flask under there?"

"What? I think I can pull off being the kind of woman who keeps a flask in her thigh strap."

I laugh out, "You are. Hadley, I feel like you could pull off being any kind of woman you want."

"You're good for me," she says with a side-eye and a smile. "You know that, right? I thought I was going to take you under my wing and show you the lay of the land, but you make me feel like a total badass."

"You are." I take a shot from her flask, her initials carved into the small, polished silver.

"Ditto, babes."

I look around the room again. "Is that Griz?" I ask, watching my friend pull apart the accordion as his fingers dance along its keys. The percussion and continuous roll of the banjo keep the tempo of the music quick and light. His deep voice starts to rumble over the microphone as he sings about a train to Memphis.

"Sure is. Just wait," she says with her eyes trained on the stage. "It's kind of a tradition."

Griz cuts out of that song and transitions the band into something slower. "I'm going to need a little bit of help up here for this next one." He scans the crowd and zeros in on where Ace was lingering. "My grandson, Grant Foxx, ladies and gentlemen. Let's go, son, we're going to need the harmonica for this one. Get yer tail up here."

I hadn't seen him there. But now that I do, I watch as he shyly nods, making his way through the crowd that's already started hootin' and hollerin' for him to get on stage. He changed from earlier, shedding his cutoff shirt for one of those black tees that seems to hug his arms just right. With it tucked into his jeans, his belt buckle shines, and the way he turns heads has everything to do with how he carries himself. The confidence on that man should be bottled and sold. Fuck bourbon. He'd make a killing off that swagger and I-don't-give-a-fuck-energy that trails behind him. I try to ignore the way his ass looks in his jeans, but if I had to bet on it, more than half the people within twenty feet of him are looking.

I shouldn't be internally overheating. I've barely danced. The sun went down, but dammit, Grant Foxx went ahead and decided to move front and center. I feel like I'm hit by a train the moment his eyes meet mine. In an entire crowd of people, he manages to find me. Only this time, he doesn't look away. And neither do I.

His mouth and his hands move against his metal harmonica in a way that drags out the notes and leads the rest of the band. He looks like a natural up there. Griz watches him and they play off each other. I swallow the dryness in my throat and take a big sip of the beer left in front of me. Because watching him also drives home the reality once more that I haven't wanted anything like the way I've started to want things here.

When the tempo picks up, Hadley grabs my hand, walking us forward to the dance floor. "We're dancing. And whatever is going on there can be figured out once we get a little more drunk and a lot more sweaty."

A few of the waitstaff from Midnight Proof are already out there. A majority of them are working through some kind of line dancing that I have no clue about, but Hadley shouts over the band, "It's like the electric slide, but throw in some hip dips and attitude. You'll get it."

When I glance around the dance floor, I'm met with smiling faces. Some are more drunk than others, and it's impossible not to loosen up. It takes only a few minutes to catch on to the way everyone is moving. And just like that, I'm sweating, laughing, and forgetting all about the one man who still has his eyes on me.

CHAPTER 27

GRANT

THE SWEAT from the water I'm chugging feels just as good on my hands as it does going down my throat. I nod at Marcus, who pats my back as I walk down the side of the stage. I smile at a few people who say, "That was wonderful," and, "You and Griz on stage like that brings back old memories." Griz has always been a bit of a show-off. So when he taught his only willing grandson how to play the harmonica, you bet I'd end up on stage with him at whatever fair was happening in the county. It makes him happy, so I do it. Otherwise, I could go without every set of eyes in our entire town staring at me. Except for one. The second I looked, I found her eyes on mine. And *fuck*, I couldn't look away. No, that set of eyes made me want to give my best performance.

I couldn't look at her earlier. I've been so caught up in my head about forgetting Fiona's birthday and the promises I made to Del that I didn't know how she fits in. Losing

Fiona and all that guilt for not being there, not catching who had done that to her myself, I've been stewing in it for years. It's been easier just to shut everyone out. Until her.

When she called me cowboy today, I couldn't figure out how to tell her that I'm trying to figure out what the fuck I'm doing. That I'm still punishing myself for something she knows nothing about and she's unfairly getting the repercussions from it. I don't know her whole story, but I know she's been through enough.

Watching her laugh with Hadley shakes me. Fuck, that woman laughs with her whole body. She doesn't half-ass anything. And here I am, fucked up over the fact that as much as I want her, I don't know how to have her. How do I keep a promise to remember someone and still move on? And in my gut, I'm scared I won't be able to keep Laney safe, especially from the way that death seems to linger near me.

I drag my palm along the nape of my neck, but it's an actual slap on the back that knocks me out of my head. Lincoln slides a beer in front of me. "You look like you're thinking about someone a little too hard over here, brother."

I smirk, because he's not wrong. And it wouldn't be worth denying it. He can be a dick, but he knows exactly who I'm looking at. He just wants me to fess up.

"Nice set up there with Griz. I didn't realize you still had it in you to play in front of a crowd. The girls are going to be so mad they missed it."

I hum in response as I watch Laney. She's swaying her hips against Hadley, and I'm not going to lie, it's so damn hot. Around the edges of the dance floor, between picnic tables and high-tops, there are plenty of people watching the both of them.

Lincoln follows my line of sight and then hollers, "Yeah, Hads!" He laughs. "Jesus, they look too fucking good." He glances around the green. "There better not be any kids still up watching this."

I lean on the high-top table, taking in the crowd, rowdy and peppered with plenty of faces I know. The band switches to a cover band, and with it, the dance floor transitions from old-timers and couples to twenty-somethings and college kids home for the summer.

Laney Young is beautiful, and not just the natural kind of beauty either. I've seen her bare faced in the morning and with nothing more than a t-shirt on, and I felt that beauty all over my body. But then she amplifies all of it when she fixes herself up in ways I don't know the first thing about. And it's so fucking sexy. Her dark lashes look longer and the make-up she has around her eyes makes the blue seem bolder. She's put together and damn near perfect. And while this version of her has everyone's attention, I'm craving the one who talks to me without a filter. The one who drank too much bourbon and stared too long at my mouth. The one who listened to me come from the other side of my screen door, and then had the confidence to tease about it. Hell, I'm sporting a semi-hard dick just thinking about her screaming lyrics at the top of her lungs in my backyard, butt naked in a horse trough, giving zero fucks while eating an overzealous amount of candy.

I fixate on the way her strawberry-tinted hair moves behind her as she rolls her hips. I want to keep it in place, loop it around my fist, and tug on it just enough to see if she'll give up some of that controlled exterior. The way she perfectly paints her lips that shade of red makes me want to see it smeared onto her chin. I want to messy her up and then lick her clean.

I let my eyes rove down her legs. The black cowboy boots are a nice touch. I must be a complete narcissist or slightly more obsessed than I'll admit, hoping that she wore them just for me. I am *her* cowboy, after all.

A few whistles come from the other side of the dance floor. And it gets a bit more crowded and a lot rowdier as the band hits the chorus of AC/DC's "Shook Me All Night Long."

"You know I forgot you played that harmonica," Del says as he leans next to me.

"Del, how you been, man?" Lincoln says as he shakes his hand.

"No complaints. How are those girls of yours?"

"Growing like weeds. It's starting to amplify how old I am. But they're incredible." My brother is nothing if not animated when he talks about how much Lark and Lily run his universe. "Del, can I grab you a refill?"

He holds up his hand. "I'm good."

"You want another piss beer, or do you want me to convince Hugo to give a sample of his watermelon moonshine?" Lincoln says to me as he wiggles his eyebrows.

"I'll take the piss."

"Lame," he says, walking toward Hugo's table.

A few beats pass before Del says, "You were right."

"About which part?"

"Your girl is a nobody." I bristle at how he says, "my girl." It makes me feel disloyal somehow, like I should have told him what was going on by now. I'm fucking up here, left and right. "It's not that she's been living a quiet life somewhere. I mean, she has no digital footprint. There was no Laney, Elaine, or Eleanor Young born in Colorado in the last fifty years. Your girl right there"—he nods toward the mass of bodies moving with the bass and drums—"is lying about either who she is or where she's from."

It wasn't hard to put those pieces together. What I'm anxious about is what's still chasing her.

"Aside from that poker game, she doesn't seem like much of a criminal."

He snorts a laugh. "WITSEC?" he asks. I didn't mention the U.S. Marshall to him, but he was a cop for long enough. He knew that *not* finding information could mean something too. "If that's the case, then you're not going to get any answers digging around unless you get them from her."

I already knew that. "What about a tie to New York?"

"I don't know, Grant. There's something going on with my contacts up there. Everyone is up in arms about some high-profile shit going on. Nobody wanted to say too much. There wasn't anything being said about a missing person, perp, or an asset that meets Laney's description."

That doesn't add up. If she was in the system and tied to Bea, Del would have found it. Fiasco is for tourists and townies—but she was neither. So why here? There were thousands of other places she could have been placed. I pat Del on the back. "Appreciate you looking for me."

"Anytime. You know that." He clears his throat. "Are you asking because she's gotten close with your family, or is there another reason?"

"Can I be honest and tell you I don't know how I want to answer that right now?" I'm not ready to have this conversation. Hell, I need to have one with Laney before I share anything more with Del.

He drums his knuckles against the tabletop. "Alright. I'm here when you're ready, then. See you on Thursday?"

I give him a nod as he walks away. "Sounds good, Del." I was hoping that'd be the case. That he wouldn't end up resenting me for moving on. Suddenly, I feel like I can breathe easier.

When I turn back, Hadley's moving toward two guys who are asking her something in the middle of the dance floor. And as soon as they start grinding up on each other, it leaves Laney swaying by herself just as the song shifts to something slower. A deeper drum beat and meandering piano riff have her smiling uncomfortably as she looks around.

I lean on the table, taking a sip of my lukewarm beer.

Lincoln comes back next to me and mimics my move.

Both of us watch Laney as she sways by herself, paired-off couples filling in around her.

"I'm about to go out there and dance with that beautiful woman . . ."

The fuck he is. I glare at my brother before I look back at the dance floor. I'm at war with myself between what I want and if I can accept the fact that I'm allowed to want it.

"After I decked Waz the other night, I wandered into Hooch's." I side-glance at him. "I forgot it was Fi's birthday." Taking a breath, I crack my knuckles. "I felt like a piece of shit for not remembering."

"Jesus, Grant." He drags his hand through his hair.

"You think remembering someone means you have to stop living. I don't know when you decided that was the rule. I'll tell you right now, if Fiona or Olivia were standing here and heard that you paused your life after they lost theirs, they'd fucking slap you."

I bark a laugh. He's right, they would.

"You don't have to choose. You loved someone. But you're still here. You can do whatever you want, you're a big boy now." He looks from my face to my feet. "You bulked up, that's for sure."

"Go fuck yourself," I laugh out.

"I'm fucked up in my own way, but Laney got to you. You're different since she's been here. And not in a bad way. In a way where I'm starting to remember why I like my baby brother again."

I take a pull of my beer, shaking my head. "Whatever she's hiding and lying about, Linc, it's going to make a mess. I can feel it."

He exhales and stares at me. "All of us are lying about something, Grant. We do it to get through the cards we've been dealt. And you've been cleaning up after Ace and me for years now. Since when are you scared about a little mess?"

"Feels like it's been you guys looking out for me, not the other way around."

He takes a sip of his small glass of clear liquid that I'm guessing is moonshine. "That's not the Grant I know. The one I know listens and lets the rest of us look good. He's the guy who knew that coming back home was what we need-ed." He clears his throat. "It was what I needed in order to stop unraveling and start healing. You've always been the best of us, Grant. And the best of us would go for it." He looks up and out over the river, and on an exhale says, "Life's too unpredictable to worry how tidy it *should* be." He nudges my arm with his elbow. "Get messy."

It sounds simple. Go for it. Live and enjoy. Pick up the pieces if they fall, but I'm already fucking scared out of my mind I'm just going to lose her.

He tosses back what's left of his drink and claps his hands. "And life is too short to watch."

I know what he's going to say. The same way I know he's about to make a move on a woman who has completely taken over my thoughts, and I can't let that happen. I drain the rest of my beer.

"So I'm going to take my shot—"

"Dibs," I cut him off, and I don't look back. He knew that was all the push I needed. There was no way I was going to watch him dance with her.

I've made up my mind. I choose messy.

When I get a few feet from the dance floor, I find her. Her eyes are focused down just as she's about to hit the edge where the wood of the floor meets the grass. But she never makes it there, because I slide my hand into hers and hold on tight as I keep walking. The momentum turns her to follow me back to the center of the dance floor. Stopping in a small space where there's room between couples swaying, I turn around to face her and pull her hand closer to guide her body into my arms. *Right where you belong, honey.*

Her eyes search mine, asking what I'm doing or where I might have come from. I grip her hand tighter and close any gaps left between us. Tilting her head back, she stands on her tiptoes as we sway in time with the band. "You disappeared on me," she says, calling me out exactly as she should.

"I know."

"Why?" Her brow furrows.

"You scare me, woman." She sucks in a breath, and I look down at her, only inches away. "Since the moment you showed up, I've felt like I couldn't catch my breath. I've forgotten about the promises I made. To myself. To other people. It's shaken up every damn thing I've tried to keep settled." My lips linger near the shell of her ear. I don't want anyone hearing this. "I know you're lying about who you are."

She tries to pull away, but I hold her tighter. The arm I have wrapped around her lower back flexes as I try to keep her front molded to mine. I can barely hear the music anymore or see the couples around us moving to their own rhythm. I only see her. Feel her.

"If you think I owe you something, then you're wrong. I'm not in the business of owing a man anything he hasn't earned. Not anymore." She grits her teeth. "Let go."

I jerk her back toward me. But she doesn't melt for it. She pulls away until I lean my head closer to hers so she can hear what I'm about to say.

"Shut up and let me finish." And while it comes out gruffer than I intended, it stops her and those blue eyes whip up to mine. "But I don't care. Lie if you need to. If it keeps you safe, then lie to everyone. But not to me, honey." It feels so good to be this close to her, my lips skim the side of her head as I breathe her in.

"Don't call me honey." Any attitude falls flat with her softening expression.

"Why, my little liar? Does it make your pussy tingle?" I growl out, low and quiet, into her ear.

With a shaky exhale against me, her body becomes less tense. "Jesus, you're giving me whiplash, cowboy."

She's staring right at my lips, and the second she looks back up at me, I won't be able to hold back. In front of the entire goddamn town, I'm going to kiss her. Plenty of eyes are on us, people I'd rather keep from witnessing the way I desire this woman.

"There are things I've told you that nobody else knows. You may not know everything, but—" She cuts off her words as I hold her tighter.

"I know your real name isn't Laney Young. I know you're not from Colorado and I know you're hiding something. Just like I know that you're all I'm able to think about," I say as I lean down and brush my lips across her bare shoulder. Lifting my head, I look around the dance floor before I focus on her again. In time with the music, I pull her arm up and let her spin. "Everyone can see it," I say when she comes back into my embrace. I rest my lips against her forehead. "This pull I feel when you're near me . . . I don't give a shit who you were, Laney. The only thing that matters is the woman dancing with me right now."

Instead of resisting any part of my hold, she leans closer, and melts into my arms. Her fingers skim along the back of my neck. Even that small touch makes me feel grounded. Heard. Seen . . .

The sounds around us come back into focus as she pulls back to look at me. I find the blues and flecks of brown in her eyes reflecting the yellow bulbs that hang above us. This moment with her hits me right in the chest. A warmth that seeps down to the tips of my fingers. "And what is it that you want from the woman dancing with you?"

There's that fire. I run my hands down her arms as unexpected nerves thrum through my veins. "You're not what I thought. Not even close." I shake my head, trying to get this out. "Mix that with—" I stop myself. I wasn't planning to be this honest.

"With what?"

Fuck it. "I want you so fucking bad that I can't think of anything else." My hand trails up her hip and toward her waist with the slightest squeeze. "You're all I think about. The things you say, how you look at me. This mouth. These lips. Do you know how many times I've pictured them wrapped around my cock? How I need to know if I picked the right nickname for you."

She hums as she tilts her head closer to my mouth.

I can't stop the smirk it pulls from me, knowing that she wants to hear more. I ghost my lips against her cheek. "Tell me, Laney, do you taste like honey, or is it something even sweeter? Either way, I'm going to savor every fucking drop of the mess you make for me."

I feel her shiver as an audible exhale escapes her mouth, "*Grant . . .*"

As she says my name in that breathy, pleading tone, I can't move fast enough. I grab her hand, and without making more of a scene than I just did by dancing with the new girl in town, I rush us off the dance floor. The retired cop, part-time recluse, and least likely Foxx brother to show any type of interest in anything, let alone anyone. I'm not going to pretend like I'm not taking her somewhere right now, away from prying eyes so I can kiss her exactly how I want.

I hold on to her hand, pulling her behind me as we walk down the main drag of the green. We weave between picnic tables and hustle toward the craft tents that are closed up for the night. "Do you need another piggyback ride?" I say over my shoulder.

She laughs out, "My feet are killin' me in these boots."

I stop abruptly, forcing her to run right into my back. Turning so she's practically in my arms, I look back at where we just were and decide that's far enough. I don't see anyone looking our way, so I wrap my arm around her waist and lift her up, just high enough that her feet dangle above the grass. She lets out a little yelp, and in about five strides, we're hidden between the dark shadow cast between two craft tents.

I set her down just a few inches so her boots hit the ground, making sure her eyes are on mine before I say, "No more lies, baby."

Her chest heaves against mine as she breathily replies, "Starting now."

So I show her my truth, the only one I want to think about with her in my arms and looking at me like I'm something special. I settle in closer, nuzzling her nose with mine, before I delve into those pouty lips. The air rushes from my lungs in a sigh of relief that she matches. She brushes her mouth along my upper lip, and I can't keep from dragging my teeth along hers. It's slow and so fucking sexy, the way she digs her fingers into my hair and lets out the lowest moan. Like we know what the other wants, our tongues caress as they explore and tease. It's the kind of kiss that you don't forget.

But it's the popping off of fireworks in the distance that breaks through our haze. *Shit*. It's the next county over, but that means they're going to start here soon too. I break away from the kiss, hating every inch of space I create. "Fireworks are going to start going off in about twenty minutes. And Julep is going to freak out if I don't get her set for the noise that's coming."

"I'm coming with you," she says as she leans back in, kissing me once more and topping it with a smile. It's damn near impossible not to smile back at that, and this stolen moment with her.

I turn us back to where we just came from, out of the darkness, and back to the crowd. We move toward the last rows of the picnic tables, where Hadley and Ace are elbow deep in some kind of staring contest. I lean into Laney. "Think you can talk Hadley into bringing you home? If you come with me right now, that's all anyone is going to talk about this summer."

Smiling, her eyes dart around the area. I'll hand it to most of the busybodies in Fiasco, they're not too obvious about watching or eavesdropping. It's the fact that not a single person is looking over here that has me certain they're ready to start talking as soon as we leave. And while I couldn't really give a shit, I don't think Laney wants or needs that kind of attention. "Am I going home or coming—?"

Too easy. I smirk at the question, not letting her finish. "You're coming at least once on my tongue. And twice on my cock, if I'm lucky."

She bites her lower lip to keep her smile from completely taking over her face.

I brush my hand over her hip and grip it once before I move a bit closer to Ace. "Hey, man, I gotta run before the fireworks start."

His eyes dart up to mine. "Yeah, fine."

The curt tone isn't anything new for him, but he looks more pissed off than usual. Hadley smiles at me, finally taking her attention off my brother. "Laney, can we pretty, pretty please find some fried dough?"

I turn toward where I've parked, along the side of the Fiasco green, doing my best not to smile like an eager kid when I hear Laney ask for that ride.

CHAPTER 28

LANEY

"YOU'RE FINALLY SEEING IT."

I stuff a piece of sugary dough into my mouth. I have a feeling I know what she's going to say. The way I melted into Grant on that dance floor did not go unnoticed. "Seeing what?"

She steers with her knee as she rips off another piece of dough. Chewing for a second, she lowers the music as we drive up the road to the distillery. "That man has been romancing you since you got here. Whatever it is he's trying to get from you..." she pauses to give me a side-eye and grins, "it's working."

My phone buzzes in my pocket.

BEA

Checking in.

She's like a big bucket of water. A reminder that I'm not here just starting fresh, but I'm hiding from another

life. Attempting to start over with the worry that something
or someone will catch up with me.

LANEY

Hi! All good here.

More than fucking good, Bea. Stop cock-blocking me.

I roll the window down for a little fresh air. I'm not
going to overthink the fact that this is her second check-in
this week. Instead, I move my fingers along the humid air
rushing by, feeling the moisture collect on my fingertips.
"What does that even mean—*romancing*?"

"He's a Foxx, so it's a toss-up whether his plan is to just
fall into bed with you. Or to make you fall for him. Either
way, it's to get what he wants out of you." She slows as we
get closer to our houses. "Grant is the quiet one. Or at least,
he has been. People forget, but I remember Grant before.
And he's persistent when he has his sights set on
something."

"And that something is me."

She laughs. "But I think that dumb idiot lost sight of
what his original plan was and went ahead and fell for you."

I pull down the visor and wipe away the bit of black
that's smudged below my lash line, then snag the red
lipstick from my pouch.

That's what we're doing, isn't it? Falling.

I dab on a bit of the red to give my cheeks some color
and smear the tiniest bit on my lower lip just to freshen up.

"You look great, by the way."

The car stops, and I open the door. "This is Grant's
driveway."

She gives me a smirk. "I'm saving you the steps."

I can't bite back the smile. Just like I can't remember ever having a friend like her. One who is equally insightful as she is non judgemental. It's refreshing to enjoy time spent with a person without ulterior motives or working an angle.

Shutting the door, I lean on the window. "Is this a bad idea?"

"I think that the kind of bad idea you're referring to is the kind we end up remembering most." She lets out an overly aggressive sigh, tilting her head back on the headrest. "He's a good man, Laney. And out of everyone I know, he could use a little fun, even if it's a bad idea."

"Thanks, Hadley."

"Thank me tomorrow when you tell me all about how many times he made you—" She honks her horn, and then floors it up the road.

I'm still laughing as I walk up the porch stairs and start knocking. Running my hands down the front of my dress, I'm suddenly very aware that the lingerie underneath is cute, but fairly sweaty from the day and dancing.

But those thoughts are wiped away as Grant swings the door open, wearing his signature smirk and the same t-shirt and jeans from just thirty minutes ago. Why does he look even hotter *right now*? Maybe it's the anticipation of peeling all of it off him.

He watches me eye-fuck him in the doorway without saying a word. But just as I start to fill the silence, he wraps his arm around my waist and pulls me into him.

He walks us past the threshold and back into the house. "Hadley dropped you off right out front, didn't she?"

"She's pretty intuitive. Said she was saving me the steps."

He brushes my hair behind my shoulder. "Hadley isn't the gossip of the bunch. It's Griz and all his girls I was worried about."

Julep barks from the living room couch, and I can't hold back the laugh when I glance at her. "Is she wearing earmuffs?" I walk over to her and give her white belly a good rub as she lays down and rolls to her back. Her coloring is as chaotic and beautiful as her big personality.

"She was the best police dog in the county." He tilts his head, watching us. "I'd bet the best in the country, but the moment she hears fireworks, all bets are off. She'll find a corner and shake until they're over. Those and her little cave tend to do the trick."

"I'm glad you got home in time, then." I smile, then what he said before I got distracted by Julep sinks in. "What did you mean, all of Griz's girls?"

Grant pulls out two Glencairn glasses and a bottle from one of his kitchen cabinets. "His book club girls. You know he's slept with half of them."

My jaw drops as my head whips to face him. "That's not true. Oh my gosh." I cover my mouth as I chuckle. "Is that true?"

"It's the one common knowledge item that everyone knows, but never talks about. Probably because they're the ones controlling all the town rumors."

"Stop it!" But even as I say it, I can see it.

"Griz likes to play the Foxx curse in his favor. Nobody wants more than some fun every once in a while. Most of them are widows. I don't think Prue ever was married. But yeah, Griz and his girls are the ones who'll start and end a rumor here."

"And it would be bad for them to catch wind of me leaving with you?"

That has him smiling. "I didn't say bad." He walks past me, hooking his finger with my pinkie as he brushes by. "Just that we'd be the only thing everyone would want to talk about this summer. It's not my favorite place to be—a part of everyone's conversations."

Grasping my hand, he pulls me along toward the far side of his open living space and through a door that I had thought would lead to a garage. But as he flicks on the lights and we move through the threshold, it's pretty evident that this is so much more than a storage spot for cars and sporting gear. The sweet and tangy smell hits me first.

"This is deceiving."

The room is double the size of his living room, but instead of comfortable couches and a cozy fireplace, there's a heavy bag hanging from the rafters and a large metal tub. It's significantly smaller than the ones at the distillery, but it holds the same thick yellow mash. The wall to my right is lined with a workbench with plenty of things I don't recognize, but the barrels and copper still give away what this space is for him.

"There's a good spot to watch the fireworks off the back."

"This is a badass hobby set-up." I laugh at how nonchalant he is about what's in here.

We stop in front of a few bourbon barrels as he puts the glasses down. "It was just a garage, but when I renovated, I wanted to have more space. I wasn't exactly sure what for at the time, but before I knew it, I had a bunch of equipment. Maybe a part of me knew all along I'd find my way back to bourbon. So, I turned this into"—he looks around and exhales—"my escape."

I run my fingers along the oak barrel. "From?"

As his hazel eyes meet mine, I can't help but lick my lips in anticipation of his. The way I feel when this man looks at me is altering. It's forever altered the way I see myself, and the way I expect to be seen. It's shifted what I ever expected, because this current between us, this undeniable chemistry that whirls to life within every inch of my body when I'm near him, has changed me. "The rumors haven't caught up to you yet, then?"

"Some have." I tilt my head to the side, thinking about how I can carefully dance around a topic I'm not sure he wants to discuss.

He lets go of my hand and moves toward his workbench. On the shelf above, he pulls down an unmarked bottle of bourbon. "It's an escape from everything. The life I chose. The one I couldn't live up to. The person I no longer recognized. And then people looking at me like . . ."

Shaking his head, he steps closer to me, erasing the space and pouring some of what he just pulled out into one of the glasses.

I stay quiet, watching and hoping he'll keep talking. But instead of finishing his thought, he holds up the glass, tipping his nose inside to smell the notes before bringing it to my lips. "This is mine." I keep my eyes trained on his as he tilts the rim of the glass, letting him do it for me. "My year." My head moves back with the motion, my tongue catching the first bite, opening my lips just enough to let more in. The warm vanilla and smoked oak flavor hits my palate first, and then a burned caramel takes over as it travels farther, coating my tongue and throat.

A few drops escape my lips, but as I move to wipe it, he stops my hand and holds it back. I search his eyes for the briefest moment before he leans forward and licks from my chin up to the corner of my mouth, making my core clench. "Tastes even better on you," his voice rasps.

"More?" I ask as I swipe my tongue along my lower lip.

I dip my finger in what's left in the glass.

He watches as I pull my pointer up and toward his mouth and drag the pad of my finger around his lips, dousing them with his bourbon. Leaning in, I kiss the trail I left. Our tongues move so slowly together, a sensual push-and-pull I'm eager to keep the tempo on.

The rumble that comes from his throat vibrates his lips, through my body, down to my chest, swooping into my belly and setting everything below it on fire. As I pull back, he hooks his finger into the thin strap of my dress, dragging it down over my shoulder, and kissing along my jaw. "I'm still thirsty, honey."

"Don't stop," I breathe out.

That's all that he needs to unleash whatever he's been keeping at bay.

He rips the rest of my strap down, exposing the pink lace bra that matches the cheeky undies under the skirt of this dress. I thank the humidity that forced me to choose something light instead of the smoothing efforts that Spanx would have offered.

"Fuck, look at you," he says as he drags his calloused fingers along the tops of my breasts, dipping just inside the cups. "So beautiful." The scratch of his touch along the tops of my nipples has goosebumps appearing in its wake. I practically pant for more. Eager for his praise and starved for his touch.

Reaching behind his neck, he pulls off his shirt in one fast motion. I've seen him without a shirt on before, but never with the undercurrent that I could touch. That even if it's just for tonight, he's mine. I don't even realize that I've started running my fingers down the front of his chest, across the tattoos that start on each shoulder and meet in the middle. My fingers lift when I hear another rumble in his throat. I can't keep the smirk off my face, knowing I'm turning him on the same way.

"Your turn now." He grabs the bottle of bourbon and takes a swig. "Let me see what I've been dreaming about sucking on, Laney."

It's not sweet or swoony, but those words make me all too eager to do exactly as he says. I roll the rest of my dress down my stomach and past my thighs until it hits the hard-wood floor, and I watch as his eyes follow. They skim up my body, never stopping until they reach my eyes again. When I flick the clasps of my bra and let it drop, he licks his lips. "The way I've thought about you, just like this. Offering yourself to me . . ." He rubs his hand across his mouth, and the look on his face is enough to give me full-body tingles.

Holding out my hand, I look toward the bottle he has looped between two fingers. He steps closer, passing me the heavy glass bottle, almost full, minus the dram he poured when he opened it. I press the opening to my lips and take the smallest sip. I let a bit dribble from my mouth, and then pull it away, tilting it just enough to trickle a path of bourbon from the top of my chest down the slope of my breast and tip of my nipple.

The smirk that dances on his lips is all I need to encourage my next words.

"Drink up, cowboy."

He lets out a quiet growl and a "Yes, ma'am." Dipping low, his tongue drags across the top of my breast, lapping up the trail of bourbon. But he doesn't linger there. Instead, his lips are back on mine in a starved kiss. His hands dive into my hair and tilt me exactly where he wants. As his mouth travels down my neck, his hips push into me, backing us against the wall. His head drops lower moments later, trailing a path of kisses from just below my ear, down my neck, and to my collarbone, pulling airy moans from my chest. One of his hands still fixed along my neck, cups my jaw as his thumb draws a path over my lips. He presses it in, past my teeth and to my waiting tongue, wordlessly telling me to suck.

"The things I've imagined doing to this pretty mouth . . ." he says, lowering to his knees and cupping my breast. His tongue swipes along the curve of the other, and then teases my nipple where a drop of bourbon waited patiently for him. "This body." It's not enough, I want more. Arching my chest, I practically drive my hips toward him for some kind of friction. I drag my free hand into his hair, my nails scraping against his scalp.

"Don't tease me."

"You want more? Then keep pouring, baby."

"I'm going to waste too much," I laugh out.

"It's the best bottle I've ever had. And it's got nothing to do with the notes or the year, and everything to do with how I'm drinking it." He leans up, licking the valley right in between both breasts, and then smiles up at me. "Now pour."

So I do exactly as he says, because if I've just realized anything, it's that I like when Grant Foxx tells me what to do. I more than like it. I'm practically getting off on his words alone.

Small rivulets of bourbon pour down the peaks and valley of my chest, toward his waiting lips. Teasing across each breast with his tongue, he makes a path down the slope of my stomach. As he gets closer to my panties, he peppers open-mouthed kisses past my navel. He looks up for permission as his fingers hook into the waist of the pink lace.

I bite my lip and give him a smiling nod. I rock my hips forward as he drags my panties achingly slow down my thighs until they reach my cowboy boots. When I step out, he tosses them somewhere behind him. "The boots stay on."

I hum at the way his hands run back up the path they just came.

"When my tongue kisses this sexy pussy, is she going to be nice and wet for me?"

I can't hold back the nervous laugh. I've never had anyone talk to me like this. His words have sparked an entirely new level of sexual confidence within me, one I want to embrace.

He nudges my legs open as he kisses and nips at the skin his hands caress. Moving from my right inner thigh, he stops just as he gets to where I want him, moving to the other side. He takes the bottle that I'm barely holding from my fingers, downing one more swig before putting it on the floor. If his mouth got any closer, I would have absolutely dropped it.

When he leans into me, his nose nudges at my slit, pulling a gasp from my lips. It's such a filthy move, but it's nothing compared to what comes next. He moans as he pulls back. "You're too quiet, honey." But he doesn't let me respond as he glides his tongue nice and slow from my opening to my clit.

The air is instantly stolen from my lungs. Like I wasn't expecting that, even though I knew it was coming. He does it again, even slower this time, savoring the taste of me by the way he releases another deep moan. "Then make me scream, Grant."

He shoves my legs wider so his broad shoulders can fit between, and then wraps his hands under my thighs. Gripping them tight, the move pushes me up the wall just enough that my feet are barely touching the ground. I don't overthink, I know he's got me. The only thing I can hold on to is his thick dark hair as my cowboy drags his tongue in punishing patterns across my clit until it's so wet and swollen that being quiet is no longer possible as whimpers and moans filter from my lips.

The thunderous booms of fireworks rumble in the background. It barely registers above the sounds he's making as he devours me thoroughly. Sucking my clit into his mouth, the scruff of his beard scrapes, numbing my skin just enough so that I can only feel the warmth of his breath, the slickness of his tongue, and my arousal. When his hands squeeze my thighs, I know he's not letting up. I forget about every detail that's kept me grounded—the room and its low lighting. The smoothness of the wall against my back. The way I'm spread out and at his complete mercy. All of it's forgotten. I only think about the hammering of my pulse and how it labors my breath. My hearing becomes muffled as my orgasm builds, leading me toward an edge I've never been so close to.

He pulls back and blows a hot breath where his mouth just left. The change in pressure has me feeling needy. "I want to see you fall apart for me," he demands. Then his lips latch onto me once more, sucking my clit into his mouth and dragging his teeth along every sensitive swipe he just teased.

With my mouth open and my head tilted only as far back as the wall will allow, I'm consumed by the pressure and sensations. My heart races and my body tenses, breaths catching in my chest. With three words, the same ones I heard from his porch, behind a screen door, a night not that long ago, he says, "That's it, honey." He slides two fingers into my pussy. "Look at me." I open my eyes, finding his, and I scream. My body jerks forward as my release barrels through me, my pussy pulsing. It's so intense that it doesn't allow any thoughts or words to break through, only complete and utter sexual intoxication. My orgasm rolls from the center of my gravity to the tips of my toes and has me gasping for air, leaving me lightheaded and wanton as he draws out the last of it. The sound of his fingers fucking me and my moans mixed with his are deliciously filthy. My thighs quiver in response, having completely succumbed to the pleasure.

"That was . . ." I let out a laugh because words are not going to be my strength right now.

"Delicious," he says, smiling as he stares up at me from his knees. His face still hovers between my legs with my arousal smeared along his lips and mustache. Lowering my legs from his grip, he allows my feet to fully meet the ground. "I thought you were sexy before, but seeing you like this with the smell of you on my beard and the taste of you in my mouth . . ." He rests his chin on my thigh, a glazed-over look in his half-lidded eyes. "How am I not supposed to fall in love with you now?"

CHAPTER 29

GRANT

THE WORDS FALL TOO EASILY, and maybe stupidly, out of my mouth. I know by the way her body tenses and she lets out a little laugh that she's thinking what I should be: that was bold. I've known her for weeks, flirted my way to a dance, dirty talked my way in between her legs, and I'm already spouting things about keeping her. It's careless and dangerous, but I'm not about to take it back.

I move up, my knees so fucking pissed off, but I couldn't give a shit. If she told me to get back down there and stay, I'd do it and ignore the pain.

"I planned to show you the lofted space so we could watch the fireworks, but—"

She finishes my thought. "We had our own fireworks in here. I barely noticed the ones outside."

I graze my teeth along her thigh. "I'm not done with you yet."

Biting at her thumbnail, she stares down at me with

those big blue eyes, like what I've just said is exactly what she wanted to hear. My dick throbs so hard that it aches, so I stand up from kneeling in front of her like she was my altar.

"I'd like it very much if you told me what to do, cowboy." She reaches her hand forward just enough to drag up the front of my jeans.

My responding growl sounds primal. I've never been so turned on and had this much fun with someone. Not like this.

"But you just may need to carry me. I still can't feel my legs."

It's the only request I need. I bend and grab just below her ass and hoist her up, her legs wrapping around my waist at the same time her arms lock around my neck. "Grab that bottle."

I have every intention of getting to my bed and fucking her senseless, but my steps falter when her breath tickles my ear. Her lips kiss just below it, and she whispers, "Are you going to ride me as good as you ride that horse of yours."

"Jesus Christ, baby." I capture her lips with mine, still trying to navigate my way through the living room.

Julep barks out repeatedly as we move past her. "She's fine," I tell my very concerned dog. "She's smiling, see?"

Turning Laney toward her, she laughs out, "I'm stealing your dad for a little while, Julep. I'll return him when I'm done."

"I think she's barking at me. She likes you more." I lean into her neck and graze my teeth along the side of it, still moving through my house, turning down the hallway, and trekking toward my master suite, bumping into the doorjamb.

She giggles the entire way, peppering in tiny moans as her fingers play along the back of my neck and into my hair. "I like her a lot too."

I don't want to hurt her as I move closer to the bed, so instead of dropping her onto it, I turn and let myself fall so she's on top. *Holy hell, this view.*

Laney sits tall, tits out, as I lean up to brush my fingers along her soft skin. Dragging them across her dusky pink nipple, I watch it get hard as she lets out the smallest moan. She grabs my hand and moves it up toward her throat.

"You like that?"

She smiles and nods.

The way I want to hear her come apart again has my cock nudging against her hips that have started grinding. I don't even know if she realizes she's doing it, but I need to feel her. Her fingers brush my stomach, lightly moving toward the waist of my jeans.

"Take it out."

She rolls her bottom lip into her mouth, biting it. Then I look down to watch her unbuckle my belt, unbutton my jeans, and pull the zipper down. She doesn't waste any time dipping her fingers into the waist of my boxer briefs and grazing the head of my cock. "Fuck," I grit out, tilting my head back against the mattress. I haven't been touched by someone else in over five years and it feels so damn good. Taking the rest of me out, she fists my length, her palm sliding up and down.

I reach for the bourbon and take a pull from it. With

our eyes locked, I slowly tip the bottle, pouring a splash along the length of my cock. "Taste it."

Eyes flaring, she gives me the sexiest smile. She shifts down between my legs just far enough to make room for her to lower her body and dip her head. Her tongue licks down the shaft and over her own fingers still gripping me. In one pass, she wraps her lips around my cock to suck and savor what's been poured.

"Tell me how that tastes."

"Like I'm still thirsty," she says with a coy smile. "I don't think I've ever wanted anyone this badly, cowboy."

And fuck, do I want that to be true.

I sit forward and wrap my arm around her, lifting her up to me and turning us over. The change in position has me on top so I can get my pants off the rest of the way. I pull away just long enough to throw open the drawer on my side table and fumble for a condom shoved in the back. Tossing it on the bed, I bring my focus back to her, splayed out in front of me like some kind of gift. "You have any idea how sexy you are, Laney?"

She reaches her arms up over her head, stretching her body out as I take in the soft curves of her hips, the way her thighs slightly part so I can see her wet cunt ready for me. "Feel free to tell me," she says with a little smirk.

I shift my weight back into the bed, nudging her legs open more. Gripping her thighs, I let my hands rove up, digging my thumbs into her skin as I move toward her pussy. I don't stop this time. I wrap my hands around her hips as my thumbs drag along the lips of exactly where I want to sink my cock. "The first time I laid eyes on you, I wanted to lift that t-shirt and sink my fingers right into here." I brush two fingers across her clit and then down-ward, letting them tease her opening. She's so wet they glide right in. My eyes practically roll back at how it feels when her pussy grips my fingers. My cock throbs, it's so fucking jealous.

She tips her head back, eyes closing with my two fingers playing inside of her. Drawing my fingers forward in a come-hither motion, my thumb circles over her clit. It pulls the sexiest whimper from her as she writhes, and then moans below me. "Show me those beautiful eyes."

Her chin tilts down to look at me, eyes opening and pleading to give her what she's waiting for.

I keep my fingers buried, and with my other hand, I give my cock a good pull. "Honey." Her mouth is open, but no sounds escape. She tilts her head back as her fingers dance around her lips. I grip my cock tighter and jerk it twice.

She moans out on an exhale, moving her hands down, cupping her tits and tugging at her nipples. And at the sight, I can't wait any longer for more of her. I slide my fingers out, but before I grab the condom, I shove them in my mouth, sucking her off of me.

"Oh my god," she says, watching my every move.

Ripping open the condom, I roll it on and rub my fingers along her pussy lips, coating them in her again so I can smear it along my length. "Spread your legs. Let me see all of you."

She keeps her eyes locked on mine and does exactly as I say. Kneeling in front of her, I slap my cock against her clit, and then start to tease her open. "Watch me slide into you, baby." She pushes up on her elbows and her head tilts to watch. I take my time and ease into her slowly, trying to savor every sensation, from the warmth and squeeze to the pressure of what it means to get completely lost in a woman I've craved since the moment I laid eyes on her. Swaying my hips, I open her more for me so I can sink into her all the way. I give her a second once I'm there to let her adjust to my size. She feels so fucking good; I don't know how I'm supposed to last here. I snake my hand up her chest, toward her neck. Cuffing my hand around her throat, she relaxes back into the bed and I settle above her, removing any space that ever existed between our bodies.

"Grant," she breathes out. "I'm so full, oh god—"

I cut off her words as I kiss her and use the distraction to roll my hips. Her tongue dances with mine at the same sensual pace that I'm fucking her. Deeply. Fully. All-consuming. On the next moan, I know I've hit her spot. It's a low and long, wordless plea that keeps her from kissing me back. I lean on my forearm, moving just enough to the side so I can watch my cock sink into her again.

Leaning up, I kiss her neck, dragging my teeth down toward her shoulder. "Look at how fucking good you take me."

She moans before she even looks. With a smile, she breathlessly says, "Why is that so hot?" We watch as I thrust into her, and the sight of it makes me fuck her harder just before I'm all the way there. I pull back slowly, trying to draw out how insanely well her pussy practically chokes my cock. We fuck each other, unhurried, and damn, it feels better than I imagined.

My cock swells, but I can tell she's close. I have every intention of feeling her come around me, so I pick up the speed. Lifting her ass slightly, I fuck her deeper, her hips meeting mine as we're both desperate for her orgasm. She doesn't stop watching as I fuck her, so it's when I see her eyes close, her body tensing, and the way she goes quiet that I know she's about to fall completely apart along her seams.

And when she does, it's with my name on her lips once again and a full-body rush that visibly rolls from her pulsing cunt, through every limb as her nails dig into my ribs and hold me close. I keep going, fast and deep, determined to draw every last drop of her release.

I'm holding on by a thread as she moans again, opening her eyes. "I'm going to come, baby."

"On me."

"Fucking hell." I don't ask if she's sure, I just pull out of her, ripping off the condom.

She pushes her beautiful tits together, and it's all the direction I need as I move up her body and jerk my cock as my orgasm crashes into me. I groan as I come across her chest, making her nice and messy. It's the hottest thing I've ever seen, and she just watches with her bottom lip perched between her teeth. All I want to do is smear it into her skin, claiming her as mine. But I don't have to, because she takes her finger and rubs it across her chest. It feels like she's just unlocked something within me, to see my cum covering her skin. *She's mine.*

I reach down and find my boxer briefs, wiping up the mess I made all over her breasts as she hums and melts into the bed. Draping my sated body over hers, I kiss her lips, only stopping briefly to smile at her. She smiles right back. Then I lean in for one more before I tell her, "Lie to me if you have to, but please tell me we're going to do that again."

"Don't have to," she says, drawing her finger along my

back as I lie on top of her. "I'm not done with you yet, either."

She closes her eyes and smiles lazily as she comes down from the high of everything we've just done. So beautiful. I trace my fingers around the edges of her arms and shoulders, lost in thought.

The moment she kissed me, I knew I wasn't going to want anyone else ever again. I didn't plan for someone to be in my life. But I wanted to make room. With her naked body nestled next to me, it felt like I was finally locking into place.

CHAPTER 30

LANEY

GRANT FOXX IS DIRTY. Even after we showered together, he whispered the dirtiest promises in my ear as we both drifted in and out of sleep. *"I can't stop picturing my cock sinking into your pretty pussy. And it is"*—his fingers traced along my lips—*"so fucking pretty."*

He woke me when he shifted between my legs. Keeping his eyes locked on mine, he licked me slowly until I came. *"You taste sweeter right after you come."* His lips traced along the back of my shoulder as he held me. *"I don't think I've had anything as delicious as you on my tongue."*

I awaken this time with his body wrapped around me and his hand between my legs with just one finger lightly teasing against my slit. I almost thought he was asleep, playing with me as he dreamt, but when I look over my shoulder, he's smirking with his eyes closed.

"Still hungry?" I study the way his lips tip up even

more. This is a beautiful man. Even up close with messy hair and puffy, tired lids, he's ruggedly sexy.

"Not sure I'll ever stop being hungry for you." His arm moves up, pulling me closer. I don't hold back the smile those words bring. This is what it's supposed to feel like. To want to be completely held by someone. And they hold tighter and lean in for more. It's impossible not to think about what he said: *"How am I not supposed to fall in love with you now?"*

My stomach growls loud enough that he lifts his head up to peer at my face.

"Your stomach is on the same page." He kisses my shoulder, and then gets up and out of bed in one quick move. I don't think my body could move that fast right now, even if I was forced to.

He walks around in the mostly dim room, that gray morning tint that comes just before the sun decides to show up above the horizon. The full-length windows show off what I'm sure is a beautiful landscape, but I couldn't be bothered with that. I'm too busy drinking in this naked man, canvassing his body from his broad back down to his full, toned ass. It's bite-worthy.

It's the first time I can really see the calligraphy-style tattoo that runs just above his V-cut and along his side toward his back. "I've been curious about that . . ."

He looks down at where my eyes are glued and smiles at me. "My brothers and I got it when we were younger. Thought it was a good way to remember our mom. She'd call us and our dad that. Her bourbon boys." He runs his thumb along the ink that he can reach. "Not much I remember about her, but I remember that."

The Bourbon Boys

"How long since—"

He pulls on a pair of sweats. "I was nine when we lost them."

Oh god. He grew up without both of his parents. I hadn't realized.

"Car accident. They didn't do much without the other. He told us there wasn't anyone else on this earth he'd rather be with than my mom. Loved her big." He smiles, looking down at his hands. "It was hard. On all of us, losing them both like that. But I don't think my dad would have survived long if only my mom had passed. It took a lot of years to realize that was how it should have been."

"Griz raised you since you were nine, then?"

He nods. "And my nana. Griz remarried when my dad was young. And then we lost her when I graduated high school."

My eyes water thinking about the amount of loss he's experienced. And I know there's more. He sits on the bed in front of me, instantly brushing the single tear that started to fall down my cheek. I want to tell him about parts of me too.

"I never knew my mom. She left my dad when I was little." I swallow down the emotion that always comes when I think about how great my dad was. "My dad raised me. Got promoted to my best friend when I was about eight. And I had a lot of great years with him. That's how I try to think about it. When I miss him too much, I remind myself about how much I got. Not what I missed."

I kiss the palm of his hand that's been lingering along my neck.

"Tell me about him sometime?"

I nod, swallowing the emotions. "Sometime."

Tipping up my chin, he presses his lips to mine. It's the simplest of kisses he's given to me, but for some reason, it means something different. Something that tastes like a promise.

"I'm going to take Julep for a quick walk. I think she forgot you're in here, because I haven't heard her whining at the door for a while."

"She really does love me," I laugh.

He stops just as he's about to open the door and looks at me like he wants to say something more. It's a serious look. One that makes me feel like the weight of the room just changed.

Nervously, I smile. "What?"

He shakes his head. "She does. I think *she's* falling hard for you."

I need to tell him everything. That there's a possibility I'll have to leave again. That I would be committing to him, and him to me, by telling him who I am.

I swallow the lump in my throat as he closes the door behind him, overthinking everything he just said as I hear him sweet-talking to Julep all the way out the door.

It takes me only twenty minutes to find one of his t-shirts, brush my teeth, and comb thru the mess of my hair. I kind of have a glow about me when I take a final glimpse in his bathroom mirror. When I head down the hallway, the coziness of his house feels even warmer than my little cottage. The style and fixtures are nearly the same, but his place has photos peppered throughout of his nieces and brothers. There're fishing poles leaning against the door in the mudroom, oversized dog beds in various rooms, and framed artwork all about bourbon hung throughout. It's masculine, but Grant has taste not too far from my own—a home that's lived in.

When he comes back inside with Julep on his heels, I'm already whisking the eggs into the buttered and heated cast iron pan.

"You making me breakfast?"

I smile upon hearing it. Julep barks and comes charging over to me, but instead of jumping up, she sits in front of me, butt wiggling and waiting for me to pay attention to her. "Almost done, Julep. One sec and I'll give you all the pets."

Slipping the pan into the oven, I set the timer.

"Hello, pretty girl," I croon as I crouch in front of a very excited dog. I rub behind her ears and along the brown coat that stops at her neck. When I look up at Grant, he puts two coffee cups down on the counter.

"You got us coffee?"

"I don't have a coffee pot anymore." He leans down and steals a kiss.

"But those are from Crescent de Lune."

"I didn't know how you liked yours yet, but I knew one of the girls at the bakery would remember. I was today-years-old when I found out what a flat white was." He pops a raspberry in his mouth. "Did Hadley happen to mention Ace's birthday is coming up in a couple of weeks?"

"Yes, she did. I'll be there. But to help. She knows I'm her girl whenever she needs me."

"That so?" he says with a smirk. "Here I was, thinking you'd be my date."

I look over at the timer on the stove, recognizing that there are about sixteen minutes left before the Dutch baby will be ready.

"Is that how you ask a girl on a date? You just assume she'll join you after you've had your way with her?" I'm still stuck on the fact that this man went out of his way for me, and I'm a bit speechless for it. But I like teasing him too.

He leans against the counter and hesitates for a second before he says, "It's been a long time since I've asked a girl out." That shouldn't be all that surprising with the way that he doesn't seem all that interested in most people. "But in case you misunderstood me, honey. When I woke up with the taste of you on my tongue and the smell of you in my beard, I considered you mine."

I blink, because the way this man talks to me feels like foreplay. And all I can think of is that I want to be his. At this moment, I want to claim him the same way he just did me.

"Any chance Julep wants to go play in the backyard for a few minutes?"

He stares at me, not understanding the request until I walk closer and drag my fingers along the outline that's starting to tent his gray sweats.

"I'd like to consider you mine, but I haven't had the pleasure of your taste on my tongue yet."

The smile that takes over his face is contagious.

I slip my fingers into the waistband, and I'm instantly greeted with the firm head of his cock tucked right there. I look up and see his surprise shift to the same kind of hunger I'm feeling.

With a smirk, he tilts his head toward it. "I was already hard when I saw you wearing my t-shirt."

"That's all it took?"

"You underestimate how highly I think about your body." He runs his thumb across my lips—a move that I'm realizing is a favorite of his. "And now that I know what's under that shirt . . ." He blows out a breath.

"Good, 'cause I got wet just seeing you bring me a coffee," I say as I sink to my knees in front of him.

"Fuck," he exhales with a laugh.

I pull down the waistband past his cock, so hard for me that it practically springs free. Eager and ready. "So big, cowboy," I say in a playful voice. But the truth is, I hadn't yet appreciated the size of him and how mouth-watering he truly is. Leaning in, I give him a little lick, like I'm testing out the flavor of a lollipop.

He groans as I wrap my hand around the base of him, but before I go for another pass with my tongue, I look up from under my lashes. "Tell me something?"

With his head tilted back and lips parted, he says, "Yes. Go. Sure. I'll tell you anything you want right now." A breath rushes out of him when I wrap my lips around the head of his cock, making him shiver.

"Who knew a cop would be so easy to get information out of?" I smile as I swirl my tongue, and his eyes meet mine.

"Honey, I'm not a cop anymore," he grits out on a moan. "And I'll tell you anything you want, but you do realize this would be coercion if I still was?"

When I run my tongue along the tip, I'm gifted with a taste of his excitement leaking along the slit.

"How long have you been fantasizing about this? My mouth on your cock." I take him all the way to the back of my throat.

He pushes air through his clenched teeth. "First fucking moment I laid eyes on you."

I pump him twice with my fist, and then focus on teasing him, dragging my tongue just along the rim.

"Fuck, fine. When I saw you again at the distillery, in the cooperage. Those red lips of yours . . . Dammit, I wanted to smear that red lipstick, fuck your mouth, and finish on those pretty tits."

I go back down again this time, flattening my tongue on the underside of his swollen cock. Then I wrap my lips and suck, hollowing out my cheeks and creating a punishing pace to get him there. The moan it pulls out of him makes me feel like a goddess rewarding her believer. Puckering my lips tighter, I let my tongue play as I move up and down, chasing my fist as it grips the base of him. I pull off him with a pop, needing to know what he was fantasizing about when I dropped off those band-aids. "When I heard you, in your kitchen?" He opens his eyes, so vulnerable, but ready for me to keep going.

"I thought about fucking your tits and your mouth." His head tilts back as I take him in my mouth again. "I wanted to know how good you'd make me feel. How pretty you'd look on your knees for me." As he hums another moan, I take him deeper while stroking him faster. "Fuck! Just like that." His breathing picks up, and the erratic wet sounds of my mouth on him, along with the curt noises that push out of his lips, have me so turned on, my thighs clench for friction.

"This perfect fucking mouth," he says as his whole body tenses, his fingers woven into my hair. "You're going to make me come."

I look up at him, saliva dripping down my chin, and he sees that I have no plans to ease off. I'm going to drink down whatever he gives me. The moment that registers, he says, "You want me to come on your tongue?"

I nod just enough to tell him he has my permission. Then I pick up the pace, taking his cock as far back as I can without gagging. His hips stutter while his hand grips my hair tighter, exhaling a shaky breath. "Drink up, honey." And he comes down my throat, chasing it with a guttural moan that might just be my new favorite sound.

The timer for the oven beeps just as I swallow, and I slide my mouth off his length. It sends visible chills rolling through his body. Wiping the corner of my mouth, I stand to turn off the timer.

He leans back like the counter is the only thing holding him up. "*That* was just for coffee?" Sinking his fingers into my hair, he frames my face.

"Nobody has taken the time to even consider how I take my coffee, never mind finding out what I like and then going out of their way to get it. And if I wasn't helping Hadley for Ace's birthday, you would have been my date to the party."

He finds his footing, tucks himself back in, and wraps his hand around my arm, pulling me into him, closing the distance. He doesn't use words, only actions as a response. The way this man kisses with his whole body, it steals the breath right out of me.

CHAPTER 31

GRANT

"HERE, LET ME SEE THAT." I hold out my hand and wait for her to give me the red nail polish she's been balancing between two fingers.

Lifting her head to look at me, she blows a piece of hair out of her face. "Why? Are you going to do this for me?"

"Yes."

Her eyebrows raise in surprise, along with a little smirk.

I wave my fingers forward. "Give it to me."

She laughs, keeping her fingers splayed to dry the coats she just painted. Julep trots back with her rope toy in her mouth and onto the blanket we've set out in the field next to where we swam with Lincoln and the girls. I give it a good toss and watch her run like hell after it, and then pull Laney's foot into my lap. "Let me have one of those," I say, nodding at the bag of chocolate-covered gummy bears she stashed in our cooler bag.

"When was the last time you painted someone's toes?"

I concentrate on the brush and swipe it slowly along her big toe.

"Lark tried to do it herself and then kept getting upset that it didn't look good, so I watched a YouTube video and fixed it for her."

Out of the corner of my eye, I see her staring at me.

My mouth ticks up, trying to hold back my smile. I know she's going to want to make a big deal about it. "What?"

"That was just not what I was expecting you to say." I turn to look at her, but instead of expanding on what she had "expected," she says, "You're not anything like I thought you would be."

I concentrate on the smaller toes. In all honesty, this isn't all that hard to do. "And what did you think I was like?"

"An asshole with a chip on his shoulder."

I bark out a laugh, almost spilling the polish.

She smiles as she watches my reaction. It's the one thing that's been consistent in all of this—she has a way of getting a reaction out of me.

"But that's not you at all." She sighs. "You're just an asshole when you want to be, but the rest of the time, you're the kind of guy girls like me hope shows up on a horse and makes just about everything . . . better."

I stop painting after hearing that. This woman is something else.

"I like you," she says, just slightly louder than a whisper.

Looking back down, I try to focus on finishing her toes with precision. With a smirk, because I have to tease her a little after that, I say, "You're alright."

She snorts a laugh. "Let's see if you feel like I'm just 'alright' when I'm riding your cock later."

"Jesus Christ." My concentration falters, and I swipe the nail polish brush all along her pinky toe.

"I'm sorry!" She lets out a small snort as she giggles, and her hand flies up to cover her mouth and nose. It's really fucking cute.

"You can't say that kind of shit to me while I'm trying to concentrate."

She leans forward and whispers, "I think you're pretty amazing, Grant Foxx."

I don't know why it hits me the way that it does, but those few words mixed with what she said before feel like some kind of vindication. That I've earned the right to show parts of myself to someone again.

It's been a helluva week since we've started whatever this is, but it's been the highlight, hands down. Just about everyone on my team at the cooperage had something they needed from me. It's been exhausting and tedious. I'm trying to delegate more of my typical tasks with a full team now. And we've started new barrels for a blend that Lincoln wanted to do in a limited run with, which meant new toasting times. *A week.* Which is why today, with her, is like the reward. It's a lazy day. The kind with no plans that I would always try to avoid. Keeping busy had always helped the days move along and kept quiet moments from turning into spiraling feelings. But right now, I'm loving every second of today's pace. It's peaceful.

The air cools down a bit as I listen to Laney talk about random things, like her favorite Little Debbie's cakes and what she would say if she ever met Michael Douglas. Just about everything on this field is bathed in wildflowers and tinted with the remnants of golden hour. If summer could only be one day, today would be it.

"All I'm saying is, I don't think I would be able to pretend like he was just some guy coming to the distillery to try out bourbon."

I make it to another toe without painting her skin. "Why not?"

"Grant, do you even know who Michael Douglas is?"

I can't help but smile at the tone of her voice. Like it would be crazy if I didn't.

"Here. Open," she says.

I open my mouth and she drops in another gummy bear.

"Why are these so good," I say rhetorically. "And yes, I know who Michael Douglas is. *Wall Street. Basic Instinct.*"

"*Romancing the Stone,*" she adds, popping another candy in her mouth.

I lift her other foot into my lap. "My nana would stay up really late and watch movies. It was her thing." Dipping the brush, I start on the next toe. "She let me watch the romance one with her. And I don't think I realized it was funny until I was older, but when I was a kid, I thought Michael Douglas was a badass."

She leans back on her elbows. "He's swoony. Don't care how old he is. The man will forever be—"

"A badass."

"In that movie, not as much as Kathleen Turner," she corrects, and I have to agree. "She was the hero." She smiles at her toes as I finish the last one. "You did a helluva job, cowboy."

I close the bottle and toss it aside. Lying next to her, I prop my arm under me. I try to commit this moment to memory. I move a piece of her hair away from her mouth. "Tell me you're not in any more danger."

She tilts her head, a little furrow between her eyebrows as her eyes lock onto mine. Maybe she hadn't been expecting the shift in conversation. I wasn't planning on it either, but I wasn't going to censor things with her. Not now. I need to make sure we can have more days like today. With the question hanging in the air unanswered, she leans forward and brushes her lips against mine. "We said no more lies, remember?"

CHAPTER 32

GRANT

"YOU REALIZE you're old now, right?" Lincoln says, swatting Ace.

"You've been calling me old for a decade, Linc. I'm not the one who wanted a birthday party. This is all you," he spits back. Ace sends me a look as we walk down the sidewalk. "I would have been fine with a good bottle and some cigars on the back patio."

Lincoln barks out, "Bullshit, Ace. You love this shit."

"Hey, Grant."

I wave at the owner of Crescent de Lune as we make our way through the bakery and down the back staircase to the speakeasy.

"You seem to have a lot of new friends lately." Lincoln jabs as he fixes his rolled sleeves.

"She's one of the sisters who owns the bakery. She's been making Laney's coffees for me in the mornings." And it's as soon as I say it that I realize what I've done.

"You're getting her coffees in the mornings?"

I shift my glance at him, and his eyes widen a fraction with amusement. "I take care of what's mine, brother."

"'Bout time you said it. You were so obvious when I was making her laugh that day at the river. And I was hoping that dance didn't go to waste."

Ace chimes in from behind us. I hadn't realized he was right there. "She's good for you." He smacks Linc in the back of the head. "You were flirting with her while your daughters were watching?"

"Ace, leave my little princesses out of it when I'm talking about women. And since when is flirting a bad look?" He points at him. "When's the big, bad Atticus Foxx going to go after who he wants?"

"Lincoln, who is it you think I want?"

A silent exchange goes on between the two of them, one I recognize well. They get along, but there's been an unspoken rivalry ever since we were kids. "I wake up alone by choice." He shoves his hands in his suit pants pockets and keeps his attention ahead of us, unfazed. "Sleepovers are too messy."

Lincoln chuckles, and I follow. "Ace, being messy is half the fun."

"Says the hot mess," Ace mumbles back.

I just smirk, shaking my head. They're my best friends. You don't go through as much as we have as a family and come out of it any other way. That was never an option for us. I hate how I've kept things from them, my feelings for Laney, the bourbon I've been making. "Mind if I talk to you guys about something later?"

"You having big feelings today, Grant?" Linc teases, clapping my shoulder.

I swat his arm away. "Get off."

Ace looks back before we push through the doors. "Whenever you're ready, Grant."

The dimly lit main room of Midnight Proof greets us, along with the smooth jazz filtering through the crowd. Servers hustle around with full trays of drinks and the main bar is stacked at least three people deep all the way around. The couches are filled with tourists, likely making their way down from the horse races or ready to finish their bourbon trail with the kind of vibe only a speakeasy can offer. We have a bit of an audience as we head up the flight of stairs and toward the private space on the second floor. The three of us together always garner some attention, but Ace has a few famous friends who I'm sure have already made themselves comfortable in the VIP space.

Lincoln throws open the double doors and the private party is in full swing with nearly twenty guys packed around a poker table in the middle of the room. I couldn't care less about the starting pitcher for Chicago about to lose a hand to the MVP of the National League. My body buzzes, eager to see Laney. I know there's a room full of men that are going to want what's mine.

I see her the second my brother shifts out of my line of sight. Her strawberry blonde hair is pinned to one side, showing off her neck and bare shoulder. *So fucking beautiful.* She moves around the bar, pouring out liquors into her mixer while she laughs at what one of the guys is saying to her. Her lips are painted in that red that instantly reminds my dick how much we love that mouth, but it's what she's wearing that has the rest of my attention. The peachy-pink color of her sheer top is just a few shades off her skin tone and draped in crystals that catch the light from the chandeliers hanging low in the room. Her black bra peeking through the sheerness accentuates how fucking exquisite her tits really are. My mouth waters just looking at her.

"Daddy's here!" Hadley croons out as she comes around from the bar. "Happy birthday!"

"Jesus," Ace mumbles, trying to brush off how much Hadley gets to him lately.

"Your brother really has no sense of humor," she says as she loops her arm in mine. "Lincoln, I need you to get me a bottle from the bar downstairs."

I smile at her. Hadley is one of the few people who can make me laugh, no matter what. And it's usually at Ace's expense. "You're an instigator. You know that shit pisses him off."

She waves her hand in the air. "People only get mad when stuff hits too close to home." Her eyes widen dramatically. "Do you think your brother is into daddy kink?"

"Hads, I don't want to think about what my brother is into."

Poking my chest, she smirks. "But I know what, or rather who, I should say, you've been getting into."

Laney watches as we get closer to the bar, pouring out whatever she was shaking up and twisting a lemon rind as garnish. I leave Hadley's statement unanswered, so she pats my chest and moves on toward the poker game happening behind me, where I hear her taunt, "Ace, it might be your birthday, but you're going to lose all your money tonight."

I get a full look at what Laney's wearing, and I'll be

honest, it's easily hitting epic fantasy levels with this woman. She looks like a vintage pin-up girl meets a modern-day goddess. Her top was just the start, the way it teases what she's working with, but her legs are strong and thick. I regret not leaving my mark somewhere near that too-short seam of her black shorts.

With a smirk, I crook my finger for her to come closer. She smiles and quickly peeks around to see who's looking.

I'm hoping it's just about everyone in here.

"What'll you have, cowboy?" she asks. But instead of my drink order, when she's close enough, I lean over the bar, tip her chin with my pointer finger, and kiss her lips. Light and sweet. Just enough to tell her I have no problem with who sees it. Pulling back slowly, her eyes find mine right away.

"Bourbon neat, honey."

She gives me a coy smile, knowing that there was nothing discreet about that. She turns back toward the row of bourbon, and I enjoy taking her in up close. The softness of her touch and the bite of her wit is really the only thing I want to drink in tonight. But bourbon will have to do while I wait.

Hadley comes up to the bar within the next few seconds, her gaze flicking to my brother. "Linc! Where's that bottle I asked for?"

Laney laughs as she comes back with a bottle of Foxx and gives me a healthy pour. "I'll grab it, Hadley. I need to run to the ladies' room anyway."

"How long?" Linc asks me. If it wasn't for Hadley shouting his name, I would've forgotten he's right beside me.

Hadley stays in her spot and listens for the answer.

"4th of July."

Holding out her hand to Lincoln, she says, "Pay up. I told you it was new."

"You had insider information," he says, pulling out his wallet.

He pulls out five crisp, one-hundred-dollar bills. "You made a bet?"

"Just about how long we thought it'd take for you to see it. I thought for sure it was right after we went to the river with Lily and Lark. The way you shot daggers at me when I was pushing her on that tire swing . . ." He laughs. "Fucking priceless."

I glance around the room for her. The poker table is rowdy as one of the guys decides to put my brother all in as soon as he is dealt. I smile, thinking about how Laney would likely give them a run for their money. It takes three more hands before Lincoln loses his chips, but instead of making a big deal about it, he yells out, "Alright, I'm too old for shots, but Hadley, let's break open that bottle of Pappy you've been keeping for me."

Looking back toward the bar, I realize Laney's still not back. Maybe she got caught up helping someone downstairs, but it's when my gut tells me something might be wrong that I'm talking over my brother and interrupting. "Hads, did Laney come back up yet?"

"No. Can you go find—"

I'm already through the double doors and heading for the stairs. In the main room, a jazz singer croons something old and romantic over the sound system, and I scan behind the bar to see if I spot her. Nothing. When I come down the stairs and look down past the ladies' room, that's when I hear her.

"You lied to me," she shouts. I walk closer to where she's standing. A man only slightly taller than me is in front of her. *Who the fuck is this guy?* He's leaner, so if I need to, I can easily muscle him out of here.

Her eyes catch mine and the small shake of her head has me slowing down as I take another step. Turning, he looks over his shoulder. "Who the hell is that, Laney?"

Eyebrows furrowing, her nose scrunches. "You have no right asking. We're not anything to each other, Phillip."

Fucking Phillip.

"How can you fucking say that?"

I don't think so. I point at him as I step closer to Laney. "Watch your mouth when you're talking to my girl."

The corner of her mouth tips up as I step forward just enough to create more space in between them. I place my hand on her lower back, and she moves just a fraction closer.

"What are you even doing here?"

"I should say the same about you. I've been calling and texting." Even though he tries to keep his voice down, it comes out rushed when he says, "We were . . ." He takes a shaky breath. "You just disappeared."

"Should've told you something." I stare him down, and she relaxes just a bit more into my hand. The tense way she's got her hands balled up at her sides and posture perfectly straight, it's obvious that she's more than uncomfortable with him.

He raises his hand up at me, as if that's going to stop me. "This is between us," he says, eyes narrowed.

I look toward the front of the room and catch Brady's attention. The sheer size of him clears a path.

When my eyes drift, so do hers, as she tilts her head to see past his shoulder. There are a few guys near the bar paying attention to this exchange. "Is this your bachelor trip?" But she doesn't let him answer. Instead, she smiles and shakes her head. "Go back to your life. Go get married and have a fuck ton of kids, for all I care. But do me a favor, forget about ever seeing me here and let me live mine."

"You don't mean that."

It's like he hits a switch with those few words, because her entire body tenses, and this time, she's not nervous. She's pissed. "You're going to tell me what I mean now? How about what I want? Are you going to tell me that too? I'll tell you what I didn't want. You. That night. I didn't—" She sucks in a breath, trying to steady her words. "I didn't want it to get that far and . . ."

"What are you saying?" he spits back. "You wanted me the same way I wanted you. Don't pretend like you didn't."

"No, I wanted someone I used to know, and you wanted to feel something before you went ahead and promised yourself to someone else. I made a mistake."

I've had enough. She's had enough. I lean into her and tell her, "Hadley's office is the last door on the right."

She looks up at me, tears brimming her eyes. "He's not worth it."

She's right, but I can't just let this guy think he's gotten the last word. He treated her like a convenient side-piece. To me, she's the only person I want to focus on. "I'm just going to make sure he finds the exit."

With a wave of my hand, Brady comes up quickly, asking him to leave.

"Are you kidding me? This is my bachelor party."

Brady just smirks at him. "Looks like your party is moving somewhere else."

I glance up at the stairs and see Lincoln watching all of this happen. He'll have my back if I need it. And right now, there's no way this guy is leaving Fiasco without a reminder of why he should never come back. I follow Brady as he escorts Phillip out the front door and through the bakery. When his feet hit the sidewalk, I don't stop.

"Now that it's just us, let me be a little clearer about exactly who I am."

He looks over my shoulder toward his friends who are on my heels. I'm outnumbered, but I can handle guys like this—all talk, barely any substance.

"I gotta head back in, Grant," Brady says from the door.

"I'll be right there. Let Lincoln know I'm out here, will ya?" I turn back to the asshole. My body thrums with a mix of anger and anxiety to get back inside to Laney. "You're going to do as she asked. Because if you don't, I have no problem sharing with some of your friends in New York, specifically at your place of business, that you're a lying cheat." I rub my palm against the scruff on my cheek. "I have a feeling your soon to be father-in-law might find that information a little bit interesting, don't you think?"

His lips part just enough to know I've surprised him. He was expecting a right hook, but with guys like him, I'd rather hit where it hurts.

"Grant, you alright out here?" Lincoln calls out from the door. *Right on time.*

"All good, just making sure my friend finds his way home."

I turn toward Phillip, his eyes shifting behind me, clearly nervous about the way I'm stalking toward him. "You're going to forget about her. You're going to forget you saw her here. You're not going to mention it to anyone."

He holds up his hands, flinching back at my proximity. "Listen, man, I don't want trouble. Is she okay?"

"She's not your business anymore. She's mine. I want you out of my town. Tonight." I take a step closer. "If I find out you've even said so much as her name again—even if it's to tell your fiancée what you did—I will make your life hell."

He doesn't say anything. A wide-eyed response and his obvious lack of backbone were enough to know he's not going to be a problem for her. I'll still make sure one of Del's New York City contacts pays him a visit in full uniform at work just as a reminder, though.

I breeze past Lincoln. I'm only interested in seeing Laney right now and making sure she's okay.

"Do I want to know what that was about?" he asks, catching up with me.

"Nope."

He stops at the stairs. "Are you coming back up?"

I ignore him and keep walking straight for Hadley's office. When I close the door behind me, Laney's leaning against the small desk and picking at her fingers. She looks less rattled than when I left her, but she needs to know there's nothing left to worry about. The small space is quiet, considering there's a packed bar and band just beyond the door and down the hall.

She stands up, starting to say, "There's something else I need to—"

I lock the door. "That's done."

Her eyes shift to the door, and then back up to me. "What?"

"With him. That's done now." I don't want her spending another second thinking about that part of her past. She's torn herself apart about the way things happened with him, and I hate that seeing him ripped it open again.

Biting her lip, she studies me. "Did you hurt him?"

"Threatened him to stay away. Gave him a good tap in the back to make sure he heard everything you said."

She looks down at her hands. "Is it awful to say thank you for that?"

I close the distance and tuck my finger under her chin, tilting her face up. The way she looks at me is something I don't take for granted. Her pretty eyes have flecks of blue and swirls of brown that remind me of my bourbon now in the dim light behind the desk and the way she looks like she's pouting when she's waiting for me to say something.

Close to her lips, I whisper, "Turn around." She searches my eyes for what I'm asking, but the second she sees it, she turns her back to me. I run my hands along her bare shoulders, over her smooth skin. This need I have to feel her, have her, is overwhelming.

Moving her hair to one side, I lean in and kiss her right below her ear, in that one spot that makes her hum when I spend enough attention on it. She tilts her head back, leaning it against my shoulder as I let my hands roam over the rough material of her top. I trace along the seams and over the crystals that meet her skin. She looks so perfect in my arms like this. I feel such a need to protect her, make her feel good, and see her for exactly who she is: strong, sexy, and exactly what I want.

I bend just enough to run my nose along the side of her neck. She has that soft floral smell, like the wildflowers behind my house, and a hint of bourbon from my lips.

"He wasn't the reason I left."

I knew there was more, but I'm not going to push. Not now.

Nodding against her, I drag my hand down the curves of her body and between her thighs. I rub her pussy over the satin of the bottoms she's wearing as I press my hardening cock against her ass.

"Can I be the reason you stay?"

There it is, at the core of why I've kept mostly to myself. Why I hated the idea of her crashing into our lives and living across from me. It's the one thing I've been scared to want, never mind ask of anyone. For them to *stay*.

She runs her hand up the arm I have wrapped around her middle, lifting it away from her body and up toward her mouth. She kisses my palm, and with a breathy exhale, she says, "Yes."

I rest my lips along the back of her neck, letting them linger so I can absorb what that does to me. It's like knocking aside far too many years of being incapable of really caring for someone. She circles her hips against me in response, and it feels so fucking good. "Do that again."

Leaning forward, she places her hands on the desk and then grinds her ass back into me.

I trail my fingers along the edges of where her barely-there bottoms meet the cheeks of her perfect ass. "Tell me what you want." My thumbs dip just past the seams to tease her.

"You. I want you."

Her words spark a heat around the edges of my skin, drawing goosebumps to the surface, and making my cock swell beneath my pants. I take a step back.

"Pull those down so I can see how much."

She peeks at me over her shoulder, a smirk on those pretty painted lips, and hooks her thumbs into the waist to pull them just past the curve of her ass. The garter belt and straps stay as she rolls down the black satin. I can't help it; she's just begging for my mouth, so I don't think as I drop to my knees, grab one of her ass cheeks in each hand, and spread her apart. Her pussy glistens, she's so wet. "Fucking hell, honey, this all for me?"

She makes the sexiest sound, a cross between a gasping breath and a soft moan. I press my face into her and flatten my tongue, trying to reach her clit. I give it a pulse before I drag it down and back all the way to her puckered asshole.

"Please don't tease me. I need that fat cock to fuck me right now."

I bite one of her cheeks because, Christ, that mouth. "I don't have a condom, baby."

Still peering over her shoulder, her lust-filled gaze meets mine as I glide my fingers along her drenched lips. "I said I want you. Now do what you're told, cowboy."

Goddamn, I like that. I rub my cock over my jeans. I'm

so fucking hard it hurts. The truth is, I couldn't care less about any repercussions of not using one. But I don't want her to regret anything. Not with me. "Yes, ma'am."

She leans forward, thrusting her ass out. "Make me messy."

CHAPTER 33

LANEY

I LEAN my forearms on Hadley's desk. Post-It notes fasten to almost every surface with reminders of liquor shipments and picking up a birthday present for her dad. I can feel my arousal drip from me as I listen and anticipate what's coming next. His belt clinks as it unbuckles. And I can't help it, I need to look again. I watch as he rips the button of his jeans open, taking down the zipper in the process. I lick my lips as he reaches into his black boxer briefs and takes out his thick cock. Hard and ready for me. My pussy tingles at the sight of him jerking himself with one hand as he fists the material around my waist.

The moment I locked eyes with him, when Phillip was in front of me, I felt stronger. Safe. I didn't care about what was in my past, what I had done, or the person I thought I had wanted to pick me. The only thing I wanted was for Phillip to forget he had seen me. And to get back to my new life. I'll worry about telling Bea when I can think. But right now, the only thing I can do is want and feel. To be present. I want Grant in a way that I haven't ever wanted anything. If he asks me to beg, I would. Wholeheartedly. If he asks me again if I'm safe, I'll bare every last detail.

He grips each ass cheek like he can't get enough in his hands and spreads me open. His gaze stays fixated at what he wants—bent over and tilted up for him. When I wiggle it, his lips tilt up into a smirk that I can't read. "So fucking pretty," he says, leaning forward, and then spits right on my pussy.

It's the dirtiest thing anyone has ever done to me. The feeling of it slowly dripping down my center ignites some kind of new fire deep within my core, and I release a long, needy whimper.

"You like that, honey? Doing whatever I want to what's mine?"

I hum as my belly flutters, and then moan some distorted version of "yes" as he pushes his free hand up my back and threads his fingers into my hair. Grasping a handful, he pulls my strands taut so my head tips back as he drags the head of his cock through my pussy to coat himself in us.

"That's it, I want to hear your moans. I don't care if this whole fucking bar hears. Don't be quiet. Not for me." And then he pushes into me all the way to the hilt, hips pressing firmly against my ass. The way he fills me steals the breath from my lungs every time.

"Fuck, it's so good." A growl escapes his throat as his head tilts back.

"So full," I exhale, along with another combination of nonsense that, at the core of it, are moans of complete and utter pleasure. His hips roll into me, slow and deep, like he needs to feel every inch he can. He fucks me carefully, intensely, like he's losing himself in my body the same way I'm lost at the rhythm of his.

The sounds he makes behind me urge me to do the same. "Grant."

"That's it, baby. Tell me." With his hand still wrapped in my hair, his other loops around my middle, pulling me up from the desk and flush against his chest. He never stops moving, his hips thrusting into me, pulling the filthiest sounds from our bodies that already have me tightening around his length.

I turn my head to look at him, and as soon as our eyes meet, he's devouring my lips. His tongue dances with mine as all my senses are overtaken. I don't want my orgasm to come just yet; I'm too consumed by this intoxicating feeling. This moment. With him.

"You feel so good, honey. I don't think—*Fuck.*"

I move so that I'm meeting his body every time he rolls his hips into me. "Harder, baby. I don't want to forget this any time soon." I plead. I try grabbing at his shirt, looking to hold on to something for purchase as he holds me up against him, his front to my back.

He does exactly as I ask, picking up the punishingly slow pace and hitting a spot so deep that my legs begin to shake. When he drags his teeth and lips down the side of my neck, I wrap my arm up and behind his neck. The heavy breathing and the sounds he makes every time his cock glides in deep are what will tip me over so quickly. Words and the world around us are suddenly muted. My body tenses, warning me that nothing is going to hold back this release from shattering me completely. Tingles whirl along the surface of my skin and a sense of cool numbness draws nearer toward my pussy. He holds me tighter with one arm under my breasts and the other snaked down to the bundle of nerves that will be my undoing. The hard fuck from behind and the pressure from his fingers has me pleading and repeating, "Don't stop. Don't stop."

I'm going to come apart any moment and he knows it. *Feels* it. Holding me tighter, I can feel him losing control too. "That's my girl. You're going to take everything I give you, aren't you?" I grip onto his arms, my nails digging into him as an answer. *Everything*. His chest rumbles as I lean my head back against his shoulder, his mouth covering my neck, and he nips at my skin. It's the sound of filthy pleasure escaping his lips, a deep, breathy sound of need and his words that have me falling completely apart. "Come for me, honey." His lips move against my skin as he whispers, "That's it. This perfect pussy. She's just made a mess all over my cock."

My hearing dulls and it's only the sounds of my own moan and his that register. Only when I fully melt with satisfaction does his body tense behind me, then seconds later, chasing my orgasm with his. He pulls out of me, and I feel his release splash against my skin as he jerks his cock between our bodies.

"Fuck, baby," he groans. He still holds me tight across the middle as his forehead rests on my shoulder. His chest rises and falls at the same deep and quick pace as mine. "Messy enough for you," he says with a grin as he rubs his cock around my lower back and down my ass where his cum drips.

"For now."

His arm snakes up between my breasts as his hand wraps around my throat, turning my head toward my shoulder so he can kiss me. "Now you look more like mine."

"I dunno, cowboy, you seem an awful lot like *mine* right now."

He lets out a laugh. "You're not wrong." Leaning in, he kisses my nose. "Let's get you cleaned up."

As I rest on the desk, he wipes up his mess with a scarf that was hung on the back of Hadley's door—hopefully, it wasn't something she'll be looking for later. Bending over, his knees crack, as he pulls my bottoms back up my legs. He leaves a path of kisses along my inner thigh as he does, and it shouldn't make me want more. I should feel sated, but in reality, he's only perked up my appetite. And the next words out of his mouth don't help matters.

"What if I don't want to go back to the party and watch you serve anyone else tonight? What if I'd rather just spend the rest of the night figuring out all the ways I can serve you?"

I peer back and watch as he trails his hands back up my body again. Wrapping my arms around his shoulders, I play with the hair along the nape of his neck. The place he loves to touch whenever he's uncomfortable or thinking. *His tell.* He leans into me, dragging his nose along my jaw, and I melt into the way this feels. Touching him this way and feeling how it softens him for me.

Kissing me once more, he looks at me like he has so much more to say. And I want to hear all of it.

"Take me home, cowboy."

Chapter 34

Laney

Three pictures. *That's all I have to remember my mother. Remember isn't the right word . . . Maybe it's to memorialize the fact that I had one, but I never knew her. I stare at the way she smiled at my dad, and the way she looked so happy in her makeshift wedding dress, The Las Vegas Chapel in the background and the champagne bottle in her hand. I always thought it was cheap and impulsive, but after spending so much time and seeing the money poured into the weddings I plan, I wonder if they got it right. Love each other and make a promise. She couldn't keep her side of it, but my dad would tell me the best part of loving my mother was that he got me. Wiping away my tears, I think about him and how disgusted I am at myself for what just happened.*

I put the photos back into the wooden box and run my fingers over the magnet from Disney World, the photo strip of us that we took on the boardwalk after celebrating the last day of 7th grade, and the tiny Buddha he said would bring me luck when we spent the day in Chinatown, wandering and eating our way down Pell Street. Tiny trinkets and pieces of paper are the only things in the entire storage unit that mean anything to me.

"Somebody—"

It's the only word I hear before the gut-wrenching scream that carries and echoes down the hall. I didn't know that I was this kind of person. That if it came down to something or someone in danger, if I would fight or flight. But I don't think. I run out of the unit so fast, but instead of away, I run toward the screaming. I leave my phone behind. My purse and wallet. I simply run to help with whatever's happening and to whom. When I turn the brightly lit corner and see the blood dripping down her neck, the torn, mutilated skin, and the way tears streak down her dirty face, I stop with my heart in my throat, but she doesn't. I don't panic. An instant need to help, find the problem, and fix it takes over me.

"Please! Oh god, please get me out of here. We need to leave!"

I glance behind her and see nothing. When I turn, I catch sight of the fire alarm. I lift the plastic cover and pull down. But nothing happens. There isn't a blaring alarm or ringing, only a light that flashes above the exits. Why is there no alarm?

That's when I hear it. Hear him. "You're mine, pretty thief."

I suck in a breath, and it feels like a weight sitting heavy on my chest. I start coughing as soon as my eyes open. My back, underneath my boobs, and along my upper lip are all damp with sweat. It's the warm hand on my forearm that grounds me. It's the one that helped wake me. I blink away the remnants of the nightmare. Small pieces of it are different from the reality of what happened, but it still amplifies my anxiety. I know that's not what he said, but hearing that voice has my stomach in knots.

Maybe it was seeing Phillip again that stirred things up. Even though Grant made sure Phillip wouldn't be a problem. If I had to guess, it didn't take much convincing if Grant threatened to blow up the inflated life that Phillip had built in Manhattan. It would be enough to keep him away and quiet.

But my dreams aren't about Phillip. They're about everything that happened in that storage facility *after* Phillip. I've woken up sweating and unsettled, remembering pieces of a nightmare, every night for the last week. And I've had enough. I'm not even upset anymore; I'm just pissed. I hate having to relive these feelings, the anxiousness, the adrenaline of being chased, the seemingly endless what ifs. I look around the room. The drapes are drawn closed, the low hum of central air keeping the temperature cool despite my overheated body.

"You're okay. It was just a bad dream," Grant says softly, rubbing small circles along the top of my hand. He doesn't know what they're about, but he still comforts me.

I sit up and scrub my hands over my face. The bed shifts and Julep jumps up, sitting on alert at the foot of the bed. "I'm okay, sweet girl," I say and wiggle my fingers for her to come closer.

Grant leans up from lying on his stomach and kisses my arm. "Want to talk about it?"

"Not really. I'm—" I don't know what I am. My body

buzzes with something that doesn't feel right. An uneasi-
ness that I'd like to ignore.

In his morning low gravel, he answers for me. "Not
okay?"

I shake my head no. He kisses where he was just
soothing on my hand.

"How about I show you what I do when I'm not
okay?" He gets up before I can respond, his black boxer
briefs molded to his delicious ass.

I roll my lips to hold back a smile as I check out just
how handsome this man is, especially in the morning. Bite-
my-fist level attractive. "Does it involve you being naked in
your kitchen?"

He throws a t-shirt at my face. "Get dressed and meet
me down in my workspace."

"Hit it again."

Almost an hour later, and I'm out of breath. It feels
good to throw my amped-up energy at a heavy bag. After I
brushed my teeth and opted for a sports bra and shorts
instead of one of his t-shirts, he had hand wraps and a pair
of boxing gloves waiting for me.

I hit the bag again.

I'm still in a mood. Pissed off and working through it,
but pissed off nonetheless. I had helped someone, and any
good feelings associated with that were washed out by
having to leave everything I had known. And I still haven't
told Grant all of it. Maybe it's more about keeping this
from him than Phillip showing up.

I hit the bag again.

Relocating, and running away, no matter how smart or safe of a move it was, made me feel like I didn't have control. Those nightmares just remind me that things are still unfinished. Unanswered. I don't know the whole story. And it's my *fucking* story.

I throw three punches in succession and then lean against the bag, glancing up at him.

"Why are you just watching me?"

"Keep going. Same combination, but add a knee at the end of it."

"You keep going," I snap back, out of breath.

"I'm watching you because you look fucking good hitting that bag."

I don't want him to flirt with me. I'm sweating and working my ass off and he's just watching. Julep too.

"That's all I am, here for your viewing pleasure, then?" I throw two jabs and a left hook.

When he smirks, it has me stopping.

"This isn't working." I yank off the gloves.

"Tell me what you need." He tilts his head to the side, sizing me up.

"Fantastic question. Why don't you tell me."

My eyes narrow as he bites his lower lip, trying to hold back from smiling. "You want someone who's going to challenge that smart-ass mouth of yours?"

"You didn't think it was a smart-ass mouth when it was choking on your cock."

He barks out a laugh, and I swallow mine down. I hadn't planned on saying that.

I can imagine what I look like right now. My hair has

escaped from its sagging ponytail, with a series of wet sweat spots spanning from between my boobs and down to the crease where my ass meets my thighs. I'm sweating in places I hadn't realized would sweat. And I'm picking a fight.

"You've been too sweet to me lately. Is that it? All that fire you have is trying to figure out where to go?"

Even as my belly swoops, I hit the heavy bag again with a huff. "What does that even mean, Grant?"

Every minute that passes, the cloud of truth hangs heavier over my head. Each punch is like a fight I'm having with myself at this point. We said no more lies, but my secret is one that has to be kept, no matter what. No matter what happens with us. It's one that could put him in as much danger for knowing as I am for living it. How can I do that to him?

"I'm telling you that whatever you need, I'm right here." He steps closer, and just his proximity softens me. "If you want to punch that bag for the rest of the morning to work through some shit, then fine. If you want to take a walk down to the stables, those horses can always help me forget the things that are too loud. If you need me to leave you alone because you need space, then I can do that too."

My chest tightens, and I grab his forearm to nudge him to come closer. "Not that one." Out of all the things I was racking my mind about what I needed to do or stop feeling in order to get out of this slump, distance from him wasn't one of them.

No more lies.

I clear my throat and close my eyes briefly before looking up at him. "You already know I'm not from Colorado."

He lets out a low hum and leans against the heavy bag. "I know."

"I was in the wrong place at the wrong time. Or maybe it was the wrong place at the right time. I told you about that night in the storage unit with Phillip."

Nodding, he loops his finger with my pinky. He wants to touch me, but he's giving me space. "Keep going, baby."

And just those words are enough to let me exhale that breath I've been holding for so long. "I was upset about what had just happened. But then, I heard a scream . . ."

I tell him the whole story. How I helped another woman escape a nightmare and the chaotic hours afterwards that led me to Ace's front porch.

"I don't know what's going to happen next. I can't even say for sure if I'm safe." I shake my head. "I just know that I trust you with my story."

"I understand what it means to hold on to a secret like yours. The kind of trust you need to feel and have with me in order to share it." He curls a piece of hair that fell from behind my ear, cupping my cheek in his palm. With his eyes locked onto mine, he promises, "It's safe with me. You're safe with me."

With eyes blurred with unshed tears, I breathe out, "I know."

Wrapping his arms around my middle, he pulls me into him.

"I'm sweaty," I laugh, trying to pull back. But he won't let me.

"Shut up," he says, holding me tighter. Then he licks the side of my neck. An exaggerated lick, right up the side where sweat drips, and I swear I feel it between my legs.

"You think a little sweat could scare me off?" Lifting me so that my feet are just centimeters off the ground, he kisses my lips and drags his teeth along the bottom. "Which candy is your favorite?"

I laugh out, "What?"

"Tell me which one is your favorite."

"That's not an easy answer."

"Tell me anyway." He smiles and gives my side a little pinch.

"Red Vines and sour gummy bears, and maybe those Modjeska things. Tied for first. Oh, and the chocolate-covered gummy bears, too."

He paid attention. He already knows that sour gummy bears are a top choice. Last week, I found unopened bags in his snack cupboard and bedside table. He told me they were "in case of an emergency."

"You're all of those to me. My favorite tastes." He kisses my lips once more. "Your mouth." He kisses my neck. "Sweat. Tears." He rubs his lips along my jaw. "Your pussy. The way she gets wet for me. How she tastes when she wants me. The way she tastes after she's had me. All of it."

I can't help but smile, giggling at his words. My body instantly warms, ready for him, as he lowers me to the ground and kneels before me.

"Thank you," he says softly.

I search his expression for what he means, but he looks back at me with such adoration that my eyes water. "For what, baby?" I smile.

He raises my hand up, placing a kiss on my wrist, and simply says, "For you."

Out of all the shit that brought me here, even if I need

to be reminded every once in a while, the moral of it all is that . . . I'm here. In front of a man who wants to be the reason I stay.

A man who is now quite literally on his knees to make me feel so damn good.

CHAPTER 35

GRANT

I LEAN against the far wall of the distillery, the one with the best view of where the tours started and ended. Right in front of the tasting bar. I still have a few things to wrap up, but I hear her laugh and it has me stopping my train of thought. She's charming a small group of people without even realizing it. And she knows what she's talking about as she pours the tasting flights.

"This is the 1936. It's going to give you those layered, richer flavors on your palate because it's double barreled," Laney says to the older couple that has just come off their tour group. "This is one of my favorites." Flipping a bottle of the newest blend, she pours and gets a few hoots out of it.

I made her a promise when I told her she was safe with me. Hell, it was a promise to myself too, because it was the one thing I was afraid I couldn't do. I had failed once before, and I won't allow that to happen again. No matter what.

"You realize you're staring and smiling like an idiot?"

I glance at my grandfather, who somehow ended up next to me, leaning against the same wall. "Where'd you come from?"

"Been watching you lately."

I take a big inhale, and on the exhale, push off to get back to work. "Why's that, Griz?"

"I always pay attention, Grant. Your brothers like to be the center of all of this, but you and I both know that it's makin' barrels, putting in the work, not having to be in the spotlight, that keeps things moving." He crosses his arms and surveys the room, the brand he built into what it is today. He was always the one looking at the big picture. "I've seen the way you're helping the new guys find their footing in the cooperage. They all actually want to be around you now," he sniffs out.

"Griz, I've never been interested in making friends here."

"It's not friendship I'm talkin' about. It's respect. They've always respected your last name, your role when you started as lead cooper, but they're respecting *you* now. You're showing them what it means to take pride in their work. Solve problems without having to ask permission. It's a powerful thing, being able to work hard and feel like it matters."

I've been doing this job for a while and haven't wanted anything other than to come in, do it, then leave. I look over at the woman pouring my family's bourbon. It feels different now. *I* feel different now.

"Heard this was the longest stint Jimmy Dugan had at one job. The hardware store didn't count. I know for a fact his father tried to fire him at least three times."

I smile at that. "He works hard. I think he just needed to find something other than the hardware store. Settle into something different."

Griz looks back at Laney. "Sometimes that's all it is. Balancing on new ground. Finding someone who'll see you as you are and not as you were." He claps my shoulder and gives it a squeeze. "Proud of you." I bite the inside of my cheek, trying to keep my emotions in check. Approval from him still feels good. "Heard the fish are biting at dusk again. What do you say, you and me show Laney what else we do well around here?"

"I'll grab the poles if you pick up the bait this afternoon?"

"I'll tell you boys right now that when it comes time for you to meet your person, you'll know it," Griz said as he cast. The way he glided the fly across the water looked like it was moving in slow motion. Just enough of a ripple to get the trout biting. Although, that late in the summer, it'd be more likely to catch bass or carp instead.

Ace shouted from his rock in the center of the river. "It's just going to be the bourbon boys, Griz. Girls just want to laugh and do boring crap."

Griz laughed to himself, and I knew just as well as my big brother, regardless of what he said, that it wasn't true.

"You're not going to think that in a few years, Atticus. That, I can guarantee you."

My grandfather was the smartest man I knew, so when he told me something was true, I believed him. Plain and simple. And if he said we had someone who would make our world more amazing than we'd ever imagined, then I couldn't wait to meet mine.

It's a memory I haven't thought about until now. How we stood in this very spot and laughed as Griz told us exactly how life worked.

"Don't care if it's with a man or a woman, but having someone—"

Linc chimes in, "Like Nana, right, Griz?"

Griz smiled. "Yeah, Linc, just like your nana."

Of course it wasn't that simple, but at seven years old, it sounded as easy as following rules and clues. I was always good at that.

Julep splashes by in the shallow bank as she chases a bullfrog. Normally, that'd be the most entertaining thing about some evening flyfishing. But it's the beautiful woman standing in hip-deep water, wearing a pair of too-big galoshes that has me entertained. "I don't think fish like me. Don't I need a worm or something?" She's holding the pole at the perfect angle to cast, but Griz still gives his speech about how a looser grip meant the line would skim the surface of the water better. I thread the line around the lore and knot it twice.

"How many times am I supposed to do it?"

I can't bite back my laugh, because I can almost hear the smoke coming out of Griz's ears. She's being loud and no one ever caught anything fly fishing when they were being loud.

"I can make you more of those zucchini chocolate chip muffins, Griz."

He pulls back his line and damn near falls in the water. "What do you mean, zucchini chocolate chip?"

"The muffins you had, they were gluten-free and had zucchini in them."

"That's what that green was in there?"

But she doesn't answer him. Instead, she flicks her wrist and almost falls back into the water as her line snaps and the pole goes flying. "Dammit, this little prick-tent, sorry-ass fucking line" is followed up with a hearty laugh when she realizes her hook got snagged on the tree trunk to my left.

Griz barks out a laugh. "I haven't heard 'prick-tent' before. Might need to use that one."

She wades through the water toward where I'm perched. With her hair piled high, a few of her strawberry and gold tinted pieces wisp along her neck. Maybe it's the way the sun hits the horizon line or the way the water ripples as she approaches, but it has my chest warming and my mouth watering. It suddenly feels like the world has decided it's time I recognize what's been happening. And maybe I was too stubborn to realize it until right now, but I won't forget this. Or what to call what I'm feeling for her. Somewhere between her swearing at me and that fishing line, I've fallen in love with her.

"Are you impressed by my skills?" She hooks her thumbs under the suspenders of her galoshes and wiggles her eyebrows.

Chuckling, I try to swallow the dryness in my throat.

When she reaches me, she wraps her arms around my neck, tilting back at me with an easy smile resting on her lips as she asks, "You alright, baby?"

Mmm. I love when she calls me that. I pull her in, wrapping my arms around her waist and kissing her pretty lips. It doesn't take any coaxing for them to part so that our tongues can meet in a slow caress. I want to linger here, with my body pressed against hers. Kissing her this way, like she's my everything. I'm afraid to blink. Afraid to let go and pretend like this is just a random evening together.

A splash and a twangy "Yeehaw" grabs our attention. Griz is laughing in the middle of the river, the water up to his hips as he reels in a fish. He yells out, "Grant, this might be the best catch of the summer right here. You and Laney stay over there so the fish come back."

"You got it, Griz," I say on a laugh, cozying her into my lap.

"Laney," Griz shouts. "Looks like your beginner's luck might be rewarding me instead, while you suck face with my grandson."

When I look back at her smiling, I pull her chin closer and lock onto those blue eyes as I tell her, "I'm better than alright, honey."

CHAPTER 36

LANEY

THE DOUBLE TAP on my front door has Julep barking.

"Come in," I yell out, my hands covered in sticky dough from today's urge to make homemade cinnamon rolls. Baking has become my clear space. I don't muddle it up with overanxious thoughts. It helps me feel close to my dad in some ways, and in others, it lets me just enjoy a task that's only meant for me.

"Hey, Laney." It isn't the Foxx I was expecting to show up at my front door—technically, his front door. I can barely hear him over some morning Ella Fitzgerald.

I jut my chin and lean down to reach the volume on my little speaker perched next to me. "Ace, what are you doing here?"

"I was going to say the same thing about you," he says, leaning against the counter. His hands are slung into his suit pants pockets and an easy smile rests on his face.

I stop stirring the brown sugar and cinnamon. "Shit.

Have I outworn my welcome? I know you said you didn't want rent, but I've been putting aside a couple hundred dollars a week in case you ask for it."

He shakes his head no. "I don't need rent. I just meant that I didn't think you would be in here. I had just assumed you were spending time at Grant's place."

"Oh." What was I supposed to say to that? Yes, actually. I've been spending a great deal of time in your brother's bed. Not to mention, the timeliness of your curiosity is interestingly accurate based on the conversation I had with Grant this morning.

I peered out of the corner of my eye as I put mascara on my lashes. Grant surveyed the bathroom counter covered in most of my things. "I'll clean this all up once I'm done."

"Is that the only make-up you have?" He globbed tooth-paste onto his toothbrush and started brushing as he watched me curl my eyelashes.

"Please don't be the guy who says, 'you don't need it.'"

He just smiled over his toothbrush, and then spit, before bringing his attention back to me. "Laney, I value my life. I would never tell you what you do or don't need." He winks.

It was impossible not to smile, especially with that navy towel tucked at the hip and slung so low.

"Eyes up here, baby." Clearing his throat, he rubbed the back of his neck before looking at me in the mirror again. "I'm asking because maybe you should grab more. To have here."

That made me pause what I was doing.

With a tight-lipped smile, he looked nervous. Grant, for all the things I'm learning about him, seeming nervous in any situation isn't one I've experienced yet. "I'm trying to get more of you."

That threw me off. And not in a way where I didn't want to hear it. It was more like, I had never heard those words before. There had never been a time in my life when someone other than my dad wanted more of me. It had always gone the other way. And some of that surprise, and albeit slight panic, must have been showing on my face.

He wiped whatever toothpaste was left behind and shifted closer, leaning down and kissing my shoulder. "Let me have more of you."

The truth was, I wanted it too. Maybe all of it was soon. Maybe it would turn into the worst decision of my life—getting closer to a man who had gone from calling me a liar to claiming me as his.

"There's room for you here. In the top drawer, space in my closet, and the table on your side of the bed is practically vacant anyway." *Dragging his teeth along my shoulder, he said,* "Think about it," *and then strode out of the bathroom, giving my ass a little smack.*

It's all I'd been thinking about. Hence the bag of skittles I already powered through after I had made a big batch of granola.

"Prue asked about having a wedding at the distillery. One of her granddaughters is looking for a small venue and she was wondering if that was something we could do. I told her that I would need to talk to my events person before I committed to anything."

I finish sprinkling the brown sugar bourbon mixture onto the rolled-out dough and move toward the little refrigerator for some butter. I really like that he came to talk to me before committing to it. The gesture makes me realize how much I respect Ace and the way he does business. The way he treats people. Especially the people who work for him. "I think if it's in the dead of winter or the heart of summer and they want it outside, it'll be tricky with the weather. But maybe if it's in the fall, that'll allow us to only worry about a tented space and not about temperature control."

"And what if we had a dedicated space for events like that?"

That has me stopping the cinnamon bun multitasking once again. "I would say the distillery is too busy during typical tour hours for a private event. But if you had a special place for things like that, then it would be something we could offer regularly."

"Is that something you would consider sticking around for? Long term?"

I'm flattered at what he's proposing. "Why?" I clear my throat. "I just mean, if hosting a wedding here for a family friend is something we can pull off, sure. But if you're talking about creating a space here that feels like a destination for weddings, well, I think it would be amazing."

He nods, not offering anything else. Just a clipped nod, like that was that.

"Alright. I'll make sure Prue chats with you directly, then. Work up some numbers for costs associated and we can see if it'll fit into her granddaughter's budget."

"Um, sure." I wipe my hands off quickly. Just before he reaches the door, I call after him. "Ace?" He must hear the question in my tone.

"It seems like you're staying. So, I want you to have

something here. This is yours if you want it." He gives me a tight-lipped smile. "You deserve good things, Laney. I don't know the details, but I've seen enough to know that whatever you ran from, it was ugly. And I'm telling you, from one hardened heart to another, that no matter what happened, you're allowed to find good things."

You can do hard things.

"And you've brought my brother back." His Adam's apple bobs as he swallows hard. "I recognize him again. I know that's got a lot to do with you."

He leaves a few beats later, and my eyes well up with tears. I don't bat a single one of them away as they roll down my face. I stare at the door and let myself feel this. The sense of belonging and care that I've found here isn't something I plan on taking for granted. I glance around the small cottage and toward Julep cozied in the corner sleeping. I feel like I have a home.

The loud whinny of a horse snaps me out of my head. I look out the front window and can see the outline of Grant brushing Tawney, wearing that damn blue baseball hat backwards. He went into the cooperage this morning and then for a ride after lunch. It's a typical Sunday for him, I'm learning. There haven't been any days when he's not at the distillery in some way or another. He loves being there and I understand it.

A text message alert from my phone dings over the speaker and interrupts my music.

BEA

Laney, call me.

I've got colleagues asking me about
Fiasco. Someone's been poking around.

My stomach bottoms out.

I look out at Grant. And I know right then, this is my fault. I waited too long to tell him. I turn off the timer for the cinnamon buns and pull them out of the oven, working through what this could mean. It's not good. I know that much.

Instead of calling Bea back, I walk outside and across the lawn, speaking before I've even approached him. "Have you been looking into my case? Asking questions?"

He turns from brushing Tawney, the smile quickly disappearing from his face. It's the way a realization takes over that stops me in my tracks.

"Dammit. What did you do?" I whisper. The repercussions of what this could mean—danger, relocating, leaving. My hands start shaking and my mouth runs dry.

He drops the brush and comes closer. "I messed up."

I take a step back.

"Before you told me everything . . ." He rubs at the back of his neck. "Baby, I knew you were tangled in something the second you mumbled Bea's name. When Ace confirmed that she was the one who brought you here, I eased up. But that night at Midnight Proof, when Waz said something about New York, it had me on edge. Guys like that are never up to anything good." He reaches for me, but I don't want him to hold me. I want him to talk, so I back away.

Dragging his hands through his hair, he releases a heavy

sigh. "I had Del do some digging. He has a lot of friends in the FBI and U.S. Marshall service in offices up north."

Shit. My eyes widen, almost not believing this. Why didn't I just tell him sooner? He was a fucking cop, of course he could have handled it!

I spin around and start walking toward my cottage. I need space and I need to call Bea.

As I hear him following me, something has my steps coming to a halt. "How would Waz . . ."

"I don't know. But Del didn't find anything about you. There was nothing that stood out. So he left it alone. And I waited for you to tell me when you were ready."

Oh god. There's no reason for Fiasco to be on anyone's radar unless a retired cop was looking into a woman who randomly showed up. I close my eyes. A roster of worry revs up within me. If I had only told him sooner, he wouldn't have tried to dig into it.

I only realize I'm basically running when he calls out to me, "Honey, wait!"

"Don't call me that right now." I hold up my phone. "You asked too many questions, to too many people, and it might have put me in danger, Grant. It might have put YOU in danger. Ace, Griz, Lincoln, the girls," I shout, my whole body shaking from the inside out. "Just asking has put *everyone* in danger." A sob lets loose as he steps closer, trying to hold me. There's too much emotion coursing through me to think about anything logically.

He rests his hands on my shoulders and then bends his knees so I'll look him in the eye. "Baby, tell me what happened?"

"You stopped calling me a liar. I told you everything.

But you know what?" I point between us, adding space as I keep stepping farther from him. "I've been the only one sharing things. You haven't told me a damn thing about you. About Fiona. How you and your family even know Bea Harper. I'm the one taking chances and trusting you. And what? For what?"

His expression reflects the stress and pain I'm feeling, and it pulls at my heart. I know he doesn't deserve all of this, but I have no one else to be angry at here. Julep comes barking up behind me, interrupting our stare-off. She knows something's wrong, but I'm too upset and spiraling to soothe her as I storm up toward my place.

"Fuck, Laney, stop!"

I stop on the top step of my porch and turn to look at him.

"Talk to me, honey. Please," he breathes out, his hands clasped together, resting on top of his head. "Tell me what's happened? Is that Bea?"

I nod, tilting my chin up and trying my hardest to stop it from quivering. "I need a minute." My eyes water as I look at him. "I don't know what any of it means, but I need to make a call."

I shut the door to my cottage and lean against it, sinking to the floor. Blowing out a slow breath, I swat away the tears that keep falling down my cheeks and call Bea.

She picks up before it even rings. "Laney, I've got two colleagues now who have asked me about a Colorado asset. And, if I've brought anyone from Manhattan into the program under the radar. This isn't good, kid. It's not just you I have to protect, you understand that?"

"I didn't know," I say, closing my eyes.

"Grant?"

"Yes. We got close and I should have told him sooner."

"It's just as much my fault. I should have given him the heads-up. I'm going to make my way down to you in the next few days."

There are plenty of other questions I should be asking, but there's only one I want to know the answer to. "Am I going to have to leave?"

She stays quiet for too long. "I promised you that I'd keep you safe. And I promised Ace that this wouldn't come anywhere near him or his family. I plan to keep my promises, Laney."

And the only thing I'm thinking about is that I promised Grant I'd stay.

CHAPTER 37

GRANT

"I NEED SOMETHING FROM YOU," I say to Griz as I stalk up their front porch.

He studies me. I feel like a wreck and I must look like it too, because he hesitantly asks, "You okay?"

"You want the truth, or will you please just get me what I want?" My tone is gruff, but I don't have it in me to sugarcoat anything right now.

Ace comes out the front door. "Grant, you alright?"

I drag my hands from my forehead and back to the nape of my neck. "I messed up."

"Well, that's fucking obvious," Griz chimes in.

Ace points to him. "Not helping."

"If I asked you not to ask questions, can you respect that?"

Ace nods as Griz folds his arms over his chest. *Good enough.*

"How quickly can we move some money around so I

can cash out of my share of the business?" I avoid making eye contact with Griz when he grunts and mumbles something that sounds like disapproval. I don't want to see what this question does to him. I know it's a panicked move, but I have to know my options. If Laney needs to move quickly, then I'll know what I'm working with.

I'm not letting her leave alone. I'm going with her.

Ace stares at me, working out what's going on with me in his head. "A few days—probably. Are you talking about cash, or can we move to offshore accounts?"

"You tell me. The numbers from the last quarterly meeting put our gross at just over 1.2 billion. I know that's not a complete split of assets if you include the properties, but I'll leave that alone."

Ace puts his hands in his pockets. "You're sure about this?"

I tilt my head back, taking in the slotted wood that lines the porch ceiling. I helped him design that. "There isn't much I've been sure about in my life. But this . . ." I look my older brother in the eye and quietly plead for him to see how much I mean it. "This is the only thing I'm sure about. What I'm asking here is a precaution. Or maybe it's inevitable, but I'm not clear on that part just yet."

Ace thumbs over his phone, working out what I'm asking. "We'll make it work. I'll get it as even of a split as I can. Any increases later, we'll put aside just in case."

"You don't need to do that. If I'm cashing out, I'm selling you my cut."

"Your last name is Foxx, which means you have a third of everything. Always," Ace says with a finality in his tone. "And then we'll figure it out again when Griz decides to finally lose his faculties or head to that deserted island I have set up for him."

Griz barks back, "Hadn't realized I was raising such assholes. The two of you, shit . . ."

It's hard not to laugh at them, always at each other's throats, but one would be lost without the other. It doesn't sit lightly with me what I'm leaving behind by choosing Laney.

The consistent breeze that's moved around the humidity today is the only reprieve to the heaviness of this moment. I fix my attention on Griz and hand him a note. I don't want to discuss it with my brothers ahead of time. I need this to be mine and Laney's first before anyone else can interject. "That's only for you to see. But it would mean a lot to me."

He unfolds the note and reads it, his eyes watering as he looks up, giving me a curt nod. His thick mustache covers his pursed lips. "She would have wanted her to have it." Clapping his hand over my shoulder, he squeezes.

Lincoln comes out the front door, almost out of breath. "Those maniacs just fell asleep. It's past *my* bedtime, for fuck's sake." But that's where he clips his words. He looks at me, and then down at Griz's hand. "What did I miss?"

An unspoken understanding passes between us. Instead of a thousand questions, I'm sure he wants to ask, Lincoln comes to my side and only asks one: "Does she love you back?"

She hasn't said the words, but I feel it. Even despite what my digging into her past may have done, the way Laney looks at me was her tell. Biting back the emotions creeping up my throat, I give him another nod yes. "She's really fucking pissed off at me right now, but yeah, she does."

But it's Ace who surprises me. "Then you go where she goes."

Lincoln grips my other shoulder as Ace takes a step forward and does the same to his. "No matter what."

"Doesn't matter where you are," Griz says as he looks around at each of us, "you're my bourbon boys. And I'm fuckin' proud."

A CREAK of the floorboards wakes me, and I know right away that it's not Julep. The movements are too quiet for her. The bed dips to my front and I feel Laney settle in next to me.

I open my eyes and slowly blink away the haze as she runs her fingers through the side of my hair. Neither one of us says anything. Just looks at the other. The way her fingers touch my neck feels so good. I knew if she didn't find her way to me tonight that I would be back on her porch by the time dawn broke in the morning. I waited up for her as long as I could. I sat on that porch past midnight, but she didn't come back out. I could see her moving around inside, blaring music, working through what was likely going to happen next. But she made it clear she wanted space. I gave her as much as I could. And I made plans.

GRANT

I'm right here when you're ready.

Don't shut me out, baby.

She didn't answer. I sat and waited until I couldn't keep my eyes open any longer.

I close my eyes as she drags her fingernails along my hairline. I know there needs to be words between us. Explanations and truths. But I'm content to feel this. Her warmth, her body so close. As her lips brush mine softly, I wrap my arm around her and pull her against me. "Tell me what's going on," I whisper, pinching my eyes closed.

She starts to say, "I'm sorry—"

"Don't." I open my eyes and find her pretty blues staring back at me. "Don't do that. You don't apologize here. I messed up. I was so hung up on what you weren't telling me that I didn't think about setting off some alarms. I didn't think it through."

I'm not a cop anymore, but I should know better.

She stretches her body, and her fingers press against mine. I search her eyes for understanding, or maybe forgiveness. "You left things out about your past, but the truth is, I was looking for a reason not to trust you." With a rough swallow, I take a second before continuing. "A reason why I shouldn't want you." I reach my hand out, curling a piece of hair behind her ear. My thumb trails the movement and draws a soft line across her jaw. "Then none of that mattered."

Her eyes are blurry, my voice raw with emotion.

Leaning forward, she kisses my lips, and I can feel every emotion within it. I don't want her going anywhere. I know that's what she's saying here. That she can't stay. But there isn't a single part of me that will hear it. To feel this deeply for her, to want something so badly, and then to let her walk away? It isn't going to happen unless that's what she wants.

When she pulls away slowly, eyes on mine again, I bring her palm to my mouth and kiss it lightly. "I'm in love with you."

She lets out a small gasping exhale as her face squints up hearing those words. Tears track across the bridge of her nose.

I kiss her palm again and soften my voice. "I'm pretty sure I started falling for you the moment you flipped me off." I try to smile, but it's labored. My chest is heavy and adrenaline pumps through me, making my hands shake as I tell this beautiful woman exactly who she is to me. "But I am, honey. I'm so fucking in love with you. This is it for me."

Chapter 38

LANEY

I've felt it. Hell, I've felt it for a while now. I haven't even been in Fiasco for all that long, but holy shit do I feel it with this man. Hearing that declaration as he draws small circles along my wrist, I blow out a shaky breath. I want to believe it, because I feel it too. "You're in love with me?"

"You have to know that. And I guess if you didn't, then I wasn't clear. I love you, Laney Young." He kisses my lips, stealing any words from me that could outweigh his. "A little more every day."

His thumb rubs across my lips, and I inch closer as I run my fingers up his chest and over the place that's beating so fast. All for me. "This is the part where you're not supposed to leave me hanging."

"Shaw," I tell him, smiling at the curiosity dancing in his eyes.

His thumb slows its movement.

"Laney Shaw. You need to say, I love you, Laney Shaw."

His mustache quirks. "You first."

With a smile and an exhale, I go first. "I'm in love with you too, cowboy."

With a smirk at hearing his nickname, he moves my hair away from my shoulder. His touch always feels possessive and strong, but right now, it feels like appreciation. Grant cups the back of my neck, driving his fingers into my hair. "I love you, Laney Shaw." And then he erases any space left between us. When his lips meet mine, it's as if we're making a promise—sealing the words with the pull that exists between us. His tongue licks along the seam of my lips and rolls with mine, setting a deep warmth in my core that flickers out across my skin. A small groan escapes his lips as we both take a breath. And anything that felt soft or simple turns into a desire to express with our bodies the way we feel for the other. His fingers sink deeper into my hair and pull tighter, shifting me on top so that I'm straddling his cock. The hard length of him pressed up against me is only separated by a few thin layers.

I sit up, and as his eyes rove along the curves of my body, it feels like the most wicked game of foreplay. Rolling my hips forward, I peel my tank off. He folds one arm behind his head and the other he reaches up, drawing a line from my navel to between my breasts. The kind of confidence I've found just by the way this man looks at me is something that I hadn't expected. I tilt my head back as he continues moving his hand along the same path to my neck.

The grit of his voice drags along my skin when he says, "You're so beautiful like this—trying to take what you need. That's my girl." Craving the friction, I roll my hips again. I hold his wrist and bring his fingers to my mouth, kissing the rough pads.

"That's it, honey. Eyes on me."

I flick them with my tongue, wetting them and guiding them around my lips. I keep my eyes on his and pull them in my mouth. His cock jumps at that, and I can't keep myself from smirking at the response.

"He wants a turn," he laughs.

I yelp out laughing as he quickly flips us both over, my back hitting the mattress and Grant hovering over me. When he settles between my legs, my smile falters and the mood moves back to the intensity from just a few moments ago.

My eyes water as I gaze up at him, the low, gravelly whisper only making them blurrier. "Don't look at me like that."

"I like looking at you. You're very handsome, you know." I smile, trying to lighten the moment to keep him from seeing how I'm cataloging everything. The weight of him. The way he breathes in, smelling my hair. The scruff of his beard as it tickles me just right. How his eyes soften when they're looking at me.

"Don't look at me like you need to remember. I'm yours, honey." I search his eyes for more, the caveat or the exception. But it doesn't come. It's a calm, quiet promise. An offering. He's mine, if I want him. And god, do I want him. To keep him. To stay. To love him.

He places a brief kiss on my lips first, then my forehead, before he buries himself in my neck. His forearms hold him above me just enough and nestled between my legs. I want him. In every single way, I want him.

"Make love to me."

The request is instantly answered as his teeth drag along my shoulder. He kneels back, pulling my legs up to rest on his shoulders. Tucking his fingers in the waistband of my pajama shorts, he rolls them off as he turns his head to kiss my ankle. Once he moves my legs back down, he spreads my knees wide, his thumb gliding up and down my pussy. He doesn't say anything, only watches his thumb play from my pussy to clit and back as quiet moans leave my lips. He kneels up and pulls down the boxer briefs that he'd worn to bed, his thick and hard cock showing exactly what it wants.

Same. I let a whimper escape.

He runs his thumb through me again—one, two, three, strokes before he leans forward and swipes that thumb across my lips, drawing my arousal around them. Hovering above me, he licks my mouth, kissing the wet away. "Better than bourbon."

I smile against his lips. Before I can say anything, his cock rubs where his thumb had, hitting my clit at just the right pace and pressure to pull the gasp from me. When he kneels back again, he starts to bury himself into me and swipes in small, measured strokes along my clit.

"Grant . . ." I breathe out.

Like I've ignited something, he wraps his arms around me and lifts me up to him, kissing me. A punishing kiss with lips and tongues lashing and consuming as I sit against him, rolling my hips and pulling him into me deeper with every thrust of his hips. The sweat that's slicked our bodies and the way he moans has my orgasm waiting patiently to let go.

"Laney . . . fuck."

"I know," I exhale. His arms stay around me tight as I hold on to him, burying my face in his neck, and running my lips from his, down his neck, and along his shoulder.

"You feel so good, so perfect." When he moans against my neck, he leans back enough to find my lips. His kiss can barely finish as his mouth opens, holding me tighter against him, grinding into me so deep, brushing that spot within me that has me trembling. "I'm going to come, baby."

I hold him tighter, not letting him move back and chasing my own orgasm. "Come."

He tips his head back to make sure he understands the demand.

So I make it clear. I want him to own every part of me. "With me."

He tilts his hips just right so that he grinds against my clit, and that's all I need. The last moment before I fall completely, he says, "If you want me to pull out, baby, you have to tell me now."

I shake my head no as I let him fuck me faster.

"Oh fuck, come now," I moan, just before I'm screaming.

His hand wraps around my hair and he holds me flush to him, and he releases a groan from deep in his chest. The sound of his pleasure is the final piece that makes my vision blur. My whole body tenses and clenches and starts to pulsate just as he spills into me. It's a succession of heavy breathing and sweat. Filth and heat. Lust and a love that feels like it radiates throughout my entire body. Across every inch of real estate on my skin.

When he falls to the side, collapsing onto the mattress, he takes me with him. We're a tangle of legs and covers as we hold each other and come down from everything we just shared.

Minutes tick by before either of us move. And I can feel him dripping out of me.

I turn my head to look at him. His eyes are closed and a small smile rests on his lips. I study his profile from the square jawline to the prominent slope of his nose. Separately, they would be severe and intimidating, but with his eyes and the way his lips meet the hair of his scruff, he's beautiful.

"You're looking at me and fucking me like it's goodbye."

How can he know me so well? "I'm telling you I love you too—"

His eyes open and he smiles big and wide, but the smile falters when he sees the tears brimming in my eyes and the way I can't smile at what I'm about to say to him. "But?"

"But I don't know if I can stay, cowboy. I can't put anyone in your family in any kind of danger. I can't risk you —" I swallow the cry that wants to come out with that confession.

He leans up, cupping my face. "Then marry me."

"What?" I search his eyes, because I didn't expect those words to come out of his mouth.

"Marry me. If you need to leave, they'll allow me to come with you if we're married."

I can't hide the smile and nervous laugh it pulls out of me. "That's crazy. Grant. We've just started . . ." My eyebrows pinch closer as I think about what he's really saying. Without even knowing the details, this man is suggesting we get married. "Do you even want to be married?"

"To you? Yes." He says it so confidently, like this isn't a rushed decision or that it's been barely any time since I've even known him.

"But your life is here. Your family. We've only known each other for—"

He tips my chin up to look at him, halting my words. "My family will always be my family. No matter where I am, I love them and they love me. But you're wrong about my life, honey. I've been treading water. Wasting time trying to keep people away. But I've only just started living again." He wipes the tear that's fallen down the side of my nose. "This woman who has no filter and calls me cowboy is the person I want to do life with. I don't need more time to tell me something I already know."

With a fluttering belly, I sit up and watch as his eyes dance between mine, searching for what I'm thinking. For what I'm going to say.

He takes a deep breath as he pushes my hair away from my shoulder. "It started with Griz's mom. Then it happened to his first wife, and then again with my nana." He clears his throat. "Then my parents." He runs his fingers along the top of my hand. "Fiasco loves saying shit behind people's backs without thinking about how it hurts. We've been hearing it since we were kids: 'The Foxx boys are cursed.' And I never put much weight on it until I lost Fiona. And then when Lincoln lost Olivia."

I can see and feel how much this has gutted and haunted him. It's beyond comprehension how he lost so many people he loved. And then to think it's somehow his fault? I wrap my fingers around his.

"I had known Fiona since we were kids. We went through school, and eventually, the academy together. I was a year ahead of her, but she was eager to fill Del's shoes."

"Is Del her dad?"

He nods. "And my best friend once I started working for the Fiasco PD. Things between Fi and me, it wasn't some long-time crush. It started as friends with benefits. Getting drunk and hooking up. And somewhere along the way, I fell for her." He smiles. "She didn't want to tell anyone about us. I did, but I knew things for her were harder. She was one of six women in the department. And she was respected; Del made sure of that." He clears his throat. "Del was my superior officer, and it felt like I was lying to him."

As he rubs at the back of his neck, I can tell how hard this is for him, and it makes me wonder if he's ever said any of this out loud.

"The morning I told her I loved her was the same night that she went on a call and"—he clears his throat again—"it wasn't good intel, but she went. The second I heard dispatch, I knew something didn't feel right. I had this gut feeling; told her to stand down. And I couldn't get there." His eyes water, and I watch as he battles with letting them fall as he tells me. "I couldn't get there fast enough to back her up." He holds my hand tighter. "After that, I couldn't do the job anymore. I had failed her and going there every day reminded me that when someone really needed my help, someone I loved, I didn't get there in time." He covers his eyes with his free hand, but as soon as he does, I move in and wrap my arms around him. My heart breaks for him and this guilt he carries.

Tilting his head down, his forehead rests on my shoulder. "And a year later, Liv left us. I put my grief aside to be there for Linc and my nieces, but I didn't want to feel anything after that. I don't think I felt anything for years. I worked, worked out my shit on the heavy bag, and made my bourbon. That was it."

I lean back so he'll look at me. I need him to see me when I tell him this. When his eyes meet mine, I wipe at the stray tear that reaches his lips. "I. Am. Lucky."

He searches my eyes for a beat.

"Ask me why I'm lucky, cowboy." I smile, and my whole body warms at the look in his eyes.

A small smile touches the corner of his lips. "Why are you lucky, baby?"

"Because you love me."

His eyes pinch closed and his nose scrunches as he hears me say it.

"Because I get to love you. And I get to marry you."

His hands frame my face as his eyes dance with mine. "Yeah?"

"Yeah." I nod frantically, a tear trailing down my cheek.

My hands cover his, that frame my face. When his lips find mine, it feels like more than just kissing the man I love. It feels like coming home. This complex and caring man who hid behind so much loss in fear of it being the only option for him.

I tip my head back, thinking about something he'd said that I hadn't put together until right now. "What do you mean, *made your bourbon*?"

CHAPTER 39

GRANT

"I REALLY FEEL like I could have ridden my own horse," she says as she leans in, her back to my front. And fuck, does it feel good to have her this close. I wanted to take her out here when she asked last night about my bourbon, but I had a plan. And we needed daylight.

"You could have, but I like you here." I nuzzle into her neck.

"This is where you go so early in the mornings?" I look around at the open landscape and listen to the way the buzzing of cicadas keeps the low hum of the morning as Tawney snorts at the bluegrass pollen that's been kicked up from the heavier winds from the past few days.

"Not every day, but at least once every week or two, I come out this far."

Before she sees it, she can hear it. "What's that—?"

When we crest the small hill we've been climbing, her breath catches. And I felt the same the first time I came out here with Griz. This is by far my favorite place in Fiasco. Beyond the distillery or the stables. This place feels big and important. It always has.

Cascading water rushes and tumbles thirty feet down its ledge, splashing across rocks and a deep pool at its end. The falls are more than a hundred feet wide, making the simplest thing, water, appear like an animated curtain of white haze and fine mist.

It's not as intense this time of year, with not as much rainfall or snow to keep the river moving, but it still roars. And it's a helluva sight.

Julep comes barking up behind us. She ran off chasing a rabbit a few miles back, which tends to be her favorite game whenever we're out here. I've only had to search for her once, when she found a burrow of bunnies and wouldn't leave. And just like those damn rabbits, she found something she loves in Laney too. My dog knew, even before I realized. I let out a short whistle. "Jules. Keep up, girl." There was no way she was staying behind with both of us heading out so early. And I want her with us for this anyway.

The sound of Laney laughing as Jules shoots by has me smiling back.

"This is a good look on you."

I tilt my head back to look at her turn over her shoulder. "Whatever it is you're about to show me, you're excited about it."

"Damn right, I am." I lean one leg down and hoist it over Tawney's backside, hitting the tall grass. I hadn't planned to ask her to marry me last night. I had planned on doing it here. Showing her a part of me, and then asking if she'd like to skip to the good part. Start our life now, no matter where it ends up. Whether or not we could stay or had to leave. When I made the decision that I wanted forever with her, I needed to know she'd want the same.

I reach up and offer my hand, but she's stubborn and kicks her leg over, holding on to the pommel and letting out a yelp as her feet hit the ground. She raises her hands up like she just landed a trick in gymnastics.

"Graceful."

"Natural talent," she jokes back.

I pull out my phone, looking at the time, then grab her hand. Still plenty of time to show her what I've spent so much of my time doing over the past handful of years. "C'mon."

"Is the water going to be freezing without any sun right now?"

I keep us moving alongside the falls. "We're not going in. We're going behind."

She laughs, but then her brow furrows. "What?"

I keep pulling her forward and Julep runs ahead. The pathway is graded, lined with tracks, and a simple climb. It's just not the easiest to find. I wanted it that way. When we come up along the falling water, the mist dances around us as if it were a wall of its own and not moisture in motion. She peers over the side. "How deep is that?"

I pull her shoulder back. "Ace and Lincoln used to run and dive in closer to where Tawney is tied up. So deep enough for that."

"You didn't go in with them?"

I swallow and look back out at the water falling into the deep pool below. I love it here, the sound of roaring water, the way the field turns into something completely else around this corner. "I tried once. Ended up belly flopping because I didn't like how it felt to fall."

She looks out over the rushing water. "How did it feel?"

"Like I didn't have control of what was going to happen to me."

"There." And with one flick, the string lights that have been placed along the crevices of the rock wall, inside the waterfall's cave, kick on and illuminate.

Her eyes dance around the space as she slowly walks in. A small workbench with just a few of the tools I need when I'm out here—gloves, oak spires, bungs, and a whiskey thief. But it's when she steps in a few feet farther, she looks back at me.

"Your bourbon?"

I smile at how that sounds. "My bourbon."

Her lips part as she takes in the racks of barrels stacked on either side, four barrels high and deep enough that she needs to walk a bit farther to see where it ends.

"I came out here when I was about thirteen or fourteen with Griz. Told me if I was smart that I'd do well to remember places that made me feel a certain way. I don't know why that stuck with me, but it did. Something so obscure, my grandfather said to me years ago." I look around the cool, damp space. "Bourbon's beauty is in the way it ages. It's one of the few things that people appreciate more as it gets older. But aside from that, Kentucky bourbon does so well because—"

"Because of the extreme weather changes," she finishes with a wink. "And the water." That day in the cooperage when I teased her about what was in the water here, comes rushing back to my memory.

"That's my girl." I love that she knows that. Laney doesn't just know the bare basics anymore. I watch and listen to her when she pours at the end of tours; she has opinions about flavors and has learned the science that Lincoln is so hell bent on teaching. It's just another turn-on.

I grab the gloves, along with the screwdriver and mallet. "I needed something in order to stay busy and out of my head." I clear my throat, not proud of how I was after I left the police department.

"So you made bourbon."

"So I made bourbon."

I crouch down to the bottom row a few feet ahead of her. "I wanted to turn this grief I had into something. A way to remember, but also to forget for a while, if that makes sense."

She runs her hand along my arm. "It does."

"I've only ever been good at a few things." I nod to the barrel I've just opened. "And knowing good bourbon is at the top of that list. I don't have any plans for it. Nobody knows about it—not even my brothers."

"What?" She scoffs at me, eyes wide, disbelief evident in her voice. "What do you mean, they don't know about this?"

I dip the long stopper into the open slot. "This was for me. And now . . ." I look down the row and see all the barrels. The sweat and time it took to make this, bringing it out here and giving it a place to change into something better, makes me proud. "Now it's theirs if they want it. I don't have a need for it anymore."

"You can't just leave all this. I can't even imagine what it took to get all of it out here. And the time to get the mash right."

My mouth ticks up. "Listen to you using the proper language."

With her hand slung on her hip, she says, "I've been living, breathing, and sleeping with Foxx Bourbon. I know what I'm talking about." She smirks at me.

"It was fucking sexy, that's what it was. C'mere," I say, reaching out for her. She leans down to where I'm kneeling. My knees kill me every second of it, but damn, do I love kissing this woman. Her soft lips drink mine, and if I'm not careful, I'll end up fucking her right here. I pull back and focus back on what I was doing. Holding up the long whiskey thief and looking at the color—a deep amber in this row. "Taste."

"The last time you and I fed each other bourbon, we ended up very naked."

I smile at the memory. "Open," I demand, holding the long tube of bourbon above her.

Her mouth opens, and I release a dram into it. Her eyes meet mine as she swallows it down slowly, giving me a little moan of approval. "It has a sweet finish. I like this."

I've been waiting to bottle it. And even if it weren't ready, I'd be forced to just so I could take some of it with me. But as I take a taste and it coats my tongue, I know this is good bourbon. Hell, with a little longer in these barrels, some of it could be great bourbon.

"You're really just going to leave it?" Lips pursing, she

looks around the damp space. The roar of the falls and the generator running have her practically shouting it from the distance she's walked. "I don't understand how you even got it all here."

"ATV and a small trailer that hooks to the back. I only made small batches. And then, once I got here, I put down rails and rolled 'em up."

"So what happens to it all?"

"Might be nice to leave it. Give it to my little flowers for when they inherit some of this."

She smiles up at me, looping her arms around my neck. I take my gloves off as I pull her closer. "You're a good uncle. Brother. Grandson. You're a good man, Grant Foxx."

"I have my moments," I joke.

But she shakes her head. "How could you just leave?" Her eyebrows pinch together, looking more serious by the second. "You can't want to leave."

I kiss her. "I want to be with you. It's that simple. Nobody asked me to choose, but it's you, baby. You're what I've been waiting on. Brave. Smart." I kiss her lips again. "Fiery and sweet. And what I want."

I push the curtain of strawberry blonde waves behind her shoulder. "I'm going to take two bottles and we'll drink them when I'm missing home. How's that?"

She rests her head on my bicep, looking up, and it's the first time in a long time that I've felt excited about something new. For an unknown.

"It's not true, you know?"

I search her eyes for what she's asking.

"You're good at more than just a few things, Grant."

She runs the tips of her fingers along my hairline, and I lean into her touch.

Julep's bark echoes throughout the cave. I lean in and brush my lips along hers. "Time for us to go."

She doesn't ask any questions, just smiles big and wide at my dog, scratching her behind her ears. It hits the right spot when I see Julep's back leg start to thump at her belly. Her coat is muddy and damp from the morning, but Laney couldn't care less; she gives Jules all her attention.

"It's beautiful here." She sets her hand on her forehead, visoring the sun that's high in the sky, reflecting off the water. When we make our way back to the horse, I swap the bottles in my hands for the shoebox-sized wooden box I stored in the Tawney's saddle bag.

I hand the box to her. "I hadn't realized I was even doing it until I had all these things that—" I cut myself off. "Open it."

Her eyes bounce from the box back to me as she drags her fingers across the sanded and glossed wood top. "Did you make this?"

I give her a fast nod, pushing my hands into my back pockets. "Used some of the imperfect oak staves that didn't make the cut for barrels. Took a while to find the right fits. But it still came together pretty nicely."

As she sits down in the overgrown grass, the wildflowers bend around her to make space. She rests the box on her legs as she pulls out stalks of dried chamomile and purple coneflower—the same ones she wove in her hair with Lark and Lily. A few of the crystals that had been stuck to her sheer shirt the night of Ace's birthday at Midnight Proof. "Some of those ended up in my boot and pocket." I smile.

The smirk that ghosts her lips lets me know that she remembers exactly why those would have haphazardly ended up in god knows where. She holds up the fishing lure that she used the morning Griz and I took her fly fishing.

But it's when she pulls out the Fiasco, Kentucky magnet, her eyes fly up to mine. I remembered what she had said about her dad and her keepsakes. Hell, I remembered everything she said. I was starting to keep stock of her different smiles and how all of her 'tells' weren't tells at all, but just mannerisms and habits that I hadn't memorized yet. I want to learn all of them.

"You're making new memories here." I tip my head. "You needed a new memory box." And the way her face squints as she tries to hold back tears, the same way she did last night, has me clearing the same emotions from my throat. Her eyes meet mine, blurry and brimming with so much that I know she wants to say, but I look back down at the box, urging her to keep going. There's one more thing in there. It was why I brought her out here today.

I know the moment she sees it. Her lips pop open just enough that I can tell she didn't expect it. She holds up a thin gold band with a simple round diamond. It might not fit perfectly, but we'll figure it out.

"That was my nana's ring. I asked Griz if he wouldn't mind if you had it. A little bit of my family with us wherever we end up." I kneel this time, on one knee, the way I would have planned if I had more time. "I love you, Laney. I want you to be mine the same way that I'll be yours. I promise that I'll make you proud to wear that ring. The same way I promise to be your family, to keep you safe, and to keep loving you a little more every day."

Tears flow down her cheeks, and she lets out a small sob as she throws her arms around my shoulders. "A little more. Every day," she says softly. "You'll be safe with me too, cowboy."

Wrapping my arms around her middle, I lift her feet off the ground. I stare at the blue in her eyes as they pick up the light from the sun. I swallow down the lingering fear that history will repeat itself. I won't let it ruin the life that I want. I've done that for long enough. I think about the night on the dance floor and when I asked her what kind of woman she was. And what it felt like to finally have her. I've never wanted anyone as badly as I want her.

"Do you remember when I asked you what you liked?"

"Yes," she whispers, her lips lingering against mine for a brief moment.

I run my lips down the side of her neck. "Show me."

She leans back to look at me with a smirk playing on her lips. She shimmies out of my arms. Then, taking a small step back, she glances around the open field. I'm buzzing with want for her and the anticipation of what she's going to do. What she'll say. When her eyes come back to me, she gazes down the length of my body.

"Take off your shirt."

I don't question it. I grab behind my neck, pulling the shirt over my head.

Her eyes dance around my tattoos, across my chest, and down my stomach.

"Now the belt."

I keep my eyes on hers as she unbuttons her shorts and works them down her thighs. She starts backing away as I unbuckle my belt. With a good ten feet between us, she says, "Now your jeans." She sheds the Fiasco Bourbon t-shirt with the sleeves cut off that she snagged from my closet this morning, leaving her in a barely-there pair of underwear and a cropped white tank.

She keeps walking, but when I look behind her, I realize what she's doing. "Where you going, Laney?"

"Feel like fallin', cowboy?"

With only a pair of black boxer briefs on, I rush after her. There's not a day I've been with her that I haven't been pushed out of my comfort zone, but this catches me off guard. "Don't!"

And instead of ignoring it, and jumping anyway, she stops right along the edge of the steep riverbank to smile up at me. "Fall with me, Grant."

I take her lips between mine in a punishing, almost pleading kiss. The adrenaline of nerves and excitement are buzzing through me even louder than the vibration from the waterfall beneath my bare feet. I'm ready. "Alright, baby, hold on nice and tight."

She does. It's a short running start before we go over the edge of the cliff and fall. It's only a couple of seconds with Laney in my arms before we plunge into the cool water below.

It's the same spot that my brothers jumped off when we were kids. It always looked so high. So much farther than the fall.

I let go of her so she can surface as quickly as she needs. When I come up for breath, she's already there waiting for me with a bright smile. I shake my head to get my hair out of my face and yell out, "Wahooo!" The echo off the water and the surrounding earth bounces the sound right back at us.

We're laughing as we swim toward each other, my hands finding her hips as her legs and arms wrap around me as soon as we're close enough.

I can't remember a time, a day, a moment when the only thing I felt was good. There's not a single thing that's been expected when it comes to this woman, and I smile as I think about the kind of life that'll be.

CHAPTER 40

LANEY

"LANEY!"

"Laney!" Lily yells over Lark as they both come running toward the stables. "Laney, we made you the most perfect flowers for your hair."

They hold up a piece of lace with the wildflowers from Grant's yard woven throughout. "Will you wear them?" Lark asks, so much calmer than her younger sister.

Lily bounces in her shoes. "Please? Please?"

"So I guess Griz told you, then?"

"That you're marrying Uncle Grant? Yes. What took you so long? He got back forever ago."

I meet Grant's eyes and smile, thinking about how we just spent our time celebrating each other. Forgetting what would be waiting here for us.

"Of course I'll wear these." I open my mouth, pretending to be shocked, but I am absolutely impressed.

"The lace was our grandma's from her wedding. And

Dad said that our mama wore it at theirs, so you have to have it now."

It was the first time I heard either of them mention their mother, and the fact that they wanted to share this piece with me hit me right in the chest. *How am I supposed to leave this? Leave them?*

Griz wraps me in a hug. "If I was forty years younger . . ."

Grant laughs out, "Hands off, Griz."

He whispers to me before he lets me go, "Welcome to the family, darlin'." I swallow down the emotions that have been so intense today. Joining this family, and knowing I won't be here to enjoy them.

Hadley walks up behind the girls and plows into me, wrapping her arms around my waist. "You bagged a Foxx, you badass!"

I can't help but bark out a laugh as I scrunch up my nose. "I know."

"I get it, Grant. I want to keep her too." She smirks at him as he comes up behind me and kisses the side of my head first, and then my lips. Leaning into Hadley, he says, "Mine." Nothing else, just mine.

He scoops up Lily, and she starts giggling as they walk toward the main house. I hear him ask her, "You know I love you, my little flower?"

Hadley loops her arm with mine. "Those are fighting words, I hope he knows that."

"Oh, he knows." It feels so good—this much love between so many people.

I wrap my arm around Lark. "Will you help me tie this pretty lace into my hair?"

She smiles so brightly, so much more mature than I would have imagined a ten-year-old would be. "Are you leaving?"

"What makes you think I'm leaving?"

When we walk along the side of the house and come around to the back patio, she says, "That lady who's fighting with Uncle Ace said she came for you."

When I look up, I see Agent Bea Harper, and my stomach sinks, all the air in my lungs rushing out. She's talking with her hands moving a mile a minute at Ace. As we get closer, she notices Grant approaching ahead of me with Lily in his arms. She stops her tirade and puts her hands on her hips, locking eyes with me next. She's not happy.

"Lark, can your uncles and I have a few minutes out here?"

But it's Hadley who answers. "C'mon, girls," she sing-songs as she steers them inside.

"Bea," Grant says with a nod. But then he walks closer to me, standing tall as he intertwines his fingers with mine. A protector I hadn't realized I wanted.

She zeroes in on me, looking down at my left hand, staring at the gold band that slid onto it just a little while ago.

"You married her?" Bea asks, looking at Grant.

He looks at me first and smiles, calmly answering, "Not yet, but I will."

Glancing at me for a beat, she then shifts her glance to Ace, like somehow this is his fault or he should have stopped it.

"Don't look at me, Bea." He holds up his hands. "I just found out too."

Ace smiles at Grant, and then winks at me.

When my attention settles back to Bea, there's something I haven't figured out. Her relationship with the Foxx family. "How do you know each other? I don't understand—"

Grant tilts his chin up higher, like he's preparing for pushback. He squeezes my hand. "You want to take that one, Bea?"

It's not lost on me the way the mood shifts, transferring the dynamic from frustration on Bea's part to a secret that seems like I'm the only person who doesn't know. She pulls out her silver case of cloves and shoves one in between her lips as she searches her suit jacket pocket for her lighter.

Lincoln wanders our way with Griz. All the Foxx men are here to listen to the truth.

Grant takes a small step closer to me, filling the silence. "What I still can't figure out is why here? Why bring her here, Bea?" He looks down at me and kisses the hand he's been holding. "I'm happy for it, but I don't get it. You would never get clearance on this if it was a legitimate WITSEC placement."

She lights her clove, pulling in deep, and taps her finger to her mouth.

"I'm waiting," Grant pushes.

Only once she's blown out a big plume of smoke that seems to linger in the midday humidity does she answer. "Because I needed a place where she would be safe."

Grant grits his teeth. "But why here? There are plenty

of places you could have gone. Why Fiasco?" He points to the ground. "Why here?"

She barely lets him finish when she shouts at him, "Because I owe her!"

I look around her face for what she could mean. *Owe her. Owe me?*

Lincoln chimes in, "What do you me—"

Her hand flies up, then drops to her side. "Because she stopped the person who killed Fiona."

My heart just about stops, and Grant tenses beside me. *That can't be right.*

"Because she came face to face with a goddamn monster. The monster who took my daughter's life."

My mind reels at what she's saying. It takes me a minute to really understand it. It's the same reaction coming from the men.

"She saved a victim. Ran right toward danger, pulled a damn fire alarm, and then gave a closed testimony that would have put him away."

Grant asks, "What do you mean, would have?"

I let go of his hand, feeling antsy as I work all of this out. "You're Fiona's mom?"

Grant mumbles, "Barely."

"Oh, fuck you, Grant. Don't pretend like you have any clue about what kind of relationship I had with my daughter," she says, stomping out her clove.

"Had more than clues, Bea," he barks back at her.

She closes her eyes for a second, trying to keep this from turning into an argument. "I listened to my gut. I'd been profiling Fiona's killer for years. I knew, just like you, Grant, that it wasn't some meth head in the wrong place, at the wrong time. Not with that kind of knife precision. And that piece of her that had been shredded from her back . . ." She shakes her head. "There was *nothing* she would have crawled through that would have caused that."

None of us say a word, all listening intently, knowing she has more to say.

"When I caught wind of a serial up in New York who had kept women and then saved parts, something in my gut said to look. Dig." She swallows. "So I did." She tips her chin up, attempting to keep any emotions from escaping. "There were souvenirs he kept. And he'd had a piece of skin that DNA-matched Fiona." She pulls in another breath of smoke. "She's here because he didn't have a name. No fingerprints? Fine. There are plenty of psychopaths that burn or cut them off." She pinches the bridge of her nose. "But there was no history. No digital footprint. No family or next of kin that NYPD or FBI could figure out. They didn't see it, but I did. I've been a U.S. Marshall for longer than I've been anything else. I knew in my gut, he was WITSEC."

Grant rubs the back of his neck, head shaking in disbelief. "You're telling me that the guy Laney had to enter witness protection for is an asset in fucking witness protection?"

Bea shifts her eyes around at the audience she's got, but she must realize even if she asked for this to be private, it would end up being discussed between these four men. "There have been a limited number of assets that have gone missing in the program over the years. Most of the time, it's folks that want to go back to their old lives and then end up disappearing—whatever they had been running from most likely caught up to them. But when I knew where to look, it wasn't too hard to start connecting the pieces."

Griz sits in one of the rocking chairs while Lincoln takes a seat on the stairs that lead to this stretch of patio. But both Grant and Ace stand, squared off and arms crossed now, waiting to hear the rest of it.

"He was placed in Montgomery, originally. About twenty miles from here. That was before I was leading any teams or a main point of contact. This one was smart. He knew what he was doing when he turned into state's evidence. He was the bookkeeper for crime families in both New York and Chicago. He was calculated. But I don't think they knew about his"—she clears her throat—"extracurriculars. So he snitched and made himself invincible for it. He helped put away a lot of people. Testified about what funds were being used for, where they went, and from whom they came. It was one of the largest series of organized crime arrests in decades. Long story short, when the Attorney General has that kind of history-making arrests that would collapse crime families, there's not going to be loose ends to reverse it. When he was arrested in that storage facility and there were witnesses to put him away, it gave those connected crime families ammunition to appeal, and potentially overturn."

"Attorney General wasn't going to let that happen, were they?" Griz asks.

"No." She stares at Grant for a beat, trying to hold in all the emotion this must be digging up. "We protected him. And they're still doing it too."

With a heavy exhale, Ace asks, "Now what, Bea?"

"Does Del know?" Grant interrupts.

"Not yet. I need to get her somewhere safe."

Lincoln holds up his hand. "Wait. You're telling me they let this guy go?"

"I'm telling you that I don't know. The hearing has been removed from the court schedule, and I can't seem to get anyone in the Attorney General's office to give me a straight answer. I'm not able to find a John Doe in holding or recently transferred either."

"Jesus Christ," Lincoln says, running his fingers through his hair.

Grant watches Bea with the same stoic glare as Ace, and I feel like I haven't taken a breath in minutes.

"I plan to keep my promises to you." She looks back at Grant and me. "It's going to be a little more complicated with the two of you now."

"And a dog," Grant says.

She shakes her head. "No."

I shrug, finally speaking up in all this. "Non-negotiable."

CHAPTER 41

GRANT

WE HAVE TWO DAYS. Forty-eight hours until I'll leave Fiasco for good. Even when I hated it here—when too many people looked at me like a charity case, or I was the topic of some bullshit rumor, it was still home. I never had any dreams about growing old here, but I think I assumed I'd end up like Griz. Surviving on bourbon and lies. Living on the few constants that we had: time and the punishingly slow and quick way it moved forward. And the gut-wrenching reminders that nothing or no one lasted forever.

My assumptions turned out to be wrong. An awakening of sorts that made me recognize home as something completely different from what I had grown up believing. That it wasn't necessarily a place, but a person. My family would always be my family, and I'd miss them every day, but when I looked at Laney, I saw a life and a family I hadn't allowed myself to picture before. It was a helluva sight.

I rest my hand on the hot silver handle, knowing that

this will be the last time I set foot in here. It'll be the last prime rib dinner with a friend whom I owe a long overdue conversation.

The bell above the door rings out, and the smell of grilled meat and the briny tang from old oak panels bathe the walls of Hooch's. There are plenty of restaurants in the county, but this place has always been the constant. I'm going to miss it. *Miss them.*

Marla shouts from behind the front counter bar, "You want the prime rib or the burger tonight, Grant?"

She throws her towel over her shoulder and squares off like I'm late to order, even though I just walked in. Her eyebrows raise at me because the only certainty about Marla is that she has no patience for much. Especially waiting.

"I'll have what he's having." I nod to Del at the far end of the counter.

He takes a sip of his coffee. "She's doing spoonbread with the prime rib tonight."

I smile at my friend. "Ambrosia?"

"Marla, tell me you made ambrosia," he shouts to her.

She yells from the kitchen, "Is a frog's asshole watertight?"

Jesus. I look around the restaurant and there's only a handful of us in here, but it's late on a Thursday night and most of the family dinner crowd are home putting their kids to bed. The air conditioning is cranking away after the heat from today.

The dead center of August in Kentucky can keep your skin slicked with sweat if you stay outside. Even without the sun out right now, it was balmy. Good for bourbon, rough for the rest of us.

"I'm going to guess that's a yes."

He glances at me. "Is the reason you're looking all sort of nervous because you want to tell me that you're in love with that girl?"

The muscles in my cheek twitch and the back of my neck heats up. There's a lot of history between us. A lot of love too, but we keep it high-level. It's always been that way, even before Fiona. "That has something to do with it." I clear my throat.

"Any chance the clove-smoking viper is the other reason?" Bea and Del's history was one of the only relationships that hadn't been gossiped about here. But I know that after Bea left, Del never dated. He never offered details, and I never asked.

"It does," I say as Marla comes back to refill his coffee and pour a fresh one for me. "Thanks, Marla."

"Food'll be out in a bit," she says, rushing off to the booths with a pitcher of water.

"Been trying to tell you, without much luck, apparently, that I'm happy for you. I didn't know about you and Fi . . . until the end. If I could have picked anyone for her to have, it would have been you, Grant. But she's not here." He pauses for a moment, swallowing audibly. "I miss her every damn day, but she had a happy life. I'm happy you had some part of that."

I really didn't want to cry tonight, but I swear if he says one more thing, I'm going to lose it.

"You don't need it, but you always have my blessing. On whomever you choose."

Dammit. I rest my forearms on the counter and hang

my head, looking down at the scuffed linoleum floor. "I hadn't planned on choosing anyone."

"Well, that's the funny thing about love, isn't it?" He looks toward the kitchen window, where Marla spoons out her ambrosia. "It tends to ignore your plans. And you can only be a dumbass for so long when someone makes you smile."

And if I had blinked, I would have missed it. The way the corner of his mouth tipped up on the side as he watched Marla. *Well, I'll be damned.*

"You shitting me right now?"

He takes a swig of his coffee, not meeting the way I'm staring at the side of his face. "It never dawned on you why I was here so often?"

I tilt my head. "Figured it was the food."

He smiles, chuckling. "Started that way."

I laugh out, "Alright." I nod, thinking about how my best friend just told me he's been with someone, and somehow not a single person knows.

Marla comes barreling through the kitchen's swinging door. "I've got medium rare for you," she says as she unloads the prime rib plate from her forearm. "And, I've got rare for you, Del." She slides the plates of spoonbread from her other forearm, and then out of nowhere, she slides out the two cups of lime green ambrosia, peppered with coconut and maraschino cherries. "I'll grab the aus jus, one second, boys."

"The spoonbread is good tonight," he says over a mouthful.

On my second bite, my ears perk up.

"We don't serve anything more than water here," Marla

says, her voice slightly elevated. I saw off another piece of the meat and glanced toward the far end of the counter at the tourist. Tall and thin, with nothing in particular that stands out about him. Slicked-back black hair, silver taking over the sides. But it's the hair on the back of my neck that stands that has me nudging Del's leg. I see him look past me —a quick glance and nothing more.

"Looks like you serve prime rib," he says with a northern accent.

"Like I said, water is the only thing on the menu for ya," Marla bites back.

I give him another glance, taking in the bold and gold ring sitting on his pinky finger. He grabs a toothpick from the holder at the register, then lets out a low laugh, like he's not enjoying the attitude. "Mind telling me if you happened to see my sister passing through?"

Aside from the news playing on the television, everyone else here is quiet and listening to this conversation.

Marla gives him one of her best *Are you fucking kidding me?* stares. "If she looks like you, then it's a no. Haven't had anybody new around here."

"Looks more like our mother. Blonde little thing. Answers to the name Laney or Eleanor."

I keep my breathing even and shovel another piece of the prime rib into my mouth, but I feel sick doing it. The only thing I can think about is that I left my phone in the car. Wiping my mouth with my napkin, I say to Del, "Gotta take a leak. See if she'll wrap this for me."

I don't look at Marla. I only walk past the two of them and toward the bathroom in the back. When I turn the corner, I hear Marla answer, "Like I said, haven't had anyone new around here." I don't catch what else is said as I move as fast as I can through the back exit and around to where my truck is parked.

I throw it in drive and call Laney, but she doesn't answer. When I try her again, it goes to voicemail after a few rings. "Baby, listen to me. Take Julep and head up to the main house. You stay there until I come to get you."

With my heart in my throat, I send a text to Bea.

GRANT

911. He's here.

BEA

Calling it in. Take her and get her out of there. I don't care where.

When I call Del, it picks up before it even rings. "He left a couple of minutes after you."

"Call it in." I hang up on him and floor it. "Fuck!" I shout, hitting the steering wheel.

My pulse hammers and adrenaline notches up, making me floor it up the private road and throw it in park. The truck is barely stopped when I get out and go running inside.

We didn't move fast enough.

As I throw open the front door, Julep wags her tail, waiting for me. If she was waiting, that means Laney's not here. "Baby, you here?" She must still be at the rickhouse with Ace.

"Jules, where's Laney?"

She barks at me. She knows who Laney is, and if anything is going to protect her outside of me, it's Julep.

"Go find her, girl." I give her a whistle. And a command she hasn't heard from me in a long time. "Jules, go! Protect."

She runs like the devil out the back dog door, so fast, like she knows exactly where she's headed.

I dial Laney's phone again, but that's when I hear it buzzing on the kitchen counter. "Fuck."

I rush to the door and shut it behind me. There are only a few places she would be, so I'll start at the rickhouse and then head to Ace's. But my steps falter as the stranger from Hooch's circles the front of his old Chevy pickup just as I step off my porch.

"Evening, sir."

"You're trespassing. This is private property. No soliciting." My firearm is in my truck and a hunting rifle is in my workshop, but not a single weapon is at my disposal right now.

He holds up his hands. "I'm just looking for something I misplaced. Thought you might be able to help me find it, Mr. Foxx."

"Like I said—"

"And I'm not sure I'm making myself very clear." He reaches for the back of his waist and pulls a Glock, pointing and aiming like he's familiar with exactly how to use it. "I have a very particular request. And I believe you know exactly what I'm talking about. You and I seem to have similar taste."

It makes me snap forward without thinking. In a breath, my right thigh is hit with excruciating pain. But that doesn't stop me from moving toward him. I'm not going down without a fight here. I rush for him and nail him in the jaw unexpectedly with a right hook. But the movement has me off balance. The gun rings out again, and this time, I can feel the bullet just graze my side. It hurts like a motherfucker, enough to take me down. I hit the ground with a thud as pain radiates up my thigh. But it's the back of my leg that burns more. The exit wound.

He hovers over me as my side bleeds and my thigh pulsates. I can hear Julep bark in the distance. Turning his head toward the sound, he smiles as he looks down at me. He digs the barrel of the gun into the wound on my thigh, and I yell so loud that my ears ring. I swallow the dryness and blink, trying to get it together. *Fuck, do not pass out.* I need to move.

"I'm going to ask you one more time. Where?"

"Go fuck yourself," I spit at him, but it's weak as my vision starts blurring.

He wipes the barrel of the gun, soaked in my blood now, along the shoulder of my shirt, but I can't even feel it. I'm fighting to stay conscious.

"I've done plenty of that," he says eerily. "Now I'd very much to play with my pretty little thief."

But I can't move to warn her. Fight back to save her. Or cause any type of damage to this piece of shit to keep him from her. I know Julep got to her in time. They'll take care of each other. I know it.

"You've been very unhelpful."

And then everything goes black.

CHAPTER 42

LANEY

"THIS WAS A GOOD IDEA." Ace smiles as he walks along the front of the rickhouse. It looks more like a rustic wedding reception space and not an old-as-dirt storage spot for bourbon.

"You could put some barrels over there." I point toward the side exit. Use that as a selfie spot for your guests, then you'll get a great backdrop of the full racks. And during the day, with the double doors open, the lighting would be good.

He eyes where I'm talking about. "I'll send Griz out here. Make sure there are no more snakes lurking at the end of the rows. That's the last thing I need—a fucking rattlesnake appearance. It's bad enough that you and Grant won't be here." He gives me a tight-lipped smile. "I'll miss him. And you too. But he wasn't built to be alone. Punished himself for long enough trying to stay that way, but my brother was always meant to be with someone like you, Laney."

I give the oldest Foxx brother a "you should listen to your own advice" smile and then wrap my arms around his shoulders. He doesn't return it, but he doesn't pull away either. "I don't think any of you are meant to be alone. There's too much love in this place."

He leans back and squeezes my shoulder. "You're family. Which means we've got you now. No matter what."

Maybe it's the way he says it, like that's already a foregone conclusion. Or that he says it with that damn shoulder grip the Foxx men do, but it makes my chest feel heavy and my eyes water. If he says anything else sentimental, I just might burst into tears.

"Alright, I need to get Twerk back to the stables."

"Twerk?"

"I'll give you one guess at who's thoroughbred he might be," he deadpans.

"I'm not even a little bit surprised." I smile.

"Sir Twerks-a-Lot. That's what she named a horse that was bred to win a triple crown."

I laugh at how easily he's riled by her. "Brilliant marketer. I'd bet on a horse with a name like that."

"Brilliant people are always slightly unhinged, so I suppose it tracks." He knocks on the door before he tips his chin. "Close up behind you?"

I nod, pulling together the last of the packaging that the string lights had come in. "Oh, and Laney, for what it's worth. I know that what brought you here was ugly, but I'm still happy you found your way to us."

Fucking Ace. My eyes blur, and I tuck my lips behind my teeth. I wait until he's out of sight before I let myself fall apart. Puffing out my cheeks, I let out an exhale slow enough to calm my shit down. Then I chuckle to myself as I hear his horse whinny. They might not be cowboys, but Grant was right when he said horsemen and bourbon boys.

I turn toward the open double doors when I hear Julep barking. Walking a little closer, I can't see much other than the lights from the main house in the distance.

"I'm here, Jules," I call out and purse my lips to whistle. It's not as loud and polished as Grant's, but it does the trick because she comes barreling into the rickhouse almost straight past me. She must be coming to see what's taking me so long. When she barks this time, it's loud, like she's talking to me, but more aggressive than her usual greeting.

"What's wrong, girl?" I look out into the dark from where she just came, and I can't see anything. "Where's your dad? Is he back yet?"

But she stands in the same spot, no butt wiggling or rolling to her back for a belly rub, which is odd. Instead, she sits tall in place, just barking at me, loudly and with conviction.

"Alright. Let's go," I say to her just as I flip off the lights.

The loud pop of a firecracker has me stopping. My body tenses as my heart pounds. I look out again at the dark, open space, and the other rickhouses in the distance are closed up, no lights on. The main house is lit, but far enough away that if Griz was lighting off fireworks, I'd see it in the sky. I glance at the workbench where I left my water bottle, but no phone. *Shit*. I left it on the counter at Grant's.

Julep sits next to where I stand, waiting for me to make a decision. Follow the sound or wait and listen. Another one goes off. When I reach to flip the lights back on, her low growl nudges at the nerves stirring in the pit of my gut. *That wasn't a firecracker. Firecrackers pop off more than once, in succession, and it would have lit up the sky. Even if it was small.*

Goosebumps rise along my skin before I even feel the chill that caused it. *Something isn't right.* I look toward the stables, and I can't see anything more than the lights outlining the stalls. I swallow down the nerves as an old pickup truck pulls up slowly, with only its yellow parking lights on. It comes to a stop at the edge of the driveway.

Julep growls by my side as the person hops out of the driver's seat. "Dave? Is that you?"

But it's not Dave, Tim, or any other of the rickhouse guys who answer. Instead, what rings out is a voice I didn't want to remember. One I've only heard once and only a few words at that. But those few words have haunted me. "Been looking for you, my little thief."

My stomach sinks, and I'm instantly lightheaded. But I don't wait to see if I'm going to wake up. I hit the lights, making it dark as night, and hustle back inside the rickhouse, whisper-shouting, "Julep, come." She follows me down the main aisle to the farthest rack aisle from the door. Even if he flips the lights back on, this is still the darkest spot here.

Julep growls another low hum, her snout pulled back.

I pet her head and slowly wrap my hand around her snout. She needs to keep quiet. I softly say, "Quiet, Jules." She listens. And we wait.

The silence as we crouch low evolves into a loud static. I struggle to listen. *Please go away.*

Mere moments tick by before the lights flip on. "You hiding like this isn't exactly what I expectin'. Hunting is my favorite part, little thief." He sounds too calm when he says, "This is going to be more fun than I hoped." He shuffles his feet. "I'm going to find you. And it's going to be *so* fulfillin' when I do." His voice echoes in the large space. "Woowee! I plan on playing with you for a good, long while too."

I shuffle back, my hand still around Julep's mouth, trying to keep her as quiet as possible.

"Come out, come out wherever you are, pretty little thief."

My hands and arms shake as the nerves and adrenaline mingle. If he walks down the other side of the building, away from where we are, we'll be able to get out through the side exit. Julep rumbles a low growl, my hand muffling it, but she still hums. She knows there is danger.

"You took my last little plaything. And all my favorite parts of the others." The echo of his voice gets louder as he moves down the main aisle. "I had a very special piece of flesh filleted and brining for a while. It would have been real nice with the little bits of you I plan on sampling."

I underestimated the level of monster this man was, but I won't let what he's saying seep in. I need to get out of here. I try shifting closer to the other side of the aisle. I just need to get to that side door. But my foot hits something and it clanks against the concrete. *Shit, shit, shit.*

It's a copper whiskey thief that someone left here. If nothing else, and he gets close enough, I'll use it like a bat. When I bend down, I hear a faint sound of buzzing like the cicadas that have been making noise all summer. My fingertips graze the cool cooper, but I freeze as the buzz is drowned out by the louder shuffle of shoes. *Oh no.*

"Awww," he says with sarcasm. "You didn't make that very hard, my pretty thief." It's like being doused with ice water. I don't move a muscle, but they tremble on their own. My fingers get tighter as they wrap around the long copper neck.

His tall, lanky stature stands at the opening of the aisle and slowly starts looming closer. He has a gun in his left hand, its barrel pointed at me as he casually motions it in a circle. "You made a noise," he tsks, like I flunked his test of how to hide from a psychopath. "That's the only rule when you're hiding. You stay quiet. Thought you would have been smarter than that." Tilting his head to the side, he canvasses me from head to toe. "Daughter of an FBI agent and all."

My body coils at hearing him speak about me like he knows me. Looking at me like he has any right to. I swallow the nerves that are clogging my throat.

"You can do hard things, Laney. Never forget it."

I grip onto Julep's harness. This monster doesn't know me. He's simply reading off facts. Surface-level details that could be found within a few minutes of a Google search if he had my real name. Which he did. But it's when he raises the gun at me that I hold my breath. I tense up and my fingers ease just enough on Julep's harness. And she feels it. She doesn't wait for the command as she launches at him, fast, precise, and catches him completely off-guard.

When she makes contact, I scream out. The gun he held drops and fires as it hits the cement. Julep's whipping head movements create a frenzy of sounds. Growls from her and howls from him. She takes him to the ground, jerking his forearm back as he yells out and curses. I cover my mouth, panicking about my next moves. I need to get away. But there's no fucking way I'm leaving here without my dog.

The gun.

I trip over myself, trying to move fast enough to it.

Julep crying out pulls my attention, and I watch as he manages to get a kick into her somewhere and she releases him. She whines, favoring the back leg where she landed. But that doesn't stop her as she tries to move back in for another bite.

I will not let this happen.

With the gun resting five feet from the wailing and bleeding monster of a man who has no other plan than to hurt me, I make a run for it. Gripping the long copper whiskey thief in my hand, my feet slap the cement without any more hesitation.

"I don't fucking think so!" he shouts as he drives his shoulder into my gut, knocking the wind out of me as we both hit the ground. The copper whiskey thief clatters to the ground on impact and slides into an empty, ground-level rack where a bourbon barrel must have been.

I try to suck in a breath and gather my wits to move. I roll my body into the main aisle and will myself to keep moving away from where we collided, but that's as far as I get, because two things happen. Almost at exactly the same time. The buzzing sound I'd heard of what I thought were cicadas wasn't a buzz at all, but a rattle. A coiled-up, very pissed-off snake juts out and connects with the monster's ankle once, twice, and then goes back for a third bite, where it latches on.

"Motherfucker," he spits out. In another gurgling moan, he yells, "Can't feel my fucking leg!"

His eyes meet mine for a split second. I'm almost stunned at the sight of what's happening just a few feet from me. I need to get out of here. But it's the flickering of a flame and its heat that jolts me and has me finally moving. Up from my side, rolling to my knees, and up as fast as possible. I should have known that gunfire and an entire room of highly flammable alcohol are going to cause one very lethal thing to happen. And it's already begun. I hustle back to Julep, because the way he's still wailing and now barely moving, he's no longer the threat. It's the heat that's licking closer that has my attention now.

My body gets jerked forward at the same time an exploding sound goes off to my right. If I'm lucky, I'll have only a couple of minutes to get out of here. I get up, my ribs aching from the impact of hitting the cement floor again. When I reach Julep, she's conscious and keeps trying to get up and stay up, but her back end keeps giving out on her. I run my hand down her side. "I'm here, sweet girl. I'm here. You're going to be okay."

The heat in the room has gotten higher and the sound of oak crackling is my cue that the racks and barrels will give way any minute now.

"We need to go, Jules." I wrap my arm around her middle and then scoop her up. She whines when I hoist her to get the right grip, but I need to run, and I need to do it now.

"We can't stop. We need to run—" she shouted at me. Her bloodied body shook uncontrollably, but it wasn't the time to ask questions. We ran and hoped the fire alarm worked.

"We're going to be okay." I repeat the same sentence over and over as my legs keep moving toward the side exit. Just like that night. *"We're going to be okay."*

I knock the door open with my shoulder just as the sounds of another explosion ring out. I need to get as far away from here as possible.

The only thing I can think about right now is getting to Grant. Getting both of us to him. My lungs are burning and my arms screaming from holding her, but I won't stop for a second, not until I find him.

Fast thumping and a horse whinnying has me straining to see in the dark until I hear his voice, and it's like a jolt to my very being. I can breathe again.

"Laney! Fuck, LANEY!" The fire starting to blaze behind me is what lights the darkness enough for me to realize that he's coming right toward me at speed.

"Here," I barely get out. "I'm here. We're here!"

I hear him exhale in a rush. "Laney!"

All the adrenaline that had spiked, pushing me to fight, pushing me to run, is fizzling, and I crack. I choke out a sob as I squeeze my eyes shut. "Grant!"

I keep Julep cradled as best I can in my arms. That fucker hurt her. My voice shakes when I tell her, "You saved my life, sweet girl," my chin wobbling as I try not to think about how she knew to come find me.

As soon as he gets close enough, he shouts, "Baby, we need to move! This place is going to go up."

"Julep's hurt. Take her."

He leans down as I try to lift her up higher. He gets a good grip on her and maneuvers her so that she's cradled in front of him across the horse's lower neck.

"Give me your hand," he says as he turns back to me. I reach up and he grips my bicep, hoisting me up on the horse that he's already started moving. Tucking myself behind him, I hold on tight. With the reins gripped in one hand and keeping a hold on Julep in the other, we take off. Twerk gallops quickly and my hair whips at my tear-streaked face. Seconds later, behind us, the rickhouse explodes. We've gotten far enough away that I can't feel the heat or the pressure from the blast. And I know that if Grant hadn't shown up when he did, I wouldn't have made it.

Fire engines with their sirens blaring fly in the opposite direction than we're going, up the narrow road toward the explosive fire. I turn my head, looking behind to catch a glimpse at the entire rickhouse burning bright in one massive blaze. My eyes blur at the roaring flames. I hold on to Grant tighter, but he twitches, tilting his side like something's wrong.

At the crest of the hill to the main house, he pulls Twerk to a stop.

"Careful, baby, not so tight," he says, wincing, and I realize with a start that he's hurt and bleeding.

His side is wet and sticky. My hands are covered in it, and I know immediately that it's blood—I've felt this before. It's not good, and my panic kicks back into gear.

"I'm fine, baby. Are you hurt?" he says over his shoulder, knowing I'm freaking out without even looking at me.

But I ignore him. "You are *not* fine." And I'm not even close to being fine, but I'm not bleeding. Both Grant and Julep are hurt, and we need help. Shaking off my emotions, I slide down from the horse.

"Where are you going?"

I turn toward the road. "You're bleeding. I'm getting help." I start waving my arms above my head, trying to pull the attention of the police cars and ambulance as they get closer. "Hey! We're over here," I shout. A set of lights slows. *Thank goodness.*

When I turn back, I see his thigh. He has it wrapped in a tourniquet with his belt. "What happened?" I try to hold back another sob that wants to escape. Not yet. Not until they're okay.

But he doesn't answer me. He holds Julep against his body and gets down from the horse, and then moves her into the grass, petting her head reverently. "You did good, girl. You did so damn good, Jules."

Still crouched over her, he turns toward me, stands, and just keeps moving. He doesn't stop until he wraps his arms around me. I breathe him in as he kisses the top of my head and into my hair, then my forehead, and then buries his face in my neck. "I tried to get there. I tried so fucking hard."

"But she did," I say, nodding to Julep. She's hurting, but her tail wags as I drop lower to comfort her. "She found me, warned me, and then got a good grip on him when he raised his gun. That's what started the fire. When he dropped it, it went off," I say, looking at the rickhouse now completely engulfed in flames.

"Fuck." He bends as best he can to pet her head again.

"He kicked her, I think, and then she hit the ground hard. She can't put any weight on her backside."

"My brave girls." Grant keeps one hand on her chest as he holds me close. He kisses the side of my head, letting his lips linger there.

I crouch next to him, and he pulls back, searching my eyes. His hands move up to my face, framing it and bringing me closer until his lips crash into mine. We kiss each other as if we both know how close we came to never being able to do it again.

When he pulls back this time, tears falling down his face, he asks, "Did he hurt you?" He looks around my face and body, ensuring I'm alright. "I couldn't get to you." He kisses me again. "Ah fuck," he says, wincing when he shifts his weight, trying to stand.

I look down at his leg, and my eyes widen at the reality of his injury. "Oh my god. Grant? Your leg."

With a small shrug, he glances down. "It was a clean shot. Went right through."

"And you're just making out with me while there's a bullet hole in your leg?"

He chuckles, but as he tries to move again, he still winces. "That one doesn't feel as intense as the one that grazed my side." When he twists to look at it, even that small movement has him hissing between his teeth.

He smirks at me. "Looks like no piggybacks for a while."

I snort out a laugh, but my eyes water. As I rest my forehead on his shoulder, both of us are starting to lose the adrenaline that has us standing and not falling completely apart.

"Ace came riding up as soon as he heard the gunshots at my place. I woke up with him slapping me in the face. We made a quick tourniquet—I hadn't bled out, so he didn't hit an artery. And there wasn't anything that was going to keep me from getting to you. I took the horse and started yelling and riding right toward where he said you were."

I hold my side as I shift on my feet, my ribs hurting with every inhale as I watch the blaze. Julep barks as another explosive sound rings out. There's no way this fire would be contained or survived. The dark sky fills with even darker smoke, billowing fast and strong.

"The fire department won't make a dent in that until it burns off."

"All of that bourbon," I whisper out.

"Look at me," he says, pulling my attention away from the almost mesmerizing sight. "None of that means a goddamn thing. You're okay. We're okay. That's all that matters to me."

". . . but your family. All that time and—"

His warm hands on my face have me unraveling, as he peels away the sweat-drenched wet pieces of hair sticking to my lips. "You are my family. And you're safe now. I have you."

He rests his forehead against mine.

"I don't know, cowboy. It kind of feels like I've got you right now with the way you're leaning on me."

He smiles. "Yeah, I suppose you do." Combing his fingers along the side of my head, he tucks a piece of hair back behind my ear. "You're so fucking brave."

My chin wobbles and my nose tingles again at hearing him say that to me.

"And I love you, my brave girl," he says, pressing his forehead to mine. "I've fallen so hard for you. And I thought—" He pauses and takes a deep breath before he finds the words to finish. "I thought it was going to happen again. That I wasn't going to be able to get to you in time. And that I"—he kisses me as tears track down his cheeks—"was going to lose you. Honey, I can't lose you. Please stay with me. I want this. Us." He blows out another shaky breath. "More than I've wanted anything else in my life."

My chest tightens with longing as I run my fingers along the back of his hairline. If men could purr, this would be Grant's special spot. I fist the front of his shirt to make sure he hears me. "You said I was yours. So unless you were just handing me a line, that's exactly what I am. It feels that simple for me. I choose to be yours the same way you've chosen to be mine. I'm not going anywhere, cowboy." I give him a teary-eyed smile.

The firm press of his lips feels like we're sealing a new set of vows in the wake of a chaotic nightmare. He smiles against my lips, his hand placed firmly on my chest just above my heart.

Behind him, the fire keeps burning, and as I watch it, I want to believe that it burns away the fears from our pasts we've let control our lives. The idea has what's left of the knots in my stomach slowly untangling. The things that had both of us in a chokehold. A monster and a curse. Seeing the flames dance over that building, feeling his arms so tightly wrapped around me, and his lips brushing against my skin, it's clear: this is the end of that.

"I don't think *he* would have made it out of there alive." Nothing could have survived that blast.

Grant looks out over my shoulder at the flames. "Neither do I."

"Julep did a number on him, but it was the rattlesnake that—"

The EMTs arrive, breaking us apart enough to start assessing the wounds on Grant. I start to tell them I'm fine, when he says, "Look her over anyway." His head whips back, registering what I had said before that. "Whoa, whoa, whoa. Rattlesnake?"

I nod. "It must have bitten him three, maybe four times. It was the only way I was able to get Julep and run." I look over at her, and she's just watching us. *My protector.* She saved my life. And with that threat gone, there will be no reason for us to leave. Relief showers over me at that realization.

He ignores the EMT who had been asking him if he can walk, and instead, wraps his hand around the back of my neck and pulls me in, fast and abrupt, as his mouth fuses to mine, whispering against me, "My wife."

I nip at his lower lip. "Almost."

CHAPTER 43

LANEY

It took four days for the fire to burn out. Five counties and an immeasurable number of firefighters battling to keep it contained. It never reached the other rickhouses on that stretch of the Foxx property, which was a miracle in and of itself. The fire burned so hot that the only remains of the monster I slayed and the nightmare I survived were his teeth and bone fragments.

He'd been erased. I searched for sadness in that, but it never came. Two nights of my life that I knew would never fully leave me, but it was done. I found comfort in that, at least. I remember asking my dad once if he was okay. It was after a case he had to travel for—it was one that had him missing opening day that year. When he came back, I knew it had been a hard one.

"Are you okay, Dad?"

He gave me that tight-lipped dad smile. The one where it felt more like a preamble to something I wasn't going to like hearing than one that had happiness behind it. We were at the diner on 22nd Street, and he hadn't finished his chocolate shake. He'd always finished his shake before our burgers arrived. I was done with my burger, and he still hadn't taken more than a sip. I knew that whatever it was that he had to do while he was away, some of it came home with him.

"Just a hard case, kiddo."

"Had to stop a monster?"

"This time, yeah. I had to stop a monster."

I leaned back in the booth, full from my disco fries and strawberry shake. I knew the possibilities at that point of what he could have meant. I also knew that if he had to hurt someone, it was to keep other people safe. "I think you're brave, Dad. You have to be brave to stop monsters."

He finished his chocolate shake after that.

He would have told me I was brave after all of this too.

I had rehashed that night of the fire and the night in the storage unit repeatedly with a therapist until I was able to sleep through the night. There was no clear-cut answer as to how Waz might have known something or someone was coming for me. Or how he knew that I had been from New York. *"But like most things having to do with Hadley's father and his associates,"* Ace said. *"We know never to let our guard down."* The conversation about it ended there and the authorities never dug deeper.

The weeks that followed were hard, but as it seemed with everything, it was time that helped ease the anxiety of the nightmares that would come to wake me. I didn't have any remorse. But I had plenty of emotions about what had happened to my loved ones in the process. For one, Grant had gone through a surgery to repair the damage of the gunshot wound to his leg and a fair amount of physical therapy.

"Where are you going?"

He stops dead in his tracks, with one foot slung into his saddle stirrup. I knew he wasn't coming down to the stables just for grooming and time with Tawney.

"The doctor said he wanted you on the ground walking, not riding."

He hoists his other leg over and winces. "She needed to go for a ride. I'm not hiking, I'm riding. I'm fine."

He really is the worst patient. Grant doesn't know how to sit down for too long. So, I resort to bribery. "I need to go for a ride."

Smirking, he looks down at the reins in his hand. "That's how we're playing this now, baby?"

"That's the deal, cowboy. You have a choice, either I get a ride or Tawney does. You choose." I turn on my heel and stride back to the house with Julep in tow. She's a far better patient than her dad.

Julep barks, her way of telling Grant, "let's go!" I pet her head and grab onto the handle connected to her hind legs. Julep's hip and one of her back legs were in rough shape, but she's out of her cast as of yesterday and the hip brace is there for added support until she's strong enough to run again. I know she misses her morning rides alongside Grant as much as he does, so I've been filling in until they both can get back to it. My girl—that's what Julep was now. As much mine as she was Grant's. It felt that way long before, but especially so after the way she saved my life and then loved me through it. Julep and I go for a slow walk to the cafe every morning and grab a flat white for me, a black coffee for Grant, and a puppuccino for her.

"C'mon, honey, I just did the hard part," he yells out to me, like he's taken a second to think about it. It makes me chuckle.

"Guess I'm not getting the *hard* part, then."

I can hear him swearing to himself, but I know he'll be about ten minutes behind Julep and me. That man's appetite for me is ravenous. But so is mine.

"You still planning on marrying him?"

I look up and see Bea leaning against her truck parked in front of our house. "I kinda love him, so yeah, I'm planning to marry him. Are you going to come?"

She shakes her head, pulling out her silver case.

"I didn't realize you were in town."

She clears her throat. "You did good, kid. More than good. Just came to tell you that the items from your storage unit are no longer evidence. Thought you might want some of your old life back." She hands me a small gold key and a key card. "I had them moved to a spot just outside of Mongomery about twenty minutes from here."

I turn over the key in my hand as I swallow down my emotions. "Thank you."

"You're your father's daughter, Laney. That's for sure." She opens the door to her truck.

"So that's it?"

"You were cleared on anything in question. Your part in his death was considered self-defense. There won't be any charges filed. You're not technically in WITSEC anyway, so yeah. That's it."

Before she gets into her car, she stops and looks down,

searching for words to whatever it is she wants to say. "You ended up rescuing yourself. Again. That's not something that comes naturally to most people—doing what has to be done in order to survive."

She pulls in a deep, lungful of smoke, and on her exhale, she says, "Just remember that the next time life gets hard, or if you're feeling like the memories of the shit you survived might swallow you, you're a badass, Laney."

You can do hard things.

"What the hell did she want?" Grant asks from a few feet away. The dirt kicks up behind Bea's truck tires in the distance.

I think about how much of what got me to this place was hard. How much of it turned me into someone I wouldn't recognize if Manhattan Eleanor was looking.

I turn to him with a smile. "Just wanted to tell me I was awesome." Even with a slight hitch in his step, he stands there so confidently. "Looks like you decided which ride you wanted, huh, cowboy?"

He rushes toward me and lifts me at my waist as I let out a yelp. "Always you, baby. I'll always choose you."

"Now might be a good time to tell us what you've been up to, Grant." I shift a glance at Griz as he prods Grant. With the 100-year celebration coming in mere days, there have been thousands of phone calls, media attention, and concerned bourbon lovers that the highlight of our celebration just went up in literal flames.

I squeeze Grant's hand, letting him know I'm here.

He looks to Ace and takes a chance. "What if you were celebrating 100 years with something unexpected?"

Ace has been stressed out and barely sleeping since that fire. There's a lot to running this company and Ace made it look almost effortless. But this was a big hit for them—they could have lost a lot more than what they did, but Grant had a solution to share.

Ace crosses his arms, leaning against his desk, and Lincoln stops texting.

"When Fiona and Olivia passed, I started making batches. My own mash bill." He wipes his palms on his jeans. "I wasn't planning for it to be anything more than a way to make time move. I wanted to try to do the one thing that my name promised—make some damn fine bourbon."

I look around at their faces. Stoic, confused, and amused between the three of them.

"Those batches are ready." He lets a smile crack, and so do I. "And it's pretty fucking good."

"Where?" Ace interrupts. "Where the fuck are you aging barrels?"

Griz starts laughing.

Grant glares at him. But his deep rumble keeps going. "What? I can't believe nobody figured it out sooner. Ya'll are damn idiots if you didn't catch on by now." He looks at me with a wink. "Except for you, darlin'."

"The caves up near the falls."

Lincoln chimes in, "Are you shitting me?"

Grant shakes his head.

"I never told you, because it was never about adding something to the brand. Or stepping on toes. I didn't want either of you thinking that I wanted to take over what you've spent your careers building."

I watch the master distiller and CEO of the brand look downright confused at what Grant just said. I don't think they would have felt that way at all.

"I had my career and left it. Making barrels kept me moving. I did what we were taught to do. The thing that's been in our blood for generations." I nod my head to Ace. "You did that for me. I made bourbon, got lost in the process and the chemistry, the nuances. I did it in small batches, with different variations until I found something worthy. It gave me purpose again. It's taken a long time to improve how I run a team of people." I smile at the way the cooperage has been running lately. "But I want this. It's good fucking bourbon."

"How much are we talking here, Grant?"

"Give or take about 250 barrels."

"Are you fucking serious!?" Lincoln barks out. "But the temperature in a spot like that must have been all over the place. Really huge extremes? Or is it chilled? What's the proof clocking out at? Is it at its sweet spot yet?"

Grant laughs lightly, his face and neck tinted pink with nerves. "I think it is, but you're going to have to tell me."

Ace looks at Lincoln and a quiet exchange passes. "You want to put it in place of what we lost?"

Griz chimes in, "The truth is, most of what burned in that rickhouse was nostalgic. I tasted too many over-oaked barrels. Maybe half of what was there was going to get dumped anyway."

He looks at Ace. "I think it's high time you each had your own bourbon. And I'm not talking about your years.

I'm talking about a mash that's special to you. You want something different to breathe life into this old girl, then you have to stop looking at me for answers."

Ace holds his hand out, looking frustrated. "You offer your answers, Griz. It's hard to tune them out."

Ignoring that, he turns to Grant. "I'm going to need a taste."

His mouth kicks up to the side. "I can do that."

"Laney, what are you thinking here?" Ace asks, brow furrowing slightly. But he's into this, I can tell.

I pull out a small packet filled with ideas and designs about what to call it, how to roll it out, and most importantly, how to make it rival something that's been hyped for years now.

"There are plenty of ways to spin it. But if what you're thinking, Griz, is that your boys should have their own craft blend, then there's only one name for this one."

CHAPTER 44

GRANT

A month later...

"It's completely sold out."

"What do you mean, it's sold out?"

Ace's eyes dance from Lincoln's to mine, and then back again.

Lincoln snorts a laugh. "I know I'm the smartest of the three of us, but there's no hidden meaning, Ace." He nods at me to finish the details. It was mine, after all.

"Foxx Bourbon's Cowboy Edition is completely sold out. We've gone ahead and created a collector's edition of a completely new and original blend in one fucking weekend!"

Ace smiles big and wide.

Griz mumbles, "Told you."

"Shut it, old man," Ace says, still with a smile on his face. "How many bottles did we keep?"

"Two cases. Everything else has been claimed for tastings that kick off in"—Lincoln looks down at his watch—"'Bout an hour. And the rest are pickups for attendees. If they don't claim their bottle in twenty-four hours, then it'll go to our waiting list.

"You think we should keep making it? Let this edition be our special edition, and then change up the bottles?"

I look at my brothers, and then over to Griz. "You're asking me?"

Ace shrugs. "Your bourbon, your decision."

I glance toward the stables, where Laney is walking with Lily and Lark. They're talking about something with their arms flailing and the girls laughing. She didn't lie about being really fucking good at throwing big parties. There are carnival rides set in the front of the distillery, where kids and families stay entertained. Local bands on a main stage behind the distillery, performing all day. And then VIP guests and ticketed lovers of bourbon filtering throughout the property. Tastings from local chefs paired with all our blends for a Bourbon Brunch. Tonight, Crescent De Lune prepared a VIP dessert tasting to top it off. The adult-only tasting also features Romey's Hemp Chocolates, and Marla opened Hooch's for one day only to tourists who wanted to try a "real Kentucky dinner."

"Let's do it."

Lincoln clears his throat. "So does this mean there's another master taster joining my team?"

"Only when you want me there. That job is all you, big brother." I clap him on the shoulder and squeeze.

"I want you there. Period."

"Proud of you boys," Griz says as he stands from the stool he's been perched on for most of the day. It's smack dab in the middle of the distillery that can be seen from every angle with the way that the double doors around the space are open. He'd said he's as much of an attraction as the bourbon itself. It's true.

Ace told him to fuck off, but people stood in line to shake his hand and talk to him about what it was like growing up and seeing his family flourish in this business.

He grasps Lincoln's shoulder and gives me a smirk. "I knew that girl was going to be good for us."

Ace drains his glass. "Grant, no more secrets like this one. It may not have started as our business, but you damn near saved us from tanking this year after losing that rickhouse." He claps his hand on my other shoulder and squeezes. And then does the same to Griz. It's the first time in a long time that I feel proud of what I've helped build.

"To no more secrets." Lincoln raises his glass, and we clink our glasses and cheers.

"What the hell, how am I left out of this circle jerk right now?" Hadley laughs out from the doorway.

Ace just grumbles and turns away to stalk off somewhere as Griz starts cackling.

"Hadley Jean, get your ass over here," Griz says to her.

Lincoln gives her some dumb-ass handshake they've been doing for decades as he leaves with me to go find our girls at the stables.

"Dad! You have got to try the stuffed croissant that Laney got for us," Lily says as we get closer.

Laney greets me with her sweet smile. Every time she

does, my chest warms, and I can't help but lean into it. The way she refused to leave my side as my leg healed, how she doted on Julep when she came home from the vet in a cast for her broken hind leg. I'd discovered that Laney was more than just funny and beautiful. She was sexy and kind. She was caring and sassy. She became my partner in every way. And I love her a little harder every single day.

She wraps her arms around my neck as I slip mine around her waist. I lift her up just enough off the ground to kiss her.

"You guys are gross," Lark says while Lincoln and the girls walk off in search of something sweet to top off their night.

That has us smiling against each other's lips. She tilts her head back. "The hat was a good choice."

She told me the only requirement she had of me today was to wear the black cowboy hat she brought home last night.

"How long have you been wanting me to wear this?"

She squints one eye, pretending to think about it. "Literally the first time I saw you."

I lean up against her cheek so the next few words are only heard by her. "Wouldn't mind seeing it on you later."

I can feel her smile against my scruff. "Just the hat?"

I give her a slow nod as she smiles.

Damn, I love it when she looks at me like that.

"Tell me what else, cowboy."

"How about I show you?" I give her a knowing smirk. But she has no idea what I have planned for her.

Her eyes flare. "Yes, please."

I link our fingers and walk with her toward the top floor

of the distillery. It's a spot that I hadn't learned about until I was in my early twenties. It wasn't something that many people knew existed. It was only meant for Foxxes and whomever else we wanted to share it with. And I want to share everything with this woman.

With her lips still painted in that red she loves so much, Laney bites it, making me want to do the same. "Where are we going? I didn't think anything was down here except offices." She laughs out, "Grant, are you going to have your way with me on top of Ace's desk?"

I stop in my tracks. "Wasn't on my agenda tonight, but now that you mention it . . ."

She laughs so loud that I do the same.

The artwork displayed along the corridor is a mix of old and new. Paintings that are worth plenty and photos that are older than Griz. But to the left of the small gallery is a Foxx Bourbon logo. The newest version that Ace had rebranded when he took things over. The wrought-iron *F* intertwined with an outline of a fox isn't there just for show; it has another purpose.

I tilt the logo up and the wall slides open as a hidden door.

Laney breathes out a laugh as her jaw drops with excitement. "Are you kidding me?"

I lead us both into the dimly lit space and close the door behind us, but when I raise the chandelier lights a little brighter, that's when she sees it.

Her hands cover her mouth as she gasps. "Grant, is that—"

"Took me a little while to find the right one. There are plenty online, but the version they had in Coney Island in the nineties was a little bit different. This Zoltar machine took a little longer to find."

I rub my hand along my neck as I watch her move closer. I hope she likes it. She quietly walks around it, examining the lever to pull. I'm second guessing myself as she says absolutely nothing in response. Maybe this wasn't a good idea, after all.

"Say something."

She smirks. "Since when does silence bother you?"

"Since I'm watching my fiancée not offer any of her tells that give away if she thinks this was a great idea or if I just tanked in the surprises department."

Tilting her head, she pinches a piece of her hair between her fingers.

I smile to myself. I did good.

"Show me how it works." She smiles with tears rimming her eyes.

I pull out a token from my pocket that's been there waiting for this exact moment and insert it into the slot. This particular Zoltar machine had been in a Manhattan museum, according to the person I negotiated with. It didn't need money in order to operate, but it needed a coin to shoot into Zoltar's mouth. Then the ticket would come.

With the coin positioned along the track, Laney studies the timing as Zoltar opens and closes his mouth. But before she releases it, she says, "This is the most unexpected—" she cuts herself off, trying to swallow the emotion that surfaces. "And I love you so much for it." Wrapping her arms around my neck, she kisses me hard. When we pull back, our foreheads stay connected for just a moment before she presses another quick kiss to my lips, and then turns back toward the fortune teller, or "future teller" as she called it.

"Make a wish, baby."

That was the point of this thing. It was a silly carnival game that held nostalgia and memories for her, which meant I'd do just about anything to give her a part of the past she had left behind.

She reaches into the covered slot to retrieve her ticket and flicks her eyes up to meet mine. "Where did you say you got this particular machine again?"

"I didn't. I worked with a guy that Griz knew." I watch her face crack, barely holding back a laugh. "Why?" I deadpan. I knew I shouldn't have trusted one of Griz's guys.

"The Zoltar in Coney Island was a little less . . . detailed. Those futures tended to be more about when to travel the world or if there was a happy reunion on the horizon, and then some lucky numbers."

I hold out my hand, but she backs up.

"What's on that card?"

She bites her lower lip and clears her throat. "When things get hard"—she looks at me and smiles—"it's up to you to take the reins. Sometimes the best types of control come when you submit. Your future is more of a penance this time around. Accept five spankings by hand or belt."

"Jesus Christ, Laney." Groaning, I drag my hands through my hair. Mortified.

She holds up her hand. "I'm not done reading my future. Hold your horses, cowboy."

"Funny." At least she's amused.

"May pleasure be forever in your favor. My lucky

numbers are 6 and 9." Looking up from the card, she smiles cheekily. "Good numbers."

I rub at the back of my neck. "Honey, I promise I didn't—"

"It's honestly an even better surprise now that I know this puppy is chock full of dirty deeds." She leans against the side of the machine where fucking Zoltar still has his mouth open. Reaching down, she grabs two handfuls of her long skirt in her fist, hiking it up higher as she watches me. "I'd like to collect on that *future* now, cowboy."

My cock is hard by the time the bottom of her skirt hits the tops of her bite-worthy thighs. I walk backward toward the same wall where the hidden door slides open and press the lock. "Belt or hand, honey?"

"Dealer's choice." She holds up her skirt high enough now that I can see her panties.

I take a seat in the brown leather club chair that's to my right. "My wife wants me to redden up her sweet little ass?"

"Not your wife just yet, baby."

"You know I like practicing. Now show me how wet you are just thinking about being spanked."

She moves her panties to the side, revealing her delicious pussy.

I fucking salivate, thinking about how she tastes. "Drag two fingers through those pretty lips and show me how wet, honey."

She does exactly as I ask. Her fingers shiny with her arousal as she holds them out.

"Taste."

She steps closer, but I stop her. "Not me. You. Taste."

With her skirt bunched up with one hand and a strap

from her white tank falling from one shoulder, I watch her lick her fingers. *So damn sexy.*

I unbuckle my belt and crook my finger for her to come to me. When she walks closer, she's such a good fucking girl that she waits for me to tell her what to do next. "Turn around."

She turns her body so her back is to me, looking over her shoulder with those big blues. "Touch your toes."

The way red flares up her neck and her eyes widen slightly, she wasn't expecting it. And fuck, do I love throwing her off.

Widening her stance, she bends forward, forcing her panties to ride up the crack of her plump ass. My fingers loop around the waistband and roll them down her legs. I lean closer to her ear and whisper, "Hands on the chair, baby."

She's going to need some leverage. Sucking in an audible breath with the demand, she does as she's told. Her skirt falls slightly with the movement, so I bunch it up around her waist and rub a small circle around right before I give her one swift smack on her ass that pulls the tiniest noise from her lips. When I rub that spot and do it again, this time, she stays quiet.

"You okay, honey?"

She inhales, and on the exhale, laughs, "More than okay."

"Good," I say, and then follow it up with three good slaps that leave her with a pinkened cheek that'll be long gone by the time we're done in here. And now, I'm hungry.

I drop to my knees and spread her open, growling into her as my tongue swipes her slit. I glide my thumbs along each side of her ass cheeks and spread her open even more so I can reach and roll my tongue against her clit. The moment I circle it, she moans, long and low, her ass wiggling back for more.

As easy as it would be to bury my cock in her right now, I want to finish out this impromptu fantasy. I stand and take a step back, admiring how perfect she looks bent over that chair.

She peeks over her shoulder. "Where'd you go, cowboy?"

I look down at the black hat I tossed on the table when we came here. The lights are dim and warm, bathing her in a hue that makes those pretty lips painted red look even more pouty than usual. She twists her body so she's sitting on that club chair, gazing up at me. "You want to try out those lucky numbers now, too?" She wiggles her eyebrows.

Chuckling, I pluck the hat off the table with two fingers and twirl it in my hand. "No, honey." I tilt her mouth toward mine and bend lower to kiss her, letting my thumb rub along her bottom lip. And then I watch that red lipstick smudge along the side of her chin. Fuck, I've wanted to see her like this—messy and willing to do whatever I ask of her.

I run my hand down from her chin to her neck and glide it past her shoulder, letting my fingers glide along her arm and down her wrist until her fingers line up with mine. I lift her hand and guide her up out of the chair. When she stands, I place the hat on her head. She watches me do it with a tiny, knowing smirk that kicks up along the right side of her mouth.

I'll never get over the way she looks at me.

She pulls the other strap of her white tank down, and

the move has the tank sliding just enough so it teases me with the tops of her breasts. The allure of her is almost as gratifying as having her. *Almost.* Grabbing at her skirt again, she drags it higher, showing me the edges of her pussy. "You taking me for a ride?"

I don't answer. Instead, I flip open the button to my pants and fold down the zipper.

She studies me doing it, biting at that lip like she can't wait to hear what else I want.

"Take it out," I demand. I can't see her eyes from under the brim of that hat, but I can hear her breath hitch when her hand finds how hard I am.

Fuck, she's good for my ego.

I sit back in the club chair. "I think it's a good time for that lesson. You wanted to learn how to ride? Be my good girl and ride me."

She doesn't hesitate. She steps closer, throwing one leg over my spread thighs and then straddling me, hovering right above my cock and lining her pussy right up. Holding her skirt nice and high, she sinks down onto my length with a sigh. I'll never take for granted how good this feels. She rolls her hips forward to find just the right spot. The sweet sounds she makes have me eager to fuck up into her, but she's supposed to be riding me, and I want this to last.

"Like this, sir?"

My eyes dart up to her smirking face, and I rub my hand over my mouth. She's playing right along. "That's it. Shoulders back, tits out, baby." I bite back the smile from this little role-play moment, rubbing my thumb along the tip of her hard nipple. "Now squeeze when you're ready to move."

Leaning back, I grip the front of her skirt that's fallen from her grasp and pull it up and tight. I want to see it. *Fuck.* The way she's rolling her hips, slow and deep, is working me over so damn good. "Look at how we fit together, baby."

I meet her gaze and then look down at where we're connected, urging her to do the same. To see the way I'm so deep inside of her and how she moves so that I can hit her just the way she likes. I lick the pad of my thumb and bring it to her clit. With a whimper, she grinds down onto me and rolls her hips faster. I'm so damn close, but I won't let go until she does. "That's my girl, making herself feel good on her man's cock."

"Oh god," she groans, and then breathily says my name. "Grant."

"This pussy is mine, isn't it?" I squeeze my eyes shut. *Fuck, I'm so close.*

She chases her orgasm that I know is quickly rushing through her. "Yes," she answers, just as her body tenses, and she leans forward, trying to hit everything she needs to get there. Crying out, her body bows, and she falls apart, her pussy squeezing me and pulsing so tight that I fall right over with her. The reality of spilling inside of her, claiming every part of her, finishes me. Her sweaty forehead meets mine as our bodies take turns working out what's left.

"How did I do?"

I smile, my eyes still closed. "Might need a few more lessons. You got a little wild there for a sec—Ow!" I laugh from her pinching my side. "Laney, that was the best ride of my life."

She nuzzles her cheek into my touch as I curl a piece of

her wild strawberry-tinted hair around my finger and tuck it behind her ear. When she sighs, the sound of it makes my chest feel even warmer. I had never allowed myself to think of a moment like this one. A life like this. The life where I get to share it with a partner. The part where I'd figure out all the ways I could love a person. Even on our hardest day, I was happy alongside her.

"A little more every day."

I run my fingers through her hair and down her back. "A little more every day," I say back to her. A promise we made when I asked her for forever.

She kisses my chest, right over my heart, before she says, "Now it's your turn. Pour me some good bourbon, cowboy, and let's go for a ride."

EPILOGUE

LANEY

"Don't," Grant said, his tone serious, but he knew I wasn't going to listen, which is why he smiled as he said it. He knew by the smirk on my face that there was no way I was listening to him. Not with an audience and armed with a piece of bourbon-vanilla cake in my hand.

Tonight was the eighty-fourth wedding I had planned. And out of all of them, it was my favorite, because it was mine.

"Open," Grant says with a forkful of our wedding cake hovering in front of me.

"Mmm, it tastes even better now," I say with a mouthful. The hammock swings gently as I let my bare foot skim the grass beneath.

"I agree, because," he says over a bite, "the first piece I had got shoved so far up my nose, I don't think I really savored the flavor."

I can't stop the laugh that bubbles out of me as he kisses my head.

He had held up a piece, and like a good husband, led it to me with minimal mess. I even licked a bit of frosting from his thumb as stealthily as I could. But when it came time to do the same for him, I went for it. I held it to his mouth, and just as he opened, I flicked my hand higher, smushing it on his mustache and slightly up his nose. He got me back. He snagged me around the waist and kissed me deeply as Italian buttercream slid around my mouth and down to my neck when he kept going. The hoots and hollers from our small wedding party egged it on. It was one of the dozens of memories from today that will never leave me.

I walked down the aisle toward Grant in a pair of white cowboy booties and the prettiest cream-colored dress I had ever seen. I wanted to wait so we could get married outside in the field of wildflowers behind our home, so I chose a short, flowy dress from Loni's, a pair of custom cowboy boots from a designer in New York, and a certain German Shorthaired Pointer as my guide. It felt only right to have Julep as my escort—she was my guardian. There was no other way to put it. And I was lucky enough to be joining her family.

"I don't smell it as strongly anymore," I say, taking a sip from the round silver flask that Hadley had given to me this morning.

"The air doesn't smell the same. It does, but I think I've gotten so used to it now that I don't notice it."

"It's because you're a Foxx now," he says in that deep

voice that hits me right in the gut and sends goosebumps down my arms.

"That's not a thing."

"You've been smelling a lot of bourbon, tasting new things, your senses are being conditioned. It's a real thing. It just means you're one of us."

I smile at that, swinging slowly on our hammock and thinking about the day.

Grant stood in front of me, holding my hand as he slid on a diamond ring to join my finger that had been wearing his nana's band. His eyes watered as he said his vows. "I promise to love you. In this life, but also in the next. You're the part I never believed in. The kind of partner I didn't understand. Until you got here, I didn't know. But now that I do, I vow to stand next to you always, behind you for backup, and in front of you for protection."

"Griz seemed to know how to whip you around that dance floor," he laughs.

"He might have strained his back when he spun me," I say, wincing a little."

The Doobie Brothers played over the speakers in what should have been the father-daughter dance, but it felt like my dad was there as his favorite band played. Griz was a great stand-in. We have a standing breakfast date every Monday morning before I head into the distillery, and he makes his way there every afternoon for a survey of the place. Grant and his brothers think it's Griz's way of keeping tabs, but I just think it's his way to stay tied to something he loves so deeply.

My husband starts humming a little Fleetwood Mac.

"Go Your Own Way" isn't a typical wedding song, but our story isn't very typical either.

"Happiest day of my life, Mrs. Foxx," Grant says with a mouthful of cake.

I smile and look up from his chest. "So far . . ."

"Yeah, baby. So far . . ."

GRANT

The humidity finally broke, and it's the first autumn night that actually feels like it. The heat lamps crackle every time a bug flies into it, but they're keeping us warm so we can still enjoy dinner out on the patio.

Ace flips the banana pancake onto the stack he just piled at the center of the table. "I didn't do chocolate chips this time. Cinnamon and banana seemed like it would be sweet enough."

Hadley chimes in, "Did you want us to skip the syrup too, Atticus?

"Atticus?"

"Is that what happens when you hit your forties? You stop adding fun to pancakes and start repeating what people say?" She looks around the table, with Griz laughing at the head.

Griz cups his ear. "Say that again?"

That gains a laugh from everyone at the table except Ace.

Hadley swats at the air in front of her. "Anyway, I have some fun news." She looks around. "I just hired a resident burlesque dancer."

"For what?"

Hadley looks at Lincoln like he's an idiot for asking. Sarcastically, she says, "For invigorating conversations." She rolls her eyes. "For Midnight Proof, obviously. I want more than just the jazz band for entertainment. It's such a good idea. Laney's idea, actually."

My wife smiles at her.

"Plus, she's a total smokeshow now. I kind of have a crush on her." She waves that off. "Anyway, I'm sure you'll see her around."

Hadley's eyes widen as she leans over the table to see where Lily and Lark have gone. I follow her line of sight, and both girls are on the couch, already engrossed in something on their tablets. She whisper-shouts, pointing at Lincoln, "You will not, I repeat, will not take my new girl for a whirl."

He sits back with a smirk. "Seriously, Hads?"

She looks around at me, Ace, then Griz. "Your slut-astic escapades are not coming anywhere near Midnight Proof. Do I make myself clear? She needs a good ol' small town welcome, not HPV as a welcome present."

"First of all, fuck you. I'm not giving anyone HPV."

"As far as you know . . ."

The two of them are like a variety show, always have been, and sometimes I do wonder if she's really our sister with the amount of grief she dishes to Linc and Ace.

"Wait what do you mean 'she's a smokeshow now?' Is she from Fiasco?" Linc asks.

She crosses her arms, giving him a glare. "No. I should have never mentioned this." She points at him. "We're not talking about her because I don't want to hear how she has to quit because you're not calling her back or how you need to know which nights she's working to avoid coming in or some dumb shit." Chugging his water, he slams the glass down, slightly out of breath.

"Are you okay?" Ace asks her hesitantly.

She rolls her eyes at him. "Yeah, Daddy, just fine."

"Jesus Christ," he huffs out as Lark calls for him.

"Uncle Ace, the Wi-Fi isn't working," she croons from the next room.

Hadley leans across the table and smiles. "It's like a drug. I can't help myself with him. It's like the how-much-can-I-make-Ace-uncomfortable Olympics."

"Gold medal work, Hads," Linc says.

She salutes him. "Seriously, though, hands off the new girl. You bourbon boys and fresh meat . . ."

Laney leans her head on my shoulder and squeezes my knee. "Was that the appeal?" She wiggles her eyebrows. "Fresh meat?"

I kiss her lips. "I hadn't had any meat for years before you showed up. It was all you, baby."

She smiles up at me.

"You two are so cute, I think I was just smiling at you both for no reason," Hadley says. "Now my face hurts."

"Calm down, Hadley Jean. Your time will come. Don't get your knickers in a bunch." Griz smiles at her over his bourbon.

"That's the problem, Griz. There's no one getting in my knickers."

"How about a little rumor for ya, then? I've got some good gossip about who is gettin' some," Griz says, resting his elbows on the table.

"Dish!" she says as she gets up, rounding the table.

Ace comes back in, sending her a disciplinary look. "Why are you encouraging him?"

She flutters her lashes at him. "He's the only one with anything interesting happening around here."

"Haven't we had enough 'interesting' for a little while?"

She laughs, clapping her hands like it's the funniest thing—which, to be fair, when she's on a run with putting my brothers in their place, it's hilarious. "Yup, it's official, you've become the boring brother. I thought Grant had you beat, but then he went and leveled up with Laney."

I couldn't help but smile at the backhanded Hadley-compliment. It was a small thing, getting together every Friday night for breakfast at dinnertime with my family. Some weeks, we had to skip it for some reason or another, but most of the time, everyone made it a priority. They became just as much Laney's family as they were mine.

When she wasn't with me, she was with Hadley, getting into some kind of trouble, but outside of that, she worked hard alongside my brothers. Building our family business as if she'd always been there. Only now, she had her own staff, a few people who helped her run the small events we took on at the distillery and inside the new barn that was erected in place of the rickhouse that had burned down.

"Thank you," she whispers to me. And I know what she means. "For a family."

I kiss the side of her head, dragging my fingers lazily along where the hem of her skirt meets her thigh. Damn, I love this woman. I lean into her and lower my voice. "What do you say we cut out of here and practice."

She tilts her head back to meet my eyes. "Practice?"

I smirk. "Want to practice making it bigger?"

She looks down at my lap. And the smile that takes over her face and reaches her eyes, crinkling them at the sides, is the best one I've gotten all day.

"It?" she says, biting her lip.

"I meant our family—"

"Looks like I'm already really good at making things bigger, cowboy."

I mumble, "Jesus Christ," as I drag my hand over my mouth.

Pushing her chair out, she drops her napkin on the table, and then leans in close. I stare at those pretty lips of her as she whispers, "And this time, I'm not lying."

"About what, honey?"

Her lips skim just below by ear when she whispers, "I'm not wearing any panties."

THE END

Want more of Grant and Laney?
Scan below for the Extended Epilogue.

The Extended Epilogue to Bourbon & Lies

Bourbon & Secrets

Who's ready for a single-dad, romantic suspense?
Lincoln's story is coming December 2024.

Scan here to pre-order it now!

Acknowledgments

There's one very important person that I want to thank. She'll only see it if time is not linear and she somehow stumbles upon this. **Nanny**, thank you for loving me big, always rooting for romance, AND for letting me stay up late to watch *Romancing the Stone* with you. There's just something about Kathleen Turner and Michael Douglas that slaps. I don't remember deciding when it became my favorite movie. It feels like it always has been. Maybe it's the nostalgia of seeing it with my favorite person. It inspired this series and is how I decided on my pen name.

To my editor, **Mackenzie**, you are an incredible editor and friend. This book would not be what it is if it wasn't for your insight, the love you have for these fictional characters, and the ways you push me to make these stories better. Thank you for the excitement and support. I am forever grateful to have you in my corner.

To the talented artist who created the most stunning illustrated cover I've ever seen. **Loni**, your talent and style are beautiful. You ended up being the creative soul that I didn't know I needed to find. Your work helped fuel me. I can't wait for what we're going to do next!

My beta readers, you are so incredibly valuable to me, and I cannot thank you enough.

Amy, you have such amazing insight into characters whom you've just met. You push me to be better every step of the way–from the bird's eye view down to the details of what ended up being some of my favorite scenes. You are simply fabulous! I am so thankful for you.

Jill, thank you for cracking open some bourbon and reading this story. I am so happy to work with you on each book. Making sure I have the right labels and triggers is the important piece, but holy shit, did I love when you went feral over Grant's dirty mouth.

Thank you so much, **Kate**. I don't think I've ever gotten so choked up after a DM before, but you managed to do it. Thank you for your perspective and insight. Most importantly, no handcuffs will be used in this series.

Sierra, it was a pleasure having you beta-read for me on this story. Thank you for your feedback and the care you took in finding what was working and what needed some added attention. I'm so happy to have you as a part of this.

Blair, with a hand enthusiastically raised, "We stole a car!" Thank you for letting my chaotic ideas run wild and for helping me reign it in with belly laughs and exaggerated hand gestures.

To my **ARC Team GIRLS**! You are THE most amazing crew of humans. Thank you for reading and taking the time to not just hype this story, but to add your creativity to all of your social posts. I will never forget that it is all of you who help my stories find new readers. Thank you for taking a chance and staying with me in a new series. I love you all so much.

To **Pamela**, thank you for hopping on a plane to Kentucky with me, indulging in my creative side, and drinking a boatload of bourbon in the name of research.

To my **mom** who will devour this book in one sitting and my **dad** who will only crack it for the dedication and acknowledgments (keep it that way, Charlie): thank you for being my biggest fans and the kind of cheerleaders every kid, no matter how old they are, deserves.

To **Mr. Wilder**, there are always bits of you in every story. You are the best thing.

Also by Victoria Wilder

The Riggs Romance Series

Peaks of Color

Hide & Peak

The Sneak Peak

A Peak Performance

Standalone

December Midnights (A holiday novella)

The Bourbon Boys Series

Bourbon & Lies

Bourbon & Secrets

ABOUT THE AUTHOR

Forever a hopeful romantic, author Victoria Wilder writes contemporary romance with deliciously witty and wild characters. Her stories range from small-town, swoon-worthy men to fiercely powerful families and lead characters whom aren't afraid to ask for what they want.

She's an east coast girl, living in southern Connecticut with her husband, two kids and Yorkie, Linus. She's always chasing the next season and believes in romanticizing whatever you can along the way. You'll always find her either reading, writing, or ready to dish about books.

f facebook.com/victoriawilderauthor
O instagram.com/authorvictoriawilder
BB bookbub.com/authors/victoria-wilder
d tiktok.com/authorvictoriawilder
@ threads.net/@authorvictoriawilder

Printed in Great Britain
by Amazon